"From cover to cover, RM Johnson's writing is powerful and bold. He deals with issues in prose that evokes all of the senses. His writing is from the heart, thought-provoking, and life-changing; he moves the reader from the first word."

—Eric Jerome Dickey, author of *The Other Woman*

"RM Johnson explores the most significant issues in our society today with a respect, a poignancy, a knowledge that makes him, undoubtedly, the writer for the new millennium."

—E. Lynn Harris, author of *A Love of My Own*

"RM Johnson has set his sights on becoming one of the most daring and insightful novelists of his generation."

—Colin Channer, author of *Satisfy My Soul*

Praise for *Father Found*:

"RM Johnson has written a remarkable novel—an intimate examination of roles and responsibilities in an ever-changing, increasingly less responsible world. *Father Found* is a literary mosaic filled with powerful, poignant characters and infused with a richness and spirit that rise far beyond the page, spilling over into real life and touching everything within their reach."

—Lolita Files, author of *Child of God*

"Johnson writes about fatherhood in this era with a boldness you don't see often. *Father Found* pulled me in from the start and never let me down. This is powerful stuff. I wish I'd written it first."

—Omar Tyree, author of *Diary of a Groupie*

Praise for *The Harris Family*:

"Johnson juggles his multiple plot lines deftly, and his lean, no-frills style keeps the action moving. . . .This novel—a *Waiting to Exhale* for men—seems ripe for filming."

—*The Washington Post*

"*The Harris Family* is real life with a touch of magic. It's a tightly knitted story of men, family, and the distance they must bridge to keep them together."

—*Black Issues Book Review*

LOVE FRUSTRATION

A NOVEL

RM JOHNSON

SIMON & SCHUSTER

NEW YORK   LONDON   TORONTO   SYDNEY

SIMON & SCHUSTER
Rockefeller Center
1230 Avenue of the Americas
New York, NY 10020

This book is a work of fiction. Names, characters, places, and incidents either are products of the author's imagination or are used fictitiously. Any resemblance to actual events or locales or persons, living or dead, is entirely coincidental.

First Simon & Schuster trade paperback edition 2003

SIMON & SCHUSTER and colophon are registered trademarks of Simon & Schuster, Inc.

For information about special discounts for bulk purchases, please contact Simon & Schuster Special Sales: 1-800-456-6798 or business@simonandschuster.com

Manufactured in the United States of America

10 9 8 7 6 5 4 3

The Library of Congress has cataloged the hardcover edition as follows:

Johnson, R. M. (Rodney Marcus)
    Love frustration : a novel / RM Johnson.
        p. cm.
      1. Triangles (Interpersonal relations)—Fiction. 2. African
Americans—Fiction. 3. Chicago (Ill.)—Fiction. I. Title.
PS3560.O3834 L68 2002
813'.54—dc21   2002075968

ISBN 0-7432-2973-8
    0-7434-4873-1 (Pbk)

Thanks go first to my family,

then to my friends, and to all

who were instrumental in bringing this project to completion.

To those of you who want nothing more

than to find your soul mates,

but have yet not found them.

LOVE
FRUSTRATION

I was getting married in less than a week, I thought, as I sat in Ozzio's, an expensive, dimly lit Italian restaurant in downtown Chicago. I was there with my fiancée, Faith, and a couple of other people. I had brought along my best friend, Asha. My fiancée gave me sideways looks for claiming her as such, but we went way back, and whether Faith liked it or not, Asha was my girl. Then there was Faith's best friend and soon to be bridesmaid, Karen. I wasn't crazy about her ass, but then again, she wasn't too fond of me either. I'd asked Faith a thousand times why she even planned this dinner, trying to squirm my way out of it, because I knew what was in store.

"Whether you like it or not, Karen's my best friend, and this will be a good opportunity for you two to get to know each other better."

"Sure," I'd said, conceding. "We'll see."

"What is your problem? Why are you looking at me like that?" And now, here was Karen talking to me from across the table, catching me giving her the death ray stare as she stole the last bread stick.

"Maybe it's because you took the last bread stick out of the basket, like you did the last basket. There're three other people here. Maybe somebody else wanted it. Ever thought of that?"

"Yeah," Karen said, taking a bite out of the very bread stick I was talking about. "And if they did, they would've grabbed it. Ever thought of that?"

1

"Maybe they didn't have time, because you grabbed at it like there was a prize for getting it first."

"Or maybe you're just mad because *you* didn't get it first."

"Just have the waiter bring some more," Asha said to me, softly, nudging my elbow.

"Yeah. Listen to your *girl*. Have the waiter bring some more," Karen said. She was no longer eating the bread stick, but holding it like a cigar, waving it in my face, teasing me with it. I didn't really want the thing at first, but now that she had it, she made me feel as though I really did want it, and badly.

"No, I won't have the waiter bring some more. We shouldn't have to race and eat fast every time we eat with Karen, because we're afraid she'll steal all the food from us."

"Okay, Jayson, cool," Karen said. "You want the bread stick? Fine." And then she stuffed the entire thing in her mouth, churned it around in there a few times, then let it ooze out into her cupped hand, and extended the gooey mess out toward me.

"Here's your bread stick, if it means that much to you."

Man, I was boiling at that point, but I remained as calm as I could and said, "You better put that back in your mouth, or else I'll do it for you."

"All right, all right," Faith said, standing up. "I don't care if you two can't stand each other, this weekend, you're going to be best friends. Jayson and I are getting married on Sunday. Can't you two please act like you have some sense until the damn wedding is over?"

I looked at Faith and knew my soon-to-be wife was right. Then I looked at Karen. I could act civilized if that's what Faith wanted, even though it'd be a stretch, considering Karen tried to do everything within her power to keep me and Faith from getting married, from even staying in the relationship.

"Faith is right," Asha said.

Asha and I were like brother and sister, although five years ago, we were involved for almost eight months. And even though I'd told Faith on countless occasions that there was nothing going on between us now, she still seemed to watch me suspiciously when I was around Asha. Faith didn't like the idea that I rented my downstairs unit to her, and didn't like the fact that I was so adamant about remaining friends with her. The truth was, I could kinda understand, because Asha was the most beautiful woman I'd ever set eyes on. She was like half Native American and half Japanese. Hell of a combination. And what resulted was a gorgeous woman with a beautiful copper complexion, like a shiny new penny. She had silky, straight black hair that she always parted down the middle and wore in long braids on either side of her head. She had a perfect body, generous-sized breasts, not huge, but definitely large enough to have fun with. Her hips and ass were shapely and tight, and her waist was so tiny, it looked as though a man could wrap his hand entirely around it.

Women were jealous of Asha, spreading all sorts of rumors about her, trying to belittle her in an attempt to make themselves feel more significant. Especially women who had low self-esteem, were less than attractive, and had to pal around with a fine girlfriend just to get men to look in their direction, which was exactly what Karen did when she hung with Faith.

"You two need to chill," Asha said. "Especially you, Karen."

"You have no place telling anybody who needs to be chillin'," Karen said, rolling her head around on her neck. "And why you always feel the need to defend Jayson. He's a grown man, or is this how things worked when you two were kickin' it?"

"Nobody's defending Jayson, and it's none of your business how we did things when we kicked it."

"Oh, I was just wondering, because the way you all up under him, it looks like you still kickin' it with him," Karen said, looking over Asha harshly, then passing a glance at Faith. "Your little ass needs to let the past alone, and start calling the date line to find yourself another man."

My entire body tightened up. I looked over at my girl, Asha, as she slowly stood up, her hands closing into fists at her sides, looking like she was about to leap over the table to get at Karen. And then, as if she read my mind, she lurched forward, lunging across the table, clawing out, desperately trying to grab any part of Karen.

Faith whipped her head in my direction, telling me to do something, with her wide-eyed, angry glare.

"I got a man. You the one who's screwing a dirty ass, busted vibrator," Asha yelled.

I shot out of my seat, grabbed Asha around the waist and wrestled her back.

"Asha, Asha! What the hell are you doing?" I said. People dining in the restaurant were craning their heads, trying to get a look at what was happening.

"Let her go! We can do it right here," Karen said, shooting up from her chair, whipping her cloth napkin out of her lap and throwing it to the floor, as if implying the same fate would happen to Asha if she were bold enough to make a move. "She's disrespecting my girl just days before she gets married, all up in your face all the time. We can go right here."

"Nobody's going anywhere," I told Karen, holding an arm out toward her. And while I was trying to make sure that Karen didn't try anything, Asha was fighting to get away from me, whispering in my ear, "Jayson, just let me go. Just let me go for a minute, so I can kick that bitch's ass once and for all. Please, Jayson."

"No, Asha."

"C'mon, Jayson. You heard what she said to me. I let that stuff go without an ass whoopin', people'll start believing it. C'mon, for one minute," she pleaded again, still struggling to get loose.

"I said no!" I raised my voice.

"Well, fuck you then!" She broke away from me and hurried toward the door.

"That bitch better leave," I heard Karen say.

I shot her a stare that if Karen read correctly said, if you say another word, I'm gonna stick both my feet so far up your ass, I'll be using you for a sleeping bag.

She looked away and I ran after Asha. I caught her just outside the front door and grabbed her by the arm.

"Where are you going?"

"Don't talk to me. And let me the hell go," she said, staring down at my hand around her arm.

"Why you trippin'?"

"You see how Karen's always coming at me, and what do you do? Hold me back. I thought you were supposed to be my boy, and you hold me back."

"Why do you even care what she says, Asha? Why do you always let her bother you?"

"I'm just tired of her shit. Every time I look in your direction, or say two words to you, she act like I got my hand down your pants. What's up with that? I'm sick of it," Asha said, looking angrier, and more upset than I felt she should've looked, considering the circumstances. There was something more going on than what had just happened in the restaurant. I just knew it by the sadness in her eyes.

"I don't know what her problem is. Maybe she's jealous of me and Faith and you and Gill. She's mad that everybody has somebody but her. But that's her problem, not yours. You can't let that get to you, you hear me?" I took her chin in my hand. She looked up into my eyes. I felt her hurting, so much more than she was letting on, and she meant so much to me that I would've done anything at that moment to stop it.

"You hear what I'm talking about, girl? Don't let her get you down. She's just jealous, is all. We both have people we love, and all she's got is that, how'd you put it . . . Dirty-ass busted vibrator."

Asha smiled, and that was all I wanted to see. I was happy. She grabbed me in a hug, kissed me on the cheek, right on the corner of my lips.

"I love you, Jayson," she said, leaning away from me, smiling.

"I love you back. So what, you coming back in?"

"Not if you don't want to see that booga bear's eyes on the end of my fingernails," she said, pretending to claw at me.

"Okay, maybe you're right. You want me to drive you home?"

"No, Jayson. Everybody's in there celebrating your wedding."

"But you came with me. I should take you back. Besides, they probably haven't even noticed that we've been gone. Faith and Karen are probably in there cackling like hens. I'll take you back," I offered again.

"Naw. You go on. I'll be all right," Asha said, turning toward the curb where there was a cab waiting.

"All right, but when I get home, I'm going to knock on your door to check on you."

"Okay, I'll be up. But really, don't worry about it. I'm fine." She got in the cab, and closed the door.

I stood there just watching as the car drove down the street and made a left. She was okay, she said. But I had known her far too long and far too well to believe that. Something was bothering her, and though I wasn't going to pry to find out what it was, I would make myself available to her whenever she was finally ready to let me know. Comparing Asha and my fiancée, Asha was the one I'd known longer, the one I'd been through the most with, and friendships were very important to me, considering I'd been deprived for so long.

I was feeling good that I'd made Asha feel better, and when I turned around I was smiling. But that smile quickly dropped from my face when I saw Faith standing outside the restaurant, by the door, not ten feet from me.

"Is everything okay in there?" I asked, walking toward her, unable to think of anything else to say, hoping, praying that she wouldn't ask questions about what had just happened, that is, if she even witnessed it.

"Is everything okay *out here?*" she said, looking at me weirdly, like I should've felt guilty about something.

"Yeah. Everything's cool. Everything's fine." I stopped in front of her, wrapped my arm around her waist and prepared to walk back into the restaurant, but she didn't move, just stood there, staring at me, that same weird look on her face.

"What?" I said.

"What do you mean, what? How do you think I feel? Days before I'm supposed to get married, and I'm putting up with these accusations that Karen makes about you and your girl. Accusations that you claim aren't true—"

"They aren't true," I interjected.

"If they aren't, why do I have to come out here and see what I just saw?"

"Faith, baby," I said, caressing her face in both my palms, looking deeply into her eyes. "She's my *friend*. That's all. I've told you this a thousand times."

Faith turned her eyes down, looking sadly away from me. "Sometimes, I just think she means more to you than I do."

"No, no, no," I cooed. I grabbed her hand, kissed her finger, very near the diamond I'd given her. "You're the one that's wearing the ring. You're the one I'm marrying, the one that'll be having my children. Now tell me who means more to me."

I saw a smile start to emerge on her lips, and when I lifted her chin, her anger and uncertainty seemed to have disappeared.

"So is everything cool?" I asked, smiling myself.

She looked at me as though she was considering the gravity of the question, as though there was more to it than just a yes or no answer.

"Yeah," she finally said. "I guess everything's cool." She grabbed my hand, almost tight enough to break the bones in it, and pulled me back toward the restaurant.

"C'mon."

2

Asha jumped out of the cab in front of the downtown brownstone she lived in. She had been renting the downstairs unit from Jayson for four years now. If things had gone the way they had planned, instead of living below him, she would've been living in the same apartment with him by now. But five years ago, when they were dating, something wasn't right. She loved Jayson, loved him more than she could remember loving any man in her past, but there was a reluctance to fully commit to him. For some reason, she couldn't imagine themselves five or ten years into the future, being husband and wife, handful of kids running around the house, the two of them growing old together. She loved what they had, but knew it wouldn't last longer than the few years just ahead of them. There was just something, some feeling, acting as a partition, a barrier, not allowing her to love him like she wanted to, like she felt he should've been loved.

Asha was worried about hurting Jayson, but there was no way to tell him that they were unable to continue. She couldn't give him a good reason, because she herself didn't really know what it was.

"We just can't," Asha imagined herself saying a million times, tears spilling over her cheeks, as she broke the news to Jayson. "But why not?" she imagined him asking. Her mind would be blank, and although she would be mentally groping for an answer, there wasn't one in sight.

But thankfully, Asha never found herself having to break his heart like that. They eventually began naturally to move apart from each other, and Asha didn't know if Jayson sensed her hesitation, somehow knew that she was unable to fully give herself to him, or if he too, was unable to commit for some reason. It was probably a combination of the two, Asha told herself. Jayson had issues. Issues with commitment. Not because he wanted to be with women other than Asha, but because it seemed, he was fearful of getting too close. He was scared of investing too much, and then her pulling away, hurting him beyond repair. He had reason to fear that, she admitted to herself.

Days before Asha was set to move in, it seemed they were both better able to see their situation for what it was. They loved each other, and promised they always would, but as friends. Mutually, they ended the relationship, but this was after Asha had given her landlord notice that she was moving out. By the time she told him she'd decided to stay, the landlord had already arranged for someone else to move in.

"So what are you going to do?" Jayson said.

"I don't know. I guess I have to find a place, and fast, hunh?"

"Well," Jayson said, "the guy downstairs is moving out on the first. You're welcome to take it. That is, if you want it?"

"So you don't have anything open in the four other buildings you own?"

Jayson looked at her and smiled, shyly. "Well, I have a couple of units open here and there, but I'd rather you be closer." He looked down at his hands, then back at her. "There. I'm busted."

"Well, I'm busted too," Asha said, smiling as well. "Because I'd rather be close to you too."

Ever since then, Asha could not imagine her life without Jayson in it, but she knew that Faith had been having talks with Jayson about her. He never mentioned it to Asha, but she was aware, could just tell by the way Jayson acted with her when Faith was around. He wasn't himself, so withdrawn, not smiling as much, laughing, or touching her the way he would normally do when it was just the two of them.

But Asha could understand. Jayson was a beautiful man, with that brassy hair, those hazel eyes, and a body that looked like it was chiseled from granite. Jayson was compassionate, sweet, and shy, like an innocent child, and owned enough real estate to start his own little town. So Asha knew that any other woman who had him would probably act the exact same way. She just wished Faith would understand that she had nothing to worry about. Jayson was devoted to her. On the day that he proposed, he ran back to Asha yelling, jumping around, hugging her, frantic because Faith had accepted, and he was finally getting married. Asha knew Jayson cared for Faith, but then again, sometimes she had to wonder if he was more excited about getting married to Faith, or just getting married, period.

"Is it her?" Asha asked, while Jayson was still hugging her, just after he told her the news.

"What do you mean?"

"I mean, if it was anybody else you were marrying, would you be as happy? Would it even matter as long as you were still getting married? Because I know marriage is really important to you."

Asha felt Jayson's embrace weaken. He pulled away from her a little, looked at her, a serious expression on his face.

"Why are you asking me that?"

"I don't know. I guess I wanted you to be sure that she was the one, that this was what you wanted," Asha said, hoping she hadn't hurt his feelings, but judging by the look on his face, she knew she had.

"Well, I want to be with Faith. Getting married to just anybody wouldn't make me as happy, okay."

"All right," Asha said, but it still seemed as though what Jayson felt for Faith was somehow more like gratitude than love. He felt gratitude toward her for saving his life, taking him out of the game of chasing and cheating, of trying to desperately convince women to consider him as someone worth seeing, worth going out to dinner with. Jayson hated dating. Asha didn't know exactly why. Maybe because he sucked at it. Maybe because regarding women, his self-confidence was buried so low that he'd never be able to find it, or maybe because of those deep-rooted family issues that caused problems with the relationship that he and Asha were in.

She had always asked him about those issues, tried to get him to open up to her, resolve whatever was going on, but he would always close up, say he didn't want to talk about it.

One evening three years ago when Asha came home from work, Jayson was sitting on the sofa in his apartment, his hands folded between his knees, staring blankly at the wall in front of him.

"What's up, baby?" Asha asked, closing the door behind her.

Jayson didn't reply, didn't turn around, didn't even acknowledge her.

"Hey, baby. What's going on?" Asha asked again, setting her purse on a chair, and moving over toward him, sitting beside him. She'd moved in to kiss him when she noticed tears in his eyes. She grabbed his face in her hands and said, "What's wrong? What's going on?"

"My mother has gotten worse. I'm going to have to put her in a home."

Asha moved in front of him, sat just below him on the carpet for a long time after that as he told her about his mother, told her a little bit about their dysfunctional relationship. She didn't know for sure, but she believed his problems had something to do with her. Now Asha wondered if Jayson had ever opened up to Faith, told her what was going on with him.

Faith should've felt lucky to be with Jayson, because he surely felt honored to be with her, and it was a damn shame that she was just too blind to see that. Asha would've liked Faith, could've even seen her as a friend if she wasn't so dead set on believing that Asha was still in love with Jayson. Faith was nasty to Asha, and every time she tried to talk to Faith, start up a conversation, she would cut her short, or simply ignore her. When Asha tried to offer her some suggestions about the wedding, saying that she'd help out in any way she could, Faith would tell her that she didn't need her help or her suggestions. "Thank you, but no thank you," she'd say, her nose turned up.

So this evening, when Asha, out of the corner of her eye, saw Faith step out of that restaurant while she was talking to Jayson, she didn't stop Jayson from hugging her. And yes, she would've kissed Jayson anyway, as she always did, but it maybe wouldn't have been so close to his mouth. And the "I love you" thing, well, she did, and she would've said that anyway, too, but maybe not quite so loud. Yeah, she knew Jayson would get an earful and have to deal with that evil witch's attitude. But Faith deserved to feel threatened, considering how she'd been treating Asha.

As Asha slid her key into the front door, she heard the muffled sound of her phone ringing. She quickly pushed open the door, ran through the large, open apartment, her heels cutting against the hardwood floor, and stopped in front of the phone. She placed her hand on it, about to pick it up, but then reconsidered. It's Gill, she told herself, still standing there, her hand on the phone, as it continued to ring. It's Gill, and this is probably his tenth call of the night, checking up on me to see if I'm feeling better or not. How she wished she had Caller ID at that moment.

The phone stopped ringing, and the immediate silence shocked her out of her thoughts. Gill was Asha's boyfriend. A good-looking, brown brotha' with an MBA from Duke, and a huge loft the size of a basketball court, looking out on the lights of downtown Chicago. He was an investment banker, went to work in beautiful suits with lovely colorful silk ties, and drove a brand-new, champagne-colored, S-type Jaguar. Gill got his hair cut every Wednesday, a manicure and pedicure every Thursday, and his teeth cleaned every first of the month. He made a ridiculous amount of money, not that Asha ever asked, and not that he made a point of disclosing just how much, but it was apparent in the way he dressed, and the things he bought. He was well versed in the arts and music and had a flair for fashion. He was perfect, outside the fact that he was from North Carolina and country as hell. He spoke country grammar like he'd just fled the state via swamps and vacant train box cars. But he "loves me some Asha," as he put it, and when he said that, he would smile so brightly, that all Asha could do was laugh even though he sounded like Chicken George.

Gill and Asha had been dating for eleven months now, but he preferred to say, "Damn near a year." It made their relationship sound so much more concrete, Asha suspected he thought.

After their first month of dating, Asha sensed the man was in love with her, although he didn't come out and say it. Asha knew it was a bad idea being involved with Gill, especially if he did truly love her. When she first met him, she told herself she needed a man, a man to make everything seem the way it was supposed to seem, to make her appear normal, and possibly, hopefully, to make her *feel* normal. But it didn't work, and why did she even think that it would? It didn't work when she was with Jayson, so why would it be any different with this man?

Asha was in no way ready to face her demons, to deal with what had been plaguing her for so long, and Gill managed to keep her mind off those things, at least most of the time. When people saw them together, they thought exactly what she wanted them to think. "What a sweet couple. You two must be so happy, and blah, blah, blah . . ."

It was working, and Asha would continue to let it work, as long as Gill didn't try to get too serious, try to take this thing farther than Asha knew it could ever go.

But Gill was raised in a family where the mom and dad had got married right after high school, still were married, and would remain that way till they died. They'd probably even be buried in the same damn coffin. He was one of six children and always mentioned how he wanted a litter of his own. And then there was the fact that he was thirty-four when they met, thirty-five now, and there must be some sort of expiration date on men's asses or something, because after a man turns that certain number, thirty-two, or thirty-three, he immediately flip-flops from that guy who's just looking for a piece of ass for the night, to the man who's looking for a wife.

Of late, all Gill could do was talk about what their kids would look like once they had them, the type of house he would buy for her, and how he wanted her big and pregnant and barefooted and not to think about going to a job. "And when I come home from work, I'll just lay next to you watching TV, and rub that belly of yours," he said, smiling happily. "I just can't wait to have some kids."

Kids! What kids? Asha thought. She had never once made mention of marriage, of getting engaged, of their relationship even lasting past another Christmas.

But Gill was insistent, as he was with everything he did, and that's why Asha had been forced to lie to him tonight about being sick. He was really feeling the idea of getting married, and the last thing he needed was to be around a couple who were on the verge of that. If he'd seen how enamored Jayson was of Faith, how happy they were talking about their future life together, Gill probably would've dropped to his knee right there on the restaurant floor and proposed, slipping a napkin holder on her finger till he could run to the store and get a ring. That is, if he hadn't bought one already.

Not a week ago, she had spent the night at his place. The next morning, when she was somewhere between awake and asleep, her eyes barely open, Asha saw Gill tiptoeing around. He was up to something, and Asha wanted to know what that was, so she lay there as if still knocked out.

She heard him moving over toward the bed, felt his weight settle beside her, and then she felt him touching her hand, her left hand. It tickled slightly, and she had to bite the inside of her cheek to stop herself from laughing. She opened just one lid slightly to see Gill with a fabric measuring tape, measuring her ring finger.

Damn! Asha thought to herself, biting down harder on her cheek and twitching in pain as a result. Gill quickly looked up to see if she had awakened. Asha shut her eye and let out a bit of snore for good measure. Gill turned away, pulling the tape gently from around her finger.

Yeah, if she knew this man like she knew she did, he had already gotten the ring, and it would be something ridiculous, like six karats, a rock that he'd gone to Africa and dug up himself with the aid of some local tribesmen. That's how Gill was, always out to impress the woman that he loved, his "Suga'puss." That's what he called her, regardless of Asha's persistent objections. It was just a damn shame that she didn't feel the same way he did, couldn't feel the same way. Because of this, she'd have to let him go.

But Asha was scared, and not just about hurting him. She knew once she let him go that she would be alone. And alone, there was no one to hide behind, no one to stick in front of that mirror while she cowered in his shadow so she wouldn't have to look at herself, wouldn't have to face up to who she really was.

That's what scared the hell out of Asha, finally facing up to and then having the world discover who she really was. What would her mother think? Were there even people like her in Japan? Of course there were, but she was sure with her mother's old world ways, she wouldn't understand. And what about Jayson? What would he think after being deceived for all these years?

Asha couldn't let her secret get out, but then again, she knew she could not continue leading Gill on like she had been doing. She would tell him, tell him that it was off, that everything was over between the two of them, and she would tell him tonight. She would just have to work on keeping her business private without using Gill as a diversion any longer.

Asha placed her hand softly back on the phone with intentions of calling Gill that very moment, when the phone started ringing. She was startled. It was Gill again, she knew, so when she picked up the phone she didn't even use his name, just said, "Baby, I have something to tell you."

"You do? Is it that you were wrong? You changed your mind?" the voice said back. But it wasn't even a man's voice.

"Why are you calling me?" Asha asked, her tone, harsh, serious.

"Because I wanted to talk to you. Because I thought we were friends, Asha," the voice said, a raspy tinge in it.

"We *were* friends," Asha said angrily, tightening her grasp on the phone. "Until you pulled the shit you did." And Asha thought about that night, the night last week when she was hanging out at her friend Jackie's house. She had only known Jackie, a thin, chocolate sister with a cropped hairdo, for a few months, but they had grown tight, going shopping together, hanging out at clubs, and on Thursday nights, getting together to have drinks at her house with a couple of other girls.

This particular Thursday, Asha had much more to drink than she should've and felt herself becoming drowsy, seeing through blurry eyes. Before she knew it, she was sleeping. The next thing she remembered, she was waking up, her head spinning, but not with intoxication, but with pleasure. Her head was still cloudy, but she felt euphoric, her entire body tingling. She looked down at herself, her vision still hazy, baffled to find herself massaging her own breasts. But what shocked her even more was when she looked down farther to find her lower half draped over Jackie's lap. Jackie had pulled Asha's jeans and panties down and was slowly, sensually sliding her middle finger in and out of Asha.

"Hey, sweetheart. I see you're liking this as much as I am," Jackie said, in her raspy, seductive voice, looking down at Asha's fingers trying to squeeze her nipples through her blouse.

Asha couldn't believe what she was seeing at first, thought she was dreaming till she felt the eruptions start to build, thought she would lose it, have an orgasm right there. Because of that, she knew that this was actually happening, no way a dream. Asha started to kick wildly as she pushed herself up on the sofa, trying to dislodge Jackie's finger from inside her.

"What the fuck are you doing to me, you sick bitch!" Asha screamed, still squirming away from Jackie, reaching down, grabbing for her jeans.

"Just let this happen," Jackie pleaded. "You were enjoying it. Just let it happen."

"No!" Asha yelled, rolling off the sofa, hitting the carpet.

"But you were enjoying it," Asha heard Jackie say over the phone.

"I was asleep. I wasn't enjoying a goddamn thing," Asha said.

"Then why did you almost come?"

Asha was quiet, couldn't say a thing for a quick minute. "I'm not like that," she finally said.

"Why don't you just accept who you are and stop fighting it. I know who you are. I can sense it, feel it. I knew the first minute I met you. So if I can tell, why is it so hard for you to see it?"

"You don't know shit about me. You hear me!" Asha yelled, pulling the phone from her ear and yelling directly into the mouthpiece. "You don't know a damn thing about me, so stop fucking calling me!"

"Fine, Asha," Jackie said, sounding somewhat hurt. "I was trying to help you through this, make things a little easier. But if you want to be like that, I'll let you do it the hard way. Good-bye Asha."

"Good-bye, sick bitch!" Asha yelled, slamming the phone down into its cradle.

Asha didn't know why, but there were tears falling from her eyes. It was because she let that queer bitch upset her was what it was. Nothing more. There was nothing more going on than that, she told herself. But she couldn't really believe that. She was crying because she had to let go of Gill. She could no longer use him as an excuse not to face the truth about herself. But after speaking to Jackie, Asha feared she just didn't have the strength to do that. It would be too painful.

Asha picked up the phone and dialed Gill's number. When Gill picked up and heard Asha's voice, he said, "Suga'puss, I've been calling you all night." His voice was very caring, very attentive.

"I've been asleep. I had the ringer off," Asha said, already feeding off his affection.

"How are you feeling? Are you all right?"

"I am now," Asha said, batting her eyelids quickly, trying to hold back more tears. And then from nowhere, she said, "I love you, Gill."

"I love you too, Suga'," Gill said, meaning every word of it.

"Good," Asha said, feeling a little better, smearing the drying tears from her face. "You don't know how much I needed to hear that."

3

The rest of the dinner was a bust. As I tried to continue eating, I would look up and catch Faith just staring at me, giving that same suspicious look she had given me outside the restaurant after she saw me talking to Asha.

I leaned over to her, whispered in her ear, concern in my voice. "What's going on? Is everything okay?"

"Why do you keep asking me that? Everything is fine."

"Well, why do you keep looking at me like I just screwed the baby sitter?"

"What baby sister?"

"You know what I mean," I said, becoming aggravated.

"Everything okay over there in lover's land?" Karen said.

"Everything is fine. Why don't you butt out and mind your own damn business," I said.

"I just wanted to know what was up. See if Faith came to her senses and finally decided not to marry your tired ass."

And I didn't know what it was about that last remark, but I just snapped. I shot up out of my seat, bumping the table on my way up, knocking over some of the glasses that sat on top of it.

"You know, I'm so tired of you!" I said, loud enough for everyone in the restaurant to hear. "Why are you always coming at me like that? What have I ever done to you? All you ever have to say are bad things about me and Faith. And you're supposed to be her best friend. When you insult me, you insult her too. You don't think Faith wants to marry me, Karen?" I asked her. She didn't respond, just looked at me like I was crazy. "Karen! Answer me. You don't think she wants to get married to me?"

Karen hunched her shoulders, looking as if she never gave the question much thought, looking as though it really didn't deserve any thought at that moment. "I don't know."

"Well, look at her. Faith is sitting right here, across the table from you. Ask her. That way you'll know. That way everybody'll know. Ask her."

"Faith," Karen said, and the way she said it, the tone she used sounded as though she was trying to wake something in Faith, snap her out of whatever trance Karen thought she was in.

"Faith, you really want to marry this man?" Karen said, a look of disgust on her face, like she just swallowed something horrible. How I hated her at that moment.

Faith looked her dead in the eyes. "Yes," she said.

"But do you *love* him?"

Why the hell did she have to ask that? Would Faith have been here if she didn't love me? I thought about this while I was waiting to hear the resounding yes coming from my fiancée. But it took a minute. Her eyes were still on Karen, and she looked up at me, as if deciding her answer. Then after turning back to Karen, she said, "Yes. I do love him."

It lacked the emotion I had hoped to hear. It sounded more like a confession, actually, but I was relieved to hear it nonetheless. She was feeling a little weird about what went down tonight, I told myself. Nothing more.

Karen didn't say anything for a long moment, just stared in Faith's face, as if giving her a chance to take back what she'd just said just in case she'd made a mistake. But after that moment was over, Karen said, "Okay, fine. I'll back off then. Faith, you my girl, and if this is what you want for yourself, then I guess I want it for you too." Then Karen shocked me by standing up and extending her hand across the table toward me.

"Truce?"

I looked at that hand like it was a claw from some alien creature, like if I touched it, she would pass me some deadly disease, and I would gag, start foaming at the mouth and shaking and drop dead right there. But I took the leap, grabbed her hand, and shook it anyway. "Truce," I said.

The trip to my place was a silent one. Faith sat in the passenger seat of my Passat, not saying a word, pushed up so far against the door you'd think I hadn't washed in weeks.

Once we got to my place, I took the stairs first, climbing the first two flights. But when I looked behind me, she was still there at the bottom of the stairs, near the door to Asha's apartment.

"Faith, what are you doing? You coming up?"

She looked up at me, her arms crossed over her chest. "I didn't know if you were going to stop in and see how Asha was doing. That is what you told her you'd do, right?"

It was exactly as I thought. She was feeling jealous and that's why she was behaving like a seven-year-old.

"Come up these stairs, woman," I said, extending a hand down to her.

"You said you'd check on her. You even told her that you would take her home. That it didn't matter that I was still in the restaurant cacklin' like a hen with Karen. That I wouldn't even know that you were gone."

"I did not say that!" I protested.

"You said something like that," Faith said, anger in her eyes. "And then you said you'd check on her, so that is what I think you should do." And then Faith had enough damn nerve to turn toward Asha's door and knock on it. She was only able to hit the door once, because I had hurried down the stairs, gotten behind her and grabbed her hand in mid-motion before she was able to knock a second time.

"We need to talk about this upstairs. Now go," I said, making her go before me, so she wouldn't try anything funny again. As I climbed the stairs, I looked back at Asha's door, thankful that she probably hadn't heard the knock, thankful that she hadn't been dragged into any more of my situation.

When we walked into my apartment, Faith just stood by the door, not taking off her jacket, not setting down her purse. I closed the door and stood in front of her.

"So, you're going to stand there all night? Gonna sleep there, are you? You're like a cow now, or what?"

Obviously, she didn't like my remarks. She clip-clopped across my hardwood floor, over to the area rug, and plopped down on my leather sofa. She crossed her arms tightly over her chest again, pressed her knees closely together, even tightened the belt of her leather jacket around her slim waist, as if she was trying to close off all pathways to her.

I walked over to her, stopped three or four steps from her, and just looked down at her. How beautiful she was. Even angry, pissed the hell off at me, she was one of the most beautiful girls in the universe. Her straight, chin-length black hair was windswept all over her head, sticking up like cockatoo feathers, but she was still beautiful. Her normally almond-shaped eyes were narrowed into slits, her mouth puckered into a tight little prune, but she still meant the world to me.

We'd been together only nine months, but I knew very early on that this was the woman I wanted to be with for the rest of my life. It could've been because until her, I hadn't been with anyone, hadn't really shared my life with anyone since Asha four years prior. I was lonely, very lonely, hating having to go out there on the circuit, prance through clubs, recite practiced come-on lines to women, hoping I'd find the one to fill the void in my life. But it wasn't as though I didn't try. There were nights when I became desperate, sitting around my apartment on Friday and Saturday nights, feeling as though no one cared about me, as if no one even knew that I was alive. I asked myself at those times, if I ceased to exist, would anyone even miss me?

I would think of Asha, go downstairs, knock on her door, my spirits immediately lifting when I heard her footsteps coming toward the door.

"Wanna rent a movie or something?" I'd say, praying that she'd be game. But when she came back with, "Naw, I got to get up early tomorrow," or "I'm going out with my girls," I would smile, as though it was no big deal, and head sadly back up to my apartment.

I would stand in front of my mirror, some fifteen minutes later, wearing the clothes that, for some reason, I never thought looked just right on me, the clothes that people wore to clubs; shiny silk shirts, baggy linen pants, loafers, crap like that.

I knew what the scene would be before I even got there, before I even left my apartment. But I told myself, either that, or sit around here and feel sorry for myself.

I would park my car, and as I walked toward whatever club I had chosen to go to, I would try and convince myself that I would be aggressive that night, that I would find an attractive woman, someone I got the feeling I could develop something with, and I would step right up and talk to her, persuade her into giving me her phone number, possibly going out on a date some time.

But when I would enter those densely packed, dimly lit rooms, music so loud that you not only heard it, but felt it move through your body, I would just lose whatever fragile confidence I had built up. The places were filled with men standing around, holding drinks coolly in their hands, their sights set on the women they intended to take home for the night. How phony they were, I would think. And the women, standing in their little circles, trying so hard to appear ladylike, as though they had absolutely no interest in the men that surrounded them. They'd act as though they didn't spend hours in their closets and in front of their mirrors preparing themselves, asking each other, "How do I look? Are my boobs sticking out of this dress too much? Do I look like a ho in this skirt?"

It was all a joke, the posing, the postulating. I would walk through that club, and I would feel the eyes heavy on me. It felt like every pair in the room, male or female. And I would hear in my head what those men were thinking, at least what I thought they were thinking. *Oh, this brotha' thinks he's the shit with his hazel eyes, wavy hair, and expensive clothes. He thinks he's gonna come in here and pull every woman out of this club, take them home and leave me with nothing.* But I thought nothing like that, thought the farthest thing from that, because I knew I had no chance, had been convincing myself of it from the first step I took into the place.

Although women, from the ugliest to the most beautiful, were staring directly into my eyes at one point or another, I could rarely find what it took to approach them. It was as if they had a sixth sense, would somehow know that I was damn near desperate, and immediately be turned off by me. The times that I had been rejected in the past never really left my memory, and I felt destined to bomb regardless of what I did.

Once I did walk up to a short, shapely, brownish woman with a fitted dress that revealed a body that was tight, but soft in the right places. She was surrounded by a number of people, had just finished speaking to one of them, but now was just standing alone, bopping her head to the music.

"Excuse me," I said, almost yelling because the music was so loud.

She turned around, looked at me a moment, waiting for me to say something else, then finally said, "Yeah?"

"I just . . . I just saw you over here and thought I'd come talk to you." I said these words, not leaning in to her, but from where I stood a few feet away, and at a normal volume, knowing that she wouldn't be able to hear them clearly. I was fearful that if she did, she would find something wrong with them, with my delivery, and reject me.

"I didn't hear you," she said, cupping a hand to her ear.

I leaned in this time, and said, "I just said, how are you doing?"

"Oh, good," she said, nodding her head, taking a sip from a glass that had nothing but melted ice in it.

I had nothing else to say. My hands were stuck in my pockets, and I was fishing around in them, as if there I would find the words to interest this woman in me. But there was nothing, and I knew that just that fast she had already lost interest, if she had had any to begin with, because her eyes were wandering about the club.

But I told myself I wouldn't let this go that easily. I mustered up the courage and made another approach, stepping up closer. I tapped her on the shoulder, and was prepared to speak, when another man, a huge smile on his face, tapped her on the other shoulder. She turned to him, and it was obvious that she knew him, for she smiled widely as well, then jumped into his arms.

I turned, lowered my head, stuck my hands back into my pockets, and walked away, telling myself it wasn't meant to be. It was never meant to be, because I hated this, everything about it. The rest of the night, as with most nights, I would spend against the wall, watching as other people enjoyed themselves, watching as the women I told myself I should've been approaching were approached by other men, men that had more confidence than me. Better men.

It wasn't as though I never got approached. There are, because of their painful appearance, always a legion of women who, since a very young age, have come to realize that they must approach men if they ever wished to have one. So every now and then, I would feel a presence at my side, or see a shadow out the corner of my eye, and I would turn my head to find a little troll with blue hair, or a round, smiling woman, barbecue sauce smeared on her cheeks, as she ate complimentary buffet chicken wings beside me.

They would ask me to dance, or try to strike up conversation, and although I was the farthest thing from interested, I would turn them away as pleasantly as I could. I would tell them no I didn't want to dance, or yes I was married, or on one occasion, to one particularly insistent woman with two gold front teeth, I said that yes, indeed I was gay, and proud, and my man played for the Chicago Bears.

"I don't mind. You want to get together anyway?" she said, smiling so brightly that I had to squint.

"I don't think he'd like that," I said, then slowly backed away from her.

One night, a few months before I met Faith, I was out, and the night had gone as it always did, dragging toward an end, and I thought about why I'd come out in the first place and what waited for me when I returned home. I didn't want to go back to that empty, lonely feeling. Suddenly, I felt a tug on my sleeve. When I turned around, there was a woman in front of me, only tolerable to look at, but her body was nothing short of amazing.

"Excuse me fo' just thayin' this, but you fine ath hell," she said to me.

Ghetto, and a super duper lisp that would not be ignored, I thought. Nothing that I would ever extend myself to try for, but it was something, a warm body at least. I swallowed hard and forced myself to say, "You're not bad yourself."

That night, I sat on the edge of my bed as this woman, if she was that, for I didn't know how old she was, and didn't care to ask, began to undress me. Her name was Trina, or Trisha, or maybe even Trixi. She unbuttoned my shirt, opened it up, and her eyes ballooned like she had finally gotten that Christmas present she always wanted.

"Man, you buffed. You tho hard," she said, smoothing a rough, calloused hand over my pecs. What did she do, sand decks with her bare hands for a living?

"You work out, don't you?" she asked, and now she was actually digging her fingers into my abdominal muscles, like each one of them were tiny individual drawers she could pull out. "I bet you tho scrong."

"Yeah. I work out every day."

"You fine," she said, kissing me on my left nipple. "I don't believe you ain't got no woman, Jaython."

I couldn't believe I actually told her my real name, and that I was single. But then again, I could've told her anything, because I was depressed, desperate to feel some sort of affection.

She started to kiss me more, suckling my nipple, then the other while she unbuckled my belt, undid the button down there. And then she was kissing lower and lower, licking my abs, trying to reach down into my boxers and grab me, but she was having a hard time with my zipper. As she tugged, I started to come to my senses, started to ask myself what would I accomplish by letting her do what I knew she was about to do? And I knew I would be accomplishing nothing.

And just then, she was successful in lowering my zipper. She pulled down the front of my boxers, pulled me out, and was about to take me into her mouth when I said, "Hold it."

"Hunh?" she said, looking up like I was stopping her from taking a bite of the dinner it took her so much time and effort to prepare.

"I think I need to take you home."

It was three months before I even thought about going out after that. I had accepted the idea that I would forever be alone. Understanding that, I prepared to begin by going to the movies by myself.

The theater was practically empty, only a few people seated in the chairs as the lights began to dim in the huge room. I quickly sat down, looked around, and noticed the back of a woman's head. There was no way I could know for sure, but something told me that she was attractive. And since I told myself that much, since I was already conjuring up my dream princess, I might as well have her be smart, compassionate, intelligent, and have a great body as well. What the hell. She looked up once, turned her head, and I caught a glimpse of the side of her face. What I saw was angelic, and I was hoping that she wasn't looking for the man that she was supposed to be meeting there.

The lights lowered all the way, the film started, and it didn't make one bit of difference to me, for my eyes were focused on the back of this woman's head, this woman who would save me from all the loneliness I'd been feeling. That was, if I could somehow find the confidence to even approach her.

When the film was over, if someone were to ask me what it was about, I couldn't have told them anything more than what I had seen on the television commercial that interested me in the first place. For that entire two hours, I was staring at her, letting my imagination conjure up a world where she and I were together, where we were in love. Love, I thought. Was there really any meaning to that word? Up to this point, I wasn't sure. But now I told myself she would be the one who would prove to me that there was meaning in it.

So when the credits started to roll, I felt myself becoming anxious, felt the pits of my arms and the palms of my hands becoming moist with perspiration, anticipating what this woman really looked like. More important, if she looked like I knew she would, would I have the guts to walk up to her?

I sat up in my chair, my eyes focused on her, telling myself to relax, not to look so much like a damn pervert. But when she finally turned around, she was so beautiful that I knew I had no choice but to say something. I felt myself standing up as she approached, watching her as if in a daze as she passed my seat.

I quickly grabbed my jacket and followed her, telling myself that I had to get to her before some other man did. When I got her back in my sights, she was walking across the carpeted theater lobby, heading for the glass doors. I stayed some ten feet behind her, telling myself it wasn't just the right time yet to approach, when really I was trying to think of something to say, trying to convince myself that I wasn't really as foolish and insecure as I felt. But I knew I had to act soon, if not that moment, because she was walking toward a beige Camry, and once she got inside her car I was doomed. If I tapped on her window, asked her to roll it down, I would've been better off asking for spare change to wash her windshield, than for her number.

So I swallowed my pride and walked up beside her. It took three or four steps before she acknowledged me.

"Can I help you?" she said, leaning away from me some, as she continued walking toward the car.

Calm down, Jayson, I told myself, then I said, "You like the movie?" The words came out clumsily, nothing smooth about them, or the way I said them. I sounded like a grade school student confronting the girl he's had a crush on since the beginning of the school year.

"What?"

"The movie. Did you like it?" I said, trying to sound a little more comfortable behind the question.

"Uh, yeah," she said, looking at me like I was crazy to ask such a thing, then looking around, as if to make sure there were witnesses just in case I tried to wrestle her to the ground and steal her panties off her, or something.

"Yeah, I liked it, now good-bye," she said, as she kept on walking toward the car.

Was that a blow-off, I asked myself, stopping at the point she had actually blown me off. Normally, I would've lowered my head, shrunk about three feet, and slithered away, but I remembered all the nights at the clubs, the lonely feelings that drove me out there, and the depression I'd experience when I'd come back from not being successful. I couldn't go through that anymore. I looked over at her as she looked for the keys to her car, and I knew, somehow I just knew that we were supposed to be together.

I started again to walk in her direction. She caught sight of me, started to fish around in her purse more frantically, but was unable to find the keys before I caught up to her. And there I stood, in front of her, my mind a total blank, unable to come up with anything more than, "So what did you like about the movie?" How lame.

When she heard that question, she was still conducting the search for the missing keys, but she stopped, her arm still elbow-deep in the purse. She looked up at me as though I'd long ago become a nuisance.

"Listen, I'm sorry. I may not have made myself clear to you, but I don't want to talk to you. So if you'd please, just please leave me alone." She said this looking directly into my eyes, and I looked right back into her beautiful charcoal-black eyes, and said, "Well, what was

your favorite thing about it? The movie that is." I couldn't believe I
continued with this pathetic movie Q&A, but I had no lines; I didn't
have the *game* all those other men had, and I really, really wanted to
start a conversation with this woman, and this was the only way I
knew how. This was Jayson Abrahms being persistent.

"What are you stupid? You have rocks in your head or something?"
she said, tapping her index finger against her temple. "Am I wearing a
sign taped to my back saying, 'Ask me about the movie'? I don't want
to talk to you. So will you leave!" She said this, both anger and a little
bit of fear on her face. She was backed up against the car, looking cor-
nered, and that was probably how she felt, and I was sorry for that, but
I just wished she knew how I was feeling.

I began to turn around, but then stopped, telling myself that I
should just tell her what was on my mind. When she saw my face
again, she looked like she was about to scream, but I said, holding up
both palms, "Hold it. I just want to say something, and I'll leave you
alone. I promise." She settled down, and allowed me to confess.

"I'm sorry I came at you this way. I . . . I don't have any lines. I don't
know how to talk to women the way women like men to, the way
other men can do. I'm no good at that, never have been," I said, feeling ashamed, trying hard just to keep my head up, make occasional eye
contact.

"I'm not going to lie, but then again, I'm sure I don't have to,
because you can probably tell. I'm a pretty sad case, chasing some
woman out of a movie theater. But I'm a decent man. No, strike that.
I'm a good man, with no more problems than any other, and I don't see
why I . . ." I blew out a long, exasperated sigh, glancing up at her just
to make sure she was still there. "I just thought you were a beautiful
woman, who maybe wasn't involved with anyone since you were here
by yourself. I just thought that maybe . . . that maybe there would've
been a chance that . . ." And then I realized just how much of a complete fool I was making of myself. "I'm sorry that I ever bothered you.
Forgive me," I said, and then I turned around and walked off.

But after taking only four or five steps, I heard her voice.

"Hey, hey, wait."

I turned around to see her walking toward me.

"What did you say your name was again?"

o   o   o

Since that day, Faith and I have been together. I looked down at her, sitting on my sofa, looking like she wanted nothing more than to tear my head off, and I wanted to laugh. How could she not know how much I loved her? How could she question such a thing, not realize that I felt forever grateful to her for saving me from all that crap that I was enduring. Could she not know this because I had a best friend who happened to be a woman? Could that one thing cast doubt over all the times I'd told and shown her that I loved her, all the wonderful times we had together? I mean, damn, we loved each other enough to agree to get married, and she didn't know how much I loved her? It was ridiculous. I shook my head, giving her a sympathetic look.

Faith tightened up all her body parts even more. "What the hell are you shaking your head at?" she said.

"You. You second guessing this."

"Me?" she said, incredulously. "We're supposed to be getting married this weekend. In four days. Four, Jayson," she said, holding up her fingers. She could be so damn dramatic sometimes. "And I'm putting up with this shit."

"What shit are you talking about?"

"That bitch downstairs," Faith spat, looking down, as if she could see Asha through the floor.

"Who, again, did you say?" I asked, letting it be known in my tone that I'd taken offense.

"Your friend . . . Asha." She said her name like they were mortal enemies.

"What does she have to do with us, with our wedding, with our life together?" I said, walking closer to her.

"Everything, Jayson. She's everywhere. You talk about her all the time."

"Bullshit, Faith. I don't talk about her, or see her any more than I see anyone else. And you know that if Asha was a guy you wouldn't be making such a big deal out of this," I said, raising my voice.

"But she's not a guy. She's not, and I feel threatened by her."

"Threatened!" I threw my head back in exaggerated laughter. But when I looked back at Faith, she wasn't laughing, wasn't smiling. Nothing. Just dead serious.

"She's just my friend, a pal, Faith. Give me one reason why you should feel threatened by her."

Faith looked at me as though I didn't have the intelligence of a soiled, crusty sweat sock.

"Well, Jayson, let me see if I can do better than that. Maybe because she's amazingly beautiful, or that you and her used to have a relationship, or the fact that she lives right downstairs. Or, maybe I'm being paranoid, and this means absolutely nothing at all," she said, looking up to the ceiling, scratching her head in fake bewilderment. "But the fact that I just saw her hugging and kissing you, and you two saying that you loved each other, that makes me feel a bit threatened, you know what I'm saying, Jayson!"

I just stood there, staring dumbly at Faith.

"So what are you going to do about it?"

"Asha is a dear friend of mine, always will be, so I can't do anything," I said, starting to anger, feeling as though I was being pushed to do something I didn't want to do. "And since you're the one feeling threatened, not me, I shouldn't have to do anything."

Faith didn't say anything to my smart remark, just sat there on the sofa, looking introspective, as if weighing her options. Then she stood up. She stood up, walked around the coffee table and past me, grabbed her purse, and headed for the door. I rushed up behind her as she grabbed the doorknob and opened the door. That's when I knew she was serious, that something was wrong. I forced the door closed.

"What's up? What do you think you're doing?" I said, standing behind her.

"I think I'm leaving," she said, not turning around, but still staring at the door.

"Leaving for the night?"

"Leaving for good," Faith said sadly.

I turned from her, threw my hands into my hair, grabbed fistfuls of it as I paced away from her. "What the hell am I supposed to do?" I asked of both myself and her.

"I'm not supposed to feel like this," Faith said, again into the door.

"She's my friend," I said, still pacing.

"I'm about to get married in four days. Four, and I should not be feeling threatened."

"She just kissed me on the cheek. She always kisses me on the cheek."

"I shouldn't have to feel like this on what is supposed to be the most important day of my life. I shouldn't have to wonder if my fiancé and his best friend are fucking or not."

And that stopped me dead in my tracks. I rushed over to Faith, pulled her off that door. "What did you say?" I said, grabbing her by her shoulders.

She said, looking straight into my eyes, "I said that I shouldn't have to wonder if you two are fucking or not. But you don't even have to answer that, Jayson. You can't answer it, because I wouldn't know if I should believe you at this point anyway."

"Then what am I supposed to do?"

"Prove that there's nothing going on."

"Fine. Fine. Just tell me, how am I supposed to do that?"

"You go downstairs and tell her that you can't be friends anymore," Faith said, pointing down at the floor. "Tell her that she can still come to the wedding, but after that, it's over."

"Faith, you know I can't do that, and you shouldn't be asking me to."

"Jayson, I know what that girl means to you. I'm not doing this to be cruel, but you have to consider how I feel. I can't go into this situation feeling halfhearted."

"But . . ." I said, trying to think of some way to reason with her.

"Bottom line, Jayson. It's either me or her."

"I won't make that decision," I said, shaking my head. "I won't."

Faith looked at me, sympathetically. "Then you just did. Good-bye, Jayson."

She pulled the door open once again, and once again, I pushed it shut.

"All right," I painfully conceded. "I'll do it."

4

This is wrong, I told myself as I took each step with the speed of a ninety-year-old man who had double hip replacements. This was my girl, my best friend I was going to dis, and I was desperately trying to make it right in my head in the time it took for me to reach that bottom step.

I thought about all that I would lose if I lost Asha, thought about all that we had been through. And then I remembered that day six years ago when I stood on the sidewalk outside my mother's house. It was only half an hour drive from where I lived then, but I saw her only once every two weeks or so, and it had been more than a month since I had seen her last.

Standing outside of this house, I just stared up at it, at the chipping and peeling paint, the lawn that had been neglected for so long that it grew to waist-length in parts, the gutter along the north side of the house that had fallen, and was hanging from the roof. This was the house I had grown up in, and it was painful to see it this way. I could only look at it for so long without turning away to regain my strength before looking back. I had left so long ago, and had fooled myself, saying that I would never come back, that I would never see my mother again because of the way she treated me, the way she neglected me.

I remembered that porch from so many years ago, when I was a sophomore in high school, before the wood had rotted, and some of the stairs caved in. I remembered when Tonya Langly sat beside me on one of those stairs. I was crazy about her, stared at her during class, and dreamt of her at night, and I wondered why the hell she was there with me. What could she have possibly seen in me that would attract her? I continued to sit there, wanting to touch her, wanting to kiss her, but knew I wasn't deserving, knew that I wasn't worth her time. I couldn't have been. I wasn't worth my own mother's time, and she'd made me painfully aware of that so often that her voice saying those words still rang in my head, as I stood out in front of this house as an adult. Every now and then, I would snatch a peek at Tonya as I sat with her, but I could not find actual words to say to her. We sat there in silence for what seemed like endless minutes, until she said, "I'll talk to you later, Jayson," pulled herself from the stairs and walked away.

She never really did talk to me after that. That hurt me more than I could've imagined. But what was most sad about it all, was that I got used to being dumped like that. It happened so many more times, me questioning my worth, me asking myself what these girls saw in me; they obviously started asking themselves the same question and realized they saw nothing.

Now my mother was sick, and the nurse said that her Alzheimer's was progressing, that she would need twenty-four-hour care, and that she alone could no longer give her the care she needed.

"I really suggest you put her in a home, Mr. Abrahms," she told me over the phone.

Me, I thought. Why should I be responsible for her? Why should I even care? I cursed my father for ever marrying her, for having me, and making her think he would be forever in our lives when he knew he wouldn't.

I looked just like him, my mother always said. Acted the same way, said the same things, and she couldn't look at me without seeing him. I felt her hatred of him in those narrowing eyes each time they rested on me. I always asked myself, was there hate in that look for me too? I thought I had never known the answer, but I was just fooling myself. The answer was right before me in the way she did just enough for me to keep me clean, clothed, and healthy. She never told me she loved me after he left, never held me, never kissed me, and it was for that reason that now my confidence regarding women was swimming below ground level in the sewers somewhere.

"You ready to do this, baby?" Asha said. She was standing beside me, outside the house, holding my hand, lending whatever support she could. I had brought her with me just for that reason, because I was afraid that if she wasn't there, I probably wouldn't have made it this far, would've made a U-turn just after leaving my driveway, and tried my best to just forget about my mother.

"But last time I spoke with you, you said she was doing fine," I had told the nurse during that recent phone conversation.

"I know. She was. But Alzheimer's can progress rapidly, Mr. Abrahms. She's blanking in and out. Sometimes she's herself, and sometimes she's not responsive at all, or doesn't know who she is, where she is. She walks around the house, hostilely breaking things. When I came in today, her hand was bleeding because she was playing with broken glass she had smashed."

"Jayson," and that was Asha again. She squeezed my hand, looked into my eyes to make sure I was still with her. "You okay to do this now?"

I nodded. "Yeah," I lied, and as we slowly climbed the worn, creaking wooden stairs, I prayed that my mother had blanked out, was in one of those spells so she wouldn't know what was happening. Otherwise, I knew she wouldn't let me take her out of that house. She'd been there too long to want to leave, to allow herself to be taken.

I slid the key in the door and pushed it open.

"Elizabeth," I called out. I had always called my mother by her name, and although I knew it was disrespectful, it was appropriate, considering she never felt much like a mother to me.

"Elizabeth," I called out again, pulling Asha along behind me, through the old, dark, musty-smelling house. All the lights were off, and I was hit with vivid memories as I walked through the living room, passing the plastic-covered sofa and chair, the piano that no one knew how to play, and I was forbidden to even try. I passed the painted portrait of Jesus that hung over the fireplace. I stopped in front of it, looked at the halo of light that glowed behind him. How that picture always scared me as a child.

"Elizabeth," I called again, still examining the painting.

"Where do you think she is?" Asha asked me.

"I don't know, but she's here. She's here," I said, pulling Asha toward the kitchen. We'd started down the long hallway, when Asha stopped.

"What's that?" Asha said, bending over and picking a sweater off the floor. It was my mother's. And when I looked farther down the hall, there were more clothes strewn about. Then at the entrance of the kitchen we saw her suitcase sitting open, toiletries spilling out of it. It was clearly the suitcase the nurse told me she had packed for my mother, before leaving for the night.

We stepped around the clothes toward the kitchen, and there I saw my mother, sitting in a chair in the dark, her graying hair wild all about her head, her cloudy, tired eyes staring blankly into the open refrigerator. Her frail, slightly overweight body was slumped in the chair, the open fridge splashing her with light, her head falling slightly forward toward her chest.

"Elizabeth," I called, but she didn't answer. "Why do I have to go through this?" I said just loud enough for Asha to hear.

"Look at the way she's sitting. Is she all right, Jayson?"

I didn't know, I thought, but I took a step into the kitchen, and felt something crack under my shoe. I reached over to turn on the light so I could see what it was.

"Oh my God!" Asha gasped.

The floor was covered with broken plates, bowls, and glasses. I didn't know what the hell was going on, but I started to quickly brush the larger pieces of glass away, making a path for us to get through. That's when I saw something smeared across the floor under the glass. These were red smears, and when I looked closely, I saw that some of the shards of glass on the floor were painted with this same color red. Blood. I saw only faint traces at first, then heavier marks as they neared my mother, until I saw two puddles of blood just under her feet. She was wearing white sweat socks, but the entire bottom half of each was saturated with a thick pad of her own blood.

"Call 911, Asha!" I yelled, pushing her in the direction of the phone in the living room. "Call 911, hurry!"

I rushed over to my mother, grabbed her by the shoulders. Her head rolled limp on her neck, then fell back, her eyes, her mouth falling open.

"Mother!"

"I'm not leaving," she murmured, her voice groggy.

"What are you talking about?"

"I'm not leaving my house. Ms. Tiffany said you were coming to put me in a home."

"We can talk about that later," I said, trying to grab her around the back, and lift her, but she swatted my arms away.

"No. I lived here . . . I lived here," and she was gasping, as if she was about to pass out. "Forty years, and ain't nobody taking me out of this house."

"We'll talk about that later," I said, trying to grab her again, but realizing even if I could get her out of the chair, I couldn't stand her up, because it was her feet that were injured.

"I got to get you to a hospital," I told her, then cried out to Asha, "Are they coming? Did you get them yet?"

"I'm not leaving this house, Jayson," she said, tugging at my shirt. But this time it sounded more like a plea than an order.

"You're bleeding and you're sick. I've got to get you out of here." I looked down at her feet, the blood dripping from the socks onto the floor, accumulating now in one wide, shiny circle of red underneath her. "Asha, dammit, my mother's bleeding here," I yelled into the other room. "Did you get them!"

"They're on the line right now"—I heard her yell into the kitchen, and then her voice dropped as she gave them the address—"1642 West . . ."

"I'm not sick, Jayson. I'm fine. I can take care of myself."

"You are not fine. You have Alzheimer's, and you can't stay in this house by yourself anymore."

Asha rushed into the kitchen, stood over me and my mother. "They're on their way," she said, winded.

"Then stay here with me," my mother said.

"What did you say?" I said, knowing full well what my mother just uttered, shocked and angered that she'd even suggest it. After all the years that she just barely took care of me, treated me like nothing more than a stranger she was charged to raise, now she was asking me to take care of her? How dare she? I thought, so angered by what she had asked me that I wanted to turn around and leave her that moment.

"I can't do that," I said, trying my best to squelch my anger.

"I'm your mother. I raised you, and . . ."

"Elizabeth, don't."

"The least you could do is . . ."

"I said, don't, dammit!" raising my voice loud enough to stop her, and have Asha look at me as if I'd committed a crime.

"Then I'll take care of myself."

"No, you won't take care of yourself! You can't take care of yourself. Look at what you did here. If we hadn't come here when we did, you would have bled to death. You would've killed yourself!" I yelled, becoming even angrier with her. "And who would've been to blame?" I grabbed her around the shoulders again, forced her to look at me. "I would've. It would've been my fault that you were dead. All my fault!" I yelled, infuriated beyond belief. And then I felt Asha's hand on my arm.

"Jayson. She's your mother," Asha said, like she had to remind me of that fact in order for me not to harm her. I looked around, as if standing outside myself, as if someone else made me grab her like that. My mother was looking up at me like I was a stranger. It wasn't the illness that made me unrecognizable to her, but my behavior. If Asha hadn't stopped me, I don't know what I would've said next, what I would've done. I took my hands off her.

"Like it or not, I'm taking you out of here," I said, in a firm, even tone. "So I don't want to hear any more protests. Period!"

And then I heard the sirens from the approaching ambulance, and I was thankful that they were coming, not solely because they would take care of my mother, but also because they would save me from this situation. They would also stop her from depending on me when she had no right, and free me from having to tell her that there was no way I'd ever take care of her like that.

"Please, son. Please, don't put me in a home," she begged. "Please. Please, son."

And after the ambulance came and took her away, after she was checked into the hospital, and after I had made plans for her to be transferred to Shady Brook upon her release, I still heard her voice, calling me, begging me, "Please, son. Please."

"She's my mother," I told Asha, near tears, that night on the stairs outside the hospital. Her arms were around me, pulling me as close as she could to her body.

"She's my mother and when she needed me, begged me for help, what did I do? Turned her down," I said, looking up toward the stars, blinking my eyes, trying to stop the tears. They fell anyway. "What kind of son am I, refusing his own mother? What kind of man am I? Why do you even love me?" I said, turning my tear-streaked face to her.

"Jayson," she said, softly. "You're doing what you're doing, because you have reason to. What reason that is, I don't know, and you don't have to tell me. But whether you do, or don't, I will never question it, because you're a wonderful man." She broke the path of one of the tears on my cheek, kissing me there. "And that's why I love you, and I always will."

I remembered those words as I descended the final stair, placing myself in front of Asha's door with orders to tell her that we could no longer be friends, that the promise she made that night to love me forever didn't matter anymore, because I no longer had the right to care for her.

I reached up to knock on the door. The watch on my wrist read a little after midnight, but I knocked anyway.

After a moment, there was no reply. I thought of turning around, walking back up those stairs, thinking of some lie to tell Faith when I saw her, but the door opened. The door opened just as I was turning, as I was counting my blessings that she hadn't answered.

"Jayson," Asha said, holding the door open. "Is everything all right?"

I turned around giving her a saddened, concerned look.

"Come in," she said, reading my expression.

I walked in, my head lowered, and headed into the kitchen, had a seat on one of the stools beside her breakfast bar. I clasped my hands together, focused my attention on them, feeling ashamed of what I was down here to say.

"Something's wrong. Tell me what it is," Asha said, walking toward me wearing a cotton nightgown that fell to just above her knees. She had been in bed, probably sound asleep, and here I was bringing this shit to her. I felt even more ashamed. I pulled my head up, looked at her face, the sympathetic expression she wore, the same one she wore the night she comforted me those years ago, and I knew I had no business doing this.

"Jayson," Asha said again, now standing in front of me, placing a hand on my hands, urging me to tell her what was wrong.

"C'mon, Jayson," she said, lighthearted, smiling a little. "You're starting to spook me here. Remember what we said, whenever there was something bothering one of us and the other person asks what it was, we would have to tell. Just tell me. It can't be all that bad."

"Faith doesn't want me to be friends with you any longer," I blurted.

The smile disappeared from Asha's face and she took one step backward, caught off guard by what I'd said.

"So . . . so why is that?"

"Because she feels threatened."

"By what?"

"By you," I told her.

"Me? Did you tell her that we were just friends? Doesn't she know that?"

"I told her, and she knows, but I don't think she believes it, or trusts it," I said, grabbing one of Asha's hands.

"So you told her that she's just going to have to learn to trust it, right? You told her that she had no right demanding who you're friends with and who you aren't," Asha said, as if expecting me to cut in and tell her how I did exactly that.

"You reminded her that I've known you longer than her, that we've been through all sorts of shit together. You told her that, didn't you, Jayson?"

I was silent, unable to admit to her that I hadn't said anything of the sort. But she deduced as much and pulled away from me, turning her back.

How could I make this make sense to her? How could I relay to her all that was at stake here?

"Faith is my fiancée, Asha," I said, timidly. "We're about to get married, and like she said, for her to feel threatened in the process of taking the most important step of her life just isn't right."

Asha didn't say anything, but I heard her sniffling, and from behind her, I saw her bring her hand to her face.

"Asha," I said, walking up just behind her. "I don't want to do this."

"Then why are you?"

"Because Faith is my fiancée, and I love her."

"And I'm your friend, and I thought you loved me too," Asha said, turning around, her eyes puffy.

"I do, but—"

"But what? That doesn't mean anything now, because Faith is on the scene? You can just toss me aside like I've never meant anything to you. Fine! Do it. I don't give a fuck. Do what you want to do," Asha said, about to move away from me, but I grabbed her by the arm, held her there in front of me.

"You think I want to do this?" I said to her forcefully. "Is that what you think? You're wrong. I have no choice. Do you know how many relationships I've been in that ended because I ended them, because I wouldn't let them continue, because I couldn't, because of how my mother screwed me up?

"For years now I've been running, avoiding commitment, and you know that. I've done it to you. And all that running has left me with nothing, with no one."

"You act like there's something wrong with being by yourself."

"I'm not saying that. I just can't do it anymore. I need someone, and that someone is Faith."

Asha just stared at me for a long moment, looking as if she were trying to burn my image into her brain so she'd never forget me. Then with the tips of her fingers, she smoothed the tears from under her eyes.

She sniffed and said, "I'm just being a selfish bitch."

"What did you say?"

"It's because you're my best friend and I love you. But Faith is absolutely right. If I was in her place, I would probably be doing the same thing."

"What are you talking about? What are you saying?" I asked. Even though not a moment ago, I was trying to convince her to accept Faith's wishes, I was now feeling betrayed that she was surrendering so easily.

"You love her, right?" Asha said, still sniffing, wiping the last tear away.

"Yeah," I said, sounding more unsure than I was.

"And you're happy?"

"Yeah."

"And that's what is most important to me. I would never want to jeopardize that," Asha said, moving toward me, wrapping her arms around my neck and giving me a hug. "Besides, after a while, she'll realize I mean her no harm, and we'll be friends again. Just wait and see."

I silently let go of Asha, kissed her on the cheek, and walked toward the door. I reached out, grabbed the knob, turned it, but could not open it. I just stood there, thinking about all Asha and I had been through, all that she meant to me, and the foolish, thoughtless thing I had just done to her.

"What?" I heard Asha call from behind me.

"I can't do it," I said. And then I turned around to face her. "And I'm not going to do it. You're my best friend, Asha, and if Faith wants me, then she'll just have to understand that we're a package deal."

Asha smiled, and at that moment I knew how much that meant to her, and I knew I had made the right decision.

When I walked into my apartment, Faith was standing in the living room, her arms crossed, as if she had been standing there the entire time I was downstairs, checking her watch, wondering why it was taking me so long. When she looked at me, I saw the expression on her face soften some. She could obviously see that I was hurting.

Faith walked over to me, opening her arms, taking me into an embrace. She kissed me on the side of my face, rubbed a reassuring hand back and forth across my back.

"I'm sorry I asked you to do that, baby. But it had to be done if we were to move on. Did she take it okay?"

"She was hurt," I lied. I wanted to tell her the truth about what went on down there, but I just couldn't do it. "I think she'll get over it, though."

"I'm sure she will, baby," Faith said, still rubbing her palm gently across my back.

5

"Can you make this thing go a little faster," Asha said, leaning forward from the backseat of the taxi so the cabbie could hear her over the loud classical music he was playing.

"What?" he said in a thick East Indian accent, without turning around to acknowledge her.

"I said, can you speed it up? I'm late for work," Asha said, louder, almost screaming. "And can you turn down that damn music!" She plopped back in the seat after the cabbie turned down the volume only a notch or two, and sped the car along congested Michigan Avenue.

I shouldn't have yelled at the man, Asha thought, slumped in the backseat of the cab, fuming. She wasn't angry at the driver, but at herself, and not for being late. She was angry because she had been dreaming again, dreaming about the things she told herself never to dream about. She wanted so much for those thoughts, those images, never to enter her sleeping mind again. At night before going to bed, she'd sit and pray, and beg God to keep them away. She had even done this last night, but they came anyway. They came and blanketed her, wrapped themselves around her, bound her so tight that she could not find her way out of sleep, could not awaken to stop herself from dreaming. But did she truly want to stop herself? This was the question that really bothered her the most.

If she really wanted to wake up, if those dreams were as troubling as she told and taught herself to believe, wouldn't she have snapped out of them instead of sleeping through them, waking in the morning feeling as rested as ever, but with an uncanny wanting, a yearning that she didn't quite understand?

At first, three or four months ago, they were innocent, just a woman in a bare-walled room with Asha. They were talking—about what, Asha could never remember upon waking. But just the fact that the woman was beautiful made the conversation somewhat enjoyable.

Each time the dream came, the conversations became more intimate. Not with regard to what was said, but *how* it was said, from what distance it was said, and how much clothing was being worn when it was said.

During the first dream, this woman was sitting way across the stark white room in the only chair other than the one Asha sat in. She was fully clothed, in a business suit, sensible shoes, glasses, her hair pulled back in a bun. But with each dream, that chair would come closer, another button would be undone on that blouse revealing a bit more cleavage, a few more strands from that bun would find their way loose. Eventually the glasses just disappeared.

Then they began to touch each other. They would touch each other's hands at first, caressing each other's fingers, each other's palms. Asha would lay a soft hand on the side of this woman's face, and this woman would lay her own hand on top of Asha's, and smile, letting it be known that she approved of Asha's touch. Then the clothes started to disappear, and Asha would find herself in this room nearly naked, only in a bra and panties, the woman wearing the same thing. This scared Asha. The woman would then take Asha in her arms, close to her warm body, and comfort her, tell her everything would be all right, that there was nothing to worry about, or to be afraid of, and Asha would feel herself relax.

And then the dream would end, and Asha would awake, feeling strangely empty and fulfilled at the same time. Asha would try to remember pieces of that dream, breathing deeply, attempting to pick up the woman's scent, because the dream was that real. And all the while she would scold herself for doing so.

The touching, the holding—that was as far as it ever went . . . until last night, Asha thought, feeling overcome by anger in the back of the cab.

Last night, as Asha was first stealing into her dreams, she had immediately woken herself up. She had propped herself up on her elbows, her eyes darting about in the dark bedroom, as if looking for the woman who had shown up so fast in her dreams. All the other times it had taken her a while. But she was right there, and something felt odd, this pulling, this attraction Asha felt within her, and she knew that this dream would be the one that crossed the line. So she cleared her mind, focused on something in the dark room, the picture of an old dirt road hanging on the wall that she couldn't see but knew was there. And when she felt that the desire was no longer there within her, Asha allowed herself to settle back into her pillows, between her sheets and blanket, and fall back to sleep.

But when she woke up this morning, she knew she had not really lost that desire at all. If anything it had only grown, and she knew that because of the voraciousness with which she had this woman, the willingness she exhibited in *being had* by this woman.

Asha tried to tell herself it wasn't really her participating, that it was another woman. She herself was just a spectator, standing on the sidelines, witnessing these unforgivable actions. But she knew that wasn't the case because of the point of view she had while dreaming, because of the angle at which she held the woman's breasts in her hands, while that woman was above her, straddling her. If it wasn't Asha experiencing those things, how could she have felt that woman's warm breath on the side of her face, felt the soft skin of her belly, felt it quiver when Asha kissed her softly there. If it wasn't Asha but someone else, how could she have heard her name every single time that woman called out her name, even though it was no higher than a whisper. If it wasn't her, how could she have known what that woman tasted like? This bothered Asha the most.

Asha clamped her eyes shut in the back of the cab, trying to force the thought out of her head, the taste off her tongue, even though the glands in the back of her throat caused her mouth to water some.

Why was this happening to her? Was it because this was what she really wanted? But no! She wouldn't answer that, because maybe if she stopped thinking about it altogether, it would simply go away. Wasn't that how it all worked? Asha thought, feeling her spirits rise the slightest bit. Wasn't that the reason she dreamt about all of that to begin with, because she was so worried about it?

That was exactly right, she told herself, forcing a smile upon her face. And besides, she had other things to think about, like bumping into Jayson's psycho fiancée this morning as she was leaving for work. Faith had been coming down the stairs just as Asha was coming out of her apartment.

"How you doing, Faith?" Asha said, trying to sound cheery, trying to act as though she wasn't pissed at what Faith had Jayson try to do to their friendship.

"Good morning, Asha," Faith said, looking sympathetically at Asha. "I'm sorry about Jayson having to end your friendship."

He didn't tell Faith that he hadn't gone through with it, Asha thought. She didn't know why in the hell not, but Asha would keep what happened quiet if that was how he wanted it.

"I told him that maybe he should reconsider, that maybe you weren't that clingy a person after all," Faith said with an air. Asha wondered just what in the hell she was talking about, what pipe she had been smoking her bad drugs from.

"But he said no. He said it was best to get rid of you because being friends with you was taking too much time away from being with me. And besides, he wasn't really enjoying your company anyway."

Asha couldn't believe her ears, couldn't believe this woman had the nerve to stand there and lie to her.

"What did you just say to me?" Asha said, catching attitude, placing her hands on her hips.

"I said, Jayson never really enjoyed being with you recently anyway. He just tolerated you."

"Oh, really," Asha said, knowing she shouldn't do what she was about to do, but she couldn't help it. The bitch deserved it.

"Yes really."

"Well, if he just tolerated me, I wonder why he didn't actually end our friendship. I wonder why after he recited that nonsense you put in his mouth, he took it all back. I wonder why he told me that if you

were to have him, you'd have to have the both of us," Asha said, grin-
ning. "Package deal, baby."

Faith glared at Asha slyly, breathing hard, looking as if she were about
to explode. "No, he didn't say that. I know him. He wouldn't say that."

"You can't know him that well, because he surely lied to you last
night."

Faith looked even angrier than before. Asha saw her fists clench at
her sides, and she welcomed the woman trying to step up and test her,
see what she was made of. But she knew Faith wasn't that stupid.

"I wonder what else he's lying to you about?" Asha said, knowing
that she was doing nothing but getting her friend into more trouble,
but she couldn't help herself.

Faith gave Asha a confused look, and Asha couldn't tell if she was
about to charge at her, or break down and cry. "We'll see who has the
last laugh," Faith spat. Then she yanked the door open, and stormed
out down the stairs.

"I said, seven dollars, forty cents," the cabbie said, snapping Asha
out of her daydream. He was leaning over his seat, one hand extended,
the other pointing at the meter.

"Oh, I'm sorry," Asha said, pulling a ten-dollar bill out of her purse
and passing it to him. "Keep the change." Asha rode up to the twelfth
floor on a crowded elevator, thinking that Jayson would have huge
problems with Faith today *and* in the future. Asha wished that she
could've saved him from those problems, and realized that if she wasn't
dealing with her own terrible issues, she wouldn't have had to save
him, because they would've probably still been together. But she
couldn't butt into their problems. Even though Asha felt Faith wasn't
right for Jayson, he would have to figure that out for himself.

The elevator doors opened on the twelfth floor. Asha squeezed her
way through the wall of people around her and got off. There was a
large reception area that opened up before her, the walls, tables, and
reception desk were all an orangish cherrywood. The carpeting on the
floor was thick and plush, a rich dark gold color, as were the two
leather sofas and chairs in the waiting area.

Behind the huge, circular reception desk, sat a cute, petite brunette, her hair pulled back in a ponytail, wearing thin, black-framed glasses and a white smock. Affixed to the front of the waist-high desk were huge black letters that read, "Phillipe Cozi."

Asha rushed up to the desk. "Susie, is my ten o'clock here yet?" she said, glancing at the clock on the wall in front of her. It read ten-thirty.

"Yeah," Susie said, "but she just walked in ten minutes ago. I sent her back, so she should be just about ready."

"Sue, you're a sweetheart. What would we do without you?" Asha said, hurrying to her client.

"No problem," Sue called back to her, smiling. "Everything is cool. Just take it easy."

Take it easy, Asha thought to herself, as she pushed her way into the locker room. That's easy for her to say. She probably didn't have a best friend who was trying to get rid of her because the psycho woman he was infatuated with was telling him to do so. And she was sure Sue didn't have to worry about her dreams tormenting her, telling her something about herself that she truly didn't want to hear. And she didn't have to worry that if she did listen to those dreams, accept what they were conveying to her, that word would get out, and she would run the very real risk of getting fired from her job.

Take it easy. "Yeah, right," Asha blew, as she slipped on some white pants, a white top, and a white smock. That was the last thing she could do. But she would give it a shot. Asha walked into the small room adjacent to the locker room, adjusted the lights, lowered the table, making sure it was clean, covering it with a sheet, and verifying that everything she needed was on the small table beside her.

She would give "taking it easy" a try, stop thinking about what was bothering her, which just happened to be the entire population of beautiful women. If she could just keep her mind off them for an entire day, then maybe, little by little, she'd lose her desire for them alto-gether. Yeah, that might work.

"Okay, Chanda. I'm ready for you now," Asha said. And out of another locker room came a beautiful honey brown woman, a body like a goddess, padding barefoot across the carpet, wearing only a towel wrapped around her body.

"Sorry I'm late," Asha said, smiling, focusing her attention past Chanda, and not on the way the bright white towel hugged her shapely brown curves. "Traffic."

"No problem. I was stuck in it too," she said, climbing on the table, and lying on her stomach.

"So what will it be today?" Asha said, feeling her entire body start to warm with anxiety.

"How about a full body massage?" Chanda said, closing her eyes, and letting out a long, relaxing sigh. "And lots of oil."

Great. Yeah, sure thing, Asha thought. And while I'm squirting it all over your fine, firm body, and rubbing it into your soft, sensuous skin, I'll just try and do what Sue said, and take it easy.

6

I woke up this morning, rolled over in bed, and was surprised to see that Faith wasn't there. I sat up, looked around the room, listened for a moment to hear if she was in the bathroom, but there were no sounds of running water, no teeth being brushed. Nothing.

When Faith spent the night, which was three or four days a week, she normally nudged me awake, bent over me, and gave me a kiss when she was leaving. "Have a good day," she'd say. Then as I fell back into sleep, she'd walk out the door, jump in her car, and leave.

This morning she didn't wake me up, and I really don't believe she kissed me good-bye. I drove her here from the restaurant last night, so I gotta assume that maybe she was still feeling a little funny about the Asha thing last night, and took a cab to work this morning, rather than deal with me.

It was probably for the best, I told myself. I had a hell of a lot of work to do. I had to look at some new buildings and check the condition of a few of my South Side properties. Besides, Faith knew the deal. She knew how much I loved her, and that whatever arguments we had, I wasn't going to give up on her.

"Do you believe that?" I'd asked her last night, after we had gotten undressed and were lying under the covers in the dark.

"Just go to sleep, Jayson. It's been a long day," she said, not seeming to care about my question.

"No," I said, leaning over her and turning on the bedside lamp. She squinted against the bright light. "I want to know if you believe that I love you, and that you're the most important thing in my life."

She rolled toward me, on her side, looking deeply into my eyes, as if searching for the answer, then she smiled a little, and said, "Yeah, Jayson. I believe you." She kissed me on the cheek, then said, "Now go to sleep."

I looked at my alarm clock and saw that it was a little after ten-thirty. Damn, I really had to start getting up earlier, I thought, climbing out of bed. I went into the bathroom, took a shower, toweled off, then stood in front of the full-length mirror, examining myself.

Not bad, I thought, flexing my left bicep, watching it swell into a tight, hard ball under the skin of my arm. I flexed my pectorals, watched them jump at my command. I tightened the muscles in my thighs, wrapped a hand around one of them, and felt the hardness there. But I also noticed that it wasn't as hard as it once was. I placed a palm flat against my belly, and although my abs still felt like an old cobblestone street, there was a thin layer of fat developing over them. It was something that I should take care of, maybe by working out at the gym more. But I knew that wasn't the reason why my body was softening. It was the way I'd been eating, the late night dinners with Faith, not caring what was on my plate, and then being okay with skipping a day or two at the gym. I mean, what difference did it really make? Faith loved the way I looked, and we were about to get married, so why did I still need to be wearing myself down, working out for two hours everyday. Staying in shape would be good enough, I had told myself. I didn't have to look like the Incredible Hulk anymore. But it had been three days since the last time I went, so I would force myself to go this morning.

When I came back home from the gym, sipping on a protein shake, I was glad that I had gone. I felt revitalized, my body felt tight under the sweats I was wearing, and I'd pretty much forgotten about the Faith and Asha situation.

I hit the shower again, adjusted the water to the hottest tempera-ture I could stand. The steaming spray felt good striking the muscles in my back. It relaxed me some, but nothing compared to what I used to get when I was dating Asha. She would massage me so well that afterward I would lie on the bed unable to move, feeling as though my body hadn't a single bone or muscle in it, as if it were made of warm Jell-O.

She was nice enough to keep giving me massages even after we had stopped dating. I know how sexual that sounds, but it was a friendly thing, innocent, helpful and nothing more. My muscles were tight, leaving me sore and aching, and she had the skill and talent to relieve that. She even did it for me after I started dating Faith.

"Now you know, if that new girlfriend of yours walked in here right now, saw you on your stomach, half naked, me straddling you, she would skin you alive. You know that, don't you?" Asha said, smoothing more oil on my back, deeply massaging the muscles there with her fists. It felt so good I wanted to pass out.

"Just massage, wench! I don't pay you to talk, but to massage. Now massage. Massage!" I said, joking. We both laughed, getting a kick out of that. But when I heard a shuffle outside my front door, and it opened before either one of us could get up, we no longer found anything funny.

Faith stood just inside my apartment door, holding two bags of KFC, home on a lunch break, no doubt wanting to surprise me. There she was, the key I had given her just the night before in her shaking hand. Her mouth was hanging open, nothing coming out but a barely audible gasp.

I quickly moved to my feet, pushing Asha off me. She spilled over onto the floor with a thud.

"It's not what you think . . . what it seems," I said, rushing over to Faith, seeing the horrid expression on her face, knowing she was about to either turn and leave or go into a rage if I didn't explain this away.

"It's really not what it looks like."

But Faith wasn't hearing me, wasn't even looking at me at first, because her eyes were keenly focused on the beautiful woman with the great body, wearing a T-shirt tied in a knot to expose her flat belly, and short-shorts to expose her toned thighs. Then Faith's glare landed on me, on my bare chest, the oil that was slathered all over me. Her eyes lowered some, then narrowed. And why did they do that? Maybe because she caught sight of, and this was a surprise to me, the half hard-on that was bulging mildly into my sweats.

Damn! I thought. That wasn't a sexual boner though, but an I-feel-great-this-massage-is-relaxing-boner. Two totally different things. And I thought for a second, just a brief second, about trying to explain that to her. But then I realized that if I could speak every language known to man, I still wouldn't be able to make her understand why she shouldn't think anything of the erection that she was staring at, and couldn't take credit for building. But what was truly the worst thing about that entire situation was that it was the first time that Faith had ever met Asha. After all the times I had been telling Faith about her, about my best friend, my buddy, and "Oh, you're gonna love her," this was how they met.

I realized that's when it all started, the suspicions, the doubting about the relationship Asha and I shared. And sometimes I asked myself, could I really blame her? Yeah, kinda. She should've gotten over those doubts a long time ago, I thought as I turned off the shower water. Just then, the phone started ringing. That was always the case. The phone always rang at the most inopportune times, while you're on the toilet, having sex, or taking a stupid shower.

I yanked a towel off the rack, threw it around me, and rushed to the phone, dripping a path of water behind me. I only rushed because I thought it was Faith calling. I wanted to talk to her, just hear her voice. But when I picked up the phone, it was Karen's voice on the other end. "I jumped out of the shower to get this. If I'd known it was you, I would've let it ring," I said.

"Well, if I'd known you were taking a shower, I wouldn't have called," she said. "I hate that I interrupted your annual ritual."

"Karen, Faith's not here," I said, bluntly.

"I know Faith's not there, that's why I'm calling now. I want to meet you."

"We've already met, Karen, and it's something I'll regret for the rest of my life."

"No, Jayson, I'm serious. We need to talk. The Starbucks on Dearborn."

"About what?" I said, patting myself dry with the towel.

"It's about Faith."

"What about Faith?"

"Nothing bad."

"Then why do we have to meet? Why can't we just talk right here on the phone? This way I can hear what you have to tell me, but I won't be forced to look at you."

There was silence on the line for a long moment, then Karen said, "I thought we had a truce. I thought we were done with that childish behavior."

She was right. She was trying to stick to what we'd agreed on, and I was the one behaving like an idiot.

"You're right. I'm sorry."

"Good, now finish shaving your legs, slip on your panties, and meet me in fifteen minutes." Before I could let her have it, she hung up.

When I walked into Starbucks, Karen was sitting at the counter, her face in a huge, wide cup of latte, lapping it up like a dog. Well, not really. She was drinking it normally, but still, it took everything within me to stop myself from making a comment. She actually looked human today, bordering on nice. Her hair was braided in cornrows. She wore a stylish, though cheap pair of shades, and the semitight jeans she had on made me realize that she truly didn't have a lower half like an elephant, but something fairly attractive.

"So what's the emergency? What's so important about Faith that you just had to tell me face-to-face?"

"Have a seat," she said, pulling out a stool. "It's good to see you, Jayson," she said, smiling, looking me over like she actually meant it.

"Yeah, yeah," I said, blowing her off. "We've agreed to be cordial, but not fall in love, all right?"

"Whatever. Do you want something? I'm buying since I brought you out."

"Yeah."

Karen motioned for the pimply-faced, slim teenage boy working behind the counter.

"What can I get you?"

"A cup of green tea and a bran muffin."

A moment later the boy with the paper hat set down the tea and the muffin before me.

"So what do we have to talk about?"

Karen took a sip from her latte then set it back on the counter. "Last night was pretty . . . I don't know . . . crazy. I mean, the way you and I were acting was no different than usual, but I thought about it, and this is almost my girl's wedding day. There really shouldn't have been any reason for that, you know."

"I never really took the time to think about it," I said, "but I guess you're right."

"Like I said last night, we really need to stop it, period. I mean for good," Karen said. "What do you think?"

"I'm with that, one hundred percent," I said, breaking a piece off my muffin, and sticking it in my mouth. "But what I want to know is, why did it ever start? From the first day I met you, Karen, you disliked me. Why was that?"

Karen looked away, scooted around a little on her stool so she wouldn't have to face me. She looked back at me after a second, like she was trying to hide something. "I don't know what you're talking about," she said.

"Really? You don't know what I'm talking about?"

"Nope."

"All those times when Faith and I first started dating and she told you that I was taking her to the show, or out to dinner at a certain restaurant, and you'd show up, sitting behind us at the movies, or a couple of tables away at the restaurant, saying that you had planned to go there before she told you we were. You don't know anything about that?" I asked, looking at her suspiciously.

"Nope."

"And all the times that you told her you saw me out with some strange woman, kissing in the park, or holding hands in the mall. I guess you don't know anything about that, either?"

"All right, all right," Karen said, conceding. "Do you know how long me and Faith have known each other?"

"No."

"Like, eight years, or something. And for that time we've been almost inseparable. We'd go to the gym and work out together. On

Wednesdays, we'd go for after-work drinks. Fridays nights we'd go to the movies, Saturday nights, we'd go out clubbin', and Sunday mornings, we'd go to church and then brunch afterward. And then you came along," she said with a grunt. "You came along and took up all her time. I barely saw her anymore."

"So you hated me for that?"

"Was I supposed to love you for it?"

"I didn't deserve that kind of treatment just because Faith decided she wanted to spend time with her man." Karen lowered her head, nodded a little. "I agree," she said, under her breath. "But it wasn't just that. Way back when you all first started dating, Faith told me about your girl, Asha. She wasn't sure if something was still going on between you two."

"But there wasn't."

"That's what your mouth says."

"There wasn't!" I objected louder.

"Really. Then how about now?" Karen asked, a cunning look in her eye.

"Now I don't know what *you're* talking about."

Karen looked at me long and hard, as if she was waiting for me to break down or something and tell her the real truth. Then she said, "I spoke to Faith this morning. She told me about everything that happened last night. Outside the restaurant, back at your place. How do you think that makes her feel?"

"I know. But, Karen, you have to believe me when I tell you there's nothing going on with me and Asha. If you only knew how much I loved Faith, how excited I am about the fact that I'm going to be married to her."

And again, Karen was looking at me strangely, canting her head, scrutinizing me from different angles. "You're being honest, aren't you?"

"Of course I am. Why would I marry her if I didn't love her. I love the damn girl."

It took a minute, but Karen cracked a small smile. "I believe you, Jayson. I think I always knew how you felt about her. I was just missing her so much. But now that I realize that this is going to happen even after all the efforts I made to stop it, and Lord knows I've tried. I know that I'm just going to have to accept you. And that's the real reason I asked you out here." Karen grabbed her purse, dug into it, brought out something blue, the size of a credit card with small holes in it. She extended it to me. I took it.

"What is it?" I asked, turning it over in my hand.

"It's a key card. The new Hilton. You know, on State Street," Karen said, smiling wide. "Tonight I'm throwing you and Faith a surprise wedding party. It's kinda my way of apologizing to both of you for acting like an ass all this time."

And, man, how badly I wanted to add something to that, but I held it in, because it seemed Karen was truly making a sincere effort to be nice.

"I want everything to start off fresh. Forget the past, forget everything we've said about each other, and move on."

I couldn't believe what I was hearing this woman say. I controlled my urge to look over my shoulder for some huge sledgehammer to swing down from the ceiling and splatter me where I sat, or for my seat to eject and shoot me through the roof of this place, as I fell victim to Karen's cunning scheme. But like I said before, she seemed really sincere.

"So what do you say? You coming?"

I gave her one final look of uncertainty, then relaxed and said, "Of course. What would a wedding party be without the groom?" And then I couldn't believe it, didn't know just what the hell came over me, but I got up from my stool and gave the woman a hug. I wrapped my arms around her, and she wrapped hers around me, and I squeezed, thinking that she wasn't that bad a person after all.

I let her go after a second, because I didn't want her to get the wrong idea and start humping on me like a horny dog trying to screw the neighbor's leg, or worse, have her running back to Faith, telling her, "Girl, he tried to come on to me, in broad daylight, right in the middle of Starbucks. That's right, girl, he had his hand all down the back of my jeans, grabbin' my ass."

But looking down at her, that smile still plastered across her face, I realized that she was past all that now. Those games were over.

"Now the room number is 1415," she said, touching the key card in my hand. "Come around ten o'clock. Don't knock or nothin'," Karen said, barely able to contain her excitement. "Just come on in. I want you to surprise her. Okay?"

"Okay."

"Good," Karen said, grabbing her purse, giving me that smile one last time, then turning to walk away. She stopped all of a sudden, turned back around, halfway to the door, and said, "Oh yeah. And bring a dozen roses. You know how your girl loves roses."

"Cool. Good idea. Will do," I said, as I watched Karen go. And again, I thought, Karen might not be that bad after all.

7

Asha sat in the small Phillipe Cozi Day Spa break room, with a couple of old, worn sofas, a small coffee table, a fridge, a sink, and a tiny microwave, munching from a bag of cinnamon-flavored mini rice cakes. They tasted more like Styrofoam than cinnamon, but her mind wasn't on what was churning around in her mouth, but on the decision she'd just made.

"Uhhhh, let me see," Asha said, speaking to a client on the phone, her finger running down the slots on today's appointment sheet. Her finger had rested on an opening, 2:30 P.M., but she didn't say anything. What was happening was that Asha was in complete turmoil. This woman on the phone, Angie Winston, had been a client of hers for only two months, but over the course of her weekly visits, Asha had managed to develop a serious problem with her.

Asha remembered the first time Angie came into the spa. Asha was sitting at the reception desk killing time with Sue when the woman walked in carrying a tiny, scruffy, brown terrier in one arm and a huge Nordstrom shopping bag in the other. She wore faded and torn, hip-hugging jeans, and a BEBE T-shirt, no bra underneath. A colorful African print cloth was wrapped around her hair and the cutest sandals exposed her well-manicured, painted toes.

"How can I help you, ma'am?" Sue said, sitting up in her chair.

"I want to make an appointment for a massage," Angie said. "And please don't call me ma'am. I'm thirty-nine but I hope I haven't hit ma'am status yet." She smiled.

Sue laughed, as she asked the woman her name, and for what day she wanted the appointment.

"Have you been here before? Is there anyone in particular you want to do your massage?" Sue asked.

Angie looked over at Asha, catching Asha by surprise, embarrassing her, for Asha was temporarily zoned out, gazing at the two faint imprints of Angie's nipples pressing against her red T-shirt.

"How about you?" Angie said. "You seem attentive." And Asha knew that she was making a comment about Asha looking at her breasts, damn near salivating over them.

"Oh, yeah." Asha jumped, turning her eyes to the floor. "I can do it. Put her in my book, Sue," Asha said, turning as red as her new client's T-shirt.

She was beautiful, Asha thought, but not in the typical, Tyra Banks, commercial, leggy, supermodel way. But in an earthy, real woman,   hair-is-kinda-messed-up-but-I-don't-give-a-damn-because-I-know-I'm-still-fine way.

Asha dreamt about her that night, Angie's face appearing on that woman in the room she always dreamed about, Angie's body under those clothes that slowly disappeared each time Asha had the dream.

On the first day that Asha was supposed to massage Angie, she was trembling all the way to work, unable to calm down, to settle her nerves. She feared she might do something or say something stupid while she had the woman on her table. Oftentimes she wondered why she continued to put herself through this nonsense, and how she had ever wound up doing this job in the first place, when women posed such a temptation. At the time she became a masseuse, she was still in denial about who she really was. She told herself then that it'd be fun, relaxing for both her and her clients, and she would meet new people, do something that she was good at. But now she realized it was more than just that. She had a hunger, and she was subconsciously feeding it. But considering how bad she often felt about that, why didn't she just turn right back around and go home. Call her boss, tell her she was quitting, and find some job where there was no temptation involved at all, like massaging men all day? The problem was, she truly did love her job. She loved talking to women, hearing them laugh, and making them feel wonderful, and who was to say that she should be jailed for getting a little innocent pleasure out of it herself.

Asha waited by her table nervously as she thought about what it would be like to touch this particular woman. Asha closed her eyes, took deep relaxing breaths as she stood there, telling herself that she would be able to control not only her nerves but her hands as well. She told herself that she would get no enjoyment out of placing her hands on this woman's body, that she would not get excited, that she would not imagine them together, imaging herself sliding out of her clothes and . . .

"Excuse me," Asha heard, and she was snapped out of her daydream before it could progress any further. When Asha looked up, she was shocked to see Angie standing by the locker room door totally naked.

Asha's eyes opened wide, she gasped, and she had to place a hand on her table because she felt a little light-headed.

"No more towels," Angie said, smiling, seeming very comfortable in her birthday suit.

"Hunh," Asha said, her gaze held captive by the fullness and the slope of Angie's breasts, by the huge dark circles that stared straight at her.

"No more towels in the locker room, Asha," Angie said, again, chuckling this time.

"Oh," Asha said, and quickly averted her eyes. "Well, I'll just have to get some more then," Angie said, her voice cracking like that of a pubescent boy getting his first glance at a naked woman.

Asha took a couple of steps toward Angie, then stopped, on quivering knees, realizing that Angie was standing just in front of the towel closet.

"Um," Asha said.

"Yes?" Angie replied, smiling, looking as comfortable as if she had never worn a stitch of clothing in her life.

"I need to get more towels, and they're . . . um . . . behind you," Asha said, only able to look up for a brief moment.

"Go right ahead," Angie said, stepping aside, but it was the tiniest step, and Asha would've had to have been paper-thin in order to get into that closet without at least brushing up against Angie, which was exactly what happened. It was by accident, of course, but she touched her while backing out of the closet with a stack of towels. Asha had grazed Angie's soft, right breast with her bare elbow. Asha jumped away from her, as if she had burned herself on a hot stove, almost spilling the towels onto the floor. She quickly turned around, embarrassed, apologizing for what she had done. Angie just stood there, shaking her head, smiling, as if she had enjoyed the brief contact.

After she had gotten over the discomfort of this incident, Asha was very proud of herself. She behaved very professionally, not allowing herself to get too involved in what she was doing. She didn't massage her too sensually, didn't slide her hands under the towel that lay over Angie's midsection, and didn't linger in any area for too long. Asha altogether avoided the area near and around the breasts, ass, and coochie, not wanting Angie to think she was trying anything funny on her. She never talked about anything other than topics appropriate for a six-year-old child. After it was over, Angie got off the table and smiled. She said that she enjoyed it, and that she'd be back next week.

Sure, there were other clients that Asha was attracted to, ones who had nice bodies, beautiful smiles, and great senses of humor, but there was something more about this woman. There was all that and something deeper, a confidence, a self-assuredness that was so appealing to Asha that at times she didn't know how she could contain herself in Angie's presence.

And then there was her smell. Something like jasmine, but not quite. Sweeter, fruitier. Asha, on many occasions, wanted to ask her whether it was perfume, a musk, or a gel of some sort, but never was able to. Probably because she felt the question was too personal, might lead to Angie thinking that Asha had some other interest in her than just being her masseuse. But the real reason Asha didn't ask her was because she knew in her heart that scent wasn't store-bought. That scent was her own natural body aroma, and Asha would daydream sometimes, close her eyes, bring her hands to her nose, pieces of her clothing to her face, smiling at the fact that the wonderful smell had come off on her, followed her home. Asha would savor that scent, telling herself that if the woman smelled that good, then she had to taste . . .

But Asha would manage those thoughts, as she did on the first day she massaged Angie. She would have to. And she did. For the next four sessions, Asha behaved just as she told herself she would. But during the fifth session, while Angie was lying on her belly, her arms above her head, her head to her side, Angie said, "That first day, when I walked in here, what were you looking at?"

Asha stopped her hands from massaging Angie's shoulders. She looked down at Angie's back, feeling very exposed, as if this woman might have had insight into what she was thinking that very moment, what she had been thinking about her all along.

"What did you say?"

"You were looking at my breasts, weren't you?" Angie said, her eyes still closed, not moving from her position, sounding very comfortable with what she was saying.

"I . . ."

"Don't say you weren't, because I know you were. My nipples started to stiffen because of how hard you were staring at them." Angie giggled a little, Asha feeling her laughter as it shook through her back, into Asha's hands, her arms, into her body, and into the pit of her stomach. She snatched her hands from Angie's body.

"And that same day, when I told you there were no towels, you were staring at me like you'd never seen a woman's body before. And then you turned away, and you wouldn't look at me. Why was that?" Angie said, still not turning up to look at Asha.

Asha stood there, shocked, still unable to find words to use in her defense.

"Is it the same reason why you've never really massaged me, why you aren't really massaging me now?" And then Angie rolled over, sat up on the table, and swung her legs around over the side of it. She was now looking directly in Asha's face, and although Asha tried to look away from her, just past her, the sight of her beautiful breasts, her confident smile, and that aroma of hers kept pulling Asha's eyes back to her.

"Is it because you like me, Asha? Because you find me attractive?"

Yes! Yes! Goddammit, yes! Asha wanted to say. Wanted so badly to say yes, then grab the woman by her sun-bleached locks, pull her face forward and kiss her passionately; but she knew she couldn't, knew it would make everything that she'd been trying so desperately to hold together fall apart. But it would feel so good, Asha thought to herself. And just imagining for a moment dropping the entire charade, Asha started to feel much better. But, again, she told herself she could never let that happen.

"Talk to me, Asha," Angie said, and Asha felt something warm grab her hand. It was Angie's.

Asha looked down at their hands touching, then she looked up at Angie, angrily almost, and said, "No. I don't. I don't find you attractive."

"Really," Angie said, and she was smiling, and Asha wondered where that smile was coming from? Was she so damn confident that even though she was telling her that there was nothing there, Angie still believed there was?

"Really!" Asha said, forcefully.

"Really," Angie said, very assured, the look on her face saying, *If that was the case, why are you still holding my hand?* And Angie gave Asha's hand a little squeeze to bring her attention to that fact.

Asha looked down again, shocked, as if her hand was doing things her mind had no knowledge of.

"I think this session is over," Asha said, pulling away from Angie.

"Same time next week?" Angie asked, jumping down from the table.

"Call and confirm," Asha said, pretending to straighten bottles on her table, not even looking at Angie.

And that's what Angie did. But it wasn't the next week, or the week after next, and Asha was relieved when Angie kept missing her appointments, but only a little. She was worried that she had lost a client, but even more worried that it was this particular client, for she couldn't get Angie of f her mind. There were days when Asha stood by the phone with Angie's info at hand, and thought of dialing her up, leaving some lame message in her geekiest voice, like, "Hi, this is your masseuse from Phillipe Cozi. Just calling to make sure you haven't forgot about your weekly massages! Okay. Toodaloo. And have a wonderful day!"

But Asha didn't dare. Instead she just accepted the fact that she blew it. But what exactly had she blown? The opportunity for a great lesbian relationship, an illegal marriage, and the adoption of some infant who would look up at her parents and forever be confused as to who wore the pants. Was she just missing some hot, sweaty ass sex on the massage table? What! She didn't know, and she told herself that it was best that she never found out.

But then the phone rang.

"Phone call for Asha Mills on line seven," Sue said over the intercom.

"This is Asha," Asha said, picking up the phone in her room.

"I know I haven't called in a while, but do you have anything open today?"

"I'm sorry. Who am I speaking to?" Asha said, knowing exactly who it was after Angie spoke the first word.

"This is Angie, Asha. I'm sorry I missed my last couple of appointments, but can you fit me in today?"

Asha had already found an opening in her book—her finger was sitting there on the 2:30 P.M. slot—but should she let her in? After having already gotten over this woman—well just about—did Asha want to go down that path again? But, just because Angie came in for a massage every week, did Asha have to succumb to her desires? Hell no, she thought to herself. And if she no longer allowed Angie to come, wouldn't Asha be admitting that she had no willpower whatsoever, that each and every time an attractive woman lay across her table, that woman ran the risk of getting molested, because poor Asha could not control her raging hormones. Of course not!

"Yeah. Two-thirty, today," Asha said, confidently. "And don't be late."

"Great. See you then."

Now in the break room, Asha popped another mini rice cake into her mouth and looked down at her watch. It read 2:15 P.M. and Asha felt a little stir inside of herself, in that lower region, but she squelched it, telling herself it was just another client, nothing to get weirded out about. She wouldn't make any special preparations, wouldn't budge until two or three minutes before the client was due to arrive as she did with all the others.

Asha put her feet up on the coffee table, and prepared to really chill when someone came into the room. It was Leslie, or as Asha referred to her, "Big Les." Of course, Leslie didn't know Asha referred to her as such, and she never would, because Asha wasn't a fool, and Asha didn't want her ass kicked. That wouldn't have been a problem for Big Les, and that was, of course, because she was so damn big.

Leslie was new by about four days, had just got the job. She was a caramel color, about five eleven, black hair that stuck up all about her head and appeared to break off at the ends if she walked through the hallway too fast. She probably put everything and anything in her hair that was advertised during the Soul Train hour to try and get that stuff to grow. All it did was damage her hair, leaving her walking around smelling like lye and looking like a brunette Woody Woodpecker.

She was quiet in an evil, suspicious, rattlesnake-waiting-to-strike kind of way. She'd never really said much to Asha in the four days she had been there, and that was perfectly fine with Asha. To her, Les looked rougher than some dudes she knew, bad dudes, dudes who lifted boxes, dumped garbage, and repossessed cars for a living.

Today, Les came into the break room with her brown bag lunch and sat down. She sat in a chair opposite the coffee table, looking directly at Asha. Les ripped the bag down the center, allowing it to double as a place mat, and revealed a huge ball of aluminum foil. She unwrapped it and exposed half a separated fried chicken. She then walked over to the sink, grabbed a paper cup, filled it with water from the tap, and sat down again.

Les took some napkins, the stray ones left on the table, and placed one gently on her lap. Then she stuffed one in the collar of her shirt, careful not to soil her white smock. After a moment, she picked up a chicken leg, sank her teeth into it and chewed, all the while staring directly at Asha.

Asha munched on her rice cakes as Les chewed on her chicken flesh, both women staring at each other.

"Wha's up?" Les said, after swallowing hard.

"I don't know. What's up with you?" Asha said, trying to sound as hard as Les.

"Shit," Les said, blandly, still staring at Asha, then ripped another hunk off the leg.

Asha kept her stare up, but it was hard, because she didn't know what to make of Big Les's stare. There was something . . . she didn't know, intimidating, something animal about it, like instead of just chewing chicken, she was imagining chomping down on Asha.

"You like it here?" Asha asked.

"It's okay, I guess." Then she said in a deep voice, bordering on masculine, "You know, I been meaning to tell you. You look good today. You look good every day. I like the way your smock fits you."

"Thanks," Asha said, and she didn't know just where the fuck that came from, but she was already pulling herself up from the sofa, and heading toward the door. She'd heard more than she needed from Big L and spent enough time staring into her frightening, bloodthirsty eyes. Before leaving, Asha dropped her bag of rice cakes on the table.

"You can have those, just in case you're still hungry after your chicken." Asha left the room, relieved to get out of there.

When she walked into her massage room, she could hear someone getting changed in the locker room, and knew that Sue had already sent Angie back. Asha paused just inside the room, feeling a chill move through her, but she let it pass, paying no attention to it. This would be a normal massage like all the rest. Asha grabbed a towel, spread it across her table, and stood behind it waiting for Angie to finish undressing.

"Ready when you are, Angie," Asha called, looking down, examining her nails, trying to convince herself she needed a manicure when she had just gotten one three days ago.

When Angie walked in she was smiling, striding into the room confidently as always.

"How you been, Asha?"

"Fine. Can't complain," Asha said, working a smile up, making a point to stare straight at Angie, letting her know that she had no problems doing that anymore.

"Good, good," Angie said, climbing onto the table and lying out across it on her belly.

Asha stood over her, still forcing herself not to look away from this woman's flawless skin, even though it was becoming a little harder now. And then she took one of those deep, relaxing, anxiety-reducing breaths she said she didn't need.

She held out both her spread hands in front of her, just above Angie's back, and Asha was relieved to see that they were for the most part, steady. She then lowered them upon Angie's skin, and started on the muscles at the back of her lower neck, feeling all the tension there.

"You have a lot of stress built up back here," Asha said.

"I know," Angie said, letting out a breath. "I shouldn't have stayed away so long, but . . . I've been busy."

"Well, next time you'll know," Asha said, smiling, because she was feeling so comfortable, not feeling any anxiety, any fear, not thinking about any of the nonsense that had been going on in her head earlier about her and Angie. Asha started to massage Angie deeper, really loosening the muscles in her neck, the trapezius muscles, her deltoids.

This must have felt really good to Angie, because she let out a moan, a sinful, sensual moan like something heard during great sex. Asha halted, feeling another chill, this one very intense, making her entire body shiver, but she paused for only a moment, telling herself, once again, she wasn't affected by this woman.

Asha smoothed her hands down across Angie's back, working on her lateral muscles, then opened her hands flat, using the heels of her palms to massage both sides of Angie's spine.

"Everything okay down there?" Asha said, still in control of herself, demanding of herself that she see Angie as just another client.

"Uhhhhh, like you wouldn't believe," Angie said.

Asha reached over to her table, lifting a bottle of warm oil, squirting some in the palms of her hands, then applying it to Angie's back.

"Ohhhh," Angie said, arching her back a little.

"It's a little warm."

"Mmm, no. It's good."

Asha worked gently and steadily down the length of Angie's spine using her thumbs in a crisscrossing motion, feeling Angie's body tense some the lower she went.

"You have to relax, okay?" Asha said, continuing to move down, still keeping herself in check, actually feeling quite strong.

She continued the massage, working on the area just above where the towel was draped, the lower back. For so many people, that was where most of the stress hid, where most problems lay. She worked the area with more oil, and each time that Angie tensed up, jerked about the table, almost losing her towel, Asha told her to relax. And each time Angie moaned or breathed out a sigh, like Asha was doing so much more than giving her an innocent massage, Asha fought against it, trying to remain unaffected by it.

"But it tickles," Angie said, unable to hold her laughter anymore. "That's why I keep tensing and jumping around."

"Okay, okay, I'll work around it," Asha said, smiling to herself, glad that she was doing so well, even though she was so close to what was at one time driving her crazy. She continued the massage, working around the ticklish area, or so she thought. Asha dug her thumbs into the space just above where the spine and pelvis meet, where there was always loads of tension, and that had to be the most sensitive spot on Angie's body, for she let out a shriek, and nearly jumped off the table. She managed not to fall, but what did fall was her towel, leaving Angie totally nude, her round, smooth behind exposed, one leg hiked slightly up to expose a hint of her straight medium-length pubic hair.

Motherfucker! What did I just do? Asha thought. And then the voice in her head was screaming at her. Pick up the towel, Asha! Pick it up! But she could not move. Then she ordered herself one last time, telling herself if she didn't do it that moment, she'd have no control of what might happen.

She took a step toward the other side of the table to get the towel, and as she took that step, she felt Angie's gaze on her.

"Don't do it," Angie said, softly.

What are you talking about? Asha said, thinking that she was speaking out loud, when the words were really only in her head. I have to pick up the towel. I have to cover you, smother the temptation, drown this desire or else I'll . . . I just have to. And she took another step.

"Asha," Angie said, and Asha felt the warm hand take hers again. "Stop," Angie said, lifting herself from the table, sitting up. Asha stopped, her eyes still focused in the direction of the fallen towel.

"You don't have to pick that up."

Asha didn't respond, almost afraid to.

"Do you want me, Asha?" Angie said.

"Don't do this," Asha whispered to Angie, almost as if she was warning herself.

"Asha, do you want this?"

"Don't do this!" Asha said, firmer, her hand shaking in Angie's. Angie squeezed her hand, trying to comfort her.

"I understand what you're thinking, what you're feeling. But how long can you fight it? How long do you want to have to fight it?" Angie said, her voice soft, dreamlike.

Asha's entire body was trembling now, her mind cloudy, her legs wanting to run, but something was telling her to stay, that this must happen.

"Asha, look at me. If you don't want this, then look me in the eyes and tell me."

"Why are you doing this to me?" Asha said, fraught with anguish, and anxiety.

"I'm not doing anything that you're not able to stop. Just answer my question, and if it's no, I'll leave you alone."

Asha narrowed her eyes, clenched her teeth, trying to summon the strength to reject this woman that she'd dreamt of so many times, that she'd imagined holding, imagined being held by, but she couldn't.

"It's okay, Asha. You've tried so hard to hide it, but I've known about you from the first day when you looked at me, and every day you massaged me. And I would lie here, hoping that you'd allow yourself to embrace it, that you'd stop fighting what you can never beat."

A tear rolled down Asha's cheek.

"It's okay, you have to know that," Angie said, placing a gentle hand on the side of Asha's face. "You have to tell yourself that, and don't worry about what anyone else thinks, because they don't have to deal with it, they don't have to live this life. Do you understand?"

Asha felt Angie place her other hand on her other cheek, felt her turning her face to look at her.

"Do you understand, Asha?"

Asha's lips quivered for a moment, and then she said, "But no one else will understand."

"I will."

"But . . ." Asha tried to say, another tear falling from her eye.

"I will understand, and that's all that matters," Angie said, covering Asha's cheek with her soft lips. She kissed Asha there, then kissed her in the center of her cheek, then placed a delicate kiss gently on Asha's lips. There came the slightest bit of hesitation from Asha, pulling back only enough for herself to notice, but then she stopped herself, for the feeling she was experiencing was true, natural, more than with any man she'd ever been with.

Angie pressed her lips slightly harder against Asha's lips, parting them gently to allow the tip of her tongue to seep out. Asha met her with her own warm tongue, her head beginning to spin, her body feeling warm, weak, her knees feeling as though they were about to give at any moment. And when she felt that she was about to fall, Angie wrapped her arms around Asha, pulled her into her soft, naked body, and kissed her harder.

Asha's head was swimming now. She wasn't sure what was happening, but whatever it was, it felt good. She could feel all the pain, all the hurt, the anger and self-loathing she had felt for herself start to wash away as she was being kissed by this woman, as she kissed this woman, and at that moment, she wondered why she had hidden from this part of herself for so long.

8

I wanted a big wedding in a huge church with hundreds of people to witness the happiest day of my life. Faith would have all of her friends and family there, beaming proudly at her as she walked down the aisle. For me, Asha would be there, maybe a couple of associates I knew from work, but no family. I was an only child, my father out of the picture, and my mother, well, she'd lasted only two years at Shady Brook. I never went to visit her, took care of everything via phone, including her funeral arrangements. I didn't even make the actual funeral; I just passed by the casket afterward. I was afraid what sorts of feelings would've crept out of me, and I didn't want anyone to see me if I felt the need to topple my mother's coffin off the platform it was on.

In that empty room, staring down into my mother's waxy face, a dress on her that I had never seen but paid for, I tried to pretend that all the love she had never given me no longer affected me. I tried to act as though I was a grown man now and had never been a child, and she had never deprived me, but I could not pull it off. I felt the tears coming before they were even in my eyes. They were introduced by a pain in my heart so strong that I felt I would double over. It dropped into my stomach when I finally accepted the fact that she was gone. Now and forever, she was gone. That thought pulled all those emotions I'd tried to suppress out of me, and the guilt, the regret, the resentment I felt toward my mother had me stretched out over her casket, holding on to it as though I feared someone were trying to take it, and my mother, away from me. I cried there for an entire hour, sobbing like the child I tried to deny I'd ever been, and afterward I felt no worse, nor did I feel any better.

I wanted a big wedding, and I didn't know if this was to compensate for the feeling of family that I never had, or if I was just so excited, so proud to be finally getting married that I wanted the world, or at least as much of it as I could fit into that church, to know. But Faith wasn't game.

"I want something simple, something small and intimate, like city hall," she said.

"City hall is about as intimate as getting married in a Greyhound bus station."

"It's not about how big the wedding is, baby," Faith said, snuggling up next to me, looping her arm around mine. "It's about how good the marriage is afterward. Let's take all that money we'll save from the wedding, and do something crazy, like go on a month-long honeymoon around the world."

"Really?" I said smiling, picturing us traveling as husband and wife.

"I don't know. Yeah. Something like that. What do you say?"

"Okay. Whatever you want, baby. Whatever," I said, the smile growing even wider.

"Sir. Sir, you're next," a voice said, interrupting my thoughts. It was the heavy black woman from behind the counter, trying to get my attention. I pulled myself from what I was thinking, and said, "Oh, yeah, a dozen of your freshest red roses, please."

The woman took her time, picking the dozen carefully, then asked, "How are these?"

"Those are great."

"You want 'em in a vase, a box, or in paper?"

"Paper's fine," I said, then hesitated for a moment, not knowing if the news of my wedding would make her any difference or not, but feeling too excited about it at the moment to hold it in.

"I'm getting married," I offered, smiling shyly. "On Sunday. In three days."

"Well!" the woman said, a huge smile spreading across her chubby face. "Congratulations!" And then she turned and yelled over her

shoulder toward a back room. "You hear that, Betty? This man's getting married on Sunday."

"You don't say," a voice came from the back room, and then
another chunky woman wearing an apron, and a scarf on her head,
and holding some uncut flowers, came out, glanced at me, and said,
"That is so wonderful." Then she looked me over harder, approval in
her eyes.

"But, boy, if it don't work out, you come on back here, all right,
'cause Betty'll gladly take you, divorced, separated, hell, still married
for that matter. I ain't no playa' hata'. I'm a participata'. You want my
pager number, baby?" Both women had a good laugh at her remarks.

"Naw," I said, "but thanks anyway. I'm sure we'll work out."

"Give that fine man half off those roses, Pat," Betty said, then
walked over to the counter, and said, very politely, "I was just playing
with you, young man. But congratulations, and I hope you have a
wonderful wedding."

That was the plan, I thought to myself as I walked through the
thick pedestrian traffic of Michigan Avenue with the roses in one
hand, my cell phone in the other, dialing Faith's number at work. I
hadn't spoken to her all day and it was already . . . I turned my wrist to
look at my watch . . . ten after four. The phone rang like six times, and
then I heard the break in the tone that meant it was skipping over to
her voice mail.

"Hi, this is Faith Sheppard at the Lincoln Park Social Center. I'm
sorry I'm unable to take your . . ."

I clicked her off. "I'm sorry, too," I said, still walking, staring at the
phone as if it were her, and it could give me answers to what she was
doing at that moment. Was she still mad at what happened last night?
Was she not calling me, and not answering my calls, on purpose? No,
that was ridiculous. She was just busy as she always was, counseling
people about abortions, pregnancy, and all the other difficult issues the
community comes to her with.

Just then my cell phone started ringing.

"Hello," I said, hoping it was Faith.

"Hey, Jayson," Faith said, not sounding very enthused to be speaking to me.

"I tried calling you."

"Really."

"Yeah," I said, still happy to be hearing her voice, even though she sounded like she could care less to be hearing mine.

"Oh, okay. How's your day going?"

"Fine now that I'm talking to you," I said, smiling.

The phone was silent. I stepped off the sidewalk, moved into the doorway of a Marshall Field's department store, and said, "What's going on with you? This morning you left without kissing me or saying good-bye, and now you're acting like . . . like you don't even want to talk to me."

"That's because I talked to . . ." Faith blurted out, but then stopped herself.

"Talked to who?" I asked, but I figured she was talking about Karen, since Karen had already told me they spoke this morning.

"No. Nothing. Never mind."

"Faith, tell me. Is it about last night? The thing with Asha?"

Again, there was silence, then finally she said, "No, Jayson. It's not the thing with Asha." But she said it like it really was that and she was pissed that I didn't know it.

"Are you sure?"

"Yeah. I'm sure."

"In four days, you'll be Mrs. Abrahms. You know that."

"Jayson, I should be going, I got . . ."

"But hold it. Am I going to see you tonight?"

"Um. Not tonight. Karen and I are going to discuss some wedding things over drinks. You don't mind, do you?"

"No. Of course not," I said, smiling to myself, knowing that's just what Karen told her to get her to the hotel for the surprise party. "I don't mind at all, as long as you don't have too nice of a time."

"Never without you, baby," she said in a tone that managed to convince me that she was telling the truth.

o   o   o

After checking out some buildings that had been foreclosed on, and going by my South Side properties, as I had planned earlier, I ate a light dinner of salad and roasted chicken that I'd picked up, already prepared from Dominick's. When I finished, I showered, and excitedly got ready for the party.

I had called Karen earlier just to make sure that everything was going as planned.

"Oh, yeah. Everything is perfect. I am so proud of myself," she said, and I could hear her pride coming through the phone. "Did you get the roses?"

"Yeah."

"You still got the key?"

"Yeah, still got it."

"And what time did I tell you to come?"

"Ten. Karen! I got it, all right. I'll be there with bells swinging from my ears, all right."

"Good."

"Good," I said, about to hang up, when Karen said, "And oh, Jayson. You're going to love this. You're really going to be surprised."

At 9:45 P.M., I pulled my car up to the hotel. The valet got the door for me, and gave me a ticket. I walked up the stairs of the hotel, through the glass doors, and past an older, well-dressed couple. The man was wearing a tuxedo, and the woman on his arm was wearing a beautiful, beaded ball gown. They were both graying slightly, the man a little more than the woman, and as I passed them, I could hear the woman chuckle at something the man had whispered into her ear. She leaned in and kissed him on the cheek. They were married, I told myself, trying not to stare, admire them too boldly. But they were married and wonderfully happy together, and that's how me and Faith will be. Ten, twenty years from now, we will be the same way, like that distinguished, madly in love, aging couple.

I stood in front of the elevator, after punching the up button, and waited for the doors to slide open. After they did, I allowed two women in jeans to step off, then I got on. I punched the fourteen button with the hand I was holding Faith's roses with, while with my other hand shoved into my pocket, I turned over and over the key card to room 1415.

I really hoped that Faith would be surprised, hoped that this would relieve some of the stress and worry she'd been having about Asha and me. Something told me it would. As the elevator continued to carry me up to the fourteenth floor, I couldn't help but think about the night I proposed to her.

"Stop it," I grunted, lying naked across her bed, gripping tight handfuls of the linen, trying with everything to control myself.

"You don't like it?" she managed to warble, her mouth still around me, her hands still busy sliding up and down the length of me.

"I'm not ready yet," I said, guiding her eagerly bobbing head away from my middle, then grabbing her around the waist and flipping her over onto her back.

"I want you to get yours, know what I'm sayin'?" I said, slyly, easing into her. But that wasn't all I had planned for her, I thought, as I slid easily deep inside her. She let her head fall back, her eyes rolling back with the pleasure she was feeling. I kissed her gently on the nose, the chin, and then softly on her lips.

"I love you," I whispered to her, as she opened her legs more, letting me farther into her warm inside.

"I . . ." she started to say, but I thrust myself into her, making her moan in ecstasy instead of speaking the words she wanted to say.

"What was that?" I said, teasing her.

"I said, I love . . ." and again, I slid farther in her, and this time she groaned long and hard, her muscles down there clamping around me.

"Stop that, and let me tell you I love you, will you!" Faith said, laughing and grabbing my butt hard with both hands. "I love you, Jayson Abrahms," she said softly.

"Really?"

"Yeah," she said, looking up at me through barely parted eyelids.

"How much do you love me?" I said, still moving in and out of her.

But she didn't answer right away, because she was lost in a moment of pleasure, her eyes, once again, swimming in the back of her head. Then she looked up at me, wearily, and said, "Oh, so much."

"*How* much?"

She breathed out hard. "A lot. Oooh, a lot."

"But how *much* is a lot?" And by this time I had her in the position, legs hooked around my arms, spread all the way open. I was pushing her toward orgasm, demanding that she come, and while I was doing that, I was fumbling blindly for something just under the mattress, finally feeling it, and grabbing it.

She cried out in a series of grunts, and curse words, unable to tell me just how much a lot was.

"You can't tell me?" I said, breathing furiously, sweat dripping from my body as I continued to make love to her, careful to stop myself from feeling all the pleasure I was giving her.

"I'm about to . . . I'm gonna . . ."

"About to what? Gonna what?" I said, feeling that she was almost there.

"I love you a lot! A whole lot! And . . . and . . ." and now I could feel her muscles, not just down there, but all over her body contracting, and she was starting to make this weird breathing noise, like a car stalling, trying to start but unable. That always happened just before she came. But I wasn't going to allow that to happen before I said, "Is that enough to marry me?"

And not a second later, she exploded, screaming out, "What!" She tried grabbing me, digging her nails into my back, as she endured the eruptions that rumbled through her body, but I grabbed one of her hands, her left one, and slid the ring I had taken from under the mattress onto her finger.

An entire minute later, after her breathing slowed to just a little quicker than normal, and the tremors in her legs settled to just a little twitching, she turned her head lazily in my direction and said, "Why did you grab my hand like that?"

"Why don't you look and see," I said, smiling.

She looked bewildered for a moment, then raised her hand, and after seeing the karat and a half, she gasped, practically choked.

"Oh my god. Oh my god," she said softly, looking down at it, but it was in a way that made me feel that something was wrong. She pulled herself from the bed, walked over to the candle that sat burning on her dresser, and dipped the ring into its light.

"Oh my god!"

"What's wrong?" I asked, concerned. "You don't like it?"

"No, no. It's beautiful," she said, quickly looking up at me, smiling sheepishly, then turning her face back down to the ring. "But you want to marry me?" she asked, in a way that made the thought seem ridiculous.

I got out of bed, practically ran to her, taking her in my arms. "What are you talking about? Of course I want to marry you. Do you know how much I love you?" She looked up at me, with what seemed like worry in her eyes. I didn't understand. This was supposed to be a happy occasion.

"Do you know?" I asked again.

"But—" she tried to say, but I stopped her.

"There is no but. I love you to pieces. Do you know that?"

She nodded her head. "Yeah," she said softly. "But are you sure?"

I didn't know what all the questioning was about, but I felt honored, thinking that she must've thought she wasn't good enough for me or something. Then I smiled, trying to make her feel more comfortable, hoping some of my happiness would rub off on her. "I was never more sure of anything in my life, baby," I said, answering her question, then I gave her a huge hug.

She wrapped her arms around me too and said, "Okay, baby. I love you, too."

"So what does that mean? Will you marry me?" I asked, pulling away from her, so I could look into her eyes.

"Yes. I will marry you," she said, smiling and hugging me again. And at that moment, I was the happiest I'd ever been in my entire life.

The elevator doors slid open with a ding. I stepped off, and followed the little arrow on the wall before me, pointing toward rooms 1401 through 1418. As I walked down the hall, I felt a quiet, calming peace about me. Yes, in just four days we'd be married, and life would be what I'd always wanted it to be, but never thought it could be. I would have the love that always seemed to escape me.

Out of the corner of my eye, I glimpsed 1413 as I passed it, and I slid my hand back into my pocket, fishing out the key card. I walked another few feet, stepped squarely in front of 1415, heard the sound of muffled voices. I slid the card into the door lock, saw the little green light illuminate, and turned the handle thinking, Faith's going to be so surprised, I can't wait to see her face. But when I opened the door, it wasn't her face that caught my attention, but her body. Her naked body, squirming on all fours, her hands and knees sinking deep into the cushions of the sofa, as a well-built, naked, brown man stood behind her, moaning in ecstasy, his bare body covered with sweat as he grabbed Faith from behind, slowly sliding himself in and out of her.

9

It was 10 P.M. Asha was seated in her favorite restaurant, an upper-end establishment by the name of Banderra on Michigan Avenue. The room was big, but the ceiling was low. At the back of the restaurant was a huge open oven, where tall flames cooked a number of chickens as they rotated over and over on a spit. At the front were long, floor-to-ceiling windows looking down on the fine stores of Michigan Avenue, and the late-night window shoppers who, hand in hand, occasionally stopped in front of them. The restaurant was dark, candles dancing on each of the tables, illuminating the faces of people engaged in intimate conversations.

Asha was also deep in an intimate discussion, but it was with herself, for she was just unable to keep her mind off what happened to her earlier.

"So what do we do now?" Asha had asked, after she slowly pulled her lips from Angie's.

Angie smiled. "I don't know. I'll leave that up to you."

"I want to see you again."

"I was hoping you'd say that, because although you may not believe it now, I wasn't coming in here just to seduce you. I really do need a massage once a week."

"So, do you want my number or something?" Asha said, feeling a little awkward at that moment.

"No," Angie said, touching Asha's hand. "Let's just keep it here for right now. What do you say?"

"Oh. Yeah, that sounds fine. So next Thursday then, hunh?"

"What if I said I can't wait that long to see you? Would you have a problem massaging me twice a week?" Angie said.

Asha smiled, slyly. "Uh, it might be rough at first, but I think I could get used to it."

"Good, well, put me down for Tuesday too, and I'll see you then."

"Will do," Asha said, and received the kiss on the cheek Angie gave her. She watched as the older woman walked confidently down the hall, watched the slenderness of her waist, watched as her hips swayed, and a sweet tremor passed over Asha when she thought that just moments ago she was holding that woman in her arms.

Asha looked at the melting candle in front of her on the restaurant table. She lifted her wineglass, and absently took a sip, making it a point to try to seem interested in what was being said to her, but still she couldn't keep her mind from thinking about what she'd done earlier that afternoon, and what kind of impact it would have on her life.

She had accepted that she was a lesbian, but how would she tell Jayson about it? And then there was Gill. Asha had to shake her head about that one. The man loved her more than any man ever had, was damn near on the verge of proposing, would probably throw himself in front of a train to save her life, and this was how she would repay him?

But it was only fair. She would have to tell him, and tell him soon.

Earlier that evening, Asha had said good-bye to Sue and the other girls she passed on the way out of the spa, then took the elevator down. It was 5:30 P.M., the same time she always got out, and the sun was still warm on this spring evening. That lifted Asha's spirits just a little as she went about the task of trying to flag down a cab in the thick rush hour traffic.

Gill and the problem about what she would do with him, how she would tell him, kept popping up in her head. Would she tell him the next time she saw him, the next time they spoke on the phone, or would she even tell him at all? Couldn't she just dump him?

"I'm tired of you, Gill. Tired of all the nice things you buy me, of how you love me unconditionally, of the sex that most women would consider the greatest ever. I'm just tired, and you just aren't enough, Gill.

Now beat it." Asha tried to hear herself saying the words. But she couldn't lie to him like that, and besides, letting him go now probably wasn't that great an idea. She was just entering this whole lesbian thing, and although it felt right, she wasn't sure how it would turn out. It would be foolish to get rid of a man who loved her at this point. So Asha wouldn't say anything to him just yet. And as long as he didn't keep mentioning marriage, she could string this thing out a little farther.

The sound of a horn had yanked Asha out of her thoughts and pulled her attention to the curb. There rolling up beside her was Gill's Jaguar, Gill smiling brightly behind the wheel. He leaned over the passenger seat and pushed open the door.

"C'mon, get in."

Asha jumped into the seat, leaned over, and received the kiss she knew he had for her, feeling a bit strange after not long ago being kissed by Angie on the same cheek.

"How's my Suga'puss feeling today?"

"Gill, I told you I wish you wouldn't keep calling me that."

"Well, if you'd stop making it so sweet, then I'd stop, but I don't even think that's possible. What do you think?" Gill said, grabbing one of her thighs.

"Guess not, Gill," Asha said, smiling.

In the booth at the restaurant, Asha's head was already feeling somewhat light as she slid her two fingers up and down the stem of the nearly empty wineglass. Just one or two more glasses of Merlot, and I'll be able to get my mind off everything and enjoy this evening, she thought. She lifted the glass to her lips and tilted it back. She felt a warm hand cover her own, the one that was resting on the table, and it made her shudder. Maybe because it had brought back the memory from when they were home just a couple of hours before.

The beautiful dress that Gill had taken her to buy after he picked her up from work was hanging from the hook on the bathroom door. It was only a casual dress, a simple, black, clingy above-the-knee-length deal, but it was three hundred dollars plus.

"Gill, you don't have to do this," Asha said. "My birthday isn't for another two weeks."

Gill laughed, pulled his wallet out, threw down his platinum AmEx, and said, "Who said anything about your birthday? This dress is because I want to take you out to dinner tonight."

Asha pulled the shower curtain back, peeked at the dress, and had to just smile. That man would've bought her the sun if it were for sale, or if there was a way that he could fly up there, lasso it, and bring it down to her.

Asha adjusted the showerhead to shoot water down on the back of her neck, and upper back. She grabbed some pineapple shower gel, squirted some in her hand, and started to lather her body, concentrating on her lower stomach, her hips, and inner thighs. With each movement of her soap-covered hand, her body was becoming more sensitive, and she felt her mind start to wander away from her. She closed her eyes, letting herself be taken to wherever she landed, and she knew it would be back at the spa. The area at which Asha washed herself narrowed to just in between her legs, and she was about to move into herself, and erase all the tension from her day when the shower curtain was yanked back.

Asha snapped out of the trance she was in to find Gill standing there, just outside the bathtub, totally naked, and totally erect.

"Is there room for one more?" Gill asked, not waiting for Asha's reply, but already stepping into the tub.

Only if you're this fine woman named Angie, Asha wanted to say, but of course didn't dare. Inside the shower, Gill went straight to lathering himself up with the bar of deodorant soap she had bought for him, because as Gill said, he didn't "want to be smelling like nobody's fruit basket." He set the bar down, and then with his brown body covered with thick white suds, he pushed himself up against Asha's back. She felt his penis slipping and sliding against her backside, and she knew that was his attempt at making her "horny," getting her "hot" as so many men perceived it. But her heat was stolen from her the minute Gill had stepped in the tub.

"You know you were turning me on when you were trying on those dresses this afternoon. You know that, don't you?" Gill whispered into Asha's ear, as the warm water continued to spray down on both of them. He was sliding in and out from between her thighs now, and although Asha knew that's not how it was going to go down, she was really hoping Gill was going to satisfy himself that way, because at that moment, her thirst for him was quite dry, her insides feeling the same way.

Gill reached around and grabbed one of her breasts, lathering it with the suds that clung to his hand. He placed the other hand on her upper back, and gently leaned her forward, no, "Baby, how would you like taking it from the rear today?" or nothing. Just pushed her over.

"I couldn't wait to get you back home, Suga'."

"Me too," Asha said, in her sweetest voice, knowing that she wasn't actually repulsed by Gill himself. She did kinda love this man; it was just his timing. She would give herself to him, because it wasn't his fault that she was thinking about another woman. Why should he be made to suffer?

Gill seemed to be having a little difficulty finding his way inside Asha, frustrating her some, considering how many times he had been there before. She reached around, grabbed him, and guided him in. She was bone dry, as she knew she would be, and thanked the fact that they were in the shower, because the soap and water acted as a lubricant. Gill wouldn't know the difference.

He was a wonderful lover, always took his time, was very attentive, never left the scene before she arrived at least twice, but at that moment, as Asha's forearms were pressed against the shower wall, the shower water crashing down on her back, pouring down into the crevice of her behind, it felt like Gill was doing nothing more than working out. It felt like he was pounding himself into her without meaning, without emotion. She heard him moaning back there, and was glad that at least one of them was getting something out of it. She felt his hands grabbing her around her waist, and although he wasn't rough with her, he was missing that tenderness that Angie had.

Angie. Angie . . . Angie . . . Angie. And before Asha knew it, she was at the spa again, in that woman's embrace again, kissing her, aroused to the point she thought she would start dripping through her panties and her slacks. And then she heard Gill say, "Oh, baby, you're getting so wet."

And Asha just shook her head, thinking, if only you knew why.

o   o   o

"Can you order me another glass of Merlot?" Asha asked Gill.

"Of course, Suga'," he said, and it was sweet of him to say nothing about the fact that it was her third. He simply raised his hand, catching the attention of the waiter, while with the other hand, he continued playing with one of Asha's fingers, her ring finger.

The waiter came, a tall, thin, distinguished man with thinning black hair, who looked far too old to be serving food for a living.

"Another Merlot for the beautiful woman," Gill said, proudly.

"Right away," the waiter said, and was about to step away, when Gill grabbed him by the cuff of his sleeve. He pulled him toward him, whispered a few things in the waiter's ear, and slipped him a bill. Asha couldn't see the denomination. The waiter smiled at Gill, then hurried off.

Asha didn't know if it was because she was far past buzzed and approaching drunk, but that gesture seemed odd. And what made it even odder was when they first walked into the restaurant, and were waiting at the bar for a table to open up, Gill had found the head-waiter on his way back from the men's room, this same guy, and had quite a long conversation with him in the back of the restaurant. When Gill came back and sat down, Asha eyed him peculiarly.

"What?" he said, taking a sip of his beer.

"What was all that about?"

"I just wanted to make sure he got us the best table."

And now as Gill looked back at Asha, as though the second conversation he'd just had with the waiter had never taken place, Asha had to ask him again.

"What did you just ask him?"

"It was nothing, Suga'. Nothing."

"No. I want to know," Asha said, sitting up in her seat. "And it better not be no thing where all the wait staff comes out here with some mini cake and sings me some slappy-happy, funky version of 'Happy Birthday.' You know it's not for another two weeks."

"Baby, don't worry. It's nothing like that," Gill said, confident.

"Then what is it?"

"I just asked him to open a fresh bottle of their best Merlot. I figured if my baby is gonna tie one on, it should be with the best they got."

Asha should've known it had to be something like that. That was typical Gill, and now she felt foolish.

The wine came, and Asha thanked the waiter, after he very gingerly set the glass down in front of her on a paper coaster, and smiled genuinely in her face. He was good at what he did, Asha thought, and seemed to care about each and every diner in the restaurant. If her memory served her correctly, she thought she'd seen him stop at all the tables and have a short, friendly conversation with everyone there.

"Thank you, baby. That's so sweet of you," Asha said.

"You're welcome. But is everything all right? You've seemed kinda preoccupied all night."

"Well, I had a little something on my mind. But everything is fine now," she said, taking a swallow of the wine. It was delicious.

"You know you look gorgeous in that dress," Gill said.

"Well, I'm glad you like it. But if this wasn't for my birthday, what is? What have you planned?"

"I have a couple of things in mind, but I really haven't decided yet."

And Asha was happy to hear that, because she knew that one of those things was probably an engagement ring. And although that worried her, if he hadn't decided yet, that meant he hadn't bought it yet, it wasn't sitting there in his pocket, waiting for him to whip it out and put it on her finger. She was hoping that wasn't what this thing was leading to, the dress, the dinner at her favorite restaurant. But then again, Gill had it in him to be a little more elaborate than this. Gill would've wanted to draw more attention to a proposal than just this.

"What is it you want for your birthday?" Gill asked, smiling.

"Besides you, nothing," Asha said, stroking his ego, knowing how good that would make him feel.

"Well, you know that won't be the case, Suga', because you know how much I love you, don't you?"

"Of course, Gill. Did you want to do dessert?" Asha quickly said, trying to change the subject, because she didn't think she liked the direction in which it was heading.

"You know I love you so much, damn near since the day I met you. You know that, right? And that I'd do anything for you."

"Yeah, Gill. I know all that," Asha said, starting to become a little nervous.

"And you know that I never want us to be apart. That I want us to be together for the rest . . ."

"Gill . . ." Asha said, stopping him abruptly, because he was going there. Oh God! He was going there, and once he really started going, she knew there would be no way to stop him. Asha told herself that this wasn't happening, not this moment, not after what just happened to her earlier at work. He couldn't be about to propose. But what if he was? What would she say? What could she say? She loved Gill, but not in that way, or at least not enough in that way to marry him. So she said very politely, and smiling as kindly as she could, "Gill, this sounds like you're talking about marriage here." And then she took a deep breath in, and let it slowly escape as she tried to remain as calm as possible.

"You aren't about to propose to me are you?" She smiled some, trying to make it seem like she didn't mind the idea at all, but would've preferred a little more notice so she could've had her hair looking a little nicer or something.

Gill smiled, chuckling a little under his breath. He shook his head, and said, "No, Suga'. *I'm* not about to propose to you."

And just at that moment, with those few words, the world seemed to be lifted off Asha's shoulders. She sat there, letting that immense feeling of relief waft over her, not noticing as the headwaiter appeared at the side of their table, raising his eyebrows to Gill as if asking a question. She was so savoring her relief that she didn't see as Gill subtly nodded his head toward the waiter, and the waiter nodded back, looking around the entire restaurant, seeming to catch everyone's attention with just his glance, then raised his arms out to his side. And Asha also wasn't paying attention as the entire restaurant full of people stood, turning their smiling faces in her direction.

And then as she exhaled the last of that satisfying breath, she was almost deafened by the sound of her own name being spoken by all the people who were in the restaurant.

"Asha . . ." Her name rang through the large room. "Will you marry Gill?"

Asha snapped out of her calm place, whipped her head about, spun in the booth, shocked to find everyone standing.

It took a moment for what was said to catch up to her, but when it did, her eyes sped directly to Gill, who was no longer in his seat across the booth from her, but on his knee, holding open a ring box with a beautiful, brilliant diamond inside of it.

Asha's stomach immediately knotted up, the alcohol was doing its thing on her head, and if she wasn't careful, she thought, she could've puked up all over Gill and his humongous ring. Her heart pounded in her chest, and every fraction of a second that passed felt like an eternity. All Asha wanted to do was run, get the hell out of there, but there was the tiny issue of that man in front of her, on one knee proposing to her. Her mind simply stopped working, and so did her vocal chords. To make matters worse, it now seemed that Gill paid the head-waiter enough to convince the diners in the restaurant that if the cute little black woman didn't respond after exactly thirty seconds, then everyone was to say, "Well? Gill's waiting." And that's exactly what they did, almost shocking Asha into yet another heart attack.

"That's right, baby. I'm waiting," Gill said, in the smallest, sweetest voice, beneath her. He looked so proud, yet so humble down there, and she knew that this would make him happier than any man living. Everything that happened that afternoon with Angie, her soft touch, the kiss, the tears, flashed before Asha's eyes in only a second. She took just an additional second to think about her answer, for one more would've disrespected Gill in front of all those people. Then Asha stood, extended her hand to Gill, and said, "Yes, sweetheart. I'll marry you."

10

I was doing seventy mph down Lake Shore Drive when the limit was forty five. The radio was blaring loudly in my car, all the windows were down, the sunroof open. Why? I didn't know. Maybe because I was trying to use everything available to numb my senses, blot out of my mind what I had just witnessed. I switched lanes recklessly, yelling over all the noise into my cell phone.

"Asha, when you get this, call me on my cell! I'm on my way to your place. I need to talk to you."

I slapped shut the flip phone, and tossed it to the passenger seat. I bore down heavier on the gas pedal, now approaching twice the speed limit, not caring that this strip was known for its heavy police presence. I grabbed the steering wheel tightly, whipped the car right, across three lanes of traffic, onto the exit ramp. If I'd flipped the car at that moment, I wouldn't have cared. Hell, maybe I was even trying to do it. I didn't know if I was suicidal or just trying to make more of an effort to stop that vision from playing out in my head again, which it did, regardless.

I'd stood there watching them, as they were so busy that they didn't even notice me just inside the hotel room door, my sweat-covered hand on the knob, the other hand wrapped around the roses I had bought Faith. I stood there, knowing that my eyes were lying to me, unable to comprehend what I was seeing taking place right before me.

Faith, my fiancée . . . her face was buried in the cushions of the sofa, as that man continued to push and pull himself in and out of her. They were groaning together, and then the man called out Faith's name. He said it with such passion, but also with so much familiarity. He said it like I would've said it, like he knew her, like he loved her.

She cried out again, saying his name I thought, but I couldn't quite make it out because her voice was muffled by the pillows. But then she made a sound that I *could* make out, a sound that was very familiar to me, and my head started to spin with the realization that my soon-to-be wife was making those car-stuttering sounds with another man. My wife was about to come at the urging of another man right in front of my face!

Something disconnected in me, making my limbs go weak. The roses fell from my hand, the doorknob slid from my grasp and the door quickly shut. Both noises shocked Faith out of her pleasure-induced trance, and she looked up at me with bulging eyes. She looked horrified, like she disbelieved what she saw as much as I did. At that instant she tried squirming free from the man, but he was still in another world, still going in and out of her. And unbelievably, it seemed Faith was still responsive to the feeling. She looked as though she was fighting against it, but was unable to stop the pleasure she was feeling. And although her face contorted with fear and frustration, the sounds she made became louder, her body seeming less in her control, until she shut her eyes, and involuntarily screamed out in ecstasy. She turned her head away from me, as if not to further torture me with the look of painful pleasure on her face. But I was far beyond saving. It had happened, and I was there to see it.

At that moment, I was so focused on Faith's climax, that it took a moment for me to realize that the man had gotten his too. He was bent over, his back arched strangely, shaking all over, like he had just been jolted with about a thousand volts of electricity.

"Ah, Faith. That was great," he said, smiling, sweat dripping from the tip of his nose, from off his chin, splashing onto her back. He looked down at Faith, his hands still resting on her behind, but when he saw that she was looking up toward the door, his eyes followed.

When he saw me there, he gasped, almost choked, and quickly pulled himself away from Faith. He staggered backward, almost falling over his own feet.

"It's not what . . ."

I heard him speak those words, even though all my attention was on Faith. I was staring at her intently, like I wanted to bore holes through her face with my gaze alone. But I heard those words, and I said softly, but with immeasurable anger in my voice, "You are not about to fucking say it's not what it looks like. Don't you dare fucking say that."

The man had obviously figured out who I was. He nodded his head obediently, frightened at the look on my face, then staggered one more step away from Faith, who had now curled herself up in a naked ball on the corner of the sofa, her arms roped around her legs. Her body was trembling, and I didn't know if these were final climactic tremors running through her, or if she was scared that I was going to lose it, tear the leg off the desk that was near me, and start beating the shit out of the both of them.

I wanted to speak, wanted to express my pain. I wanted to ask her why? Why in the fuck would she do something like this to me? What had I done wrong that I deserved this? But I couldn't find any words. And even if I had, I didn't think I'd be able to coax them out of me, for all the things that made speech possible seemed to be gone from within me. I felt hollow, like all my insides, my heart, even my soul, had been violently gouged out of me, leaving me with just enough sensory perception to feel pain.

A tear spilled from my eye, and I saw the sadness on Faith's face deepen when she saw that tear. She didn't want this to happen, for me to catch her. I had to tell myself that, because I feared that was the only thing keeping me off her, from shaking her, from forcing her to spell it all out for me. And it was also all that was keeping me from that man.

He was frozen, had backed up in a corner now, his shirt balled up in his arms, holding it close to him, as if for protection. Although I wasn't much bigger than him, he was smart enough to realize that even if I were half his size, I could've killed him with my rage alone.

"What are you going to do?" he managed to say.

What was I going to do? I looked about the room at the clothes strewn about the floor, like my fiancée and this man couldn't wait to get at each other. Glared at Faith, folded up on that couch, at her body, which I had thought was so beautiful but now viewed with disgust. I saw the man pushed up against the wall, trying to cover his nakedness with that shirt, looking like his life was in jeopardy, and he was right. I scanned him up and down, trying to find what he had more of than I did. I scanned his body slowly, taking in his face, his torso, his now shriveled penis. And I had to think a moment, but I knew I hadn't seen him pull a condom off, and just to make sure I quickly scanned the floor around them for the jettisoned slimy bag of rubber, or its fluorescent green packaging, but I saw nothing. She was having sex with this man without using protection. Just more salt on the wound. I looked at my feet, saw the roses there on the floor. The card had fallen open:

I'LL LOVE YOU FOREVER, FAITH.
YOUR FUTURE HUSBAND

What was I going to do? The question rang again in my head.

"Nothing," I said, softly, more to myself than to them, but I'm sure they heard it, for I heard the man exhale, and saw a bewildered look appear on Faith's face, as though she deserved some form of punishment, and felt there was something gravely wrong since she wasn't receiving it.

"Nothing," I said, again, even softer than before. What good could anything have done. What was done, was done, and I could not beat the event into reverse. No amount of yelling could magically erase it from my brain. There was nothing I could do, so I turned around and walked out of the room.

I came to a screeching halt in front of my building, yanked the key out of the ignition, not bothering to close the windows or the sunroof. I needed to talk to someone, to Asha in particular. I ran around the car, jumping up the stairs, and quickly pushed my way through the outer door. All the while I was praying that Asha would be home, knowing that if she wasn't, I would have nowhere else to go.

Trying to contain my anger, my pain, I knocked on her door as softly as I could. After only two seconds, I knocked again; then putting my ear to the door, I listened for movement, for her feet moving across the wooden floors, but there was nothing. I started to panic, now banging on the door harder.

"Asha. You in there? I need to talk to you." Then I banged again. And then I called her again. "Asha. Answer the door, Asha." And as though there was no possibility that she just could be out, I flipped open my cell phone and dialed her number. I heard the phone ringing in there, and waited for her to pick it up, needing her to pick it up. But she didn't. The call was directed to voice mail, and after the beep, there was so much I wanted to say, that I was unable to speak a single word of it.

I called back again, this time saying, "Asha, wherever you are, if you check your messages, please call me. I need to talk to you. This is an emergency." I paused before hanging up, making sure there wasn't anything else I needed to tell her, then I pressed End.

I turned around and looked at Asha's door, knowing that even if she wasn't there, just being inside her apartment would make me feel better, feel safer. And then I remembered that I had a key. I thought of going upstairs to get it, going into her apartment and waiting for her, but I talked myself out of it. I'd never just walk into her place without her knowing. Instead I slid down the length of the door, and sat there against it. She would have to come home sometime, and until she did, I would do what I could to work all this out in my head.

11

I had awakened a number of times, stirred by dreams of Faith and that man, but instead of picking myself up off the floor, walking upstairs, and going to bed, I just continued to sit there at Asha's door like some weary, loyal dog who had managed to find its way home after getting lost.

When I was awakened for the last time, it wasn't by a dream, but by a steady nudging.

"Jayson. Get up."

When I lifted my head off my forearms, I saw a blurry Asha start to come into focus.

"Jayson, what are you doing down here on the floor?" she asked, looking worried. "Why didn't you just go inside? You have keys to my place." She extended a hand down to me.

"I wasn't going in your place without your permission."

"Oh, Jayson, please," she blew.

"I really needed to talk to you. What time is it?" I asked, seeing that it was daylight outside.

Asha opened up her door. "It's about six in the morning." She watched me as I walked slowly past her, collapsed onto her couch, and threw my face into my hands.

"Now what was so important that you had to camp outside my door?"

"I caught her," I said, and couldn't say anymore at that moment, for fear that I would lose it, start bawling like a little girl.

"Caught who? Doing what?" Asha asked, standing in front of me, both her hands on her hips.

"Caught Faith with some other man. Fucking some other man," I said, not even looking up at her.

Asha quickly came to my side, threw her arm around me, smoothed her palm over my back.

"Oh my God, Jayson. No. Are you sure?"

I gave her a look like she was crazy, a look that read, how in the world could I see someone screwing my woman, and just think it was Faith when it wasn't?

"Of course, I'm sure. It was her. I walked in on them right in the middle of it."

"Damn, Jayson," Asha said, feeling my pain.

"She sounded like she was enjoying it," I said sadly, under my breath.

"Aw, damn, Jayson."

"She even had an orgasm right after she realized I was there."

"Goddamn, Jayson!" Asha said now, shooting up from the sofa. "That bitch. I knew I should've kicked her ass yesterday morning."

"Yesterday morning? What are you talking about?"

"We bumped into each other yesterday morning while we were both heading out."

And that had something to do with it. I just knew it. That was the morning after I was supposed to have told Asha we couldn't be friends anymore, but didn't.

"What did you tell her, Asha?" I said, quickly getting up from the sofa.

"I told her the truth. That you didn't break things off with us. I told her that we're still friends."

"Damn!" I threw my hands over my face, turning and pacing away from her. "Why in the fuck did you tell her that!" I yelled, walking back to her.

"Because that's what the fuck happened!" she yelled back, taking offense at the fact that I'd yelled at her. "I'm not the one who asked you to give your best friend the boot. So don't you go getting pissed at me."

"I'm sorry. It's just that I told her something different."

"I know," Asha said, still looking at me like she was ready to slug me one if I raised my voice again. "She was coming at me like I was the one lying and not you. Why didn't you tell her the truth?"

"Because I knew she was just angry about what happened that night, seeing us out there talking. She would've gotten over that, and it wouldn't have made a difference if we were still friends. But to admit to her that I didn't end it when she was so adamant about it would've been like choosing you instead of her. It just would've made things worse, so I lied. But when she heard that I had lied to her, she probably thought I was telling lies to her about everything involving you. She probably thought there was something still going on between us, and that's probably why she went out and found someone to sleep with."

"Hold it. Hold it, Jayson," Asha said, grabbing me. "I know you aren't going to blame this on yourself. I know that you aren't about to think that just because you happened to tell a little lie, she had the right to go out there, find some dude, and open her legs to him."

"I don't know, Asha."

"So what did you do? Did you whip his ass? Both their asses?"

"I didn't do anything. I walked out of there, before I could allow myself to do anything. I wasn't sure if I had the right."

"Had the right. Had the right, Jayson! You have more than the right. You have the reason. You walk into her crib and find her . . ."

"This wasn't at her place. It was at a hotel."

"A hotel?" Asha said, looking at me strangely.

"The new Hilton on State street."

"How did you know she was going to be there?"

"It was going to be a surprise wedding party. Karen called me yesterday morning to give me the key card, and . . ."

"Oh hell, no!" Asha said, her eyes wide, shaking her head. "Something more than you think is going on here. Karen called you?" Asha said. "Karen, who can't stand you called to give you a key card. For what?"

"Like I said, a surprise wedding party. She said she wanted to start off fresh, put all of those bad feelings behind us and . . ."

"And she gave you the card, told you where to be, and you walk in and catch Faith with her ass in the air. Jayson, something is going on."

"That thought crossed my mind earlier, but why would Karen set her best friend up to get caught, and I know, sure as hell, Faith wouldn't set herself up."

"I don't know, Jayson. But something fishy is going on here, trust me, and if you want to find out, you need to find Karen's ass, because I think that bitch set this whole thing up."

12

She set me up! That bitch set me up, Faith told herself as she drove her car in the direction of Jayson's building. She had tried getting hold of Karen all night. Tried calling her at least ten times at home throughout the night, and about half that many times on her cell phone. Karen never answered.

Faith remembered her first call, it was right after Gary left the hotel room.

"Karen. Karen! The worst thing just happened. I don't know how, but out of nowhere, Jayson walked in here and caught me . . . he caught us. I don't know what to do, girl. Call me as soon as you get this."

At that point, Faith was half dressed, wearing slacks and just her bra, as she walked about the hotel room gathering her things. She was trying to get everything straight in her head, what she would tell Jayson, whether it would be a lie, or the truth, or a combination of the two. But as she slipped on her blouse, and buttoned it up, the question of how Jayson found her out kept begging to be answered.

Jayson didn't know where she was going to be, Faith thought, as she sat to slip on her shoes. Karen had gotten the room. She would call her friend who worked there sometimes, and if a room hadn't been reserved for the night, she'd let Karen have it for next to nothing. Every now and then, Karen and Faith would invite some of their friends up for drinks, or she would use it as a private rendezvous spot to take care of some "immediate personal business" was how Karen phrased it.

Tonight, they were going to meet for drinks, watch a little pay-per-view, and probably order up some free room service, but Karen had said she'd have to leave by nine.

"Girl, you can either leave too, or stay the night and do your thing, if you know what I mean," she said, chuckling slyly. Karen knew that Faith wasn't going to give away a free night's stay at a posh downtown hotel.

Faith hadn't told Jayson any more than that she would be having drinks with Karen, purposely not saying where. At that moment Faith froze, bent over, about to pull the strap through the tiny buckle of her shoe, struck with the realization that it had to have been Karen who had told him. There could have been no one else.

Faith thought back to just before Jayson walked in. She remembered that her mind wasn't focused on anything in particular but how incredible Gary was making her body feel. She was very near orgasm, grasping one of the sofa cushions, about to rip the damn stuffing out of the thing, when she turned her head, and there he was. Jayson, standing just inside the door. She never even heard him walk in, so he didn't bust the door open, didn't jimmy the thing with a screwdriver. The only way he could've entered was with a key. But that was impossible, Faith thought. Even if for some strange reason Karen was crazy enough to tell him where she was, she wouldn't have given Jayson a key. She just wouldn't have done that, Faith thought. But then again, wouldn't she?

Faith's eyes were resting on the dozen roses that Jayson had dropped on the floor just after he had busted her. She slowly got up from the sofa and walked over toward those roses, knowing what she would find under them before she even lifted them. She would find the key card to the room, and it would only prove that Karen had given it to him, because the hotel sure as hell wouldn't have done it.

Faith stood over the roses, paused for a brief moment, then stooped down to pick them up, and just as she had imagined, there was the key.

She immediately ran to the phone and called Karen again, but this message was nothing like the first. This message was filled with curse words, accusations, and threats. And then Faith finished by saying, "When I find you, you got a lot of motherfucking explaining to do."

Later that night, Faith pulled up in front of Karen's small house on the South Side of Chicago. All the lights were out, and when Faith jumped out of her car, the thing still running, the lights still on, and ran down the driveway, pressing her face to one of the windows of the garage, she saw Karen's Altima sitting there. She was home, Faith thought, angrily. She's in there, lying low, the lights off, trying to pretend that she's not, because she knew I'd be coming over here.

Faith stomped her way back down the driveway and up to the front door. She pressed on the doorbell until her thumb started to hurt, and then she started pounding on the door with the side of her fist.

"Karen, open the goddamn door!" Faith yelled at the top of her lungs, not caring if she woke every neighbor in the area. "I know you're in there. Open up!"

Still there was no answer. Faith moved over to the window nearest her, peered into the dark living room, but saw nothing but the same modestly furnished room she had seen all the times she had been here before.

Faith went back to pushing on the doorbell. She rang it for almost thirty seconds straight, then she dialed Karen's home number on her cell phone. Faith hung up three times just before the voice mail picked up, knowing that Karen wasn't going to ever pick up the phone. She wasn't going to pick up because she knew what she had done to Faith was wrong.

"Why did you do it?" Faith said, yelling through the door, because she knew Karen was there, could almost feel her.

"What did I ever do to you? You were supposed to be my girl, and you fucking do this to me. Why, Karen? Why?"

Faith stood there, silent for a moment, as if actually expecting an answer to come through the door. When it didn't, she all of a sudden attacked the door, banging on it with her fists, kicking at it with her shoes, screaming at the top of her lungs again.

"What the fuck did I ever do to you! Tell me! You tell me. You tell me right now," she said, her face, covered with tears, against the door.

Again Faith waited a moment for a response, and when nothing came, she simply said, "Fuck it," pulled herself together, and walked away. Just on the other side of that door, on the floor, Karen sat, hugging herself, tears running down her face as well.

"I'm sorry, Faith. But it was best for everybody," she said, softly.

Now, at seven in the morning, when Faith pulled up in front of Jayson's building, she was glad she had decided to go on home after Karen's and force herself to sleep. It had probably given Jayson some time to cool off, and it had given her time to think about what really needed to be done here.

Faith got out of her Camry, walked up the stairs and into the building. But as she was closing the door behind her, the door beside her was opening, Asha's door, and Jayson was walking out, Asha just behind him.

Jayson jumped, as though he had seen a ghost, and then immediately averted his eyes, as though he had reason to be ashamed. Asha on the other hand was shooting daggers out of her eyes into Faith's skull.

But Faith didn't pay her any attention. What she did take note of was the fact that it was a little after seven in the morning, and this Negro was walking out that woman's apartment. The same woman that Faith had told him he had to stop seeing just the night before. And it was like a gift that had fallen in her lap. Her defense was set just like that.

Faith screwed her face up and said in an accusatory tone, "And what are you doing coming out of her apartment?"

Jayson looked thrown by the question as Faith knew he would be, almost guilty. But before he had a chance to answer, Asha pushed him aside and said, waving her finger wildly at Faith, "I know you, Miss Ass in the Air, are you asking questions about who's coming out of where?"

"I wasn't talking to you, Asha. So you can just be quiet," Faith said, calmly waving her away with a hand, turning her attention back to Jayson.

"You should be ashamed of your damn self. Three days before you . . ." Faith heard Asha say, and in return Faith, not even looking in Asha's direction replied, "I said, shut up." Faith was about to say something to Jayson when she felt her hair being grabbed from behind and felt herself being thrown forward. The next thing she knew her face was up against the wall, absorbing most of the impact of Asha's weight slamming up behind her. Faith felt one of her teeth pierce the fat of her lip, tasted blood as it quickly spilled into her mouth and ran outside her lip.

"Don't you tell me to shut up. Jayson's my boy. He's a good man, and he don't deserve to . . ." Faith heard Asha saying, just before Faith quickly spun around, swiping at Asha's face, but only catching the collar of her blouse, yanking all the buttons off with the downward force of her movement.

"You bitch!" Asha said, looking down at herself, her bra exposed.

"If I'm a bitch, come get some of this bitch," Faith said, breathing hard, her bloody lip starting to swell.

"All right, all right," Jayson said, pulling Asha back, stepping in between the two of them. "Faith, what do you want?"

"You know what I want," Faith said, dabbing at her lip with a tissue she pulled out of her pocket. "I want to talk to you."

"Tell that bitch you don't have nothing to say to her, Jayson," Asha said.

"Asha," Jayson said, turning to give her a look.

"Jayson, I want to explain what happened last night."

"You weren't trying to explain anything when your ass was in the air, and you were backfiring like a cheep ass car, were you?" Asha added again.

Jayson spun to her once more, this time his arm extended, pointed to the inside of her apartment. "Go."

"Jayson. You shouldn't have a single word for that woman," Asha said.

"Go, Asha."

"You two were engaged and she fucked around on you."

"I said: Go!" Jayson said more forcefully. Then he softened his tone a little, looking in Asha's eyes as if thanking her for her concern, but letting her know he had everything under control. "I'll take care of this."

Asha gave one last evil look to Faith, which Faith returned. Then Asha walked into her apartment and closed the door.

"Asha's right. I don't want to hear a word you have to say. Everything I need to know, I saw last night. I know it all."

"You're wrong, Jayson," Faith said. "You do want to hear what I have to say, because if you knew it all, last night would've never happened."

Upstairs in his apartment, Jayson paced back and forth in front of Faith like a caged animal ready to attack. He stopped directly in front of her, looked her angrily in the eyes, and said, "I should be hitting you right now for what you did to me."

Faith remained calm, and said, "But you wouldn't do that."

"And why wouldn't I?"

"Because you know you're the reason for what happened."

"What did you just say to me?" Jayson said, appearing more angry, grabbing Faith by the shoulders and shaking her.

"Let go of me!" she said.

"I'm the reason you go to some hotel room and spread your legs like some street ho for some motherfucker even though you know you're about to get married in less than a week."

"I said, let go of me."

"You tell me it's my fault, because you get caught fucking somebody else!"

"Just like you're fucking Asha," Faith said.

Jayson squeezed Faith even tighter now. "I told you I'm not . . ."

"Then why did you lie about her the other night?" And Faith knew she had him, felt Jayson's grip on her loosen some. "Why did you tell me that you ended your friendship when you really didn't?"

Jayson's eyes glassed over as if he was trying to recall the reason but couldn't, and then he let go of Faith, and paced away from her.

"She's my friend, and it wasn't right to just tell her that we couldn't be friends anymore because you were jealous," Jayson said, his back to Faith.

"No, Jayson. It was because you were fucking her," Faith said, spitefully. "You were fucking her like you've been doing the entire time we've been seeing each other."

Jayson spun around to face her. "I told you, that's not true."

"So that's why I find you walking out of her apartment this morning?" Faith said, and she couldn't believe her good luck. This was working out better than she could've imagined. She was the one who was guilty, the one who was caught in the act, "her ass in the air," as that skinny slut, Asha, chose to put it, but here she was, convincing Jayson that he was wrong. Faith knew he wasn't still seeing Asha, but she always accused him of such to allow her an easy escape route if she got caught doing something she shouldn't have been doing, like she had, and also because she just didn't like Asha, and was tired of always seeing her by Jayson's side. And it was all working. She knew because she could see the guilt cover Jayson's face when she asked him that last question. He looked so guilty, that if Faith hadn't known just how much this man loved her, hadn't known that, almost beyond a shadow of a doubt, he wouldn't cheat on her, she would have started to question if he *was* actually screwing the girl.

"You find me with some other man, and feeling distraught, you go running to the one person you always run to. The person you always ran to."

"I told you that's wrong!" Jayson said, raising his voice.

"Do you love her?" Faith asked, and this was the topper. She knew he wouldn't be able to answer no to that. And although Faith knew he only loved her like a little sister now, she would act as if she'd misconstrued his answer, as though there was no way that he could only love her like that. Jayson didn't answer the question.

"I said, do you love her?" Faith asked again.

"You know how I feel about her. I've made that no secret to you. But you know I only love her like a friend," Jayson said, seeming unsure of even his own answers now.

"I see," Faith said softly, knowing she had him right where she wanted him. And now she would beautifully bring together all the incriminating evidence against him better than Johnny Cochran could, shifting the suspicion from her to him, allowing her to walk out scot-free.

"You love the beautiful girl who lives downstairs from you, the girl you used to date, the girl you still spend almost as much time with as me. You say that you're no longer going to be friends with her, and then lie to me when you're unable to bring yourself to do it. And then you come out of her apartment, after spending the night there, doing God knows what."

"I was talking to her."

"And I wonder how many other nights you spent down there just talking?" Faith said.

"Just because you think there's something going on between us, that gives you the right to go out there and screw around on me?"

"What do you think, Jayson?" Faith said, standing up to him, looking him sternly in the eyes. "When I ran into Asha yesterday morning, and she told me that you lied to me, lied in my face, how do you think that made me feel? You knew that one thing could jeopardize our entire relationship, our entire marriage, and you lied about it. I'd known you'd been fucking around with her the entire time we've been seeing each other, but if you'd ended it right there, I would've seen it as a fresh start, and we could've gone on from there. But you couldn't let her go, could you?" Faith said, and she hoped she wasn't laying on a little too much drama. But it didn't seem like it, because he wasn't saying anything in his defense, as if he too now believed that he was actually guilty.

"So I went out, found some man to cheat on you with to make you jealous."

Jayson looked at Faith oddly, as if he was puzzling something over in his brain. Faith quickly reviewed in her mind what she had just said and didn't see where she could've tripped over anything.

Then Jayson said, "Make me jealous? How was that supposed to happen if I didn't know about it? I bet the only reason you're telling me about this now is because you got caught. You got busted because I walked in on you."

And he had a point, Faith thought. But she thought quickly, hoping she was right about what she assumed Karen had done. "But that's what I wanted to happen. I gave Karen that key to give to you so you could walk in and see for yourself. So you could experience what I've been feeling, firsthand."

Jayson looked at her, the anger on his face starting to dissolve, replaced by sadness, regret, and something that could've been even sympathy for Faith. He lowered his head, as if pondering it all for a moment, then lifted it back again, and said, "You only did that because you thought I was still seeing Asha?"

"Of course," Faith said, now knowing that she had pulled it off.

"I wasn't seeing her," Jayson said, moving closer to Faith, the anger no longer on his face.

"That's what you say."

"It's true. I wouldn't lie to you, Faith. I never lied to you about this, because I loved you." Jayson lowered his head, then said, under his breath, "Still do. You know that, don't you?"

"Yeah, Jayson. I think I know that," Faith said, as though it didn't matter one way or the other . . .

Jayson paced away from her again, his head still down, tapping a knuckle against his upper lip. When he returned in front of her, he said, "It's going to take a lot of love, understanding, and effort to get over this, but I want us to try." He cracked the biggest smile he could muster, which wasn't big at all, almost undetectable considering the circumstances. "What do you say? We can put all this behind us. Still want to be Mrs. Abrahms?" he said, trying to sound upbeat, but failing miserably.

"I don't think so, Jayson," Faith said.

"What did you just say?"

"I don't think so, Jayson. Now that everything is out in the open, I think it's better that we just end it right here, right now. There was too much going on for us to think that it would've worked between us anyway."

"But you said you loved me, that you were happy that we were getting married," Jayson said, grabbing Faith by the arm. "What about all the plans we made, our life together?"

"Jayson, if it was supposed to happen, it would've happened smoothly. But obviously it's not," Faith said, looking down at his arm on hers, as if expecting him to catch the hint and let her go.

"So what? That's just it. It's over. We're done, like that? How am I supposed to be able to just accept that?"

Faith twisted the engagement ring on her opposite hand a couple of times and slid it off that finger, handing it to Jayson. "Think about what you saw last night," Faith said, pulling her arm away from Jayson's grasp. "I'm sure that'll make it easier to accept."

13

It was lunchtime and Asha stood just outside the break room at work.
She had three clients this morning, all full-body massages, and she did
her job very professionally without once thinking a thought that she
shouldn't have been thinking. She didn't know what that was, but had
a feeling that maybe, subconsciously, she saw thinking about another
woman as a slight to Angie. But that was ridiculous, wasn't it? she asked
herself, as she was massaging her last client. And then she went as far as
to try and force herself to think of the beautiful dark-skinned woman
beneath her in a sexual way. But nothing came. She was nothing more
than a client lying practically naked on her table. Asha dragged both
her hands down the woman's smooth back. The woman moaned sensually. Nothing. With the same motion, Asha pushed the towel down
some to expose the woman's firm behind. She let her hands rest there,
high on her behind, then she applied pressure, pushing down into her
soft flesh. It was enjoyable for the woman, Asha knew that, could feel
her body softening even more under her touch, could feel the movements that let on that this felt good to her, erotic, but it did nothing for
Asha. She was immune, at least to everyone but Angie.

And that was wrong, Asha thought.

It was wrong for Asha to feel some sort of loyalty to Angie, when
obviously she didn't feel any toward Gill. Asha had been having sex
with Gill for almost a year, and during that time, had been turned on

by every woman who walked past her. But she shared a peck on the lips with Angie, and now she's walking around like a nun?

Last night there was nothing she could do to stop Gill from going on about the wonderful life they were going to share. He talked about it on the way home from the restaurant, talked about it from the car to the house, through the bathroom door while he was on the toilet, while they were showering together again, and in the middle of making love, through his grunting and moaning, "Baby . . . it's gonna be . . . just like, unh . . . this all . . . ooh . . . the time."

He fell hard asleep after that, on his side, his left arm thrown heavily across her. Asha lay there, staring up into the darkness, stroking the short hairs on his forearm, trying to envision some of what he was saying. She tried to see "Asha in a wedding dress," "Asha in rubber gloves doing dishes," "Asha in a maternity dress soon to give birth," "Asha as mother and housewife, pushing a stroller to the market to shop for the family," and it just didn't come together, at least not like it did for Gill.

Asha knew the "Yes" thing in the restaurant was a mistake, but what else could she have said at that moment? He wanted it so much, and since she gave her answer he had been so happy. Asha leaned over and kissed Gill's forehead and told herself, somehow, she would find a way to fix it all.

Now, outside the break room, Asha dug into her pocket and pulled out the huge ring that Gill had presented to her last night. She had taken it off to massage her clients, as she did with all her jewelry. She wasn't putting her watch back on, or her other rings, just this one. Since she had it, she thought there really wouldn't be much harm in flaunting it.

Asha opened the door of the break room and walked in like it was any other day, but making a special effort to swing her left arm out farther in front of her than normal, grabbing the fridge handle with her left hand, when normally she would've grabbed it with her right. When she sat down, she opened her lunch pouch slowly, wanting everyone in front of her to see each individual finger, and possibly get a glance at what was on one of them.

Three girls sat at the table with her. Nicole, Rhonda, and Paula. Paula was Italian with dark blond hair, and a somewhat large nose. Nicole was cute, mocha brown, but just a little overweight, and was in the middle of finishing her second Oscar Mayer Lunchable prepared box lunch. She was making a tiny pizza, spreading some pizza sauce over a crust the size of a Ritz cracker with a plastic stick that was supposed to function as a knife.

"You steal your son's lunch, or what?" Rhonda said, popping a baby carrot into her mouth.

"No, but maybe if you ate some lunch once in a while, your clothes wouldn't weigh more than you do."

Rhonda was very thin, but she still managed to have tiny curves at her hips, ass and breasts.

"Well, at least I know that if I want pizza, I'm not going to go to Oscar Mayer expecting to get a decent one."

"Ladies, ladies, stop with all the squabbling," Asha said, waving her left hand, as if attempting to stop them, but it was back side out, which looked rather ridiculous. "I'm trying to eat here, and . . ."

And before she could finish her sentence, Nicole said, "Oooohhh, girl, no, you didn't walk in here with that big-ass Z-ring on your finger."

Asha just smiled, knowing it would be Nicole who noticed it first.

"What are you talking about?"

"Rhonda, Paula, look at the size of the rock on Asha's finger. What did you do, knock off Rodgers and Holland's?"

"Asha, let me see that," Paula said, pushing herself up from her chair and rushing around the table. Rhonda followed her. The three of them stood over her, ogling the ring, as Asha sat there loving the attention.

"That has to be a karat," Paula said, holding Asha's hand in hers.

"That's a karat plus," Rhonda said.

"Karat and a half," Asha corrected, smiling.

"So is it Gill?" Rhonda said. "That fine-ass bamma that be sending you flowers and calling here all the time?"

"He's not a bamma. He's from North Carolina. And yes, it is Gill," Asha said, feeling proud, knowing that she had no right to, considering she wasn't going to go through with it.

"Man, you are so lucky, Asha," Nicole said. "I wish I could find a man like that to come and marry me."

Just then, the door opened and closed, and the women's heads turned to see Big Les standing inside the break room, a crumpled brown lunch sack in her hand.

"What's up with the huddle?" Les said.

"Les, come over here and look at this ring Asha got," Paula said.

Les lumbered over and took Asha's hand from Paula. Asha cringed a little as her soft fingers rested on the rough callouses on Les's palms. Big Les, without saying a word, examined it much longer than Asha felt comfortable with. And when Asha tried to gently pull her hand away, she felt Les tighten her grip. Asha yanked harder and took her hand back. Les looked up at Asha, giving her a stare that suggested she should be more careful whom she pulls her hand away from.

"Is it real?" was all Les said.

"Hell yes, it's real," Nicole answered for Asha.

"Yes, it's real," Asha answered softly, looking directly into Les's eyes.

"You gettin' married or something?" Les asked, maintaining eye contact with Asha.

"Naw, Leslie. She got hired as a hand model," Rhonda said. "Of course she's getting married"

"Gill gave it to her," Paula said. "That's her fiancé."

"That's all right," Les said, not taking her eyes away from Asha. Then she turned around, had a seat, and began to eat her lunch.

Asha's last client came late, as she always did for her appointments. But Asha was okay with it. It was Friday, and she really wasn't in any hurry to get home to deal with that drama that Jayson was facing. And she definitely was trying to avoid seeing Gill just yet; it was too soon to have to deal with his overwhelming excitement about the idea of their getting married.

It was a nice evening, so all the girls had left some time ago. Asha sat in the employee locker room, her locker open, half changed into the clothes she had come to work in. She wore a denim button-down shirt, white ankle sport socks, and her panties. Her jeans were lying draped over the bench behind her. She was about to put them on when she caught sight of the ring on her finger again, and she just stopped, lowered herself to the bench, as if she was just too overcome with all that she was facing to stand. She sat there for a moment, gazing down at the ring, admiring how beautiful it was.

Asha was startled out of her thoughts by the sound of a locker door slamming. She'd thought she was just about the only person left in the spa, and definitely thought she was the only person in the locker room. She didn't see anyone, so she called out.

"Hello," Asha said. There was no answer, and that brought Asha to her feet. "Hello," she said again, looking in the direction from which the sound came. And from that direction came the person who had made that sound, Big Les, and she wasn't wearing a stitch of clothing.

"It's me, Asha. I was changing to go home," she said, her wide body, rounded shoulders, heavy breasts, and barrel-shaped hips in plain view for Asha to see.

"Oh, sorry, Leslie. I thought I was the only one left here," Asha said, shyly looking down at her feet.

Les stood there quietly, not saying a word, but not moving back toward her locker either. Asha felt her unmoving presence there, but stopped herself from looking up.

"You shy or something?" Les said, in her deep voice.

"No. Why you ask that?"

"Because you ain't looking up at me. You acting like you gonna turn to stone or something if you look at my body. We rubbing on naked women's bodies all day, and you acting too shy to look at mine."

"I'm not acting too shy, I'm just looking at my ring," Asha lied, directing her eyes to her ring now.

And then she heard the faint slapping of Les's bare feet across the tile floor of the locker room coming toward her. Asha focused harder on her ring, feeling her body becoming tense. She tried to tell herself to calm down, that there was no reason to be tightening up. And there wasn't. What had Les ever done to her?

"Yeah, if I had that, I guess I'd be looking at it all day too," Les said, and now she was standing right next to her. Asha had been looking down at her ring, but now she was looking down at Les's bare feet. And for such a brutish woman, they were surprisingly dainty, and well manicured. Les was standing so close to Asha that she could almost feel the heat coming off her bare skin, could almost smell the scent creeping out from between her legs.

"It's a nice ring," Asha said, looking up at Les, finding her staring at Asha's naked thighs.

Asha quickly grabbed her jeans and covered her legs with them.

"You love that guy?" Les said, out of the blue. "The guy who gave you the ring?"

"Yeah, I love him. And he loves me too, that's why he gave it to me."

"People say you supposed to be all happy when you in love. You believe that?"

"Yeah, I believe that."

"Then why don't you seem happy? Why does it always seem like you missing something? You missing something, Asha?"

"I don't know what you're talking about."

Les looked down at Asha, a knowing smirk on her face. "Yeah, I bet I know what you're missin'. He doing you right?"

"Of course he's doing me right. He's a good man."

"Naw, Asha," Les said, smiling slyly, "I mean, is he *doin'* you right?"

Asha knew what the hell she was talking about the first time she'd asked, but she was trying to play dumb, hoping that Les would drop it. She really was starting to get on Asha's nerves now.

"You know what, Les, that's none of your business whether he's *doin'* me right or not," Asha said with attitude.

"Hey, hey. No need to get catty, baby. I was just checking to make sure your fine ass was getting taken care of. Because if you weren't . . ." Les said, reaching to touch Asha's face. Asha smacked her hand away, and said, "Like I said, that's none of your business, and you need to be keeping your hands to yourself, if you like having hands." Asha said this in her toughest voice, even though her heart was beating so hard, she thought Les might be able to see the imprint through her shirt, see just how scared she truly was.

"It's cool, it's cool," Les said. "But if you ever want to be done right, I mean really right, you just let me know."

"I don't swing that way," Asha said, with as much conviction as she could muster.

"Yea, whatever," Les said, turning her big self around and padding away on her bare feet. "But you think about what I said. I'm leaving the offer on the table." And then before she disappeared behind the wall of lockers, she swatted her butt cheeks with both palms making a loud smacking sound, and said, "You might like this better than you think." She laughed a deep, almost masculine laugh, making Asha feel as though she had just been violated in some way.

14

It was Monday now, and I was sitting in my car, outside of the Lincoln Park Social Center where Faith worked, thinking about how hard it had been to make it past yesterday, Sunday, my wedding day. All day Saturday, I'd sat on the floor of my silent apartment, the cordless phone in my hand. Every time it would ring, I would tell myself that it wasn't Faith, really hoping that it was, and when I looked down at the Caller ID to see that it wasn't, I would just let it ring until it finally stopped. I continued to sit there thinking about the steps I had taken to get to where I was, the mistake or mistakes I must have made to allow Faith to feel as though she had to be with another man just to get my attention.

The phone rang, and I eagerly, foolishly, looked down at it, only to see that it was Asha calling and not Faith. She had been calling me all day, for the past couple of days trying to make sure that I was all right, that I wasn't swinging dead in my bathroom, hanging naked from a necktie I'd somehow fixed to the ceiling.

I was clearly depressed. I stared at the walls a little longer, trying with everything in me to keep that awful memory from playing out in my head again. Although up to this point, I had not been very success-ful. Every time I closed my eyes, I would see, as Asha so crassly put it, "Faith's ass up in the air." And I wouldn't just see the images, I would hear the sounds, that man calling out her name as though he knew her intimately, Faith making the sounds she always made before she climaxed. Somehow, I couldn't convince myself of what I so truly wanted to. I couldn't deceive myself into thinking that, yes, she'd slept with that man, but she didn't enjoy sleeping with that man, that she suffered through it, just to make her point. Because something told me she loved it, just as much as she enjoyed being with me. Possibly even more.

Yesterday morning, Sunday, I woke up sore. I'd slept on the floor, on my area rug right in front of the sofa. I don't know why when I could've easily walked to my bed, or at least hoisted myself up to the sofa. Maybe I felt sleeping on the floor was a form of punishment for being so stupid about Faith. I felt the entire thing was my fault. She'd let me know how threatened she was by Asha, had let me know pretty much by day one, and what did I do? Ignore her concerns, as though they meant nothing to me, as though she meant nothing.

I picked myself up off the floor, wincing just a little at the dull pain in my back, and walked to the bathroom to grab a shower. I combed my hair and dressed, and sat back down on the couch, where I'd spent the last day and a half.

A knock came at the door. It was Asha. I knew it, could tell by her knock. She'd decided to come up, since she probably knew I was never going to pick up the phone.

"C'mon, Jayson. I know you're in there. Your car is parked out front. Open the door."

I acted as though I heard nothing, just looked down at the phone, expecting it to light up and start ringing for some reason.

"Jayson," Asha said. "It's not the end of the world."

I knew that, even though it felt like it was.

"I mean, it's not like it's something worth killing yourself over," she said.

I knew that too, even though, for like a millisecond, the thought had crossed my mind.

"And there are always other women out there."

I knew that. I didn't think they'd all of a sudden disappeared.

"Better women than Faith."

And there she was wrong. There was no woman better than Faith.

"And eventually, you'll find her."

Wrong again, Asha, I thought.

"So please, Jayson. Will you let me in?"

The answer was no. I tried to send her this message telepathically, hoping that she would get it. Because if she didn't, she would just have to stand out there till she realized herself that I wasn't opening that door.

"You're not going to open the door, are you?"

Ah. One of the reasons I liked her, she was so damn swift.

"No."

"Are you okay in there? Outside of the obvious, everything is cool, right? You aren't hurt, are you?"

"It's nothing. Just my pride . . . my ego . . . and my heart . . . I guess." I said these words as if I was speaking to myself, not knowing if she was even able to hear them.

There was silence for a few moments, then Asha said, "Do you need anything?"

I didn't answer her.

"I can run to the store and get you whatever, and if you don't want to open the door, I can leave it out here, and you can get it when I go."

Still, I gave her no response.

"Or if you really don't want to open the door, I could just buy really thin stuff, like bologna, pizza, and Fruit Roll-Ups, and slide them under the door."

I smiled a little at that, which I'm sure was her intention.

"That was kinda funny, wasn't it? You don't have to say it, but I know you're laughing in there," she said, through the door.

"Yeah, I am, Asha," I said, not loud enough for her to hear.

"Well, if you need anything, you know where I'll be."

I nodded my head, looking at the door.

"And, Jayson . . . don't worry whether Faith loves you anymore. I still do, and I always will. I'll see you when you're better."

"Thanks, Asha," I said, softly, needing that more than she probably knew.

o   o   o

I got out of my car, feeling nervous, thinking about what I would say to Faith when I saw her, wondering if I could remain calm, or if I would throw myself at her feet, beg for forgiveness.

I walked through the doors of the community center to the smiling face of an aging, gray-haired woman. Mrs. Pilsen was the receptionist there, had been for the year I'd been coming through those doors to see Faith.

"Good morning, Jayson. How are you today?" she said in her usual cheery manner.

Faith obviously hadn't told her what happened. But then again, why would she? And then I asked myself, did Faith tell anyone? Did it even matter that we didn't marry?

This would be awkward, confronting her at her place of work like this, but she gave me no choice. I tried calling her a thousand times, left messages, but she never returned my calls. I thought about going by her house, but I couldn't bring myself far enough out of my depression to do it. Besides, I figured she wouldn't have spoken to me anyway. But she would have no choice here. She had to go to work, and here she would have to listen to me. I would tell her that I was wrong, that she was right, and we could still have the life together that we had planned.

"I'm fine, Mrs. Pilsen," I answered, trying to match her level of cheerfulness. "Can you call Faith's office, and tell her that someone's out here to see her. But don't tell her it's me," I said, putting a finger to my lips. "I want it to be a surprise."

"I'm sorry, Jayson. She's not here this morning."

It was almost as if the words didn't register at first, because I was so expecting to see her this morning, wanting to resolve this so we could move on. I gazed at Mrs. Pilsen for another second, expecting her to correct what she just said, before speaking. "Oh, um. Do you know if she'll be in this afternoon?" I asked, disappointed.

"I don't know, but I can leave her a message that you stopped by," she said, reaching for a pen.

"No, no. That won't be necessary," I said, walking away, wondering where she could be.

15

Karen had been ducking her, Faith told herself, as she pulled up in front of the bank where Karen worked. Faith had been calling her all weekend, but the girl wouldn't answer and wouldn't return any of her messages. But that was fine. It was Monday morning and Karen had to go to work, and Faith would corner her there, make her tell her just why in the hell she had given Jayson a key to the hotel room.

Faith walked through the glass doors of the bank and into the lobby. She looked in the direction of Karen's station, and there she was, finishing up with a customer. When Karen caught a glimpse of Faith out of the corner of her eye, Faith could see she knew exactly why Faith was there. Karen quickly finished with the customer and threw a Teller Closed sign in the window. She spun around and was about to head for the back when Faith rushed the counter, saying, "Don't you even think about it."

Karen halted in her tracks, her back still facing Faith.

"If you don't come back here and talk to me, I'm going to make a scene, and say such foul shit about you that they'll have no choice but to fire your ass. Now come back here."

Karen turned around, barely able to look Faith in the eyes, as she walked back to the teller station. She removed the sign and said with little enthusiasm, "How can I help you today?"

"Cut the shit, Karen. Thursday night Jayson walks in and busts me in that hotel room. Why don't you tell me just how that happened?"

"I don't know what you're talking about, Faith," Karen said, but the tone in which she said it was hardly believable.

Faith leaned over the counter and whispered into Karen's ear. "Karen, you're bigger than me, and you'll probably kick my ass, but if you don't tell me what I need to hear there is going to be a catfight right on top of this fucking counter."

Karen looked into Faith's eyes to see if she was telling the truth.

"If you don't believe me, try me."

"All right, so I gave him the key."

"Why in the hell . . ." Faith began to shout.

"Keep it down."

"Why in the hell did you do that?" Faith said, lowering her voice.

"Now is not the time to talk about it. I'll tell you later."

"Bullshit!"

"I'll tell you later, Faith," Karen whispered loudly, looking over her shoulder to make sure no one was listening. "I'm at work. After I get off, I'll come by your place and tell you everything."

"Un uh," Faith said. "I'm not going to be sitting around waiting for you, looking stupid when you don't show. I'll be at your house at six o'clock. And for each minute you're late, it'll be another brick I throw through one of your windows. So don't keep me waiting."

At five minutes to six, Faith had been sitting on Karen's porch for ten minutes and was already scanning the ground for the best rock to throw first, when Karen's car came to an abrupt halt in front of her place.

Once inside the house, Faith didn't take off her jacket and head toward the fridge as she normally did. Instead, she stood just inside the door, as if this was the first time she had ever set foot in the place, and the owner of the home was a stranger to her.

"Aren't you going to come in, sit down?" Karen asked, putting down her purse, taking off her jacket.

Faith reluctantly walked into the living room, stood in front of the sofa a moment, then had a seat, not taking off her jacket or making herself comfortable.

"You want anything?" Karen said, looking as though she was about to go to the kitchen.

"Yeah, I want you to tell me what happened Thursday night."

"I will, but I'm thirsty."

"Drink later!" Faith said, shooting up from the sofa. "Tell me why you gave Jayson that key."

Karen paused for a moment, then had a seat in a chair on the other side of the living room. She folded her hands between her knees, and lowered her head. She looked very nervous, very unsure, and slightly scared.

Faith sat there, looking at her, becoming very impatient waiting for Karen to open her mouth.

"Dammit, Karen, for the fiftieth time, just tell me."

"You didn't need to be marrying him!" Karen blurted out.

Faith looked oddly at Karen. "What did you say?"

"I said, you didn't need to be marrying Jayson. And besides, you didn't love him."

"Hold it," Faith said, shaking her head. "I know you aren't telling me who I shouldn't be marrying, and who I should, and who I love, and who I don't."

"You loved him, Faith?" Karen asked, very seriously.

"Yeah."

"Then why were you sleeping with Gary?"

"You know why."

"Oh yeah, the same reason you've been sleeping with him since before you even met Jayson. Hoping that something in that pussy of yours would finally make him leave his wife. It ain't going to happen, Faith, if it ain't happened yet."

"That's where you're wrong, baby. Thursday night, after Jayson walked in and caught me and Gary, Gary saw the look on his face, saw how hurt Jayson was, he realized just how much competition he had. He knew that if he didn't do something me and Jayson were really going to get married. So he told me then that he was going to finally leave her, that he was going to finally file for divorce."

"And what if he hadn't changed his mind? What if he'd just told you that you could take your ass on and marry Jayson, that he didn't care?" Karen said.

"Then that's what I would've done. Believe it or not, Karen, I do love Jayson. But I have to marry Gary."

"Have to? What are you talking about?"

"I have my reason. It's none of your business. I could've married Jayson and been happy, but that's not what's going to happen," Faith said, smiling smugly. "The plan worked just like I thought it would."

"And that's fine with you?"

"Why wouldn't it be?"

"Hurting Jayson like that, even though you know how much he loves you? That's fine with you?"

"Hold it," Faith said, raising a finger at Karen. "I'm not the one who gave him the key to that room, when you knew I'd be getting my thang on. I'm not the one who hurt him. You are. And when the hell did Jayson all of a sudden become your concern?"

"I just feel he didn't deserve what you were doing to him. I never felt he did. I mean, what if that were me in his situation, what if it were me who felt that way? I know how much I'd be hurt. So by giving him the key, I was saving him."

"Oh, saving him, hunh," Faith said, looking slant-eyed at Karen as though she had been betrayed. "I see. So it didn't matter that all my plans got fucked up, as long as you could make yourself feel like some saint?"

"But your plans didn't get fucked up. Everything worked out just like you said, just like you wanted."

"But you didn't know that. You didn't know what was going to happen when Jayson walked in that room, but you gave him the key anyway. I can't believe you!" Faith said angrily, standing and walking over toward Karen. Karen stood as well.

"What would've happened if everything went wrong, if for some reason they both decided they wanted nothing to do with me?"

Karen didn't say anything, just lowered her head.

Faith grabbed her by the arm, gave Karen a shake. "I said, what would've happened then, goddammit!"

"Everyone would've been better off," Karen said, softly. "Jayson loves you too much for you to be marrying him if you don't love him the same way."

"What the fuck is that!" Faith yelled. "Why are you so damn worried about Jayson?"

"I'm not worried about him," Karen said, her eyes on the floor. "I just know what's right and what's not."

"You obviously don't. What's right is my girl not running behind my damn back, giving one of my men the key to the hotel room I'm going to be in so he can catch me getting done by my other man."

"Maybe if you were getting done by just one man, you wouldn't have had to worry about getting caught by another one," Karen said, her voice still soft, her head still lowered.

It didn't even take Karen finishing her entire sentence before Faith knew the point she was making. That was the icing on the fucking cake, Faith thought, as she pulled back and threw a wild punch into Karen's eye. She hit her mark squarely, sending Karen reeling, clutching the side of her face with both hands, letting out a short, loud squeal.

"Maybe if you were getting done by at *least one*, you wouldn't have had the time to be all up in my business," Faith said, breathing heavily and brushing a few wild strands of hair out of her face. "I could understand this coming from some bitch I half-assed knew, but you—you of all people. We were supposed to be tight and . . ." Faith felt herself on the verge of crying, but she smoothed a hand over her face and remained strong. "Me and you are through. You know that, don't you?"

"Faith, I didn't want it to—" Karen said, looking up, her eye already starting to swell.

"No, Karen. Fuck that," Faith said, throwing up a finger in front of Karen's face to shut her up. "We're through after this shit. I never want to see your ass again, never want you to call my house. I don't want to look out my car window and see your ass driving down the same street as me, you hear what I'm saying?"

Karen answered with a single tear spilling from her eyes.

"I'll take that as a yes. Good-bye, Karen," Faith said, spinning around and walking out the door.

16

Tuesday morning when Asha walked into the locker room at work, none other than Big Les was sitting there on the corner of the bench, looking as though she was waiting for someone, looking as though she had been waiting since the last time Asha had seen her on Friday.

Asha moved around Les, not paying her any mind, acting as though she wasn't there at all. She stepped in front of her locker, started turning the combination of her lock.

"No good mornings today, ring girl?" Les said, and although Asha wasn't looking at her, she could hear Les chuckling at the little joke she'd made.

"How are you, Les?" Asha was curt.

"I don't know. I've been thinking over the weekend about our little conversation on Friday, been having dreams and things."

Asha turned her head quickly to snatch a glance at Les. She was sitting there on the bench, leaning back some, one hand rubbing her belly, as if her stomach was pleasantly full with the images she was talking about.

"Woke up yesterday morning after a dream so damn good, I was about to come up in here on my day off just to see if you was as fine as you were in my dream. But then I said, naw. She's fine, but not fine enough to be giving up no damn day off," Les said, and then she laughed. "Know what I'm sayin'?"

Asha turned from her locker again and gave Les her full attention.

"Just who are you talking to? You act like you're having a conversation with someone, but I know that person's not me. I don't know who you think I am, or what you think this is, but you better curb that shit, and quick."

"Or what?" Les said, and now she was standing right up against Asha's thin body. Les was towering over her, looking as though she was going to bump into her, send her flying backward into her locker.

"What you gonna do, but keep on listening, and maybe finally come to your senses?" Les said, looking sternly into Asha's eyes. And at the end of that sentence, Les rested one of her heavy hands on Asha's hip. She placed it there, still looking into Asha's face, giving her a cautionary stare, as if to imply that her hip just as much belonged to her as it did to Asha, and if she was smart, she wouldn't dare try to move it.

Asha stood there recognizing what was going on, wanting to slap that woman's hand away, but having the sense not to. After a moment, Les took her hand back, a cunning smile on her face, and said, "That was smart. You a good girl, and you train fast like I thought you would. One of these days, me and you gonna have some fun."

You're out of your damn mind, Asha thought to herself, eyeing Les as the woman backed away a few steps, still looking at Asha hungrily. That would never happen, though at this point, Asha didn't even know how she would stop Les from continuing to creep up on her, short of shooting her with an elephant gun.

When Asha thought it was safe, she turned back around, went into her locker, and pulled out her uniform, preparing to change.

"You mind? I'm about to change," Asha said to Les, not turning around to look at her.

"Naw, I don't mind. You can change in front of me if you want to," Les said, settling in on the bench, as though she were about to watch a striptease. Asha pulled her things out of the locker, cradled them in her arms, and took them into her massage room to change. Something would have to be done about Big Les, Asha thought as she walked away, and it would have to happen soon.

o o o

That evening, Gill came to pick Asha up for dinner at his place. When she opened the door, Gill was smiling wide, holding a bouquet of flowers. Happily, he threw his arms around her, squeezed her tight, and said, "How's my Suga'puss doing this evening?"

"Good, baby," Asha said, smiling, her face against his shoulder.

He stepped back from her. "You looking fabulous as always."

"I'm casual today, Gil," Asha said, who was wearing a yellow pullover and blue jeans. "You said we're just eating dinner at your place, remember?" Asha had made sure that he wouldn't be taking her to any more fancy restaurants to spring any more news on her.

"Aw, baby. I haven't forgot. Nice quiet evening, just like I said. Now bring your fine ass on."

They drove downtown toward Gill's loft, but stopped at the grocery store on the way. Gill walked down the aisles, holding Asha's hand proudly as they went, recognizing each time another man's head would turn in Asha's direction, each time another man's eyes would gaze over her body longer than they should've. These things just seemed to make Gill even prouder.

They stopped in the wine section. "What do you feel like tonight, baby?" Gill asked.

"What are you cooking?"

"Fish."

"Let's do white. How about a Pinot Grigio?"

"Your wish is my command," Gill said, reaching to open the refrigerator door. He pulled out a bottle, was about to step away, then grabbed another one.

"Can never have too much Pinot," he said, smiling.

On the elevator up to Gill's loft, he was very quiet, just staring at the doors in front of him.

Asha moved a little closer to him, grabbed his hand, and said, "What's wrong? Is everything all right?"

Gill kept his eyes on the doors a moment longer, then looked into Asha's face, mild concern in his eyes.

"Am I doing this right? I mean, this is what you want, right?"

"Gill, what are you talking about?" Asha said, brushing up even closer to him.

Gill was holding Asha's left hand. He spun the ring he had given her around on her finger.

"This. My life. You want what I'm trying to give you, right?"

And what, did the man have some kind of sixth sense, because she knew she'd never let on that she wanted anything else. But he had obviously picked up on something. Was it becoming that apparent? Was this her cue to tell him what was really going on, what had been happening with Angie, the phenomenal thing that happened with her earlier today at work? Or was he just feeling a little nervous and unsure of himself, which would be perfectly normal.

"Of course it's what I want," Asha said, leaning in to give him a soft, long kiss on the lips, knowing that if there was a time to tell him how she really felt, this wasn't it. Although she had feelings for Angie, she wasn't sure where they would lead, and she wasn't going to go dropping this man who she'd invested so much in on the possibility that something might develop between her and Angie.

"You're what I want."

Gill smiled brightly when Asha pulled away from him.

"We better now?" Asha asked, squeezing Gill's hand.

"Much better now," he said, squeezing her back, as they walked off the elevator to his door. "And I'm sorry about asking that, but I just really needed to know for sure tonight," he said, as he stuck his key in the door and started to turn the knob.

As the door opened, Asha asked herself, why tonight? But the question was answered as soon as the door opened fully, and she saw the two people in Gill's loft. One was an older lady walking about the kitchen, wearing an apron, the other, an older gentleman, sitting in front of the sixty-inch TV screen, a beer resting on his knee, his hand sunk into a bowl of Cheese Doodles. The door closed behind Asha, snapping her out of the momentary state of shock she had slipped into.

"Asha," Gill said, "I want you to meet somebody." The woman stepped out of the kitchen, taking off the apron, rolling it in a ball, and setting it aside. The man got up from the sofa, brushing cheese off his hand onto his pant leg, and walked over to Asha.

"Mom and Dad. This is Asha, my fiancée."

o   o   o

After the pleasantries were exchanged, there was a mandatory meeting in the bathroom. Asha had yanked Gill in there, shutting the door behind him.

"I thought you said no surprises tonight," she whispered loudly.

"I said, 'no surprises at fancy restaurants.' Didn't say anything about no surprises," Gill said, smiling.

Asha was really pissed, felt that everything was moving way too fast, was getting out of her control.

"What is the reason for all of this, Gill?"

"All of what, Asha?"

"Flying your parents in from out of town, having them here to meet me."

"Asha," Gill said, looking at her worriedly, as if she hadn't heard a word she'd just said. "Think about what you just asked me. The reason for all this is because you're the woman I love, the woman I'm going to spend the rest of my life with, and those are my parents, the people responsible for bringing me into this world, for raising me into the man that I am. I know that they wanted to finally meet you, and I figured, and maybe I was wrong, that you wanted to meet them too."

Asha stood there staring at Gill, this stupid look on her face, feeling even more stupid than she looked. He was right, and if nothing else, her words had shown her just how much she really didn't belong here.

"I'm sorry, Gill. You're absolutely right. I just thought you would've warned me the night I was supposed to meet your parents. I mean . . ." and it took her a second, but only a second to think of a good excuse for her behavior. "Look at how I'm dressed. I would've worn something nice if I'd known they'd be here."

"Don't worry, Suga'," Gill said, kissing her on the forehead. "They'll love you no matter what you're wearing, just like I do."

The dinner was like any dinner from hell with the parents. There were a lot of awkward questions and situations, a few misunderstandings, and even one apology.

Gill's father wore a beard so long and thick, he must've started growing it when he was five years old. He was dressed in a suit, even though anyone could tell he never wore them except to funerals and on the rare occasions his wife got him to church. Asha figured Gill probably forced his father to wear it tonight to look good for her. As he stuffed his face with catfish, he would occasionally throw his heavy arm around Asha's shoulder, pull her into his huge body, and give her a squeeze. He was immediately taken with her.

"My future daughter," he said, almost as proud of her as Gill was. "My son sure picked right this time. Yes, you did, son. Because that last one, the one with the bushy eyebrows that connected in the middle to make one big eyebrow, every time she looked at me, I didn't know if she was mad at me, or if it was just that big caterpillar-looking eyebrow doing its thing." He laughed out loud at the joke he made. "What was that girl's name?"

"Katrice, Dad."

"Yeah, the Kat with the bushy Cyclops eyebrow," he said, laughing again, and taking a swig from what had to be his fifth glass of wine. Now Asha knew why Gill had bought that extra bottle.

"It wasn't that bad, Pops," Gill said.

"What do you mean, that bad? She was a beautiful woman from Carolina," said Gill's mother. Asha could tell she was all into that old-fashioned, housewife act the moment she walked in and saw her plump butt tooling around in the kitchen, her hair in a bun, wearing that polyester flower-print dress, the apron wrapped so tight around her waist, she looked like an inflated balloon twisted in the middle.

"She made a wonderful living as a marketing director for some big company and had plenty of investments as well," his mother said, scooping some more rice on her plate from a platter on the table. "And what was it you said you did for a living, Asia?"

Asha clenched her teeth and gave Gill a dirty look before speaking. "My name is Asha, not Asia, and I never said what I did for a living."

"She's a masseuse at a spa, Ma," Gill said, cutting in, and Asha cringed when she heard that, because she knew his mother would take it and run with it.

"So you rub naked bodies all day. I know a few women still do that illegally in parts of Florida, California, and Vegas, but I can't believe some people actually make a legal profession of it. Do they cut you a payroll check, or do you just get paid cash under the table?"

Why the hell is this old woman coming after me like this? Asha wondered.

"Ma, I think that's enough. Don't you?"

"I just want to find out what type of lifestyle you and Abba will be living. Do you have a degree in something? But then again, what would a masseuse get a degree in?"

The question was directed to Asha, even though Asha had a sneaking suspicion his mother knew that she probably didn't even have a degree, but she was at least glad she didn't call her Asia again.

"I don't have one."

"Now see . . ." Gill's mother started.

"That's enough, Mable," his father said. How did Asha just know that that woman would have a name like Mable, and then have the nerve to make fun of her name.

"I was just trying . . ."

"Well, whatever it is you're just trying to say, you can stop," Gill's father said getting up from his seat. "We all know how much you loved Katrice and wanted her to marry our son. The only problem with that is our son didn't love her. He loves Asha." Gill's father tugged on Asha's arm, and she stood up, allowing him to wrap his arms around her yet again, and pull her into his soft body.

"Our boy is gonna marry this beautiful woman, and we're gonna be there for that. And they gonna have lots of beautiful babies, and we gonna be around to be proud grandparents for that too. And over the years, you gonna forget about Kat the one-eyebrow woman," Gill's father said, "and start to appreciate this woman here. Because she'll be the mother of our grandkids, and the woman that makes our son so happy he won't know whether he comin' or goin'. And that's what really matters here, what makes our son happy. Because, Mable, he's the one that's marrying her. Not you. Understand? Now I want you to apologize to our future daughter."

Mable looked up at Asha, then down at her plate.

"C'mon, now, woman. We ain't got all night, it's gettin' late and these kids need time to start working on our grandchildren before they go to bed."

Mable looked up at her husband, then at Asha. "I'm . . ."

"Why don't you stand up and say it?" Gill's father said, smiling.

Mable gave her husband an evil glare, then stood. "I'm sorry . . ."

"Her name is Asha, Ma," Gill said, still sitting.

"I'm sorry, Asha, for making those remarks. If Gill is happy and wants to marry you, then I'm happy too." Mable said these words as if she were ill and about to vomit. "Do you accept my apology?"

"Yes. I do accept your apology, Mildred," Asha said, smiling to herself.

Gill took them to their hotel. Thank God, Asha thought, as she sank lower in the warm bubbles of the bath she'd drawn for herself. If she was unsure before, Gill's mother was definitely a good reason *not* to get married. But then there were other reasons as well. The whole 'lots of beautiful babies' thing, as his father put it. Asha knew that to have lots of beautiful babies, there would have to be lots and lots of sex, and lately, sex with Gill had been almost completely devoid of pleasure. And in light of what she'd experienced earlier today, it seemed that there would soon be reason to stop having sex with Gill altogether.

Asha didn't know exactly how her average, innocent conversation and massage for Angie had turned into something X-rated. One moment they were talking about shopping, shoes, and lingerie, and the next, Angie was asking Asha what kind of panties she wore. Asha told her something from Victoria's Secret, but that didn't seem to be enough information for Angie. She obviously wanted to know how they felt, for while she was lying on her back, and Asha massaged her legs, Angie's hand went wandering over Asha's skirt, up the side of Asha's leg. She traced the curves of Asha's hips first, then the roundness of her behind. All the while, Asha acted as if none of it was happening.

Angie let her hand fall, then moved it in front of Asha, and started pulling up her skirt. Angie continued to pull it up, until she got her hand all the way under it, was gently touching the lace of Asha's panties.

"And why do you like Vicki's panties?" Angie asked, as she traced the band around Asha's waist, then the one around the inside of her thighs.

"I don't know," Asha said. Her heart had started beating fast, and her head was becoming light. "I just like the way they feel against my body."

"I like the way they feel against your body, too," Angie said, now focusing deeper in between Asha's legs, at the warmth and moisture she felt there. Angie applied the slightest pressure with her thumb and forefinger, and Asha almost doubled over with the overwhelming sensation she experienced. Asha was no longer massaging Angie, but rubbing her hands up and down the woman's thighs sensually, holding on tight to her, trying to anticipate the next jolt of pleasure Angie was going to give her.

"Is everything all right?" Angie asked, in a soft, throaty voice, now pulling on the panties gently, slowly urging them down Asha's hips.

Asha didn't know exactly what was happening, or if she should even let it happen. She raised her spinning head and looked over at the door, wanting to go over there and lock it, but not wanting to stop this moment. It would be okay, no one ever walked in while she was massaging, she told herself. She allowed herself to relax just the slightest bit as she continued smoothing her hands over Angie's firm, tight thighs, up her flat belly, and around her waist.

Asha felt that Angie had coaxed the panties from her hips and bottom, and then a moment later, she felt them drop down around her ankles. Asha continued the facade as best she could, pretending as though nothing more was happening than the innocent massage she was giving her client, even though at this point, Asha was rolling her palms over Angie's large breasts until her nipples stood hard.

And then Asha felt it, Angie's finger sliding freely inside her, and she almost buckled over entirely. She let out a guttural moan.

"Oh, you like that?" Angie said, already starting to concentrate on her most sensitive part, and Asha wondered just how she even knew where that was.

"Do you like that?" Angie asked again, slightly quickening the speed at which she played with her, then changing the angle, which gave Asha even more pleasure. Asha couldn't answer but grunted something, now squeezing Angie's breasts in her hands, lowering her face to them.

"Is that making you feel good, Asha? Does it feel good down there?"

All Asha could think was, fuck yes it feels good, but she couldn't say it, because now her mouth was filled with Angie's breast, and she was squirming all about in front of her so much that she worried she might knee Angie in the face. It was all because Angie was doing what she was doing, sliding her finger in and out of Asha, making Asha so wet that she felt her moistness sliding down the inside of her thighs, and all she wanted to do was grab Angie's hand, and push it as far into her as it would go. She even tried a weak attempt at it, but Angie brushed her away, smiled mischievously, and continued focusing on that one little spot that was driving Asha insane with pleasure, until all of a sudden, Asha felt a tingling at her toes, her fingertips, the tips of her nipples, and at the edges of her lips. Then the entire sensation moved in, gripped her entire body until she felt both paralyzed and raging with rapture at the same time.

Asha was bent over Angie's nearly naked body now, groping at her, biting softly at her skin, but Angie did not seem to mind. Her attention was focused on bringing Asha all the way, making her explode like she never had before, and after just four more strokes, Asha started to cry out. Angie quickly slapped her other hand over Asha's mouth and continued giving her pleasure, till Asha's body jolted a number of times, then went limp, slowly collapsing onto Angie's bare stomach.

Asha got a chill just thinking about what had happened, as she sank deeper into Gill's bathtub. It was strange, but the more she thought about Angie, the more she missed her. The phone sat on the floor by the bathtub, and Asha looked down at it, foolishly thinking about picking it up, dialing Angie, if for no other reason than to hear her voice, talk to her about nothing in particular, share a short laugh. What the hell was that about? Asha asked herself, abandoning the thought, not even knowing the girl's number by heart. Could it be that she was starting to fall for her? Ridiculous, Asha thought. The woman made her have an orgasm one time, and now Asha was thinking she was in love. Asha smiled and laughed at herself for thinking something so insane. Then she found herself remembering Angie's smile, and she had to fight to get the woman entirely out of her head once and for all.

She had more pressing matters to think about, like Gill, and how to stop what had recently turned into a runaway train. But if she got rid of Gill, would she be alone? Would Angie be there for her? She knew that shouldn't be the reason she either stayed with him or got rid of him, but it seemed like Angie played a huge part in her decision. Asha knew that she would have to have a conversation with her before a real decision could be made.

17

For the better part of the day, I'd been trying to busy myself with work. I put on jeans, work boots and a heavy work shirt, and went to one of my South Side buildings to see if there was something I could do. It was all an attempt to get Faith off my mind. But while I was painting some stairs, trying to repair the mechanism on a garage door opener, replacing a basement window that one of those bad-ass kids who lived in the building had broken, I could not seem to think of anything but her.

I went to the gym afterward, trying to work off some of the anger and stress I was feeling. As I did dumbbell curls, pushing myself till my biceps ached, I asked myself why Faith was running from me. There was something I was missing, something that I'd done wrong that she couldn't seem to get past so we could reconcile and get on with our lives together.

I lowered myself onto the bench press and stared at the bar loaded with weights hanging over me. I was focusing deeply in on it, because I was trying to stop myself from thinking that the only reason Faith was continuing to avoid me was because Asha was still in the picture. I knew that had to be it, though. If I wanted her back, I had to do something about Asha, and I had to do it now.

I didn't even pick up the bar. Instead, I moved quickly to the locker room, not showering, just throwing my clothes over my sweaty body and heading home. Driving there, I kept trying to rationalize what it was I knew I needed to do, but in no way wanted to do. I would make Asha a sacrificial lamb. I would kill our friendship for the sake of my relationship with Faith. It was what Faith wanted me to do in the first place, what I should've done.

When Asha opened the door, she was just coming out of her shower, wearing a bathrobe, her hair all over her head. I followed her into her bedroom, where there were a couple of outfits laid out across the bed.

"What's up?" she said, looking down at the outfits. Then before I could answer her, she said to herself, "I know I'm wearing these jeans, but should I go with that yellow pullover, or that orange button-down?"

I stood there just behind her, trying to find a way to make this sound right, not to make myself seem so much like a monster.

"Jayson. Orange or yellow?" she said, looking over her shoulder.

"Oh. Orange."

"Thanks. I'll wear the yellow," she said, picking the other shirt off the bed and hanging it up back in her closet.

As she did that, I couldn't help seeing how carefree she seemed, as she hummed some soft song that sounded vaguely familiar.

"Where you going tonight?" I asked, avoiding what I was there to do.

"Oh, Gill's taking me to his place for dinner. Nothing special. Or at least it better not be."

I felt a tinge of jealousy come over me, knowing that she had someone to spend her evening with, someone that loved her. I looked at her hand, at her ring, just as beautiful as the ring I had put on Faith's finger, the one she had given back to me. I hadn't returned it yet, because I thought, I knew, there was still hope for us.

I thought about those things, and I not only started to feel jealous, but a bit angry as well, believing that it was all Asha's fault that I was standing here watching her get ready to go out for dinner, instead of making plans to go out with Faith myself.

"Asha," I said, looking down at my feet.

"Yeah."

"You happy?"

She smiled, but didn't say anything.

"Are you happy?"

"There's things going on in my life now that need some clarification, but for the most part, I'm happy. Why?"

"Are you happy that Gill's marrying you?"

"I'm happy that he wants to marry me."

I walked closer to Asha, who looked at me sadly all of a sudden, as though I was about to tell her something like I only had a day to live. I rested both my hands on her arms, and looked more at the collar of her bathrobe than her face.

"Asha, I don't want you to say anything. I don't want this to be open for discussion. I want you to know that I want to be happy too. That at this point, I'm willing to do whatever I have to do in order to accomplish that, and the only way to do that is to get Faith back."

I closed my eyes, took a deep breath, exhaled, opened them, and then continued.

"I'm going to go and try to find her now, and tell her whatever she wants to hear, do anything she wants me to, and if she still wants to hear that I will no longer be friends with you, I'm going to have to tell her that, too. And it will stick this time. I'm sorry, Asha."

I stood there, my arms still on her shoulders, looking at her, as she looked back at me. She wanted to say something to me, but I suggested she not by the look in my eyes. I squeezed her gently, as if saying good-bye for the last time, then I turned around to leave.

"I understand, Jayson," I heard her say from behind me. It took everything in my power not to turn around before I left.

I had parked my car down the street, out of sight of Faith's house. I didn't need her to see my car from there as she was about to turn the corner, and then all of a sudden race away. I'd been sitting on her porch for the better part of three hours now. I told myself I was going to leave at the start and middle of each one of those hours, but never found the courage to.

I heard a car coming and leaned forward some to see that it was Faith's Camry. She pulled up, her mind obviously occupied by something enough to stop her from noticing me until after she'd parked and pulled her key from the ignition. I stood, and she looked disappointed to see me there.

She grabbed her things out of the backseat, and took forceful, businesslike steps toward me and up the porch stairs. When I tried to say something, she said, "Jayson, we've already been through this. I have nothing left to say to you."

"Faith, I know this can't be it. There has to be a chance for us to fix this."

Faith was fumbling with her keys, trying to shove the right one in the lock.

"There's nothing to fix, because we don't have anything anymore."

"Just like that?" I said. "One moment, we're in love, eating dinner at a restaurant with all our friends, days away from getting married, from spending the rest of our lives together, and loving the idea of it, and now we don't have anything anymore?"

Faith looked up at me from the lock a moment, and said, "That's right, Jayson," as if she had never loved me a day in her life.

That's when I snapped. I don't know exactly what it was that did it. Was it because of how calm she seemed about this whole thing, when I was sitting up nights, seeing her face on everything I laid eyes on? Or was it the fact that she seemed to have absolutely no emotion in her whatsoever when I was practically pleading for her forgiveness?

I smacked the keys out of her hand, moved up very close to her, breathing in her face. "So that's it? Period? It's over?"

"How many times do I have to tell you that," Faith said, not intimidated at all.

"I want to know why? Why just so damn all of a sudden?"

"It wasn't all of a sudden, Jayson. It was a long time coming with that girl. I told you all this before. Now if you don't mind . . ." she said, looking at me, then down at her keys.

I was standing over them, and I guess I was supposed to move out of her way so she could get them.

She picked them up and was searching for the right one on the ring again. "This was your fault, Jayson. Not mine."

"I'm ready to do the right thing now," I said. "I'm ready to end my friendship with Asha, for real this time. I even told her so earlier today. You can call her if you want," I said, knowing that Asha would curse Faith out if she ever picked up her phone and heard Faith on the other end of it. But I was desperate, willing to do anything.

"I'm not calling anyone, Jayson. It's too late for that. Way too late. We're done. It's done. I just wish that you would move on with your life and stop coming around here, because it won't make any difference."

"You don't mean that, Faith," I said.

"I do. I really do."

"Then tell me that you don't love me. If that's how you really feel. Look me in the face and tell me," I said, staring intently into her eyes, knowing she wouldn't be able to do it.

She looked sternly, deeply into my eyes, not blinking once, and said slowly and firmly, "Jayson. I do not love you anymore." After that, she continued to hold that unblinking stare, as if proving there was no question of her certainty.

There were still so many questions I needed answered. What about that man? Where did he come in? But after those firm final words she spoke, I knew all the questioning in the world wouldn't make one damn bit of difference.

After a moment, I lowered my head and walked away from her, off the porch, down the street. I did not look back, almost afraid to, afraid that she would still be there, looking out over her banister, her arm outstretched, pointing at me, the other hand covering her laughing mouth. When I got to my car, I fell into the seat, rewound the tape in my head, and played over all that was just said. Still, two and two weren't adding up. It was just too damn quick of a change of heart for me to believe that she didn't love me anymore. There was something else that she was hiding, maybe afraid to come out with.

She wouldn't tell me, but maybe there would be someone else that could. I grabbed my cell phone, scanned through the directory, looking for Karen's number. She was probably the last person who would want to help me save my relationship with Faith, considering she was Faith's best friend, considering that now things were probably just how she always wanted them to be with Faith and me, but I had no one else to turn to. No one knew her better than Karen.

It was a little after nine. The phone rang three times, and I was praying that she was home. It was funny, but I never thought I would be praying to speak to this woman.

"Hello."

I was silent a moment, not knowing what to say, fearing that if I said the wrong thing she would hang up in my face.

"Karen."

"Hello?"

"Karen. It's me, Jayson." There was silence, then after a second pause, she said, "Hi, Jayson." Her voice was low, she sounded depressed.

"Before you hang up on me, I just wanted to say that I figure you probably already know what happened to me and Faith."

"Yes, I do."

"And I've been trying to talk to her, do whatever I can to get her to come back to me, but she won't even listen. I know that she loves me, but there must be something else that she's afraid to tell me about, afraid I won't understand. I was hoping that maybe you could find out what's really going on, that maybe you could talk to her."

There was another short pause, then I heard Karen sigh heavily over the phone.

"Jayson, I *know* what's going on. But the real question is, do you really want to find out?"

"Of course I do!"

"Fine. You've come to the right person."

18

Angie parked her Mercedes in front of the day care center. It was a little after four, and things had been busy at the downtown clothing boutique she owned. She wanted to take care of most of the customers herself before she left her assistant in charge for the rest of the evening.

Angie stepped into the day care center and clip-clopped across the hallway tile floor toward Room 101. She peered inside the glass and saw three children sitting on a large area rug with the ABCs and 123s stitched into it. One of them, a brown, round-faced boy with curly, sandy brown hair, looked up at her, smiling. He got up, ran toward the door, and Angie opened it to receive his hug.

This was her son, Kyle. He was six years old and the most important thing in her life. Angie grabbed her son's hand, walked him back over to where he'd been sitting, and grabbed his Pokémon backpack off the floor.

"Is everything in here, Ms. Rodgers?" Angie asked of the girlish-looking day care teacher who was walking toward her.

"He's all set," Ms. Rodgers said, patting Kyle on the head. "See you tomorrow, Cowboy."

Angie strapped Kyle in the backseat of the car and began heading home. She had soft music playing, her favorite Chicago radio station, Smooth Jazz, WNUA. She tapped her finger to the music against the steering wheel as she drew to a stop at a red light. She was peeking up into the rearview mirror when her cell phone rang.

Angie fumbled with her purse, pulled the phone out, and glanced at the Caller ID, as she always did. Then she pressed the Receive button.

"Hello," she said.

"Hey, where you at? You got Kyle, yet?" the man on the other end of the phone asked. It was Deric, who knew full well that Angie had picked him up already. Every day he called between 4:15 and 4:30 P.M., and asked that same question, and Angie would always answer him with, Yeah. I just got him, and we're on our way home, or to the store, or stopping by the post office.

"Is he awake back there?" Deric asked.

Angie peered back, and said, "Yeah, and you don't have to ask. Here he is." Angie handed the phone back to Kyle, which he happily grabbed and pressed it up to his chubby cheek, smiling.

"Hello?" he said.

He waited a moment to hear who it was, then said, "Hi, Daddy."

Angie smiled herself, shaking her head, accelerating as the light turned green. Kyle loves himself some Deric, and Deric wouldn't know what to do with himself if there wasn't any Kyle. He loved that boy like any man would love his son, more even, and that said a great deal about Deric considering the boy wasn't even really his son.

Kyle was the son of a very handsome man that Angie had seen for all of three months. He was married, had three kids already, and was a huge corporate success. He was perfect for what she wanted him for, and that was nothing more than donating to her cause.

Angie was thirty-two years old, had not a single man in mind to marry and probably never would, because she loved women. But she did want a child, and she wanted to have one before she got too old.

Angie would see this man once or twice a week, whenever he was able to distance himself from his job, his wife, and his kids. He'd show up, they'd grab a bite to eat and a couple of drinks, then head off to a hotel.

It was always relatively quick sex, and that was fine with Angie, because she wasn't in it for the pleasure anyway. Angie no longer even referred to him by name, but only as "Donor."

A month and a half later Angie ended up pregnant. He almost had a heart attack when she told him the news.

"But you're on the pill," Donor said, pacing back and forth, infuriated.

"It is still possible to get pregnant on the pill. It's like a 1.25 percent chance but it's still possible."

Donor stopped his pacing, lowered himself down beside Angie. "Don't worry. I'll be there for you, and I'll pay for everything," he said, holding her hand, a comforting expression on his face.

"I'm not having an abortion."

After that, for the next two weeks, he kicked and screamed, tried to bribe her into getting the abortion, offering cash, a car, anything. He was concerned about paying child support, about his wife finding out, about his kids having a half sister or brother. Angie assured him that he had nothing at all to worry about.

"You can keep your money. I have my own. This will be my child. You won't have anything to do with us, and we won't have anything to do with you. As far as I'm concerned, this can be the last time we see each other."

Old Donor seemed happy with that arrangement, and Angie was ecstatic, already thinking that she could feel the little life growing inside her.

"Mommy," Kyle called from the backseat, holding out the phone. "Daddy wants to talk to you again."

Angie grabbed the phone. "Yeah, baby."

"What do you feel like eating tonight?"

"Uh, I don't know. I was thinking about pork chops or something."

"Okay, well, don't you worry about it. I'll be home in about an hour, and I'll . . ."

"No, baby, I'll cook," Angie said.

"I said . . . ," Deric insisted, " . . . I'll be home in about an hour, and I'm cooking. You got that?"

"Yeah, I got it," Angie said, smiling.

"Love you."

"I love you, too," Angie said, then hung up. It came much easier now, those words. The first time he'd said them to her, Angie didn't know what to do. She didn't love Deric, and knew she wouldn't fall in love with him, so her first instinct was to run. But then she told herself to look at it differently—to look at him differently. He was a friend, a dear friend of hers, who would do anything for her, and for that reason, she'd learned to love him in a way.

Four years ago, Deric, a handsome thirty-year-old, whose good looks were hidden behind a Clark Kent get-up—out-of-date clothes, and geeky glasses—opened a bookstore next door to her boutique. It failed, but during the six months it was open, Angie and Deric became good friends, having lunch every day, and dinner at least three times a week.

Angie told Deric about Kyle, how hard it was to find a baby-sitter sometimes, and he said he loved kids. He started baby-sitting now and then, and grew attached to Angie's son. Then when his store closed, and he had to move out of his apartment to conserve money, Angie offered up her place.

"I have an extra bedroom that I claim is an office, but is really more like a storage room. You can crash there for a while," she said.

He moved in, and after six months, he was no longer sleeping on the futon in the extra bedroom, but in Angie's bed. At first it was truly nothing more than just a "friend thing." They both enjoyed having the comfort of having someone to lie next to while they slept. But as time passed, during the nights Angie could feel Deric's arms around her while he slept. She could feel him holding her like they were more than just friends, like he was dreaming they were, wishing they were.

"I want us to be together," Deric said one night after they put Kyle to bed. The boy had already taken to calling Deric Daddy, and whether or not Deric encouraged it while she wasn't around, Angie didn't know, but she didn't stop it from continuing. It somehow seemed right.

"We *are* together. If we were bunched up anymore on top of each other, you'd be inside me."

Deric gave her a sly look, as if to say, "Exactly."

"Angie, you can pretend like you don't know this," Deric said, scooting even closer to her, pulling her into him by the waist. "But in the year that I've known you, I've grown to love your son, all that we have, and I love you."

And there were those words that had sent her running in the past from countless relationships. When men said that to her, Angie had to leave them, because she knew nothing could come of it, considering her preferences. And when women shared that little tidbit of info, again, she had to jet, because even though she loved women, she wasn't ready to tell the world, start marching in gay pride parades. And once she had a son to consider, she definitely wasn't affixing any rainbow colored bumper stickers to the old Mercedes.

That night, she'd been so close to shoving Deric out of that bed and telling him to hit the road, but something he had said stopped her. "All that we have." He was right. They had really managed to build something. Something like a little family. Slightly dysfunctional maybe, but it was nice. Kyle had the father figure that Angie so desperately tried convincing herself he wouldn't need all the time she was carrying him, though she knew he really would. Deric had a woman he said he adored. And Angie had comfort as well as stability and security.

She had been in worse places in her life, with worse people, and although she knew she could never be truly in love with Deric—lustful love, like thinking-of-that-person-every-moment-of-the-day love—she could settle for what she had. It had its advantages.

So that night, she gave Deric what he wanted and had been giving it to him every night since. But still, she loved what she loved, and not a month later Angie was seeing a beautiful Jamaican woman who shopped in the store from time to time. After that ended, she was seeing a personal trainer at her gym, a well-put-together sister who knew how to coax pleasure out of every muscle in Angie's body.

Angie would try to keep these relationships at a distance. She didn't need them encroaching on what she considered her "real life," her "serious life." But eventually, Angie's privateness regarding that life wouldn't satisfy these women. They wanted to know more about her, wanted to see her more, wanted to give her more, and get more from her. They wanted a "relationship." And that was just impossible. Kyle was getting older, very near the age of understanding, and she didn't need him at school, the teacher and kids looking over his shoulder, as he mashed two Barbie dolls faces and torsos together, telling everyone that "This is what Mommy does."

There were times when Angie thought about those women, and

the relationships she didn't give a chance to blossom, and she felt kind of sorry. She was happy, and she did love Deric in a way, but would she have been happier with someone she was truly in love with?

Angie pulled into the driveway of her West Side townhome. She got out of the car, opened the back door, reached in, unbuckled her son, and pulled him out. He fell limply into her arms, his eyes closed, his head rolling about on her shoulder.

"I'll let you sleep another fifteen minutes, Cowboy. After that, it's wakee time. Don't need you climbing the walls at one in the morning."

Angie managed to open the front door while still not waking Kyle. She walked in, set her son down on the sofa, then kicked off her heels, and sighed in relief at the feel of the cool, smooth floor against the soles of her feet.

She was about to walk over to the fridge to see how she could make Deric's job a little easier when he came in, when her cell phone started ringing again. She rushed over to her purse, grabbed it, and the Caller ID said "Mills, Asha."

Angie looked down at it another second, letting it ring another time. She knew that she was smart to just give out her cell number, because eventually the phone calls would always start, and she didn't need her women friends calling her house.

"Hello."

"Hey, Angie, it's Asha. Am I bothering you?"

"No," Angie said, feeling slightly bothered, looking down at her sleeping son, knowing she would make this conversation a short one. "What's up?"

"Oh, nothing much. I was just thinking, and you popped into my head, and . . ."

"You were thinking about yesterday, weren't you?" Angie said slyly, moving into the bathroom, out of her son's earshot.

Angie could hear Asha laugh bashfully.

"It's okay, Asha. Did you like that?"

"Mmmmmmm. I just . . . I've never felt . . . I mean, the way you touched me, I just wanted . . ."

Angie felt a quick chill race up her spine at the sound of Asha's voice, and pushed it away. "I know, I know."

"You know what you do to me, don't you, Angie?"

"Of course I do. I know exactly what I'm doing. That's why I do it. That's why I'm going to keep on doing it," Angie said, laughing mischievously.

"Well, you aren't the only one who can have fun."

"And what are you saying?"

"I'll whisper it to you next time I see you."

"Mmmmmmm, now you got me purring."

"Just like a kitten," Asha said, laughing.

"Oh, yeah. *Just* like a kitten," Angie said, laughing with her.

After a moment, Asha said, "I was really calling, because there's a couple of things I need your opinion about."

Angie hoped that this wasn't already going where she thought it was, then said, "Shoot."

"There's a new girl at the spa, I don't think you met her yet. Her name is Les, but this chick has all but thrown me up against a wall, and strip-searched me."

"What are you talking about?"

"She's telling me that she wants to get with me, that she wants me and her to do that thang, if you know what I'm saying. I would've whooped her ass by now, but she has like three of them, and she's damn near six feet tall. If we were in prison, we wouldn't be having this conversation, because I would've been her bitch a long time ago."

"She's like that, hunh? I've had to deal with women like that," Angie said, lowering the lid on the toilet and having a seat. "So she's harassing you?"

"Yeah, and I don't know what to do."

"Well, it is what it is. If it was a man stepping to you that strong, you probably would've let him know that if he keeps it up, you'd go to the supervisor. Tell her the same thing. That should back her big ass right off."

Asha was silent for a moment. "Yeah, you're probably right."

"I am. So do that, and let me know what happens, okay. But I gotta be . . ."

"Hold it, Angie. There's one more thing."

Angie leaned forward on the toilet, looked out the bathroom door to see if her son had awakened or if Deric had walked in yet.

"Mmm, hmm?"

"There's this uhm . . . this really kinda sticky situation that I've been in involving this man, and I was wondering . . ."

"You know, Asha," Angie said, getting up from the toilet, as if Asha could actually see this action and realize that Angie was truly in a hurry to go somewhere, "I was really on my out the . . ."

"I was just going to ask your opinion, considering all that happened, do you think . . ."

"No, Asha, really," Angie said, and she spoke those words very deliberately, almost in a way that Asha could do nothing but understand that they held a double meaning. "I can't talk right now. I'll see you for our appointment tomorrow?"

Asha didn't respond until after a long moment. "Oh, yeah. Tomorrow." She paused again and said, "That'll be fine. I'll see you then."

"Good. See you then," Angie said, hanging up the phone before Asha could say anything else, and flopping back onto the toilet seat cover. She was going to try to drag me into it, Angie told herself. She was going to say something about some boyfriend, or fiancé, or even husband she was having second thoughts about now that Angie had helped to open the closet door. She was hoping Angie could save her from all that doubt, whisk her away on some magic carpet so she wouldn't have to contend with any of it. Angie wouldn't involve herself in that. That was Asha's business.

Angie had finally found the right recipe, all the ingredients needed—not to make the best-tasting soup in the world, but one that was at least nourishing enough to live on—and she wasn't about to go messing all that up just to get mixed up in another woman's problems.

Angie quietly walked back into the living room to see that her son was still sleeping. She sat down beside him, rubbed her hand across his curly hair. Asha was a beautiful woman, and Asha was cool people, and Angie was almost certain by the way Asha paused before answering her that she had gotten the message. Decisions like those Asha would have to make herself. But if she didn't, if she tried to make this more than what Angie would allow, could allow, then once again, Angie would have to walk away. And she didn't want that, because it had been a long time since she'd started to like someone the way she liked Asha.

19

The next morning, I was nervously sitting in Starbucks, on the same stool I had been sitting on when I last spoke to Karen in person, when she'd given me the key card that had started all of this. I thought back and I realized now just why she'd been so excited. "You're gonna be so surprised." That's what she'd said. She obviously did as Faith asked, gave me the key and told me when to be there. So why was she meeting me here now to talk to me, to help me? At least that's what I assumed this conversation was going to be about.

We were supposed to meet at 10 A.M., but I got there at 9:30, unable to control my urge to finally find out what was going on, what was stopping me from getting Faith back. I sipped on a rapidly cooling vanilla coffee, even though I knew the caffeine did nothing but make me more nervous, more jumpy.

I was sitting facing the counter, my head lowered over the cup, trying not to look at my watch, or silently count the minutes in my head as they ticked by. Every five minutes or so, I would spin on the stool and look out the glass walls of the store, down the street in the direction I thought Karen would come from. The fifth time I did that, I finally saw her walking toward me. She wore a long, lightweight trench, huge dark glasses, and carried a purse that she clutched like she was carrying millions of dollars' worth of diamonds in it.

Her expression was blank as she walked in the door and sat down next to me. She didn't take off the glasses, didn't even turn toward me, but addressed the same boy who was behind the counter when we were there last, who always seemed to be behind the counter.

"Double espresso," Karen said, then to me, "How you doing, considering everything, Jayson?" She still didn't turn around, but her head moved slightly as she followed the movements of the boy making her coffee.

I wanted to say, How do you think I'm doing? I'm ready to shoot somebody, or myself, if I don't find out what's going on. But I just said, "Not bad." Then, "What's up with the tinted goggles?"

"Sunny outside," Karen said, coolly.

I turned to look out the window, and the sky was still mostly covered by clouds. Whatever.

The espresso came. Karen paid the boy, then took a sip. She finally turned toward me now, gave me a long look, and said, "You look like shit. I'm sorry about all of this."

"Well, I'm not blaming you. You only did what Faith asked you to do. I mean, you're her friend more than mine so I understand. It just bothers me that everything just seemed to turn around all of a sudden. I mean, one minute we're in love, we're fine. We're talking about honeymoons, about the children we're going to have, and then next thing I know, she's asking you to give me some key, and . . ."

"She didn't ask me to do it." Her face turned to the side again.

"She didn't ask you to do what?" I said, feeling as though I missed a beat somewhere.

"To give you that key. She didn't know I gave it to you."

"Of course she did. She set it up that way. She had you give me the key, so I could walk in and—"

"Jayson," Karen said, turning toward me, holding both her palms up at me, trying to calm me, because she had to see that I was beginning to get riled. "That's what happened, but she didn't want that to happen. That's what I'm here to tell you."

I looked at her, as though she were crazy.

"Hold it, hold it. I'm not understanding. What are you trying to say?"

"It was going too far. You were all crazy in love with Faith, and with each day that passed, the more you actually thought you two were going to get married."

"What are you talking about, *thought*? We *were* getting married."

"No, you weren't, Jayson. It wasn't going to happen, at least not if Faith got what she wanted."

I was really getting annoyed at that point. "Karen, make it fucking plain," I whispered loudly.

"What aren't you getting!" she whispered back. "Faith didn't love you. At least not enough to marry you."

And that was as plain as she could make it. Too plain, actually, and I sat there frozen on the edge of that stool like a stone statue, threatening to topple off. Even if what she said wasn't true, just hearing it made my heart disintegrate.

"That's bullshit, Karen. She had sex with that guy because she was trying—"

"—trying to get him to marry her. Jayson, I don't know what she told you, but that just wasn't some guy she met in a club that night, or pulled off the street. His name is Gary, and she knew him even before she knew you. She was in love with him, still is, but he's married, has kids. He's been back and forth with his wife though. His wife would put him out, and he would stay with Faith before she met you. And then he would go back to the wife again. He always said that he would leave her and marry Faith, but he never seemed to have enough incentive. And that's when you came along." Karen paused to sip from her cup again and wiped her mouth with a paper napkin.

"The day you met her at the movie theater, what a loser she thought you were. No game. But you were handsome, more so than Gary, and Faith's wheels started spinning the way they do, and she found a way to use you."

Found a way to use me, Jayson thought. This wasn't happening. Karen didn't know what the hell she was talking about. She was lying. She just had to be.

"You're trying to tell me that for almost a year Faith has been seeing somebody else, that she never loved me, let me buy her a ring, make all the preparations, and she never intended on getting married in the first place?"

"What preparations, Jayson? Getting a time slot at city hall?"

"I wanted to do more. To have a big wedding, but—"

"But Faith said she wanted something small, something intimate," Karen cut in. "Didn't want to make a big fuss over anything. She said that, Jayson, because she never had any intention of it actually happening. I think she loved you in a way, but not enough to spend the rest of her life with you."

"I don't believe you," I said, shaking my head. "No." I shut my eyes, thought about all the times we had together, tried to remember if her mind seemed elsewhere, if while making love, her body didn't seem totally invested in what we were doing, but that never seemed to be the case. "I would've known. I just would've."

"You don't give women enough credit. We can hide things better than you think. Men think we can't be anything but open with our emotions, but we could care less for a man, remain with him, and never have him doubt that we love his dirty drawers," Karen said, looking me intently in the eyes through her dark glasses.

"There's more, Jayson. September. Not long after you met her. The two weeks you couldn't have sex with her."

I had to think a moment about that. How did she even know that much about our sex life? "She had a yeast infection," I said.

"No, Jayson. She had an abortion. She was carrying Gary's child, but he convinced her that she shouldn't have a baby before they got married."

And again I found myself traveling back in my mind. Wouldn't I have known all this if it were the case? No. This just wasn't happening. None of this was true. I turned away from Karen, lowered my face into my hand. I was trying to keep all these bits of information from coming closer together, because I knew that if they did, they would probably fit perfectly together like a puzzle, forming a picture that fully supported what Karen was saying.

I turned back to her, feeling as though I could barely hold myself up on the stool.

"Why did she do this to me?"

"I told you, because she wanted to make Gary jealous, agree to leave his wife before she married you."

"And what if he didn't? Would she have married me, anyway?" I asked, and for some sick reason, I was almost wishing that was what would've happened.

"She said she would've, but I don't know, and I didn't want to find out. That's why I gave you the key, Jayson."

"And what happened. Did he agree to marry her?"

Karen looked in the other direction for no reason, then looked back at me through the wide dark glasses. "That night after you caught them, she said Gary realized how much she must've meant to you. She said he got jealous, and he finally agreed to leave his wife."

"So that's why, no matter what I say to her—that I'm willing to forgive her, that I'm willing to never see Asha again—" (and how worthless I felt at that moment for agreeing to sacrifice my friend like that)"—no matter what I say, she won't hear it, because she's gotten what she wanted from the start."

Karen agreed with me by nodding her head.

"Why are you telling me all this?" I said.

She took another sip from her coffee, which had to be near gone. "Because she did you wrong."

"But you were never too big on doing me right yourself," I said, looking at her suspiciously.

"There's something else," Karen said, changing the subject, digging into the purse she was holding on to so tightly. She pulled out a video-cassette and placed it on the counter between us.

I looked down at it oddly. "What is it?"

"It's them. That night. The night you walked in on them."

And what kind of sick shit was this? Why would they have taped it, and why would I have wanted it?

"They taped it? Why the hell would they do that?"

"I . . . I don't know," Karen said, looking away. "Maybe they . . . I don't know."

"Well, why would Faith give it to you?"

Karen didn't answer and her face was still turned away from me. I scooted closer to her, trying to look into her eyes.

"Faith did give this to you, didn't she, Karen?" I asked her, raising the tape, holding it in her face.

"Yes, she did," Karen said, snatching a look at me, and then looking away. Something wasn't right here. This just didn't make any sense for that to have happened. I looked down at the tape again, then decided to play my hunch.

"She didn't give you this tape, did she? And if what you say is on here actually is, the only way you could've gotten it, would've been for you to have been the one who taped it. That's right isn't it?"

Karen slowly turned back around, resting those big black lenses on me.

"Why did you do it?" I asked her, trying to find the answer in my own mind.

Karen didn't answer right away, as if judging whether I was really on to her or not. Finally she sighed and said, "If when you walked in, they weren't in the act, I didn't want her to be able to lie and say that she wasn't involved with him. So I taped it."

I shook my head, barely able to believe any of this. "How did you do it?" I asked her.

"Simple. I hid the camera, pointed it toward the couch and programmed it to start recording around the time I knew they'd be there. I didn't think they'd do it right there on the couch. I just thought I'd catch them saying something, kissing a little. But like I told you," Karen said, looking sympathetically at me, "I thought it was going too far. I thought you were really going to get hurt, that's why I did it."

"You never cared if I got hurt before. As a matter of fact, you always seemed intent on hurting me."

"Seemed, Jayson," Karen said, under her breath.

"What do you mean by that?"

"Nothing," Karen said, looking down into her empty cup of coffee.

"No. Tell me what you mean by that."

"I said it was nothing," she said again, spinning away from me on the stool. I grabbed her by the arm, but she pulled away hard, and when she escaped from my grasp, she almost fell off the stool. She caught herself before she did, but the dark glasses dropped from her face and hit the floor. I quickly bent over to retrieve them and held them out to her.

Karen's head was turned, as if she was trying to hide something, blindly reaching for her glasses.

"No. Let me see," I said, softly, placing my other hand on her shoulder, and turning her to face me. Her left eye was slightly closed by swelling, and the lid was discolored.

"Where'd you get that?"

Karen didn't answer the question, just reached for her glasses in my hand. I didn't release them.

"Faith was that mad at you, hunh?"

"I don't care. She was wrong," Karen said, pulling on her glasses again. I let her have them, but she didn't put them back on.

"She *was* wrong, but why did it matter to you?"

Karen stared me sadly in my face, shook her head, as if deciding if she was going to disclose what she was thinking, then stood as if she was going to walk away. I grabbed her, this time not as forcefully, but by the hand.

"Karen, you have to understand what I'm going through, all that's just happened to me. Now I'm trying to make sense of this but it seems like you're hiding something from me. Just tell me. Please."

"I was always mean to you, because I didn't want her to know how I felt about you. At first, I just thought it was a passing thing, but over time, Jayson, I . . ." And then Karen just stopped speaking, as if she all of a sudden ran out of words. I sat there, staring at her, my mouth open, waiting for her to continue.

"You what, Karen?"

She looked as if she had reconsidered what she was about to say, then slowly continued. "I fell for you, Jayson."

"What do you mean, *fell* for me?" I asked, after a moment, as if I didn't understand English.

"You know. I fell in love with you. I think I still love you. That's why I always tried to break the two of you up. Yes, I didn't want you to get hurt, but I also didn't want to see you with anyone but me. I didn't want you to marry Faith."

Me and Karen. I allowed myself to think this thought for only a fraction of a second. Any longer, I would've barfed all over the Starbucks floor. "That's why you gave me the key card?"

"Yeah," Karen said, very softly, nodding her head. She stared directly into my eyes afterward, and wouldn't look away.

"What?" I said.

"I want to know what you think. If, maybe we could—"

And I cut her off before she even had a chance to get the question out. "I still love Faith, Karen. Regardless of what she's done. I know she has a good reason, and I know she loved me once, and still does."

Karen's face fell.

"But if I wasn't still with her," I said quickly, trying to save her feelings.

She looked up at me.

"Well . . . you know," I said, implying that it could've been me and her, which would always be the farthest thing from the truth.

"I'm sorry," I said.

"No. Don't be. It was wrong of me to even say anything," she said, slipping her glasses back on, slinging her purse over her shoulder. She stood up and extended her hand, and we shook hands like civilized people.

"Take care, Jayson, and good luck." She turned and headed toward the door.

"Karen," I called to her. "What about the tape?" I reached for it, held it out to her.

"I don't want it," she said, turning around to face me.

"Well, I don't want it either," I said, looking down at it like it was a piece of filth.

"Hold on to it, Jayson. You never know, you might need it for something."

What the fuck was she trying to say? I wanted to ask her, but I was done dealing with talking to her. I was done with this entire situation.

"I won't need it for nothing," I told her, as I turned to walk toward the opposite door.

"Fine, leave it for the next person who sits down then," Karen said. She exited and left me standing there a few feet from the tape.

I stared at it for a moment. I looked around quickly to see if anyone was paying particular attention to my movements. Then when I saw that they weren't, I quickly walked over to the tape, grabbed it, tucked it under my arm, and left.

20

Karen was in love with me? I thought about this all the way home and I still couldn't believe it. Why didn't she just pull me aside one day, and instead of cursing me out, calling me names like some third grader who can only express her feelings by slugging you, just tell me what was up? She could've let me know how she felt and we could've worked all that out right then and there.

I could've said something like, "Woman, are you crazy? Have you been sniffing glue? Get that nonsense out of your head and bring your ass back to reality." It wouldn't have been quite that harsh, but she would've gotten the point, and all of this hotel setup, with a complimentary keepsake tape of the event would've been avoided.

I sat there now, in my apartment, on the sofa, that tape sitting right in front of me on the coffee table. I had been sitting there for the past two hours trying to ignore it, trying to stop myself from grabbing it and sliding it into my VCR. Why the hell did Karen give that thing to me, and why hadn't I thrown it away on the way back up here? I should've, I wanted to, but something sick inside of me obviously wanted to see it more than I wanted to toss it.

I extended a trembling hand, fearful of touching it, as if thinking that the mere feel of it could hurt me as much as what was recorded on it. I picked it up, pulled back the cover that protected the actual video tape, and thought of yanking the shiny ribbon right out of it, but I couldn't. Dammit, I couldn't.

I walked over to the television, turned it and the VCR on, and slid the tape in. I grabbed the remote, and on nervous legs walked back over to the sofa and sat down. I clicked the TV to channel three, and noticed that I was trembling, that my hand was shaking and sweating so much that the remote almost slipped from my grasp.

But what was I afraid of? I asked myself. There was nothing on this tape that I hadn't already seen. There was no more harm that this thing could cause me, for I had been there when it happened, absorbed the full brunt of its pain. I couldn't be hurt any more than I had already been. Telling myself that, I pressed Play.

The screen went black, there was a flash, a horizontal line ran up the length of the screen, and then the image appeared. It was Faith and that man. The picture was grainy, the light was bad, and it reminded me of those cheaply made porno flicks. He was undoing the buttons of her blouse. He started kissing Faith's neck, and she was sensually turning her head to the side, giving him more access. She was moaning, clawing at his back, as he rubbed his hands up and down her, settling them on her behind. I felt myself getting weak, as beads of cold sweat started to roll down the side of my face, accumulate under my arms.

Karen must've known exactly what she was doing when she positioned that camera, or Faith and this man had to have secretly known it was there, for they seemed to be playing to it. They were directly in front of the camera, allowing me to see everything that was happening, and the camera caught a direct shot of Faith's breasts as they fell out of her bra when that man removed it. I felt the need to avert my eyes, as if embarrassed by what was happening before me, as if I had no business watching this. He threw the bra to the floor, and started to grab at the button on Faith's jeans but was interrupted when Faith yanked his T-shirt up and over his head. He went back to her jeans, unzipping them, as Faith kissed him about his neck, his collarbone, started to suck on his nipple, and then started to undo his jeans.

After undoing her jeans, he slid them and her panties down her shapely ass and hips. She stepped out of them, totally nude, as beautiful as she had always been when I had undressed her. She was excited, and it was clear by how engorged, how erect her nipples were, and by the desire in her eyes as she feverishly worked on that man's zipper.

And at that moment, something told me to turn it off, because I knew what was going to happen, and I knew I wouldn't be able to bear it. It would've been the worst thing I could've possibly seen, the worst thing any man can see. I would rather have seen her getting her brains fucked out as I had, than see what I thought was about to happen. But I didn't turn it off, because I was hoping, praying, that she wouldn't do it, that she couldn't do it. I was hoping that at that time something familiar would strike her, something that reminded her of us, something that said that there were some things she only did with me.

But that didn't happen, of course, for when she did snatch his pants below his hips, and his erect penis jumped out at her, she quickly put her lips around it, taking him all the way into her mouth.

Everything stopped for me at that moment. I froze up, could barely breathe, having only enough strength to push the Stop button on the remote. I sat there, staring at the TV, that image of Faith on her knees, taking that man in her mouth, burned on the screen. I continued to stare at it angrily, foolishly imagining that even though I had stopped the tape, that somewhere inside the television, she was still pleasuring that man, tugging on him, sucking him, massaging him, till he was on the verge of erupting. As she had done so many times for me, as she had probably done so many times for him.

I thought about the times we were together, the times I would kiss her passionately, the times I would go down on her, and now I was seeing this. My stomach all of a sudden flipped, spun, and all my insides seemed to liquefy. I felt as though I would lose everything right there, but I covered my mouth with my hand and swallowed hard, which relieved the urge. I wiped my hand across my brow, and pulled away a palm covered with sweat. I took three deep breaths and told myself that none of this was happening this very moment, that it had already happened and it was over.

Telling myself this, and although I knew I shouldn't have, I grabbed the remote, pressed Play, and watched the rest of it.

21

Asha had been at work for three hours already, and surprisingly she hadn't bumped into Les yet. It wasn't because she was avoiding seeing her either. Asha was just so busy that she had been in her room most of the morning, and she hadn't had the opportunity to run into Les. She wasn't even fearful of the woman anymore after talking to Angie. Angie had told Asha exactly what to do, and when Asha was finished with her last client for the morning, she took long, quick, businesslike strides toward the break room. She knew Big Les would be there, probably gnawing on a six-foot sub and drinking a gallon of chocolate Nesquik.

When Asha pushed her way into the break room, Big Les was the only person in there. Immediately something drained from Asha. Some of her confidence seemed to have magically disappeared.

Les looked up at her, grinned in her face, then pulled a spoon of Fruit Loops up toward her mouth and quickly ate them. Asha looked at the bowl full of milk and cereal that sat before Les, then looked at the plastic shopping bag there at Les's feet, and saw a huge family-size box of the colorful Os, and a quart of milk. She would've laughed right there in Les's face if the whole scene hadn't been so pathetic, and she wasn't starting to lose her nerve.

"You all taken up with my box of Fruit Loops," Les said, catching a line of milk that spilled out the corner of her mouth with her spoon.

"If you want some, just ask. I think there's another bowl up there in the cabinet."

"Naw, Les," Asha said. "You go right ahead. I had Fruit Loops yesterday for lunch." Asha was about to turn around and walk out of there, because with each moment she looked at the big woman, sitting there like a grossly overweight four-year-old, she became more intimidated. And besides, since Les hadn't said anything inappropriate to her, maybe she had planned on dropping the entire affair. If that was the case, why should Asha even bring it up again?

Asha moved to the door, grabbed the knob, and was about to turn it when Les said, "Oh, yeah, girl, had another dream last night."

Asha didn't turn around; she stood there, her hand still on the doorknob, squeezing it so hard she felt she could've crumbled it into dust at any moment.

"I had you wide open, girl," Asha heard Les saying between her crunching and slurping of the milk and Fruit Loops.

"I was doing my thing, and it was gettin' so good to you that you were crying for it, you was beggin' for it." What she was saying was sickening Asha. It was angering her so much that if she could've ripped that knob from the door, and slung it at Les, hit her in the eye, she would've. Anything to make her shut up.

Asha spun around, holding a finger up before her. "You can stop that shit right there."

Les's eyebrows raised, as if she was questioning if Asha was actually speaking to her. She looked left, and right, as if she was really unsure.

"What did you just say?" Les said, coolly.

"You heard what I said. You can stop talking that shit, because I ain't gettin' with you, and I ain't ever gettin' with yo' big stank ass."

With those remarks, Les looked as though she had been slapped across the face. She forcefully pushed her chair back, which made a loud screeching noise as it slid across the tile floor. She slowly raised her huge body from her chair, as if to remind Asha just who she was talking to, and how foolish it was to say what she had just said.

"I think you got who you talking to a little mixed up in your head, sweetheart," Les said, pushing the chair aside, coming around the table toward Asha. "'Cause I ain't none of your little friends who got a little crush on you, and you tell them where to go, and they leave you the fuck alone. Let me tell you something, baby," Les said, now right up in Asha's face, "If I want you to get with me, then you gonna get me with me. Know what I'm sayin'?"

"Then you must not like working here," Asha said, standing her ground, even though she was pushed up against the door, Les towering over her. "Because this is sexual harassment, and if I go back to Margee's office, and just *tell* her that you've been harassing me, it'd be enough to start an investigation into getting your ass fired. But if I went back there with a black eye, or a bloody lip . . ." Asha said, feeling that Les had intentions of doing just those things to her, " . . . then they'd fire you on the spot, and probably bring criminal charges against your butch ass."

Asha saw that what she was saying to Les was having an effect on her, and although she looked like a chimpanzee trying to understand a complex physics equation, something sunk in, for she looked a little more timid than a moment ago.

"Now back your big ass off me," Asha said, feeling that she could've blown Les over with a strong breath, she had her so punked.

It took Les a moment, but she backed off Asha. "So you comin' like that, hunh? Trying to take my job, my money."

"I'm not coming like nothing. You trying to lose your job, trying to give away your money, all up in my face with what you were talking. You keep away from me, and you don't have nothing to worry about."

"Yeah, that's cool," Les said, backing away from Asha a couple more steps. "I'll keep away from you, but don't you ask me for shit, you hear me."

"I got you, Les. I won't be asking you for shit."

"You should've seen her elephant ass," Asha laughed as she told the story to Angie, while she massaged her later that afternoon. "She couldn't do nothing. Nothing! I could've spit in her face, and all she could've said was, 'Mmm, taste good,' I had her so punked."

"Oh, yeah. Big bad Asha," Angie said, looking up at her.

"That's right!" Asha said, waving her arms about, pointing her finger in her chest. "Don't mess with big bad Asha, unless you got a death wish, ya' dig!"

They both laughed, and then they quieted, allowing Asha to continue with Angie's massage.

"You know, I really got to thank you for telling me what to do," Asha said, rubbing Angie's neck.

"It wasn't a big deal. I'm sure, eventually, you would've come up with the same thing."

"Yeah, probably, but . . . sometimes it's just nice knowing that you got someone in your corner, someone you can turn to, even if they do nothing more than just support a decision that you've already decided to make. And speaking about decisions, yesterday when we were on the phone I was going . . ."

Angie quickly sat up from the table, threw her legs over the side and faced Asha.

"Asha don't."

"Don't what? You don't even know what I was about to ask you."

"I do. And I don't think it's wise."

"You don't think what's wise? Tell me what I'm talking about first, Angie, before you start telling me what you think is wise and what isn't."

Angie blew a sigh of frustration, lowered her head, then looked back up at Asha.

"You were about to bring our outside lives into this. Don't do that, Asha. It's just us right now. This is our special thing," she said, squeezing Asha's shoulders. "Why do you want to ruin that with the outside world?"

"What is the outside world? Other people, other places? Our lives before we met each other, decisions that we have to make regarding each other? This outside world that you're talking about must be everything outside this room, because I never see you outside of it."

"Well, you never said you wanted to."

"What? You think the only time I want to see you is when you come in so we can squirm around on the table for half an hour. You get off, smile, kiss me on the cheek, and go home. See ya' next week?"

"Asha, let's not go there."

"No!" Asha said, forcefully objecting. "Let's do go there. I want to see you outside of here. I want to do things, go to the movies, to dinner. Or are you ashamed of me?"

"No, Asha."

"You don't care for me? Don't have feelings for me?"

"Now you know that's bullshit. You know how much you mean to me."

"Then what is it?" Asha said. "How come we have to be always bunched up in this little room like we have something to hide?"

"So what. You want to walk down State Street tongue kissing, bra-less, our hands in each other's hip pockets and proclaim how free we are, how unconcerned we are with what other people think?" Angie said.

"No," Asha said, pausing, giving Angie a serious look. "I just want to have dinner with you."

"Asha, I said, don't do this," Angie said, now rubbing Asha's shoulders, trying to soothe her into understanding. "Everything is so good just like . . ."

Asha swatted both Angie's hands away. "So good for who, Angie? So good for you, because you get to have your little closet girlfriend tucked away in a little secret compartment, so you can get off on her anytime you want to without anyone knowing, like some pervert getting off on his daughter."

Angie was struck hard by Asha's insult. She jumped off the table, wrapped a towel around her, and quickly headed for the changing room.

"What are you doing?" Asha called to her.

Angie didn't answer.

"I said, what are you doing?" Asha said, now coming up behind her.

Angie quickly spun on her, stared her dead in the face with her angry eyes. "How dare you compare me to that? How dare you talk to me like you know what's going on in my life, like you have experience in this. I opened your eyes to something that you've been trying to fight all your life, make you come a couple of times, make you think you're falling in love, and now you think you own me? Now you think you can make demands of me?" Angie said, shaking her head, waving a finger at Asha. "You don't even know me." Angie turned to leave.

"Wait," Asha said. "You're wrong."

Angie turned back to face Asha.

"I do know you. And I don't think I'm falling in love with you. I know I am."

Angie didn't say a word, couldn't say a word. She looked into Asha's eyes, and Asha knew that she was looking there to see if she was telling the truth. She wouldn't have to look that deep to know that she was, Asha thought.

Angie kept her eyes on her for a moment longer, then said, "Good-bye, Asha," and turned and left.

22

"Good-bye, Asha." Just what the hell did that mean? Asha pondered as she gave the cabbie his money and jumped out of the taxi. All during the ride home, she wanted to call Angie, wanted to ask her if it was over. But was it? Angie claimed that Asha didn't know her, but Asha knew that wasn't true, because if it was, she couldn't have felt the way she was starting to feel about her. It was love, she knew that it was, even though she had to stop and ask herself if it was merely something physical. Was it because of the incredible way she made Asha feel, or was it because she had opened the door to all this for Asha? Was it like a young boy falling in love with the first girl who made him aware that pleasure could be derived from that thing that grew hard in between his legs? She didn't think so. Although Asha had never been with a woman before, she knew what puppy love was, and this definitely wasn't it.

She wouldn't call her, Asha told herself. It seemed as though Angie wanted her distance because she had things to sort out. Maybe she was feeling the same feelings that Asha was starting to feel and just didn't want to admit it. Or, maybe she was truly using Asha as a toy. Maybe Angie had half a dozen women around the city that she visited every couple of days out of the week. How Asha didn't want this to be the case. But if it was, and good-bye meant forever, then maybe that was for the best. After all, she herself had issues of her own that she really

needed to resolve before she started getting involved in a serious relationship, mainly Gill.

She slid her key into her door, pushed it open, telling herself she
would call Gill as soon as she got settled in. He would be wanting to
see her tonight, and she would have to tell him that maybe it was a
bad idea, push it off until tomorrow, if not the day after.

She stepped inside, closed the door behind her, and almost jumped
out of her skin when she saw Jayson standing in the middle of her living room, aimlessly looking toward the ceiling, as if waiting for rain,
something in his hand.

"It's not a problem, Jayson, because I knew that you could never
stop being friends with me, but I thought you said you'd never just
come in here."

Jayson didn't say anything, just looked strangely down at the television set, looked as though he was angry with it.

"Jayson," Asha said, setting down her purse, and walking over to
him. "I said, it was cool. It's your building. You can come down here
anytime you want to, just don't freak if you see my panties in the sink."
Asha laughed, hoping that would trigger something in Jayson, but
nothing happened. He continued looking at the TV that wasn't
turned on, and then down at his hand, where he held the remote to
the television.

"What is it?"

"There's a tape of it in the VCR," Jayson said, his voice low, dis-
turbed.

"Of what?" Asha said, pulling the remote easily from Jayson's hand.

"Just watch it," Jayson said, struggling to raise himself from the sofa,
then without looking back, he disappeared into her bedroom.

What was on the tape, Asha asked herself, her thumb hovering
over the Play button. She knew it had to be something horrible, so
why should she watch it? Because Jayson asked her to, and he was still
her best friend, and the man was hurting, and she would've done anything for him, short of giving her own life, and who knows, if it were a
spur of the moment thing, she would probably have done that too.

Asha pressed Play and the image of Faith on her knees appeared on
the screen. She was sucking off some man. The man who ruined
Jayson's life, and he was enjoying himself far more than seemed possi-

ble, and he made it known by the horrible faces he was making and the way he was moaning, loud enough to make the speakers on the TV vibrate. Asha quickly thumbed down the volume, thankful that Jayson had closed the door.

The man lifted Faith off the floor, dumping her onto the sofa, her legs falling open. He bent over her, taking her breasts in his hands, sucking them, then working his way down. Although Faith's face was obscured, it was apparent that she was losing her mind by the way she was writhing about on that sofa, the noises she was making, the way she grabbed that man's head, pulling him closer, wrapping her legs around him. Then the man flipped Faith over on her stomach, and entered her from behind.

Asha frowned, a sickened look on her face, and she told herself that Jayson couldn't have seen this, he just couldn't have, and not thrown himself off the top of this building.

Asha pressed the Eject button, yanked the tape out of the machine, walked swiftly into the kitchen, and dropped it into the trash. She then went to her bedroom door. She put her ear to it and knocked softly.

"Jayson."

"Don't come in here," she heard him say through the door.

"Jayson, I just want to talk to you," Asha said, slowly turning the knob, gently pushing the door open.

"I said, don't come in here."

Asha came in anyway.

Jayson was sitting on the edge of the bed, and when she walked in, he scooted around to the other side of it, turning away from her.

Asha sat down near him, but again, Jayson turned away from her. She stood up, moved around in front of him, then lowered herself to her knees, pushed herself in between his knees. He was covering his face with his hands, but she gently pried them away, held them tight, to reveal his tear-streaked face.

"Jayson, it's not your fault," Asha said to him in a soft voice.

He looked away from her, still trying to hide his face, even though he could not use his hands.

"Jayson, did you hear me? You did not cause that. Nothing you did sent that woman to that man," Asha said, more forcefully, trying to make him understand.

Jayson shook his head, his lips starting to quiver as he was about to speak.

"All I did was love her. All I did was love her, and then she . . . and then she . . ." And more tears spilled from his eyes, leaving him unable to finish.

"Jayson, she was a fool," Asha said. "Don't cry for her. She isn't worth your tears."

But tears continued to come from his eyes, as if he hadn't heard a word she said.

"She didn't deserve you, Jayson. You have to know that," Asha said, releasing his hands and grabbing his face in both of hers, turning him to look at her, even though he was still trying to look away. "You're a good man, and she was just too stupid to realize that. Don't cry, Jayson. Please don't cry," Asha pleaded, as she tried to wipe away the tears that did come. But they kept coming, and so much heartache seemed to seep out of him that Asha could feel it actually starting to cause her pain. All she wanted to do was make it stop for him, say the right words, comfort him the right way, deliver him past this anguishing moment.

"Jayson, Jayson," Asha said, tears now falling from her eyes, as she still tried to dry his face with her now wet hands. "Jayson, please stop." But he wouldn't, and she knew he wouldn't soon. It was a pain so deep that he had no control over it, a pain that she shared with him now, and there seemed no way to stop it, so all she could hope to do was smother it by throwing her face into his, pressing her lips against his. It was all she knew left to do. They had experienced pain together in the past, and as they kissed passionately, their cheeks brushing against each other's, their tears joining, it seemed oddly familiar, safe, and secure, like a home left years ago and then returned to.

The sobbing stopped, but the crying still continued, and the pain was transformed into something that no longer hurt them, but something they fed off, something that strengthened the bond between them. And as Asha felt her clothes being peeled off her, and as she disrobed Jayson, she knew this was something that he needed. In some strange way, it was something they both needed.

23

"So, I'll see you tomorrow, right?"

"Of course, baby," Gary said, kissing Faith on the lips, patting her on the behind, then walking out her front door.

Faith stood there on her porch and watched till his car pulled out of sight. It was only eight o'clock, but he was leaving after being there for only two hours.

"I have business to take care of," was his excuse, but Faith wasn't some fool, or at least she wasn't when it came to him. She had been dealing with Gary long enough to know the code words for "I need to be getting home to my wife and children." That's what it was, and even though she didn't want to let him leave, felt like a fool allowing him to, considering that they were supposed to be in a relationship, supposed to someday be getting married, she let him walk out that door.

It was partly because she knew that this was the last of it. Gary had already started to move his stuff over to Faith's house, and that meant commitment. The overnight bag that he had brought over today and was now sitting in Faith's hallway closet proved it. He would be finally filing for divorce tomorrow. His wife wouldn't like it, and she would try to talk him out of it, as she had always done in the past, but this time, he wouldn't allow that to happen. Gary said so himself. This time, he would pack up the rest of his things and head on over to Faith's house and that was where he would stay. As soon as the divorce cleared, the way would be freed for the two of them to get married.

"You almost got away from me, but I ain't gonna let that happen again," he said, referring to how serious he thought things had gotten between her and Jayson. He'd seen the look on Jayson's face when he walked in the room, and knew the man loved her. There was no faking the hurt that was on his face. As Faith was still getting taken from behind, she herself could see the moment Jayson's heart broke into a million pieces.

But why was she even thinking about that? That chapter of her life was over. Yes, she'd spent a year of her life with him, playing relationship, planning to play house with him, and although he was a good man, she was after other things.

Faith stepped back into her house, closing the front door behind her, wondering if there had been no Gary, could things have worked between her and Jayson? She didn't want to admit it to herself, but she thought it was possible. There were times when she would almost forget that it was a game she was playing with him. She would almost lose herself in the excitement of planning for their marriage. There were times when she would go with him on his little imaginary journeys into the future, and she would see the two of them ten, fifteen years from that moment, see their two or three children, and she would smile with Jayson, a warm feeling in her heart, until she awakened and realized it would never happen.

And why wouldn't it? Because she was in love with Gary of course. She was in love with married Gary. Gary with kids, kids representing obligations that he would have for the rest of his life, and that meant a relationship that he would have with his wife for the rest of his life as well.

"You are the stupidest woman I've ever known for playing Jayson like that for tired-ass Gary," Karen had told her so many times. "Jayson is fine as hell, he's paid, no kids, no wife, and he loves your holy ass panties, and you want to sacrifice him for some brother who has to spend all his money on his family, and will always have to spend at least half of it on them. That is, if he ever leaves them."

Faith felt a pain in her heart as she thought about Karen. Even after what that woman did to her, she missed her, because Karen was her girl. They'd shared too many good times together for it to have to end like this. Faith still couldn't believe what Karen had done to her, but in her heart she knew it was because she was jealous. She was just jealous because Faith had two men at her disposal, and she had nothing. Sure there were men who stepped to her on occasion, but nothing that her high-standard-having ass would ever lower herself to.

Faith plopped down on her sofa, grabbed the remote, and thumbed through all one hundred plus channels in twenty-five seconds, realizing that there was nothing on TV worth watching. She thought for a moment about what she could do, but there seemed to be nothing at all. Normally on a day like this, after she had just finished seeing Gary, she would call up Jayson and they would go to dinner, or go for a walk downtown, or along the lake, and he would shower her with affection, tell her how much he loved her, and how happy they'd be together once they finally got married.

Faith quickly shook those images out of her head, but it took a little longer to shake the smile that was on her face. She wasn't missing him, Faith told herself. She wasn't, because she had exactly what she wanted now. And she knew she couldn't be missing him, because if she did, that meant that she had feelings for him, and she knew she had done a hell of a job at keeping her heart guarded from him. If that wasn't the case, she would've felt more than just the minimal amount of sympathy for Jayson when he walked in and found her with Gary. If she really had feelings for him, she wouldn't have been able to turn a deaf ear to Jayson, to be so cold to him when he tried to come back to her, to bargain his way back in her life.

Faith thought back for a moment, remembering some of the things she had said to him. Did he deserve to be treated like that? No. Not really. All he did was love her. But she had to get her point across, Faith reasoned. She loved Gary, and she would be with him. She loved him so much that when she got pregnant, she yearned to have his baby, wanted to have it so much. And when he told her that it wouldn't be a good time, that it would be better once they were together, she loved him so much that she aborted that child.

Afterward, she cried for it, as though she had been the one who killed it, as though she had been the one to stick that vacuum up inside her and suck it out of her. But Gary was there for her, allowed her to cry on his shoulder, and he cried with her, until he had to get up and leave, go home to his family. But while he was there, he said all the right words, words that comforted her, words that made her look toward the future.

"That baby's not gone, sweetheart," he said, holding Faith, kissing her on the forehead. "It'll be back next time. That baby will be back when we're together," he said, and that calmed her. It was the promise that Faith held on to. While she was playing the game with Jayson, while she was trying to continue to convince Gary to leave his wife, that thought was with her. She was doing everything she did because she needed to bring that baby back, the baby whom she had killed, she needed to bring it back, and she couldn't do that without Gary.

That's why she was so hard on Jayson. He had to know that there was no way that he could ever get back into her life. No way. But now when Faith thought about it, she realized that she had been far too harsh on him. And there was something else she realized. She had never once apologized for being caught with Gary, for subjecting him to such a thing.

Faith thought it over for a brief moment, then reached for the cordless phone there on the table before her. She punched Jayson's number in it, and listened while it rung.

"I can't take your call. Leave a message, please," was what Faith heard.

She thought about leaving a message, but then hung up. Considering all that she had done to him, she knew he wouldn't have called her back. She would have to call him while he was at home, or better yet, apologize to him in person.

24

When I opened my eyes and looked at the clock, it was 8:45 P.M. I turned my head to find Asha's cheek resting against my shoulder. I craned my neck to get a look at her to see if she was awake. She was sound asleep, on her side, one arm draped across my middle, a leg thrown over my legs.

I kissed her head and caressed the smooth skin of her bare shoulder with my fingertips. I didn't know exactly how all this happened. One moment I felt I was on the verge of dying from a broken heart, and the next minute, Asha's warm lips were pressed against mine, her tongue finding its way into my mouth. Amazingly, that action seemed to stop the pain I was feeling, to fill the hole that allowed everything to seep out of my heart. I didn't know if what we were doing was right or not, but I didn't have the time to answer. Nor did I really want to know the answer. It was what I needed at that moment, and I told myself I would search for the answer later.

Now I was lying there awake, next to this beautiful woman, this woman that I once loved as a woman, then as a friend, looking down at her, feeling her soft, warm breath grazing the hair on my chest. Did I ever really stop loving her as a woman? Even though I regarded Asha as only a friend, did Faith see something deeper in that relationship? Did she know something that I didn't?

I had to admit that I'd never stopped being attracted to Asha. She was, and still continued to be, the most beautiful woman I'd ever been with, and that included Faith, even though I loved Faith harder than I had ever loved another woman.

But Faith was history now.

"She didn't deserve you," Asha said. "She's not worth your tears," and although I was crying so hard I could barely hear what she had said, somehow the words did get through, and now I was starting to believe them. It was definitely time to move on.

But move on to what? Again I was looking down at Asha, lowering my lips to her soft, long hair, smelling its sweet scent, kissing her there again. Was it a mistake to ever have stopped things with her? And now I had to think back to exactly why we had broken it off to begin with. She was preoccupied with something; I felt that there was something stopping her from allowing me to get as close to her as I would've liked. At first I just thought that she needed time to get to know me better, that eventually her occasional aloofness would pass, but it didn't. So we settled for being friends.

But now that I looked at her and thought about what had happened just hours ago, I wondered, where did we stand?

We'd just made love, and yes, it could've been something that she did for me because of the pain I was in, a way to distract me from thinking about Faith. But it seemed like more than that. As she rode atop of me, there was nothing quick about her actions, as if she were trying to get it all over with. There was nothing forced, nothing mechanical in her movements. I may have been wrong, but I really felt she was doing what she was doing, not just because she wanted my mind on something else, but because she wanted me to feel good. I remembered her looking down at me through partly opened eyes, as she gyrated her hips about on top of me, asking "Does it feel good to you? Is this good?"

All I could do was nod my head. I could not speak, because it felt so good. It felt as good as it had when we were together, almost better. When we were both satisfied, her body collapsed upon my chest, and we held each other. We held each other, and I felt her body start to relax even more, felt the characteristic twitching in her arms, and legs before she fell all the way off to sleep. She woke herself just to give me a kiss on the lips, and say, "Everything will be just fine, Jayson. Don't you worry," and then she fell right off.

Those didn't seem like the actions of a woman who was giving charity sex.

I was about to move her around a little bit, so I could wrap both arms around her, hold her in a tighter embrace, when I heard something. I raised myself up a little, listened again. It was someone buzzing the front door. I hoped that it didn't wake Asha, but when I looked down at her to see if it had, she was already stirring and opening her eyes.

Is that someone at the door?" she said, in a groggy voice, slowly raising her head.

"Yeah, but don't worry about it. Go back to sleep. They'll go away."

"No, no. I should get that," she said, and she was pulling herself from the bed, reaching into her closet and grabbing a thin robe. She threw it around herself, and tied the belt around her waist as she left the room.

I watched her as she went, asking myself if I could envision myself with her again. It didn't take me a second to answer: Yes.

"Who is it?" I heard Asha ask into the intercom. There was a reply, but I didn't hear it. I heard her buzzing whoever it was in. I continued to relax, knowing that she would soon get rid of the person and come back to bed.

I heard her unlock the bolts on the door, and I imagined her doing it, seeing her slim fingers twisting the locks. I envisioned her entire body, the robe cinched tight around her slim waist, conforming to her round behind.

"Gill, what are you doing here?" I heard her say and immediately I was brought out of the little fairy tale world I was living in.

"I thought I was supposed to be seeing you tonight, Suga'puss. Give me a kiss," and I actually tried to listen for the sound of his lips smacking against hers, feeling more jealous than I had ever felt about her before. But what gave me the right to do that, to feel this way? Yeah, for some reason I had forgot all about Gill, but that didn't mean just because I forgot him, Asha did too. She was his woman, she was wearing his damn ring on her finger. That meant something. But she had just slept with me, and unless I'm mistaken, that meant something too. But nothing could happen between us with Gill still hanging around.

"Damn baby, you looking good tonight. Give me a squeeze."

"This is not a good time, Gill," I heard Asha say, and I imagined her pushing away from him.

"Aw, Suga'. Any time is a good time for me. Now come on over here and let me see what you have on under that robe," he said playfully, chuckling.

"Stop it, Gill," Asha said, and the threatened tone in her voice pulled me quickly out of bed. I raced over to the door, naked, grabbed the knob, and put my ear to the door. I should walk out there, I kept telling myself. I should walk out there, and yes, it would surely ruin things with Gill and Asha, but if we were about to restart something, wouldn't that be okay?

I looked around, looked down at my clothes on the floor, but felt it would take too much time to put them all on. I grabbed the blanket from the bed and wrapped it around me, quickly getting back to the door and listening again.

"Gill, I don't have to give you a reason why. I just said it was a bad time, and you've got to leave," I heard her telling him.

"Asha, why you doing this? Why you acting like this?"

"I can't explain it, at least not now."

"You can't explain it to your fiancé, to the man you're about to marry, to the man you love, or are supposed to love," Gill said.

"And what is that supposed to mean, Gill?"

"Just what I said. We supposed to be getting married, and you keeping secrets, kicking me out of your house for reasons you can't tell me. This don't seem like the actions of a woman that loves her man."

"That's what you think?" Asha asked, sounding a little hurt by what Gill had assumed of her.

"Yeah. That's exactly what I think."

I didn't hear anything for a second, and I was starting to get worried, ready to open the door and walk out there, until I heard her say, "Think what you want, Gill, but right now, you have to go." I heard her open the door again.

"Asha, I'll be at home when you're ready to explain this to me."

"I know you will, Gill. Good-bye," and then I heard the door close.

That was it. That had to be it, I thought, as I went back to the bed, threw the cover back on it, and slid back under it, so as not to seem that I had ever gotten up. She did want us to get back together, and she proved that by putting me before Gill. Her man had come to the door, wanting to see her, but she would rather spend time with me. There was no question about it, and when she walked back into the room, pulled off her engagement ring, set it on the nightstand, then bent down right into my arms, I knew that I had been right.

"Is everything all right between you two?" I asked her.

"I don't want to talk about that right now, okay?" she said, kissing me on the lips.

"Okay," I said, kissing her back, and lowering her down to the bed to make love to her once again.

25

Angie had been through all this before, gotten the same mess from another woman who couldn't control her feelings and emotions, got demanding, wanting Angie to commit to her, and Angie had had to cut her ass loose, forget about her. It was easy, and it didn't even take a day for her to forget everything about the girl. She could do that, wipe these women out of her mind like they were simple notions, ideas that she entertained just before falling asleep at night. She was good at that.

But if she was so good at it, why was Asha still on her mind? Sure she had only told Asha good-bye a matter of hours ago, but in the past, by this time, Angie was more consumed by what she would have for dinner, than her feelings for the woman she'd just dumped. This was different. From the moment she'd left the spa, she couldn't get her mind off what had just happened, and just before stepping out that door, she paused for a moment and thought about turning around and apologizing to Asha, seeing if they could come to some accord. It was only the slightest second, but in the past that would've never happened.

On the drive home from picking up Kyle at day care, she was non-responsive to her own son because her damn mind was so clogged up with what Asha could've been thinking at that moment. Was she crying? Was she hurting? Or did she take it in stride? She was a beautiful woman, and she was sure that there had to be a number of other women who were just as attracted to her as Angie was. These could've been the same women that Asha massaged routinely. One of those women, or maybe a new one, like Angie had been, could feel something for Asha. A woman could come in, lie on Asha's table for the first time, and when Asha placed her magical hands on her body, making all the stressful tension melt away, exciting a new, lustful tension, making her body warm and wet in that familiar place, that woman could fall for Asha, just as Angie had.

When Angie thought about this, she wanted to yank the wheel of her car hard to the right, do a U-turn, and race back to that spa to tell Asha that there was nobody else that she could be with but her.

But she couldn't do that. And why was that? she asked herself, as she walked across her driveway. She didn't have to search hard for the answer. It was holding on to her hand at that moment, walking floating a half-wrapped Snickers bar through the air like it was Superman.

When she got into the house, she released Kyle and let him run free and do what he normally did after they got home: go crazy. Angie went to her purse, pulled out her cell phone, hoping to see that Asha had called, but when she didn't see her number on the phone, she told herself it didn't matter.

Deric had called while they were on their way home, as he did every day. Just before she heard the phone ring, she had been wishing that once, only once, he would just miss one day of calling. He was the last person she felt like speaking to.

"Hey, baby, you pick up Kyle yet?"

And he knew the answer to that, had always known the fucking answer to that, but he asked the ridiculous question anyway, which made no sense to her. It was like him calling and asking her, "Hey, baby, are you still black?" Or, "Hey, baby, you still female, still have two legs, two eyes, and a freakin' nose in the middle of your face?" Yes, yes, yes! "Yeah . . . he's in the backseat. Wanna talk to him?"

And before she even heard Deric's reply, she handed the phone back.

"Cowboy, phone for you."

"Daddy!" And the ritual continued.

The boy seemed so in love with that man. That was another reason

Angie couldn't just drop everything and hook up with the first woman she could possibly see a future with. She would in essence be taking her son's father from him. And considering that when Kyle was conceived, she'd thought she would be bringing him into the world fatherless, it would seem like a hell of a cruel thing to do, to snatch the man away who had happily taken on the responsibility of being a father to him.

But would it really matter to her son in the long run?

"Cowboy," Angie called loud enough for her son to hear her from upstairs, as she dug three Double Stuff Oreo cookies out of the Cookie Monster cookie jar. "Come down here a minute, would you please?"

His footsteps pounded quickly above Angie's head, and then she heard them coming down the stairs. A moment later he was standing in front of her, a beach towel hanging from his neck like a cape, and a headless GI Joe in his hand.

"Yeah, Mommy."

"C'mere, let's sit for a minute," she said, placing a hand atop his head, and leading him over to the sofa. He crawled up on it, and she sat down beside him.

"Want a cookie?"

"Yeah!" He said eagerly, plucking one out of her hand, pulling it apart and licking the cream filling.

"Is that good?" Angie asked him.

Kyle nodded his head and started eating the crunchy cookie.

How was she supposed to go about this? Angie thought to herself. But there was no tactful way, and even though she knew the answer, knew the reaction her son would have before she asked the question, she asked it anyway.

"Do you like Daddy?" The question sounded even more ridiculous aloud than it did in her head.

Kyle looked at her like, "Duh!"—like she was crazy for a moment— and he had every right.

"I like him. I like him a lot."

"A whole lot?"

"A whole, whole lot, Mommy. He's Daddy," Kyle said, as if enlightening her to information she hadn't already known.

"And how would you feel if Daddy had to go away? If he couldn't be here with us?"

Immediately, Kyle's face started to wrinkle, his chin started to col-
lapse, and before he could let out his first whine, Angie said, "No, no,
no, don't do that. Daddy's not going anywhere."

"Then why did you say that?" Kyle asked.

I don't know. Just wanted to know if you'd miss him if I dumped
him and replaced him with a woman, traded in Daddy for another
Mommy, she was thinking. But as she had known, and now as Kyle
had just confirmed, she couldn't do that.

"I don't know, I was just wondering," Angie finally said. "Here,
want another cookie?" she said, handing her son another, and eating
the last herself.

That was hours earlier, and now she was sitting at the dinner table.
It was a small round table, really meant for two, but since Kyle was just
a child, he could fit in, and it made things very cozy. At least that's
how Deric saw it. He'd picked up the table from a resale shop, and
stuck it under the skylight windows in the kitchen. "Let's eat on the
Table," he would say with a smile sometimes if he'd made a special
dish, or if he had something exciting he wanted to talk about, or if he
was just feeling like he wanted to bump elbows when he ate. That's all
that was happening at that moment, which wasn't a good thing, considering how every little thing was aggravating Angie at that moment,
and especially considering since what to do with Deric was at the root
of her aggravation.

"You want some more gravy, sweetheart?" Deric asked, picked up
the pourer, dousing her pork chop with more gravy before she had a
chance to answer.

"No, I didn't. But since you wanted me to have some more, I guess
I'll take it," Angie said, not sparing his feelings.

He looked at her, hurt, the cup of gravy still in his hand, still dripping over her pork chop.

"I'm sorry. I was just trying to . . ."

"Well, I don't need you to try to do anything for me, all right?"

"I guess that includes making this dinner, hunh?" Deric said.

"I didn't ask you to make dinner. You just came in and made it like
you always do."

"Yeah, and I thought that would've counted for something," Deric said, pulling his napkin from his lap, balling it up, and throwing it down onto his half-finished plate of food. "But I guess me being thoughtful and helpful around here doesn't mean anything to you." He stood, picked up the plate, and took it over to the kitchen sink.

"What's wrong, Mommy?" Kyle said, holding a half-eaten pork chop in his hand, a worried expression on his face.

"Yes, I would like to know that too. What's wrong with you, Angie? You've been acting funky like this since I walked in this evening."

Angie wanted to say it was nothing, wanted to say it was work, or her period, or she just didn't know, but she knew exactly what it was. It was that damn girl that she'd been thinking about all day. If Deric hadn't been around, would she be with Asha? She wasn't one hundred percent sure, but she did know that if he wasn't in her life, she would at least have the opportunity to look into it.

"Did you hear what I asked you?" Deric said, pulling Angie out of her thoughts.

She looked up at him, realizing that he was right. He was nothing but caring and helpful, and because she was having personal issues, he had to be hit with her being a bitch today.

"I'm sorry, baby," Angie said, pushing herself away from the table, walking over to him, taking the plate out of his hand, setting it down, and then hugging him and giving him a kiss. "It was just a really rough day at work, and I wasn't able to shake it before I came home. Do you forgive me?"

"Well, what happened? We can talk about it."

"No. I'm done thinking about it. I'm done ruining our evening," she said, turning and directing what she was saying to her son as well. Kyle was smiling now. The worry was gone from his face, and that made Angie know that she couldn't possibly do what she had entertained, even if she really wanted to. Her son's happiness was directly linked to whether this man was around, and she couldn't see putting her desires in front of her son's well-being. She just couldn't. She would have to get rid of Asha, once and for all.

26

The next morning, I woke up in Asha's bed. She had already gone to work. I had heard her moving around as quietly as possible, getting ready, trying not to wake me. It was just like it was so many years ago when I would stay the night at her place, and she would kiss me before going to work.

She did the same thing this morning, and as I lay there in her bed, tangled up in her sheets, smelling her scent, I felt happy that we were back together. No, it wasn't exactly official, we hadn't shaken on it or anything, but I'd known her long enough to know that we were back on.

Our second session of lovemaking was as phenomenal as the first, with only one shortcoming. Although she seemed as though she was loving every moment of it, she also seemed somewhat distracted, like something was seriously on her mind. I assumed it was Gill and the argument they had just had. And considering they were supposed to be getting married soon, considering they had almost been together a year, of course, she should've felt a little bad for dumping him just like that for me.

But things were better this way, for everyone, I thought, as I climbed out of bed. Gill was a nice guy, but from my point of view, Asha never seemed to be as into him as she should've been. Then again, she wasn't that into me back then either. But after last night, things between us seemed different.

Everything seemed to have worked out for the best, because if I hadn't caught Faith with that man, then I wouldn't have gotten back with Asha again, and . . . I had to stop thinking about Faith, because whenever I did that image of her with that man would pop into my head, and I would have a sharp second of torture.

Now that I was back with Asha, I would forget her soon enough. I was sure of it.

I walked into Asha's kitchen, opened the fridge, pulled out a gallon of O.J. and a peach yogurt. I poured myself a healthy glass of juice, peeled off the foil top of the yogurt, and was about to drop it in the trash when I saw the tape sitting there.

I held that little foil top over the trash, not letting it go, just looking down at that tape. I knew what had probably happened. Asha was so outraged, so upset over the tape, that after she viewed it, she yanked it from the VCR and tossed it in the trash, telling herself that it was best that I never saw the thing again. She was right, I knew that. But if I really did know that, why was I still standing over that trash can, that messy yogurt foil top still in my hand, still staring down at that tape like it had some kind of power over me.

Walk away, Jayson, I told myself, and that's what I did, without throwing away the trash in my hand. But when I noticed that I was still holding it and went back to discard it, I quickly plucked the tape out of the trash before doing so.

Would I look at it again? I seriously doubted that. I had, against my will, copied everything on that tape onto my brain anyway. So I didn't know why I had to keep it. I just did.

When I walked into my place, I sat the tape down on top of the TV. I took two steps toward my bedroom, but then turned around, grabbed the cassette, opened the entertainment center glass doors, and put the tape down there with all the other videotapes. I was about to close the doors, when I reached back in, took out the tape, and against my better judgment, pushed it into the VCR. I turned on the television and the VCR, pressed Play, and stood in front of the TV, my arms crossed over my chest, preparing myself once again for the imminent pain.

The hotel room appeared on the screen again, but what I was looking at was myself. Asha must've left off at the moment I walked in that room, and just looking at that picture of myself transported me back there, to that moment, and how shocked, horrified, and hurt I was.

"It's not what . . . ," the man said, finally seeing me, and backing away from Faith. The camera caught just his face. He looked to be in as much shock as I was, his eyes white and round with fear. It was a different shock, but shock all the same, and I had to hold on to that image.

I quickly picked up the remote and paused the tape, staring at his face. This was the first time I'd really paid attention to him. Like any other man would've done, I should've beat his naked ass down, right there in that room, left him bleeding and barely breathing on that hotel room carpet. If I had, I probably would've been feeling better by now, or at least not as affected by this tape. But I had done nothing, and he'd got away clean with fucking the girl I loved, and ruining the rest of my life. If I heard Karen correctly, which I'm sure I had, he knew that I was supposed to be marrying Faith, and for that reason alone, he shouldn't have had anything to do with her.

Filled with hate, I looked at his frozen face again there on the television screen. And I knew, considering what he had done to me, what he had taken from me, this couldn't be the last time I saw his face.

I picked up my phone, dialed information to get the number where Karen worked, and then I called her.

"What was his name?" I asked Karen the moment I heard her voice.

"Well, hello, Jayson. I thought I'd never hear from you again," Karen said.

"I never said that."

"That's what it seemed like."

"I'm sorry if it seemed that way. But considering what happened, and all you laid in my lap, it wouldn't be wrong if I never did speak to you again," I told her.

"I told you I only did it because—"

"I know, Karen. And I know, someday, in some strange way, I may appreciate it. But for right now, can you tell me the name of the guy Faith was with?"

"Why?" Karen asked, suspicion in her voice.

"Just tell me!"

"Gary. His name is Gary Robinson."

"Gary Robinson." I said his name softly to myself.

"Yeah."

"And where does he live?"

"Why do you want to know that?" she asked, sounding even more suspicious. "You aren't going to go over there and put his son's rabbit in a pot of boiling water, are you?"

"What are you talking about?"

"*Fatal Attraction* shit. You saw the movie."

"Just give me the address, Karen, and I promise I won't hurt the man, or his son's damn rabbit."

"What makes you think I'd have his address, anyway?"

I wondered if she thought I was stupid. "For as long as you say Faith has been seeing this man, you being her best friend, she's never told you where he lives, and you never asked?"

Karen seemed as though she was seriously thinking it over.

"I told you, I won't do anything foolish. Just give it to me."

Finally, she told me it was the big brown brick house, with red awnings, halfway down South Oakley Street.

"So just why do you want it?" Karen asked. "What are you planning on doing with it?"

"I don't know. Maybe nothing, but I just needed to have it. Thank you," I said, getting off the phone before she tried to get into conversation about anything involving the two of us.

I waited till 4 P.M. when I got into my car and headed toward the South Side of Chicago. I think I remember Karen telling me he was a banker or something like that, and I figured he wouldn't have gotten off work any time before then.

I exited from the expressway and headed west toward Beverly. It was a quaint residential area, once considered upper class, and inhabited by only whites in the seventies and early eighties. Now it was at least half black, and moving more in that direction every day.

The houses were nice, brick buildings, beautifully designed architecture. The lawns were manicured, the properties well maintained. I took a left off Ninety-ninth Street onto Oakley. I was looking for this

big brown house, and thought, could she have been any less descrip-
tive? Of course there was more than one of them, but I saw the red
awnings and figured that to be the one. It was 7326 South Oakley. I
slowed down some, eyeing it, scribbled the address down on a scrap of
paper, and stuck it in my pocket, just in case, for some reason, I needed
to remember it another time. The house was as neat and clean as the
rest of the houses on the street, a black wrought-iron fence around the
property, a red mailbox just outside the fence that read The Robinsons
in white block letters.

I came to a stop, half expecting someone to walk out the front door,
maybe him, maybe the wife I'd heard he had. But when no one came
out, I placed my car in park and just sat there continuing to stare at his
house. I looked at the windows trying to see inside, even though it was
impossible from this distance. I wanted to see if there was anything in
that house that would've helped me understand what led Faith to this
man, what kept her dealing with him, even though she knew he had
this sort of obligation.

I wondered if Faith had ever been here, and if she had, what she
thought of this place. Did she imagine that once they were married,
the two of them would share something similar, or better? Faith probably saw this place and liked it, I thought, slumping some in my seat
and turning off the engine.

She probably could've had it a week ago. But now it was too late,
for there on the front lawn was a huge Century 21 sign, declaring the
house sold. I figured that after Gary gave his wife the news, maybe she
could no longer afford the place on her own, or maybe she just didn't
want it any longer.

Sitting out here in front of this man's house made me start to wonder why he would leave the situation he had. Not that Faith wasn't
worth it, but he had a wife, and a couple of kids, boys I think Karen
said. What happened to make him want to leave? How did his wife
compare with Faith? Suddenly I had to know the answer to that, I had
to get a glimpse of her.

I thought about continuing to sit out there, hoping that maybe she
would come out if she was in the house, or that she would drive up if
she wasn't, but I didn't feel like waiting.

I pulled the key from the ignition, got out of my car, and slowly moved around it toward the house. I walked up to the fence, pulled down on the lever, and thankfully, it was not locked.

I whistled a couple of times, making sure there wasn't some blood-thirsty rottweiler laying low waiting to attack. Then I went up the stone path to the front door of their house.

I can't believe I'm doing this, I thought as I climbed the final step. In front of the door, I raised a finger, preparing to ring the doorbell, when I stopped myself. What if the wife didn't come to the door, but Mr. Robinson himself? Would he look at me, a strange expression on his face, then take a deeper look, finally recognizing me? And what would happen if he did that? Would he shut the door in my face, or upon seeing him, would I go crazy, push my fist through that screen door, grab him by his throat, and try to break his neck.

I turned around, looked at my car, and thought about walking back down those steps, and just driving away. But then I thought, to hell with that. Yes, I was intruding a bit by trying to get a look at his wife, but that was nothing in comparison to the intrusion he made upon my once future wife. I turned back around and rang the bell. I waited a moment, and then after no answer, rang it again. Still there was nothing. I peered through the square glass in the door, but saw nothing but an empty hallway.

No one was home. I turned, about to go back down the steps, when I heard the door opening behind me. A beautiful, dark-brown-skinned woman with long curly hair and green eyes was at the door.

She was wearing a faded green flowered print spring dress that brought out both the color of her eyes and the shape of her body. I was caught off guard with how beautiful she was, and for a moment, I couldn't say anything after she said, "Hi. Can I help you?"

I stuttered, staring into her eyes, gazing at her rich, dark complexion, then said, "Uhhhh, is Max home? I'm looking for Max."

"Max? No, I'm sorry, there's no Max who lives here. Are you sure you have the right address?"

I dug out the little piece of paper I had written this address on, and glanced down at it. "Uh, yeah—7326 South Oakley, right?"

"Yeah, this is it, but still, there's no Max," she said, smiling sadly.

I was about to turn around and leave, feeling satisfied, no, actually privileged that I was able to lay eyes on this woman, when she said, "You have a number where you can call him?"

"Uh, yeah. You know I do," I said, caught off guard again. "But I don't have my cell phone with me. Would you mind terribly if I um . . ." and I made a gesture with my hand like it was a phone, putting it up to my ear.

"No, sure. That's no problem," the woman said, opening the door, and welcoming me in.

I stepped inside, walked down the hall, and now I really couldn't believe what I was doing. I came to look at the man's house, then wanted to see his wife, and now I was walking through his home. I took in everything around me, the pictures of Gary, his wife, and his two sons, hanging from the walls, and sitting on the mantel. Judging from those pictures, they all seemed so happy. Gary looked like the model husband and father. Oh, how pictures can lie, I thought.

The house was expensively and tastefully decorated with fine furniture and beautiful paintings. Gary must've been making nice loot, I thought, considering his wife stayed at home.

"This is a beautiful place you have," I said to her, as she pointed me to the phone.

"Thanks. If you would've come by a week ago, it could've been yours. It's sold."

"I saw that. Why are you leaving, if you don't mind me asking? Those cold Chicago winters?"

"No, we just think we'd benefit from a change of scenery," she said, looking somewhat melancholy. "Get a fresh start."

I wanted to know who "we" were, but I figured she was referring to her two sons, considering Gary was leaving this woman for Faith. What a shame, I thought.

"Where are you guys going?" I asked, and only after asking it, I realized how nosy I was being. "I'm sorry. I'm prying. Never mind," I said, picking up the phone. "You were kind enough to offer your phone to me, and now I'm talking your head off."

"No, it's quite all right. I don't mind. Sometimes I get lonely sitting around the house all day waiting for the kids to come home," she said, brushing a hand over her curly hair. "We're relocating to D.C. My husband put in for a transfer out there. I went to college there. I think it'll be nice for the kids."

"So your . . ." and I had to stop myself from asking if her husband was going with her, because I know that was what she just said. But how could that be the case if he was marrying Faith?

"I'm sorry, what did you say?"

"Oh, I was just saying, so you're from D.C.?"

"No. I just went to school there; Howard. I was born here. But let me let you make your phone call, because now I'm starting to talk your head off." She turned to leave the room, and although I didn't want to, I couldn't help but take a look at her behind as she walked away. Very nice, I thought. Very, very nice.

After leaving a message on my own voice mail for the fictitious Max I was looking for, I walked back toward the living room. She was there, standing, thumbing through an *Essence* magazine.

"So thanks a lot for letting me use the phone."

"No problem. Did you find Max?" she asked, sounding genuinely concerned.

"No, no. But I left a message on his machine. And thanks again." I extended a hand to her, for what reason I don't know. Was this a situation where you would shake hands? Anyway, she took my hand with one as soft as a baby's belly, and shook it.

"Lottie," she said, smiling that beautiful, gleaming smile of hers. "Lottie Robinson."

"And I'm . . . Jay. Jay . . . Atkins," I said, choosing not to tell her my real last name. We stood there, still shaking, looking into each other's eyes, smiling weirdly, and I felt compelled to say, "You have really pretty eyes."

Lottie smiled shyly, lowered her head, and slowly pulled her hand away.

"What, oh, I'm sorry. I don't normally do that. I mean, I shouldn't have . . ."

"No, it's okay, Jay. It's nothing that you did wrong," she said, still looking down, occasionally glancing up at me. "It's just when you've been . . . um, well. It's just when you've been married so long, you kind of get used to not getting compliments, and when one does pop up, it kinda takes you by surprise, that's all."

"So, I haven't offended you?"

"No, no, not at all," she said, still smiling, shyly. "That actually made my day."

"Well, good," I said, smiling widely, feeling proud that I was able to do that. "Well, I guess I ought to be going now," I said, and the words seemed to shake her a bit, as if she thought I was going to stay there forever.

"Uh, yeah. That's right. Let me show you to the door."

And she did. She opened it and stood there by it, just looking at me as though I was supposed to kiss her good-bye or something. I know that wasn't what she was thinking, or expecting, but it just felt that way. There was an awkwardness about the moment, like we had just gone on our first date.

"Well, nice meeting you, and nice talking to you."

"Yeah, likewise."

"And who knows," I said, making an effort to store away as much of her appearance in my memory as possible. "Maybe we'll bump into each other again."

"Yeah, who knows," she said, looking like she doubted it very seriously.

27

For the past week, Jayson had been acting really strange, like they were back in a relationship again. All right, she thought to herself, that wasn't fair. Maybe he had reason for behaving like that. Maybe it had something to do with the two times she'd slept with him that night last week. But she couldn't believe he'd misconstrued friendship sex at a moment of desperate need, for love sex.

He was hurting, beyond hurting, and she couldn't take it, and she would've done anything, everything, to make him feel better, and that's what she'd done, but she hadn't expected things to go the way they'd been going.

For the past week, he had been calling and coming down to her place every night after she got off work. When she answered the door and let him in, he would always take her in a tight hug and kiss her on the lips before walking in.

"So what are we doing tonight?" Jayson had asked last night.

"I didn't know we were doing anything. I didn't know we had plans. Besides, we've been out practically every night this week, and I'm kinda tired."

"All right then, tomorrow," Jayson said, smiling, taking her face in his palms, and kissing her on the lips again. "I guess I have some things I need to do anyway."

She didn't have the heart to tell him that she was really going over to see Gill—to try and decide what she was going to do with him. He had been calling like crazy as well, and Asha thought it was funny. Everyone was calling her home, trying to speak to her, except the person she really wanted to hear from. Angie. It had been a week, and nothing. And for her last two appointments, she didn't show. As Asha waited at work, in her massage room, she worried that she might have ruined everything with this woman. Day and night Asha thought about calling her, but she knew that would only push Angie away more. It was the reason she was staying away now. Why hadn't she just let things take their course and not forced the issue? Everything would've worked out okay, just like Angie said, and things would've still been fine between them. Just when they were seeming to really start getting close, Asha had forced them back twenty steps by trying to catapult them forward ten. And now, it was really starting to hit her, realizing just how stupid she had been.

She had to rectify this, Asha thought as she hurried to the phone. She had to fix this before she lost the woman she was falling in love with. Asha dialed Angie's number as fast as her fingers would allow. It rang and rang while Asha stood there beating herself up, knowing that Angie wouldn't pick up the phone, because that would give Asha the opportunity to apologize to her, and Asha knew, after her behavior, she didn't deserve that opportunity.

The phone stopped ringing, there came the usual clicking, indicating that the call was being transferred to voice mail.

"It's me, An-gee. Sorry I can't take your call. But drop a message in 1,2,3." The beep sounded.

Asha stood there, unable to speak, wondering if she should just forget about trying to apologize, because it was probably too late, or speak her piece there, because she knew she would get no other opportunity.

"Angie," Asha said, her voice soft, uncertain. "This is Asha. You missed your last two appointments, and I know it's because you don't want to see me anymore. I know I messed up by demanding everything right here, right now, when you were trying to take it slow so that it would work. Angie," Asha said, swallowing hard, trying not to let her emotion be heard over the phone. "I am so sorry for pushing you faster than you wanted to go. I still want this with you. I just sometimes get worried that, maybe . . . that maybe . . . I don't know. Just call me back," Asha said, desperately. "Yeah, just call me back, and I'll make everything up to you, and we'll try it again, and I swear I won't ever . . ." A beep sounded, cutting her off.

Asha lowered her head, hanging up the phone. Angie wouldn't listen to the message, and if she did, it wouldn't make one bit of difference, Asha thought to herself. But Asha needed to finish telling her how sorry she was. She was about to lift the phone again, when someone said, "You swear you won't ever do what?"

Asha spun around and saw Angie standing there just inside her room. "How much of that did you hear?"

"All of it. You swear you won't ever do what, Asha?" Angie asked again, closing the door behind her.

"I swear I won't ever push us faster than we need to go, demand things that we don't necessarily need just now," she said, walking quickly over to Angie and stopping just in front of her, wanting to hug her, to kiss her, but not knowing if she still had that right.

"Angie, I don't want us to end."

Angie looked as though she was thinking over what Asha just said, and then she said, "Asha, I've been really thinking and—"

"Angie, don't say it, if it's what I think you're going to say," Asha said, moving very close to Angie. "I'm sorry about last week, and we can take it however fast or slow you want to, just don't leave."

Angie shook her head, seeming sorry in advance for what she was about to say. "Asha it's just that . . ."

Asha wrapped her arms around Angie's waist, placed her cheek upon Angie's, and whispered in her ear. "You don't want this anymore? You don't want me?"

"No. It's not that. I just think . . ."

"Don't think, Angie," Asha said, kissing her softly on the ear. "Do what you feel. You don't feel this?" Asha touched the tip of Angie's earlobe with the tip of her tongue. She felt a shiver run through Angie's body, felt Angie's arms find their way around her waist.

"Why don't you think about it. Just don't say no, Angie," Asha said, taking Angie's earlobe into her mouth, sucking on it. "Will you do that?" And then Asha gently eased her warm, wet tongue into Angie's ear. She felt Angie's knees weaken, and then Angie turned her face to Asha.

"Okay, I'll think about it," Angie said, kissing Asha.

"I missed you so much," Angie said, as they continued kissing.

"I missed you too," Asha said, pulling Angie toward the table, help-ing her up, unable to pull her lips from Angie's as she sat up there.

"I kept telling myself how crazy I was to let you walk out of here," Asha said, as she pulled Angie's T-shirt up and over her head, exposing her bare torso. "I kept telling myself that if I ever saw you again, I would make you feel how much you mean to me." And now Asha was unzipping the skirt Angie was wearing, sliding it down from her hips. "I was hoping so much that I'd see you again, and now you're here," Asha said, her tone feverish, taking a moment to savor the sight of Angie's caramel thighs as they spread out across the table. And then she reached around and grabbed the waistband of the thong Angie was wearing and slid that off.

Angie was sitting in front of Asha naked, and Asha placed both her warm palms on Angie's knees and gently started to pull them apart.

"What are you doing?" Angie said, seeming in a dreamy state, her eyes partly open.

"I think you know exactly what I'm about to do," Asha said. "Have any objections?"

Angie slowly shook her head, not saying a word.

Asha slid a hand up Angie's thigh, feeling how increasingly warm it got as she moved farther in between her legs. She touched Angie with a single finger, watching her eyes roll back in her head, feeling how wet she had become, and then Asha lowered herself to her knees. Asha urged Angie's legs open just a little wider, when all of a sudden, the door swung open.

"Asha, you got some clean towels in—oooohhhhhh!" Big Les howled, her eyes popping damn near out of her head.

Asha leapt up from her knees, throwing Angie's skirt in her lap, try-ing to cover her up, as if it wasn't too late to stop Les from seeing all that was about to happen. But Asha knew there was no hope. Judging by the looks on Les' face, first, shock, then delight, Asha knew she had been found out.

"I was just massaging my client," Asha quickly offered.

"Don't worry, Asha. I know exactly what you were doing," Les said, winking. And before she closed the door, she said, "I'm sure I'll rap to you later."

28

After being busted by Les, Asha had Angie quickly grab her things and get out of there.

"Are you going to be all right?" Angie said, turning to her, even though Asha was steadily trying to push her toward the door and out of the room.

"I hope so. I don't know."

"You call me and let me know what happens. You hear me?"

Asha nodded her head and opened the door for Angie, quickly closing it behind her. She fell back against it, knowing that she was in a world of trouble and had no way of getting out of it.

For the rest of the day, Asha tried to pretend nothing had happened, as though Les hadn't seen anything. Asha took the rest of her clients, trying not to let them see that something was really bothering her. During the course of the day, she tried her best to steer clear of Les, but that was impossible. When she did see Les, Les didn't say a word, really didn't even acknowledge Asha, which she thought was strange. Maybe Les didn't plan on making a big deal of this after all. Maybe, after seeing how Asha had stood up to her a couple of days ago, she had decided that Asha shouldn't be messed with.

Asha closed her eyes, praying that was the case as she finished massaging her last client.

"All right, Belinda, that'll do it for today," Asha said, pushing her cart of oils and other bottles aside.

"Thanks, Asha. I'll see you next time," Belinda said, climbing down from the table, and walking toward the changing room.

Asha went over to a chair and fell into it, wondering what she would do when Les finally approached her. What would she say? The time would come, Asha knew. All that nonsense about Les not bothering her, she knew that was garbage. Before the day was out, Asha knew Big Les would be up in her face, gloating at the fact that she had something on her.

A few minutes later, Belinda stuck her head back in the room, making Asha almost jump out of her skin.

"Thanks, again," she said, and then left.

"Okay. Bye," Asha blew, slumping back in the chair. She kicked one of her legs over the arm of the chair, let her head fall back until the top of her skull hit the wall, and went back to trying to find a way out of all this. Then she heard a noise. Asha quickly pulled her head up to find Les standing in front of her, smiling mischievously.

"What do you want?" Asha said, sneering, after Les didn't say anything, just continued to stand there smiling.

"Hmmm," Les said, rubbing her chin. "What was that you said? 'I don't swing that way,'" she said, in a baby's voice, mocking Asha. "It sho' looked like you were swinging that way earlier, baby," Les said, laughing to herself. "Looked like you were swinging that way, like you were born with a little rope in your hand made just for swinging. Know what I'm sayin'?" Les started to pace in front of Asha. "But I can't blame you, because that piece you had on the table was fine as hell. I would've went down on her myself. I bet that pussy tastes good, don't it?" she said, stopping in front of Asha, sticking her face in Asha's face. "Or did I interrupt you two before you could get your hot little tongue all up in there."

Les was still smiling, making a joke of all this, while Asha sat there, anger starting to rage within her, but she knew she could do nothing but sit there and take it. Les had her right where she wanted her.

Les stepped away from her, and started her pacing again, her big fat hands folded behind her back, as if she was questioning a witness.

"So how long you been eating pussy, Asha?"

"I don't—"

"I seen you with my own two eyes," Les said, pointing to them. "But what I should be asking you is, how long you been eating the pussies of your clients?"

"What the fuck do you want!" Asha said, shooting from her chair.

"No, no, no," Les said, shaking her head, waving a finger at Asha. "It's not what I want, but what Phillipe Cozi wants. How did you put it? 'I don't think that's behavior befitting an employee of Phillipe Cozi.' Is that what you said, Asha? Something like that."

"Cut to the motherfucking chase, fat girl," Asha said, frowning, ready to attack Les if she hadn't known for sure that she'd get her ass beat.

"Oh, so you're talking about my weight now. But that's okay, sweet thang. Because you're gonna love all this fat ass before we're through." Les rubbed her chin thoughtfully, and looked up toward the ceiling. "I think now that we've established that you're just as much of a dyke as I am, and I caught you in here on your knees about to give one of your clients a tongue bath, I'd think you'd want to keep that quiet. What do you think?"

"What do you want?" Asha spat.

"I want the same thing that lucky girl was about to get. But not no twenty-minute quickie. I want it for as long as I want it, whenever I want it."

"Fuck that," Asha said, sitting back down. "That shit won't happen."

"Oh it won't. I think you better think about that, baby. You could lose your job for not wanting to do what you were about to do anyway."

"Fuck you, Les. I can work anywhere."

"Oh, you're probably right," Les said, turning toward the door. "Well, I guess you'll just have to do that, because when I leave this room, I'm going straight to Margee's office." She went to grab the door when Asha said, "Hold it. Wait."

"Yeeessssssss," Les said, turning and smiling.

"I'll do it. You'll have me for one hour."

"One week," Les said.

"Hell no. One day," Asha said, still knowing that it would never happen, but she needed something to put Big Les on pause while she thought this whole thing through.

Les looked as though she was giving it thought.

"Take it, or you and this job can go to hell."

"Hmmm, you being my bitch for twenty-four hours. All right. I can roll with that. Friday night, brush your teeth, have your pussy smelling fresh, and no bra or underwear. I don't like fucking with details. We'll leave from here, and go wherever the hell I want. Till then, sweetheart."

The next day, Les didn't come to work, which Asha was thankful for. She was probably at home, playing with herself, fantasizing about the night she thought she would have with Asha. But there was no way in the world that shit was going to go down. It just couldn't. But was she ready to lose her job? Asha allowed herself to see the image of her head in between Big Les's legs, and she almost heaved that very moment. She quickly kicked the thought out of her head. She needed to find her way out of this. She needed to talk to Angie, see what she thought about this. Asha had called her already three times today. She hadn't called back, and Asha was just starting to get worried when she heard, "Asha Mills, line seven. Asha Mills, line seven," on the overhead speakers.

Asha quickly picked up the phone. "This is Asha."

"I just got your messages," Angie said. "You don't sound too good. What's going on?"

"I'm not too good. Everything is fucked up, and this heifer is threatening my job. She wants me to . . . she wants . . ." Asha said, sounding nearly hysterical, unable to get all the words out.

"Asha, look. I have to go right now, but don't worry. Everything is going to be all right. Let's meet tonight, and we'll figure it all out then, all right?"

Asha was breathing hard, trying to calm herself down. "Yeah. All right."

"Now, I have some things to do, so it won't be till late, but I'll call you. Cool?"

"Yeah, cool."

"You all right, baby?"

"Yeah, but I'll be better when I see you."

It was 11:30 P.M. and Asha and Angie were sitting inside Red's, a casual lounge on Stony Island Avenue, listening to old R&B tunes. Asha was finishing her third Long Island iced tea, Angie had had a couple of glasses of wine. They had been talking for an hour and a half, and Asha was starting to feel a little better. Angie didn't tell her exactly what she had planned, but reassured her. "I'll work something out. Don't you worry. Like I said, I've dealt with people like her before, and I always come out on top. All right?" Angie said, resting a hand on Asha's shoulder, then touching her cheek.

"All right, but like I said, something needs to be done by Friday, because that's when she thinks we're getting together."

"I know, Asha. It's Wednesday. That gives me all of tomorrow. That's plenty of time. Now let's get you home, before you pass out on that stool," and Asha laughed, but that very well could've happened, considering how light and fuzzy her head was feeling. She got up from the stool, stumbling, and would've hit the floor if Angie hadn't grabbed her.

"Oh yeah. It's time to get you home."

It was a short drive to Asha's apartment. She would've had Angie drop her off a block away so that Jayson wouldn't see them together, but Asha thought she would have enough trouble walking from the car to the front door, let alone from the next block. Besides, it was just about midnight, and she knew Jayson was always in bed by ten-thirty or so.

"There it is, right there, 1343," Asha said, tapping the windshield of the car, pointing to her apartment. "All right, Angie. I'll wait to hear from you," Asha said. Then she felt for the door handle, opened the door, and almost fell out of the car.

"Hold it, hold it," Angie said, getting out of her side, slamming her door, and rushing over to grab Asha. She carefully put her hands under

Asha's arms and pulled her up. Asha got to her feet, and Angie leaned her against the car.

"Baby, are you okay?" Angie said, grabbing her cheeks between her two palms.

"Yeah, I guess I just had one, two, or three too many Long Islands," Asha said, smiling, and then the smile all of a sudden disappeared from her face.

"What?" Angie said.

"Have you been thinking about what we talked about? You've been thinking about it, right?"

"Asha, baby, this is not the time."

"You won't leave me, will you?"

"Asha, we're just fine right now. Okay?"

"Yeah?"

"Yeah, let me walk you in."

"No. That's okay. I can make it, really. I just had to get my bearings."

"All right, but I'm going to watch you until you get inside."

"Okay," Asha said, sounding like a tired two-year-old. She was about to turn and go, but Angie wouldn't let her.

"What? I don't get a hug good-bye?"

"Oh, I'm sorry," Asha said, falling into Angie's arms, squeezing her. When they were finished, they pulled away from each other, smiling.

"And what about a kiss?" Angie said.

Asha frowned a little. "But I've been drinking. I've got to smell like a bottle of something."

"Don't be stupid, and give me a kiss, girl."

Asha smiled, and let Angie pull her face close until their lips touched, and they were kissing passionately.

Meanwhile, upstairs, Jayson had been sleeping for about an hour and a half, but it never failed—just when he was about to really get into some serious sleep, he would feel that pesky poking at his bladder, and he would have to get up and relieve himself. He really needed to stop drinking that glass of water before bed.

Jayson stood over the toilet, shaking away the last few drops that never seemed to want to fall free, when he heard a car door slam outside of the apartment. He flushed the toilet and walked slowly, blindly, through the dark apartment. He parted the curtains slightly, looked out the window, and saw a huge Mercedes, and a woman rushing around the car to help a younger woman who appeared to be falling out of the passenger door. The woman helped prop the girl up against the car, and Jayson could see that it was Asha and that she was drunk.

He chuckled to himself, knowing that in the morning if he went down there, she would be talking that nonsense about how she's never going to drink again, like she always had in the past.

Jayson let his eyes rest on the woman who was talking to Asha. She wasn't that bad a looker. Actually, she was pretty. Jayson wondered why Asha had never introduced him to that one.

Asha stumbled away but was pulled back to give the other woman a hug, which was so typical of women, Jayson thought. Men don't give hugs. Men give dap. Why don't women just give dap too? He mused to himself, and then Jayson thought that there must've been globs of sleep still in his eyes or that he had not really awakened at all, because he could've not been seeing what he thought he was. Asha, the woman he'd known so well for so many years, and loved, was down there, her tongue buried in this other woman's mouth. They were hugging and kissing, and feeling all over one another, like they loved each other, or something.

"Now see. You didn't taste that bad," Angie said, wiping some of her lipstick off Asha's mouth.

"If you say so," Asha said.

"You sure you can make it?

"Yeah. I'm fine. I'll talk to you tomorrow. And thanks, Angie," Asha said, turning to walk toward the apartment.

Jayson had almost thrown himself to the floor trying not to be seen when Asha turned around. He hadn't been seen, but what had he just witnessed? It was a stupid question, he told himself. He wasn't a fool, or a naïve child, and he was starting to put two and two together. This was the reason why Asha didn't want to go out with him last time he came by. Come to think of it, she'd seemed a bit reluctant to go out all those other times as well. He couldn't believe it, and he told himself not to. But was this the reason why she'd seemed so distant years ago with him, why she was distant with Gill. Jayson closed his eyes, threw the thought out of his head. It couldn't be. She's my best friend, he thought. She would've told me something as serious as this. She wouldn't have deceived me for all those years, told me lies like that. She just wouldn't have.

But there was no denying it, something was going on. He had proof. She was seeing that woman who was driving away, and Jayson didn't know to what extent, but it was more than just friends. Asha had lied to him, like he thought she never had or never would. He had trusted her in the past, was trusting her now, and look what she had done to him, betrayed him just like Faith had.

29

It had to be a dream, I thought sitting up in bed. Asha wasn't kissing some woman outside my building last night. I placed a hand to my head, assessing the condition it was in. Had I been drinking? No. I hadn't even gone out last night. Was it some strange fantasy that was always hiding in my subconscious and finally decided to show itself in my dream? I didn't think so, because that had never been a fantasy of mine, and I distinctly remembered getting up to use the bathroom, and then . . .

I was ready to rush down the stairs and confront her, ask her what the hell was going on. But something stopped me. It wasn't the right time, for I was far too angry, and judging by the way she was wobbling around outside, she was far too drunk to make any sense anyway. I told myself I'd let her sleep it off, and confront her about it in the morning.

But now, getting up, and looking over at the clock, I saw that it was already after nine, and I knew that she had gone to work by now. I pulled myself out of bed, slid on some jeans and a long-sleeve T-shirt, and just paced about the house for a while.

I should've eaten something, but my stomach was still twisted in knots from what I'd seen last night. I walked over to the phone, picked it up, and dialed Asha's work number. Something had to be said to her. I had to find out what was going on, and for just how long it had been going on.

"Phillipe Cozi Day Spa," a cheery voice answered.

I didn't say anything, wondering if this was the right way to handle this situation or not.

"Good morning, this is Phillipe Cozi Day Spa."

I hung up the phone on whoever that was who was so happy to be working at Phillipe Cozi. This wasn't something that I needed to be confronting her about while she was at work, or discussing over the phone. I had to address this shit face-to-face. I'd just wait till she came home. I'd be downstairs, sitting on the outside steps waiting for her cab to pull up, and we'd get to the bottom of this, I thought.

I ended my pacing in front of the sofa, and for lack of anything else to do, I sat down. It was silent, and I stared at the walls around me. I didn't want to think about it, but it was happening to me again, this time with Asha. No, it wasn't exactly the same thing. We weren't engaged to get married, and no I didn't catch her butt naked with that woman, but they were kissing, and kissing usually came as a thank-you after the act was done, or as a teaser in preparation for.

A quick image of Faith and Gary flashed through my head, both their faces contorted in pleasure. Then I saw a quick glimpse of Asha down there on the front lawn, her head twisting and turning, her tongue sloppily dipping into the other woman's mouth, and I couldn't take it anymore. I shot up off that sofa, knowing I had to do something, had to find out why this was happening to me. Why she would do such a thing.

I raced toward the front door, grabbing my keys off the kitchen counter as I passed them. I ended up downstairs at Asha's door, knocking softly at first, then banging relatively hard.

There was no answer, and then I did what I'd told myself I would never do. I slipped my master key into her door, and walked into her apartment with the intent to look through her things.

"Asha, are you in here?" I called, thinking up some kind of lie I could tell her, if indeed she was still there.

I stood there in the living room, feeling strange again to be there without her being in the place with me, or without her at least knowing I was there. I shouldn't be doing this, I told myself, but I had to. I had to find out something.

I glanced over everything that was out, that was open. Loose change atop the television, a pack of gum and a beaded bracelet on the coffee table.

I walked over toward the kitchen, saw a crumpled piece of paper on the counter. I opened it, saw some numbers scribbled across it, balled it up again, and placed it back. I opened the fridge, half expecting to see a huge strap-on dildo sitting there in the middle of it, between the gallon of skim milk, and the leftovers from last night. When I didn't see anything more than I normally saw, I closed the door, leaned my back against it, and shook my head.

"Why, Asha?" I said aloud, disappointed, not so much because I caught her kissing another woman, than in the fact that I *caught* her. Why didn't she just tell me? I'd thought we were as close as two people could be.

Next I went into the bathroom and riffled through the cabinets both under and over the sink, finding nothing but what women normally have in their cabinets. Crap for hair, crap for nails, lotions, ointments, and gels that smell like every fruit and every combination of fruit imaginable. I encountered huge pads for heavy flow days, and thin napkins for when there's just a trickle, and all sorts of remedies for PMS that don't work one bit. There was nothing there that gave me any info, any insight, into what led her in the direction she was going in and why she felt the need to hide it from me.

I went toward the bedroom next, halting within the doorway. Just a week ago, I was in here, and we were making love, and now look what's happening. I considered leaving, but only for a moment, still feeling compelled to find something that would explain her actions.

I walked over to the bed, looked at it suspiciously for a moment, then sat down gently on it. I smoothed my palm over it, stopping there in the center of the bed, wondering if that woman had ever been here, pressing my palm deeper into the blankets, as if I could've felt her warmth.

I stood, yanked back those blankets, examining the sheets, feeling foolish, feeling guilty, but also feeling justified. I went to the dresser, pulled out all the drawers, and went through each of them from the bottom, where her jeans and sweaters were, to the top, where her lingerie, socks, and wraps for her hair were. Inside the last top drawer, I found her address book. I quickly picked it up, flipped backward through the pages, seeing numbers scribbled all about, some in pencil, some in ink, black and red, but not knowing which had relevance to me, and which ones didn't. I closed the book, and tossed it behind me.

I went to the open closet door, pulled the string on the light, and stepped in.

I pushed through the shirts, coats, and pants hanging there, randomly going through the pockets of some of the garments. I grabbed some of the purses from the hooks they were hanging on, and went through them, tossing them out on the floor, after finding nothing.

I was annoyed, growing angry and frustrated that there was nothing to support what I had seen. Nothing that said I wasn't indeed dreaming. I looked up, and saw there was a shelf above me. I threw an arm up there, and swept everything off that was on top of it. A couple of shoe boxes fell down, opening up, knickknacks, hair barrettes, CD cases, and things of that sort falling out at my feet. A photo album came down as well, which I quickly picked up and opened, confident that I would find something in it.

I flipped through the first ten or so pages of black-and-white photos of Asha's parents, of Asha as an infant, and the faded color snapshots of her as a little girl with the pigtails on either side of her head, wearing tiny white shorts, and knee socks. I continued turning past homecoming, her smiling teeth covered with braces, and prom, her standing next to a handsome boy she didn't appear to like, but probably thought was handsome all the same.

I was about to turn past the next page, when I saw my face staring back at me. The first photos Asha and I had taken together on our first date. We'd gone to the Navy Pier, off Lake Michigan, and jumped into one of those one-buck photo booths that take four snapshots.

I looked down the row of shots, at our smiling faces and remembered how happy we were then. I slowly turned the page, and saw more pictures of us. The time we went to Cancún, when we were on the beach, and I had buried her in the sand. There was a photo of the time we went skiing in Vermont, pictures of the great time we had at Mardi Gras, and a snapshot of me and Asha standing in front of the first building I purchased. I was holding up a bottle of champagne, and she had her arms thrown around my neck and was kissing me on the cheek. We were so happy. I thought we were going to get married then, and even now, standing in her closet, looking down at that photo, I couldn't help but smile.

I turned the next page, and immediately, the smile dropped from my lips. It was another picture of Asha and me. We were sitting on a bench in the park, my arm around her. I was smiling, but she was looking in the camera with the saddest, guiltiest eyes I had ever seen. She looked like she wanted to cry, even though it was apparent she had made some effort to smile.

She was wearing a white sweater with long sleeves, and frilly French cuffs. We had gone out earlier that day to buy that sweater to hide the white bandages around both her wrists. The wounds under those bandages were the reason I had suggested going outdoors, hoping that the air and sunshine would cheer her up.

Two weeks prior to that, Asha was driving down to Atlanta with her younger sister Toi, who was about to start school at Clarke University. It was a long trip, and they took turns driving. When it was Asha's third turn, she was tired, but she knew she had to be back at work the next morning, so she took the wheel anyway.

"Are you sure you don't want me to keep on driving so you can sleep a little more?" Asha's sister had asked.

"No, no. I'm fine. You go ahead and go to sleep, and by the time you wake up, we'll be there," Asha said. But when Asha woke up, the car was flipped on its top, the windshield shattered, smoke coming from everywhere. And when Asha looked to her side, she saw that Toi hadn't been wearing her seat belt. She was upside down, all her body weight pressing down on her neck, and Asha could tell by the extremely unnatural way that her sister's head was canted, that her neck had snapped, and there was no way that she was still alive.

It was all her fault, Asha kept crying when she called her mother from the hospital to tell her the news. Her mother kept telling her it wasn't, and insisting that saying so wouldn't bring back her sister. That didn't make Asha feel any better.

Asha went back home to stay with her mother for a week in Indianapolis, but after those seven days, she told me that she could no longer take being there, walking the halls that she and her sister walked as kids, seeing her pictures in her room, her clothes still folded neatly in her drawers, as if waiting for her to come and put them on.

That would never happen again, and there was no one else to blame but her, Asha still told herself. Almost every night, Asha would cry atop her sister's bed, clutching her sister's favorite stuffed animal, wishing that she could've gone back to that night, accepted her sister's offer to drive like she should've. She would've still been alive if she had, if Asha hadn't been thinking about herself, about some damn job. She sacrificed her sister's life so she wouldn't be late for work. When she thought about it in that way, Asha realized that she should be the one dead and not her Toi.

When Asha came back to Chicago, she didn't go to work for another week. She barely spoke to me outside crying on my shoulder when she felt the need, which seemed like always. Every morning during that week when I would check on her, all the way into the evening when I'd come back from work, Asha would be there in her apartment in the same place, staring at the wall, leaving me uncertain as to whether she had moved an inch in all those hours.

Then came that one evening when I walked in, and she wasn't sitting in front of that wall. I smiled thinking that she was up and about, but when I called for her, she didn't answer, and when I searched most of her apartment, I couldn't find her. I went into the bathroom and saw nothing but one of her legs dangling over the rim of the tub. I stood there in the doorway, afraid to take a single step further. When I finally forced myself to move into the room, look down into the tub, I saw that she had slit both her wrists, blood everywhere, splattered across the walls of the tub, covering the tub's floor, and slowly seeping down the drain. The white T-shirt she was wearing was, in some places, soaked dark red with her blood as she lay there barely breathing.

The guilt was so bad that she took a razor blade to both her wrists, telling herself that she was no more deserving of life than her sister.

Yeah, I remembered this picture, I thought, as I continued to look down on it, and I remembered all we'd gone through to get past that, and here I was rummaging through her shit like she was no one to me, like she meant nothing. Yeah, she had lied to me, but that was something that I needed to talk to her about face-to-face. Bottom line, this was wrong. I needed to clean up the mess I'd made of her room, and get out of here, pick this up with her later, the right way.

So I closed the photo album, placed it back on the shelf, and turned around to walk out of the closet. But as I did, Asha was just walking into her bedroom. She looked at me, shocked, as though she had never seen me before. She looked at her dresser, all the drawers pulled out, clothes hanging over the sides of them. She looked at the shoes and purses that I had thrown out of her closet, then she looked back up at me, and said with more disappointment than anger, "What are you doing in my damn bedroom?"

I couldn't answer because I was caught off guard at first. I just stood there, busted, this stupid look on my face, waiting for her to say something else, because I knew I wouldn't.

"Jayson, I said, what the hell are you doing in my damn bedroom?" she said again, but this time anger was apparent in her voice.

Still I said nothing.

"You're going through my shit? You're going through my shit!" She said it twice, as if she couldn't believe it the first time.

"I cannot believe this. You of all people, always saying that you wouldn't come down here unless I allowed you, and here you are, my shit all over the place," she said, looking over the mess on the floor again with disgust. "Just what the fuck are you looking for, Jayson? Maybe I can help you. That is, if you haven't already found it," she said, angrily kicking one of her shoes.

Still I didn't respond.

"Did you hear me? Are you deaf?" She continued ranting. "Tell me one thing. Is this the first time, Jayson? Or do you come down here every week, every couple of days, and tear through my shit? Hunh, Jayson?"

I stood there frozen, still too ashamed to utter the slightest sound.

"Answer me, you lying motherfucker!"

And then it seemed as though my shame all of a sudden just disappeared. "What did you call me?"

"I called you a liar. This is my private shit. I pay rent to you, and you said you'd . . ."

"I'm a liar, Asha?" I said, really starting to get angry, remembering all that I'd seen last night, forgetting all that I'd just seen in the photo album.

"In all the time I've known you, all the time I've been dealing with you, I've never lied to you once," I said, taking a step toward her.

"Because we meant more to each other than that, I thought. Our relationship, and our friendship. But obviously I was the only one who felt that way."

"What are you talking about, Jayson? I never lied to you."

"Never, Asha?"

"No, never, Jayson. And what the fuck does that have to do with you tearing up my shit?" Asha said, her hands on her hips.

"Where were you last night?"

All of a sudden Asha was dead quiet.

"I asked a simple question, Asha. Where were you last night, and don't try to lie about it, because it'll only prove what I'm saying now is right. And it wouldn't do you any good anyway, because I know, Asha. I fucking know," I said, now standing right over her, right up in her face.

"I was out."

"Out with who?" I asked.

"That's none of your damn business."

"Yes it is if you're out sucking face with some woman when we're trying to get back together."

Asha looked like she had been physically assaulted with the comment I had just made, then she said, "Get back together? We're not trying to get back together. We had sex last week because you were trying to get Faith and that damn tape off your mind. You were in need of that, and to tell you the truth, so was I, but I wasn't trying to get back together with you."

"That wasn't just sex we were having, Asha. We were making love."

"That's because I love you, Jayson. That's why I did it. But I don't love you like that anymore. And you no longer love me like that, because you still love Faith."

I was silent for a moment, had to think about what she had just said. It couldn't have been true after all that Faith had done to me, but I wasn't sure, because I never considered it. Every time I thought of her, the only emotion that I would allow myself to feel was anger and betrayal. I'd never thought about whether or not there was still love in me for her.

"But you still lied to me," I said. "I saw you downstairs last night kissing some woman, and don't say she was just a friend, because friends don't kiss like that. Not even woman friends."

She looked at me, guilt written all over her face.

"When did that start?" I asked her. "All the time you were with Gill? All the time you were with me?"

"Yes, dammit. Yes! Is that what you want to hear? All the time I was with you, but I never cheated on you, and I never lied to you."

"All those years you had that going on in your life and you never came to me, never told me. It's like all those years we were together, I never really knew you. It's like I barely know you now," I said.

"That was my personal life," Asha defended. "You didn't need to know about that then, and you didn't need to be sneaking in my fucking apartment, going through my shit to find out about it now," Asha said, snatching the purse I'd thrown on the floor from the carpet.

"You don't like it?" I said, spinning around, fed up with the entire argument.

"No, I don't like it," Asha said. "So get the hell out of my apartment."

"Naw. How about this? Why don't you get out?" Asha's face went blank, because she knew exactly what I was suggesting.

"What did you just say, Jayson?"

"You heard what I said. You feel you don't have to be on the up and up with me, then you need to pack up all your shit and leave."

Asha looked as though she was considering a thousand different combinations of words to say to me, but settled on, "Okay. All right, if that's what you want. But I need to the end of the month."

"Fine. You have fifteen days."

30

Asha couldn't believe what just happened. She couldn't believe that she'd left her apartment just to go down the street to get some coffee to try and get rid of the massive hangover she had, and had come back to find her best friend ripping through her personal belongings.

It was a good thing she'd called in sick today, because if she hadn't, she would never have found Jayson down there, she thought. She would've never known that he had known about her and Angie until he confronted her about it, and she wouldn't have had any idea when that confrontation would come.

Asha sat on the edge of her bed, a purse in one hand, one of her slips that had been hanging out of one of the dresser drawers in another, feeling violated. She thought about what Jayson said, that she'd lied to him all the years that they'd known each other, that he really didn't know her, and she had to admit that there was some truth to that. But did this have to be the punishment for that, she thought, looking over the mess he made of her place.

For a brief moment, Asha thought about going upstairs and apologizing to Jayson, and demanding an apology from him in return. But why would she try to communicate with that man when he told her that he wanted her gone. He didn't want to talk. And by the look in his eyes, it seemed he never wanted to see her face again. And now that Asha thought about it, hell, it was probably for the best. Her heart was breaking that their friendship had to come to an end this way, and the thought of never seeing Jayson, never speaking to him again, just didn't seem real. But she was about to enter a new phase of her life now, and maybe just as Angie was supposed to be a part of that new life, Jayson wasn't supposed to be.

Asha remembered her mother telling her that people come into other people's lives for a reason, a season, or for life. She didn't know which of the first two Jayson was there for, but she knew now it wasn't for life.

She would have to go to the hardware store and get some boxes, start packing if she was really going to be getting out of there. Then she would have to find a place. She had no idea where to start looking, and thought for a moment, that it would be so nice if Angie offered to allow her to live with her. But Asha had no idea what Angie's living situation was like, and Asha didn't even want to mention the fact that she was being kicked out, because Angie would probably think she was giving her that information hoping that she would invite Asha to stay with her.

She wouldn't say a thing, but Asha did go to the phone and dial Angie's number. She was feeling bad, and she knew just hearing Angie's voice would make her feel just a little better.

"Hello," Asha said, after Angie picked up the phone.

"How's your head, baby? You were messed up pretty bad last night," Angie said, a smile in her voice.

"It ain't that bad, but I called in sick today because it ain't that good, either," Asha said, placing a hand on her forehead. "And I also didn't feel like dealing with Big Butch at work."

"Well, like I said, don't worry about that. I'm working on it, and we'll take care of it, one way or another," Angie said, confidently.

"Can you tell me in what way?"

"I'm working on it, Asha."

"Well, will all the work be done by tomorrow, because I told you, tomorrow she'll be going to my supervisor and . . ."

"Asha."

"What?"

"Didn't I say I got you on this?"

"Yeah."

"Then stop worrying, okay?"

Asha paused, attempting to forget about all her worries that very moment. "All right."

There was silence over the phone for a few seconds, then Angie said, "Are you all right? You don't sound that good."

Asha wanted to tell Angie all that had just happened, wanted to tell her that she had just lost her best friend, lost her place, and felt like she was in the process of even losing herself, but she didn't. There would be sobbing and tears. She would appear helpless and needy, and it would all be too much for Angie.

"No, everything's fine. It's just the hangover."

"Are you sure?"

"Yeah, positive. But I gotta go. I got a lot of things to take care of. So will I talk to you tomorrow?"

"You'll see me tomorrow. I'll come up there, and we'll handle this little situation with Big Les. I promise."

When they'd hung up, Asha thought about all the things she had to do, and there were a hell of a lot of them. But the most pressing of all was dealing with Gill. Again, all that Jayson accused her of, echoed in her head.

"So was this going on all the time you were seeing me, all the time you were seeing Gill?"

It was wrong, and she'd always known, but in the past, she felt she had options, and she felt she had something to cover up. Now, since Jayson knew, her secret was out, and she realized that marrying Gill wasn't even an option anymore.

She picked up the phone and dialed Gill's direct number at work.

"Hello," Gill answered.

"Gill, it's me."

Gill paused for a moment, then said, "You calling me back to apologize for throwing me out of your place last time?"

"Yeah, I am. I'm sorry about that, Gill. That was wrong of me. But I also think we should get together tonight around eight."

"You want to get together?" he said, sounding a little too excited, not taking it the way Asha intended on him taking it.

"Yeah, Gill."

"Want to go out to dinner?"

"No. Not out to dinner. I'll just meet you at your place."

"Want me to pick you up?"

"No. I'll just meet you at your place," Asha said again, in the same bland tone.

"This isn't nothing bad, is it?"

Asha didn't want to lie to him, but what was she going to say. Of course, it is, Gill. I'm coming over there to spit in your face, give you back your ring, and walk out of your life forever.

"No, Gill. It's nothing bad. I just want to see you," Asha lied, not needing to get into all of that this moment.

Asha didn't use the key to Gill's place he had given her only six months into their relationship. She rang the buzzer. She didn't want him to think that things were just as usual. She wanted him to feel that things were different, that they had something to discuss the moment she walked in the door. Asha hadn't changed out of the torn jeans and oversized T-shirt she'd put on right after she got out of bed. She didn't do her hair, didn't even shower. She wanted to look as unattractive as possible, so when she did break the news to him, he would look at her and think to himself, humph, she's not that much of a loss anyway.

"Asha. What are you doing down there?" Gill said, his voice coming through the intercom, knowing it was her, because Asha was sure he was looking at her through the tiny camera that pointed down at her. "Why didn't you use your key?"

"Can you just buzz me up, Gill," Asha said, looking into the camera.

A second later, the buzzer sounded, and Asha pulled the door open.

When she stepped off the elevator, Gill was smiling, waiting at the open door, looking as though he'd dressed just for this occasion, wearing nice linen slacks, and a beautiful loose-fitting cotton short-sleeved shirt.

"Hey, Suga'," Gill said, his arms open wide for a hug. Asha moved into his embrace, allowing herself to be hugged, but making no effort to return his affection. After he was finished, she stepped back from him. Gill looked at her.

"We definitely aren't going out to dinner, I see," he said, commenting on her attire.

"Sorry, but my sequin gown is in the cleaners," Asha said, walking past Gill into his condo, and standing in the center of his living room.

He followed her in, closing the door behind him. "Is there a problem, Asha?"

Yeah, there's a damn problem, Asha wanted to say. I'm mad as hell that I have to come over here and tell you that I care nothing for you anymore, that I don't want to see you again, when all you did was love me, treat me like a queen, and attempt to devote your life to me. That's my fucking problem. But all she said was "I just have something on my mind."

"Then tell me what it is, baby," Gill said, rushing over to her, taking her hands in his, looking as though he was willing to do whatever was in his power to solve her problem.

"Gill, no," Asha said, pulling her hands away from him.

"No, what?" Gill said, looking at her strangely.

"It's just that you're always so caring, always so willing to sacrifice anything for me, and—"

"And that's bad?"

"No. It just makes it harder to . . ." Asha stopped speaking, walked away from him, toward the couch, then behind it, dragging a single finger across the top of it. Gill watched her, a bewildered look on his face, until she stopped and faced him again.

"Harder to what, Asha?" Gill said, and he looked like he was holding his breath while he waited for her answer.

How could she save his feelings? Asha thought to herself. How could she spare him from the pain she felt she was about to inflict on him? And even if it could just be by a little bit, she would do whatever it took, because he didn't deserve this. She knew lying to him would only cause him more harm. She also knew by lying to him, she'd be continuing to lie to herself, and she had accepted who she was by now. She would just tell him the truth. The whole truth.

"Harder to do what, Asha?" Gill asked again, walking over toward her, but stopping a few feet from her, when Asha took a step back.

"Harder to . . ." Asha said, starting to twist the engagement ring on her left hand, " . . . harder to let you go, Gill."

Gill looked as though what was just said to him was incomprehensible, as though he didn't understand a word of it.

"I . . . I . . . I don't know what you're saying to me. Let me go. What do you mean?"

"Gill, don't make this harder than it already is. I can't be with you anymore. I can't marry you," Asha said, looking directly into Gill's eyes.

He held her stare for a moment, then had to look away, saying, "No. I can't accept that, Asha. No. I just can't accept that."

"I'm sorry, Gill, but you're going to have to," Asha said softly, painfully watching as Gill paced about in front of her, his hands clutching his head. "I can't," he said.

"You have to."

"But I can't!" Gill said, raising his voice, rushing back toward Asha. Asha jumped, surprised, because it was the first time Gill had ever raised his voice to her, ever threatened her in any way. He backed away from her, realizing that she was scared.

"Why, Asha? Just tell me why," he said, lowering his voice, taking a less threatening stance. "What have I done wrong?"

"You haven't done anything wrong. This has nothing to do with you."

"How could it have nothing to do with me. You're telling me that you're leaving me. We're getting married, Asha. You've met my parents. I've been looking at houses. We're getting married, and you just one day come here and tell me that none of that matters, that none of it's going to happen. You have to tell me why. You have to give me a goddamn reason why."

"I just changed my mind," Asha said.

"No!" Gill said, grabbing her by the arms. "A real reason!"

"You don't want the real reason."

"Why? Are you cheating on me?"

"No?"

"Is it another man?"

"No," Asha said.

"Then what the hell is it?"

"I told you. You don't want . . ."

"Just tell me, dammit!" Gill yelled.

"It's another woman!" Asha said, raising her voice over Gill's.

He was stunned. Asha could tell by the dead look on his face. His arms went limp and fell from her body. He staggered two steps backward away from her, shaking his head, a look of grief so intense on his face, it made Asha want to cry.

"I don't believe you," he said, his eyes seeming to focus on something deep in his mind, like the possibility of what she said being true. "I just don't."

"I'm sorry, Gill."

"What? Are you friends? Are you just attracted to her. I'm sure it's something that'll—"

"I love her, Gill. I've been with her, and I love her. I'm so sorry, but I can't marry you knowing this about myself."

Gill stumbled back another few steps. "What? Did you just wake up one day last week, and you were gay?"

"No, Gill. I've known for a while, but I've never acted on it till now."

"How long is a while?" Gill said, hesitating to look up at Asha.

"For years."

Gill's eyes opened wide. "Before me? All the while we were together, you knew this, and you never told me?"

"Gill, I'm sorry," Asha said, moving toward him to comfort him, but he leaned away from her, threw up his arms a bit as if fearing her touch.

"You knew how I felt about you, how much I loved you, the plans I had for us, and even though you knew this, knew you could never marry me, you allowed me to keep on thinking that we would be together?"

"Gill, I never meant to hurt you," Asha said, still trying to touch him, trying to ease his pain some.

"What did you think would happen? How did you think I would take this?"

"Gill, I'm so sorry."

"Get the fuck out!" Gill said, pointing toward the door.

"Gill, let's talk about this," Asha said, extending her arms out to him.

"I said, get the fuck out, Asha. I don't ever want to see your ass again. You hear me!" he said, yelling.

Asha gave him a long look, searching his eyes, trying to make sure that he really meant what he was saying. His eyes meant every word he had just screamed. Asha dropped her eyes, knowing there was nothing else she could say, nothing else she could do. She walked sadly toward the door.

"Asha," Gill called to her. Asha quickly spun around.

"Give me back my ring."

Asha twisted the ring off her finger, and started to walk it over to him.

"No. Just place it there on the table," Gill said. "I don't want you near me."

Asha did what she was told, then left.

31

After I told Asha to leave, I didn't know what to do with myself. Was it the right thing to do, I kept asking myself, threatening to turn back around, walk down those stairs, and tell her to forget it. "You can stay," I could say to her. "Just don't ever speak to me again. And when you have to pay the rent, just slip it under the door."

No, that wouldn't work. I'd done the right thing. We were supposed to be friends, best friends, and she'd lied to me. She lied to me for as long as we'd known each other, and considering that I had just been hurt by someone who was supposed to have loved me and lied to me, I had no tolerance for anyone else doing the same thing.

So again, there I was, back in my place, sitting on the sofa with nothing to do. I'd had my fiancée taken away from me, and had thrown away my best friend, and now I had no one.

I tried to think about someone whom I could call, someone I could talk to, someone I would want to talk to at a time like this, but no one came to mind. I thought some more, and then I remembered Lottie, Gary's wife. Yeah, it was wrong for me to think of her at a time like this, but I was sure we shared a little something special that time I spoke to her. Besides, she was beautiful, and Gary had spent time with my future wife, so it would only be fair for me to return the favor with his present one.

All of a sudden I was kind of excited. I jumped in the shower, threw on some clean clothes, nothing special, jeans and a pullover top, and headed out. It took me only about twenty minutes to get there, for I was driving a little faster than I normally did, excited to see her again. Why? I didn't know. It was foolish for me even to think the way I was thinking. This woman was married to the man who supposedly was going to marry my ex-fiancée, but still I was looking forward to seeing her. I just wanted to talk to her again.

There was a Jewel food store on the way to her house, and I pulled into the parking lot and cut off my engine. I did that for two reasons. One, because I was starving and needed an apple or something, since I'd been unable to eat anything in light of what happened earlier. And two, because it just dawned on me: How was I going to initiate seeing Lottie again? Was I crazy enough to think that I could just walk up to her door, ring the bell, and tell her something crazy like, "I was just thinking about you, and thought I'd drop by." She'd look at me like I was trying to rob the place, slam the door in my face, and call the police.

I walked into the grocery store, went over to the produce section, picked out a couple of apples, dropped them into a plastic bag, and headed over toward a small coffee café that was attached to the store. As I walked, I continued to think about how I could bump into her. I could just slowly circle around her block, passing in front of her house until I see her step out to go somewhere, to get the mail or something. Then I could stop my car, and yell out the window, smiling, "Hey, funny seeing you again as I was just passing by." Yeah, right, Jayson. Funny seeing her in front of her own house, after I drove around it a hundred times like a maniac psychopath. That wouldn't work at all.

I walked up to the counter, asked for a large vanilla coffee, and a bran muffin. I paid the girl, and moments later she gave me my order. I turned around looking for a place to sit, when I saw a woman sitting at a corner table, a trashy romance novel held up in front of her face.

I walked over to the table, stood in front of it for a second, and then said, "Lottie?"

The woman lowered the book, and it was indeed her. She took a second to recognize me, then that beautiful, gleaming smile appeared across her face.

"Jay Atkins, right?"

"Yeah, yeah, that's right," I said, happy that she remembered the phony name I had given her, because I sure as hell hadn't.

"What are you doing over here?" I asked her.

"Sometimes I come here for coffee, and to escape to a world of love, romance, and mystery," she said, sarcastically, holding the novel, with the big-breasted woman, and bare-chested man on the cover, up for me to see. "But I should be asking you. What are you doing over here?"

"Oh . . ." I said, not ready for that question. "Um, just coming back from my friend Max's house, and was hungry and thought I'd stop to get a muffin and some fruit." I held up my bag of apples for her to see.

"Well, you can join me if you'd like. Nothing's going to happen in this book that I don't already know will happen."

I happily pulled out the chair in front of her, and sat down. I set my bag of apples, my muffin, and my coffee on the table, and looked up at Lottie, smiling.

"Why are you smiling?" she asked me.

"You're smiling too," I said, a little bashful that I was smiling.

"Yeah, I know why I'm smiling, but I asked you why you're smiling."

"You tell me, then I'll tell you," I said.

"Well, promise you won't laugh or think I'm socially deprived or something, but I thought the little conversation we had was nice, and as you left my house, I was thinking that he would be a nice guy to have as a friend. But I knew I would never see you again, but now, here you are. That's why I'm smiling. I guess I'm glad to see you, Jay Atkins."

"You know, that's the exact same reason I'm smiling, Lottie Robinson."

"Get out of here," she said, waving a hand at me, blushing.

"No, I'm serious. It's weird, because I kind of feel like I already know you."

"Hey, me too. That *is* weird."

"Maybe we met in a previous life."

"Did you meet any African queens in your previous lives, because I've always been a queen," she said.

"I don't think so, but I think I'm meeting one now," and right after I said that, I wished I could've taken it back, because her smile disappeared from her face, and there was an awkward, silent moment. We

looked at each other, as if wondering just what to do with the comment I'd made, and then she burst out with an embarrassed grin,
lightly swatted my hand, and said, "Oh, you go on. You're just the big-
time, handsome, smooth flirter guy."

"*Au contraire,*" I said. "If you only knew how bad my luck is with
women."

"Yeah, I bet you tell them all that. But that stuff won't work on me,
because I'm married."

"Darn!" I said, joking. "You wouldn't mind if I practiced on you
though, would you? Telling you how beautiful you are, you know, stuff
like that?"

Lottie smiled slyly and said, "I really shouldn't. But since I never
get it at home, and it's just practice, go ahead and knock yourself
out."

Lottie and I sat at that table until it was time for her to go pick up
her kids from school. We had wonderful conversation for a little more
than two hours, and standing outside her Volvo station wagon, she
said, sadly, "It's a shame that we just met now that I'm moving soon.
You would've really been a good friend to have."

"I feel the same way about you."

"I'm glad," Lottie said, smiling kindly. "It's been a pleasure knowing
you, Jay Atkins."

"And you as well, Lottie Robinson," I said, extending a hand to her.
She looked down at it, as if to say, Don't you know women don't shake
or give dap, we hug, silly. She moved forward, threw her arms around
me, and gave me a tight hug. I hugged her back.

"Don't tell anybody this, or I'll deny it. But if I weren't married,
you'd be in serious trouble," she said, squeezing me tighter with the
remark.

I smiled, thinking that if I were going after what I truly deserved,
you'd be the one in serious trouble, but I just said, "You are so sweet for
saying that."

When I made it back to my place, I fumbled with the keys in my
pocket, trying to get them out in a hurry and get the front door open,
because the phone was ringing. I finally got it open, ran to the phone,
and snapped it up.

"Hello?"

There was no answer, only silence, and just when I was about to say something again, a voice said, "Hello, Jayson." It was Faith.

I didn't know what to say, didn't know why she was calling me, thought this was some sort of mistake, but I said, "Yeah. This is me."

"How have you been?"

"What kind of question is that?" I snapped.

"Look, Jayson. I'm just trying to make contact, all right. Don't bite my head off just—"

"Just because what? Just because I caught you screwing some guy days before we were supposed to get married," I said, angrily.

"Jayson, will you hold on a minute," Faith pleaded.

"What?" I was breathing hard, gripping the phone like it was Faith's neck. I wanted to squeeze it till it snapped, I was so mad.

"I've been thinking, and I called to apologize. I called to apologize for you having to have to see that."

"I see. You apologize for me seeing it, but not for doing it. That's just like you, Faith."

"I apologize for everything. I'm sorry that things had to work out the way they did."

"They didn't *have* to. We could've worked things out. I told you that."

"No, we couldn't have," Faith said.

"Why not? It's because of that man you were fucking, isn't it?"

"Jayson, no," Faith said, trying to sound sincere, but failing poorly.

"Then what happened to him?" I said, trying to calm down. "Are you still fu— . . . still seeing him?" I was giving her a chance to tell me the truth, to drop the entire game now that she had no reason to keep playing it.

"No, I'm not still seeing him. I told you that it was just to get back at you," she said, sounding so phony, and I thought, couldn't she hear how unbelievable she sounded. She must've thought I was a complete idiot not to hear through that lie. I wanted to tell her that I knew everything, that I'd found out from Karen, but something held me back. Then I thought about how she was about to get played herself, or at least it seemed that way. This guy Gary, whom Faith still expects to get to marry her, was moving away, and it looked as though he had no intention of informing Faith of that fact.

"So like I said, I was thinking about how everything went down, and I was feeling kinda bad, so I wanted to give you a call and apologize."

"Feeling kinda bad, hunh?" I said, mocking the way she said it. "And what, you expect me to accept this bullshit apology so you can feel kinda good again? It ain't gonna happen."

"See, I should've expected this shit from you. I'm trying to be nice, calling you up, trying to make peace with your ass, and here you go, making a big deal over it."

"Oh, I'm making a big deal over this? What should I do, Faith? Just accept your apology and get over it?"

"Yeah, that's exactly what you should do. Get the fuck over it, Jayson. It's over, it's done. There's nothing else that can be done about it. Yeah, you caught me fucking somebody, and it probably stung some, but now it's time to move on."

"Stung some," I said, chuckling pathetically. "That's the feeling you thought I experienced when I saw you. A little stinging? And now you're telling me it was no big deal, get on with my life?"

"That's right."

"It's really easy for you to say that, Faith. But what if it were the other way around? What if you had caught me fucking some woman. You could just get over it, and get on with your life, hunh? You could accept my lame-ass apology when I called to offer it to you and act like it was no big deal?"

"That's right, Jayson. I could do that, because I would know that if a man did that to me, at that point he had stopped loving me, and I would stop loving him. It would be that simple," she said, sounding very confident. "Now do you accept my apology or not?"

"I hope it's never you in that position, Faith."

"Do you accept the apology or not, I said?"

"Because you'll see that there's a little more involved than just a little stinging."

"Jayson, I'm offering this apology one last time then I'm hanging up. Do you accept it or not?"

I paused, thinking for a moment, then said, "If you only knew how I felt for . . ." but before I could finish, she had hung up. I was listening to the dial tone. I pulled the phone from my ear, gave it a hard look, then placed it back to my ear, not believing that she'd actually hung up on me. I slammed the phone down, understanding that she truly was calling not because she wanted to apologize but because she wanted to get relief from what little guilt she felt about getting caught.

I picked up the phone and thought about dialing her back, telling her about Gary, that he was out of here soon, that he had no intention of leaving his wife and family, and that she would be left out in the cold just like she had left me. Man, how good that would feel, I thought, as I dialed the first three numbers. But then I stopped. That would be a short-lived victory, and it would help her more than hurt her. It would be giving Faith a heads-up, instead of her looking up one day and finding the man she thought she was going to marry suddenly gone. Now that would sting a little, I smiled to myself, hanging up the phone. But that would mean that Gary would be getting away with using my woman for whatever pleasure he decided to use her for, then packing up and escaping. And there was the issue of his wife, Lottie, who I had to admit felt like a friend now. He would've gotten away with cheating on her, and that just wouldn't be right.

I considered telling Lottie everything that I knew about her dear husband, Gary, and my ex-fiancée Faith over coffee tomorrow, but then I stopped myself. I thought about everything Faith had just said to me, that arrogant-ass attitude she had, and then I thought about Gary's naked ass on that tape, screwing the hell out of her in front of my face, and then, amazingly, it came to me, and I knew exactly what was going to be done to settle everything among everyone. I grabbed my jacket, the keys off the counter, the tape of Faith and Gary, and left again.

32

It was ten o'clock, Asha had already seen two of her clients, and still there was no sign of Angie. Asha stood by her closed door, needing to go out into the lobby so she could restock her room, but afraid that she would bump into Big Les, who she knew was out there lurking, waiting.

Asha went to the phone, dialed Angie's cell phone number, but she didn't pick up. Angry, Asha hung up without leaving a message.

"Damn!" Asha said. She knew that any minute Les would be knocking on her door, and what would Asha do then? And just as she had imagined it, the knock came. It startled Asha, making her glance around the room, at the cabinets, under the table, as if she was searching for a place to hide.

She felt herself getting nervous. What would she do? What would she say when Les asked her what she was going to do? Would she actually be, as Les put it, "Her bitch for a day?" Hell no! But she didn't want it to come to her having to say it. She didn't want to face the repercussions of what she did coming to light in this place. There had to be some third option.

The knock came again, a little harder this time.

"All right, all right," Asha said, reluctantly going to the door. She breathed in, let it out, then pulled the door open.

"You look like you just seen a ghost, girl," Rhonda said, standing in front of Asha. "What's going on in there?"

"Oh, nothing," Asha said, relaxing. "What's up?"

"We're ordering from Ranaldi's for lunch. You want something?" Rhonda said, extending a menu to Asha.

"Naw, I'm good. I don't think I'll be able to eat a thing by lunchtime. But thanks."

Asha closed the door and walked back into the room, still thinking about what she was going to do, when the door quickly opened up behind her. Asha spun around to find Big Les there, closing the door gently, a sly smile on her face.

This was it, Asha thought, quickly trying to weigh all her options, decide which was truly the best route for her to take.

"I stopped by because I wanted to know what you gonna be wearing tonight. I want a visual, so I can start getting all worked up for you," Les said, walking up to Asha. Asha was taking steps backward, when she bumped into the massage table.

"You . . . you shouldn't be in here. I have a client changing," Asha lied.

"You ain't got no client changing. I looked at your book. You're clear until lunch. And guess what?" Les said, leaning in so close to Asha, that she could see the light shadow of a mustache growing above Les's lip. "So am I. So I was thinking that we could start our little party early." Les reached around, placed a hand in the small of Asha's back, and gently started to massage her there.

Asha didn't jump away from her, didn't scream, didn't spit in Les's face. She just stood there, trying with everything inside of her not to move, allowing Les's hand to do what it was going to do, and then after a moment, hoping Les would step away. Les pushed her body close to Asha's. Asha could feel Les's huge, heavy breasts push against her own chest, and could smell the big woman's slightly sour breath. She felt Les's fingers dip into the waist of her trousers, heading farther down.

Asha squirmed away from Les, pushed her back, and said, "What's your goddamn problem!"

Les looked shocked. "What you talking about? I'm just rolling with our agreement. Know what I'm sayin'?"

Yeah, Asha knew what Les was saying, but it didn't matter, because there was no way that she could go through with that. No fucking way.

Les would just have to go to the supervisor's office, say what she had to
say, and Asha would have to defend herself as best she could. It would
be her word against Les's.

"Well, we ain't got no agreement to roll with no more," Asha said,
pulling up the back of her pants.

"Really? You sure about this? Because you know, I ain't joking when
I say I'll go to Margee's office. I'll go, and I'll tell her about the little
party I caught you having back here, and your ass will be gone."

"At least I won't have to see your ugly face no more," Asha said,
defiantly.

Les nodded. "Cool then." She turned around, opened the door, and
walked out.

"Shit!" Asha said, under her breath. "Where the fuck are you,
Angie?" Asha stood there in her room another second, knowing if she
let Les go, this could very well be the last time she stood in that room.
She loved her job, and she loved working at Phillipe Cozi. There had
to be some way to stall Big Les a bit longer. She ran out of the room,
down the hall, stopping Les at the front desk.

"Les, Les, wait." Les stopped, but didn't turn around.

"Our agreement is still good," Asha said to the back of her head,
still trying to give Angie a little more time to fulfill the promise she
had made to Asha.

Les turned around, smiling. "Really?"

"Yes," Asha said, her head turned down.

"We can go back to your room, and you'll prove that to me?"

Asha nodded her head without looking up. "Yeah," she said, unsure
what she was going to do in the next second. But then, thank God, the
front door of the spa opened, and in walked Angie with three other
beautiful women, two of them black, one white.

They all walked right past Asha and Les without saying a word, not
even Angie. They stepped up to the front desk, and Angie said to Sue,
"Hi, we have an appointment to see Margee Simmons."

Asha looked gratefully at Angie and the other women like they
were saviors.

"What's your problem? C'mon," Les said, grabbing Asha by the
arm, trying to pull her toward the massage room. Asha yanked away.
"Sorry, Les. The agreement's off again."

"It's off again!" Les said, looking angry. "Oh, okay. Cool. You wanna play like that. Bet!" She turned to walk away from Asha, but then turned back, waving a finger. "And this time, don't come back talking about it's on again. This is it, so you might as well start packing your things." She walked up to Margee, an athletic, but overweight, middle-aged, blond woman who had come from her office to greet Angie and the other women.

"Margee, can I talk to you? It's very important," Les said, jumping in front of Angie.

"Leslie, it'll have to wait. Can't you see I have these ladies to speak to?" Margee said, ushering them toward her office.

"But, Margee . . ." Les said, walking up behind her.

Margee turned to Les. "After this appointment," she said, sternly, then walked away.

For the next half an hour, Asha sat in the break room, watching some ridiculous soap opera, unable to change the channel, because it was the only one with decent reception. Les sat across the room from her, sucking on a huge sour pickle, wrapped in a paper towel, taunting her. "As soon as Margee's finished in there, you're going to be finished out here. Know what I'm sayin'?"

"Whatever," Asha said, paying Les little attention, because she knew whatever Angie had planned, it would take care of this situation once and for all. "Why don't you just keep sucking on your pickle and shut up."

"That's cool. Act like it don't matter now. But let me see how cool you are in half an hour."

Asha got up and raised the volume on the television, when Sue stuck her head in the door.

"Leslie, Margee wants to see you."

Les looked over at Asha, a confident smile on her face. She wrapped the pickle back up in the paper towel and placed it in the fridge. "Don't you eat my pickle," Les warned.

"I'll try and fight the urge," Asha said, smugly.

When Les entered Margee's office, she saw Angie, two other younger attractive black women, and the one white woman with dark brown hair and matching eyes. They sat in chairs in front of Margee's desk, all of them with their legs crossed, looking at Les, as though Les had wronged them all in some way.

Margee sat behind her desk, her hands crossed on top of it, a solemn look on her face.

"Close the door, Leslie," Margee said. "Do you know why I asked you back here?"

"Yeah," Les said, standing in front of her desk, the four women sitting behind Les. "Because I said I had to talk to you."

"No, Leslie. These women have all accused you of harassing them while here at the spa, and they're urging me to take action."

"What are you talking about?" Les said, spinning around to get a look at the women who were trying to get her fired. "I didn't do anything to these women. I don't even know who they are." Then her eyes rested on Angie. She hadn't recognized her when she'd walked in because of the wrap she had on her head, and the dark sunglasses, but now she remembered. That was the woman she caught Asha about to go down on, and . . . hold it. Wait a minute, Les thought. And now she knew what was going on. This was Asha's defense against having to be her bitch for a day. Her and the woman with the shades were in this together.

"Hold it, Margee," Les blurted out, after putting the pieces together. "I'm being set up."

Margee looked at Les like the woman was overly paranoid. "By these women? Why would they want to do that?"

"I'm telling you, Margee. I'm being set up. I can explain," Les said, desperately.

"Well, you're going to have to if you plan on keeping this job."

Half an hour later, the soap was ending, and Asha was pissed, because it was actually starting to get good at that moment. She got up to turn the TV off when the door flew open, and Les walked in. She stood just in the doorway, staring menacingly at Asha, then walked right over to her. She stopped in front of her, only inches away, still staring, still not saying a word.

"So that's how you play?" Les finally said. "Because you got caught doing something you weren't supposed to, you took my job."

Wow, Asha thought. She knew Angie was going to take care of the situation, but she didn't think she could permanently take care of it. "You tried to take mine," Asha said back.

"I need this job. I have a kid at home."

Asha didn't say anything for a long moment. It had never occurred to her that Les could possibly be a mother. "I'm sure you'll find another job."

Les glared down at Asha like she was working hard to stop herself from grabbing her and twisting her into a pretzel. Les walked away, but before leaving the room, she turned and said, "You watch your back. You hear me, girl? Watch it hard." Then she left the room, leaving Asha with a huge smile on her face, chanting to herself, "the giant is dead, the giant is dead!"

The rest of the day had been a great one. Asha was able to walk freely about the spa like she used to, not worrying about Les making advances or undressing her with her eyes.

After work, when Asha stepped outside, the day was so beautiful and she was in such high spirits, that she decided she was going to walk. She took two steps in that direction, when she heard a car horn. Damn. Gill, she thought, but when she turned around, she saw that it was Angie. Asha quickly hopped into the passenger seat of the Benz, happily gave Angie a kiss, and they drove off.

"So tell me how it went down?" Asha said, sitting in her seat, excited. "How did you work all of that out?"

"Well," Angie said, leaning back in her seat, all the windows down, the sunroof of the car open. "A lot of my customers go down the street to Cozi, that's how I found out about it. I told a few of them, the ones I consider friends, that I needed a favor, that there was a woman who worked there who was harassing another one of my friends, and would they help me out? They agreed to do it, because they've all been harassed, be it by men at work, or women on the street, behaving like men. So I called your supervisor, told her me and three other women needed to talk to her about one of her employees who was harassing us sexually."

"And she believed you?"

"Yeah," Angie said, not seeming very proud of what she had done.

"Even though Les fought with everything she had. There were four of us, never seeming to have another connection to each other than the spa. Why would we have brought charges against that woman like that if they weren't true?"

"So Margee just fired her?" Asha asked, sitting on the edge of her seat.

"No. She told her that she could either resign and nothing more would be made of it, leaving her able to find a job somewhere else. Or have those complaints put in her personnel file, and next time she came up for evaluation, probably get let go anyway. If that happened, she'd have to deal with those complaints when she tried to find work anywhere else."

Asha threw herself around Angie, giving her a huge hug, and big kiss on the cheek.

"I'm free! I'm free! I thank you so much for this," she said, throwing her arms over her head, and stretching out in the passenger seat, a wide smile on her face. A second later, she turned to see a bothered expression on Angie's face.

"What's wrong?" Asha asked.

"Nothing. Just stuff on my mind."

"What stuff. Tell me."

Angie exhaled, sinking a bit lower into her seat. "After I get off work, I always pick up my son. I know I never told you I had a son," Angie said, glancing quickly at Asha, then back out the windshield in front of her. "But I do. Had him six years ago. The father's not in the picture. Anyway, I pick him up everyday from day care, and just as sure as the sun sets at night, Deric calls to make sure that I picked him up, and that we're both okay."

"What is your son's name?" Asha asked, softly.

"Kyle."

"And who is Deric?"

"He's the man I live with, the man Kyle thinks is his father." Angie glanced over at Asha, but Asha looked away from her at that moment.

"So what's going on with that?" Asha asked, sounding a bit jealous.

"He's a friend, someone who used to work near me, and needed a place to stay," Angie said, in a tone that suggested there was nothing to be concerned about. Angie brought the car to a stop at a red light and felt Asha's eyes on her.

"Do you love him?"

Angie turned to her and said sincerely, "That's not really important. He's a father figure to my son, and a respectable representation of what people think my life should be like. Okay?" Angie gave Asha a slight smile, which Asha tried to return but couldn't.

"Anyway, on the way home, Kyle wasn't his normally cheery self. When I got him home, it took me half an hour and eight cookies to get him to tell me that some bigger boy was picking on him. I did what I could to cheer him up, said what I knew about situations like this, which was nothing at all. Needless to say, he remained depressed for the rest of the evening. When Deric came in, I told him what was going on. He told me don't worry about it. Then he walked over to Kyle, said, 'Come here, Cowboy.' We call him Cowboy. He threw him on his shoulders and walked him upstairs. 'So, I hear some kid's been messin' with you, hunh?' I heard him say as they climbed the stairs. When they came down a little while later, Kyle was his happy self again.

"Mommy, look what Daddy showed me," Kyle said, and Deric threw up both his palms, and Kyle went to attacking them like a little Mike Tyson. They both looked so happy," Angie said, a smile on her face, still staring out the windshield.

"Deric, because he was able to help Kyle, and Kyle because he had Deric there to help him."

Asha sat up in her seat, and the content smile on Angie's face made her afraid to ask her question, but she did anyway. "Why are you telling me this?"

The smile fell from Angie's lips, and she turned toward Asha.

"Because I can't do this with you anymore, Asha. There are things that my son needs, that I can't always give him, and that another woman wouldn't be able to give him either. He needs a man in his life. He has one, and what kind of mother would I be to take that away from him?"

Asha couldn't believe what she was hearing. It had to be a dream, a nightmare of some sort, for her to lose her best friend, her fiancée, and the woman she had fallen in love with all in a matter of a few days. It just couldn't be.

"No," Asha said, shaking her head, then lowering her face into her hands. "No. You're the one who brought me into this. You're the one who made the move on me, convinced me to let go, and now you're telling me you can't do it. No. I can't hear this," Asha said, raising her voice.

"Asha, calm down," Angie said.

"I won't calm down! Do you know what I sacrificed for this, for you? Angie, I love you. Did you know that?"

Angie just looked at Asha, not speaking.

"Did you know that I love you, Angie? Yes, or no. Answer the question."

"Yeah. You told me you did."

"And what? That doesn't mean a damn thing to you?"

"Asha. It means something. I just have to put my son first. Deric is an important part of his life."

"Is Deric an important part of your life?" Asha asked.

"Yes. He is."

"Do you love him?"

"That's not what's important here."

"I see. So you're letting me go for a man you don't love, but who's important in your son's life," Asha said, wiping a tear away from her cheek that had fallen.

"That's right, because I love my son."

"And I'm sure he loves you too. But I wonder would he like to know that you stayed with someone you didn't love for his sake, when you could've been with someone you really did love."

"But he loves that man. Deric makes him happy," Angie said, fighting with her emotions.

"And is that the only thing that's important. Kyle would love anyone you love, don't you know that?" Asha said, taking one of Angie's hands in hers. "I know it seems right to have that man raising your son, but don't you think sooner or later he's going to realize that you aren't happy?"

"His happiness is worth the sacrifice," Angie said, looking away from Asha.

"Do you love me?"

Angie pulled off the road and stopped the car, still averting her eyes, not answering.

"Angie, just tell me. Do you love me?"

Angie slowly turned her face to Asha. There were tears streaming down Asha's cheeks.

"Yeah. I think I do love you," Angie said, managing to keep her own tears from falling.

"And you still want to end this with me?"

It took a moment for Angie to answer, but she simply said, "Yes."

More tears seemed to roll from Asha's eyes. With both her hands, she brought Angie's hand up to her lips and kissed it. "Then I should be going," Asha said, only able to look into Angie's eyes for a second, before pushing her way out the car, and walking away. Angie watched her go, and finally a single tear fell.

33

Yesterday evening, after leaving my place, I drove back over toward Gary's house. I parked two houses down, sitting there in my car, the music low, the windows rolled down, because it was a particularly warm evening. It was half past six, and I didn't know if he had already come home from work or not, but I was hoping that he hadn't. Lottie already knew my face, so I had to catch him before he got to the front door.

I was sitting out in my car for almost an hour, ready to start the engine and drive off, when I saw their front door open. I ducked some behind the steering wheel, trying not to be seen, but slowly raised my head, when I saw two boys, somewhere between the ages of eight and twelve bound out the door, onto the front lawn, tossing a football back and forth.

They threw the ball four or five times, when the door opened again, and this time it was their father who came out. He was still wearing his white-collared shirt, obviously from work, but he had taken off the tie, unbuttoned it some, and had thrown on a pair of old jeans, the shirt halfway tucked in.

"Throw me the ball," he said, running out across the neighbor's lawn. The older son threw him the ball. He caught it and walked back toward them smiling. He rubbed both his sons on the head, and told them to run out for a pass.

They ran as fast as they could, jostling for position, smiling and laughing back at their dad. What a picture perfect scene this would've been, I thought, if their father wasn't into ruining the lives of other people by fucking the women they loved.

I watched that man play loving father and devoted husband, watched him laughing, wrestling with his sons, watched him as he looked into their faces with pride, and how I hated him at that moment.

He had such a wonderful life, or so it looked to me, but this wasn't enough for him. He had to have more. And what he'd decided to take was mine. He was wrong about that, and he had to pay, I thought, as I stepped out of my car and started to walk toward the house.

Gary had overthrown the ball to his younger son, it dropped ten or so feet in front of him, rolled some, and landed at my feet. I bent down and picked it up, and held it till his son came to take it from me. When he grabbed for it, I wouldn't let it go, and said, "What do you say?" in an overly nice, sing-songy voice.

"May I have my ball, please?" the boy said.

"That's right. Yes, you may," I said, handing him the ball.

"Thank you, mister," the boy said. I noticed he was missing his two front teeth.

"You're very welcome," I smiled and rubbed him on the head like his father had done. When I looked up, I noticed there was something near worry on his father's face.

I raised my hand to wave at Gary, not knowing if he remembered just who I was or not. But then the expression changed from slight worry, to extreme surprise, and I knew he recognized me.

"Rodger," he cried for the boy. "Come here, son."

"See you, mister," the boy said, looking up at me.

"Okay. Run along."

When Rodger reached Gary, his father grabbed him by both his shoulders and quickly examined him, as if I had somehow secretly molested the child in six seconds, right there in front of him.

Gary started walking toward me, and I started toward him.

"Nice boys you have," I said.

"What do you want?" he said with a serious tone that sounded like he was ready to lay down his life in defense of his family.

"And nice house, too." I looked it over, as though I had never seen it. "How did you find out where I live?"

"Calm down, Gary. You sound pretty riled. I don't know why you should be so upset. You have a beautiful home, a wonderful family."

"You leave my family out of this," he warned.

"All that, and my fiancée to boot. You should be the happiest man in the world."

"What do you want?" he asked again.

"Dad, you still playing?" the older son called, tossing the ball up and down in his hand; Rodger, his younger brother, standing near him, wanted to know the answer to this question as well.

"You guys go ahead. Dad's talking, he'll back in a few minutes."

"Uh, no he won't," I said.

"What did you say?" Gary said, turning back toward me.

"You asked me what I wanted. I want you to come with me."

"You know what?" Gary said. "You need to get off my property."

"Or what?" I said. "You'll call the police?"

"Or I'll throw you off."

"I'd like to see you try that," I said, looking at Gary, as if comparing his smaller, less muscled body to mine.

It seemed he was doing the same thing, because then he said, "Fine. Stay out here as long as you want. I don't have to stay out here with you. "Boys," Gary called, turning to walk away.

"No, you don't have to stay out here with me," I said, walking behind Gary. "But you have to go with me, or I'll go in that house and tell your wife everything I know about you and my ex-fiancée Faith, and the years you all have been dating, even about the time you got her pregnant and convinced her to have an abortion."

At that remark, Gary spun around, looking at me as though I had spoken of something that never should've been heard of again while he was alive.

"I'm not going to hurt you or anything like that, Gary. I just want you to come with me. It's that, or the consequences. You choose."

By that time, his boys were standing in front of him with their ball, like two eager dogs waiting for their owner to throw their favorite stick.

"You two go on in and tell Mommy that I went to the store with a friend from work, okay?"

"Okay," the older boy said, looking suspicious, while the younger boy just smiled innocently at me.

"Go on now," Gary said, watching them as they went in the house.

"That was a very smart decision," I told Gary as we walked toward my car.

When I turned the car off, we were in the parking lot of a Circuit City electronics store.

"What are we doing here? You didn't take me away from my family to go shopping, I know," he said.

"Just get out," I said, pulling the key from the ignition and getting out of the car myself.

Once inside the store, I walked over toward the televisions and VCRs. They were all lined up on three shelves, the smaller models on the top shelf, the larger ones, the thirty-two- and forty-seven-inchers, on the bottom. This wouldn't do, I told myself, and walked away from that section, heading down an aisle where the portable TVs sat. Gary followed dumbly behind me, questioning me with each step I took, but I just ignored him.

After finding the set I was looking for, a small one, down a vacant aisle, with a VCR attached to it, I turned it on, the volume low, and stood in front of it.

"So you brought me out here to get my opinion on a fucking TV?" he said, looking like he wanted to beat me, if he could.

"No, I brought you out here to tell you what I want you to do for me."

"I'm not doing anything for you."

"Oh, but you are!" I said, smiling kindly in his face. "You are, because you have no choice. You don't do it, and your wife will know everything. Now, are you ready to hear what's going to happen?"

"Go ahead," Gary grunted.

"You're still seeing Faith, aren't you?"

Gary didn't answer, looking as though he was trying to decide the best way to answer the question.

"Are you still seeing her or not?"

"Yeah."

"And I assume you have a key to her house."

"Yeah."

"Good," I said. "What's going to happen will be a kind of reenactment of what already happened."

"What are you talking about now?"

"You know how I caught you with Faith in that hotel room. You're going to get caught again, but this time not by me, but by Faith; and not with Faith but an escort I will arrange and you will pay for; and not in a hotel room, but in Faith's house."

"Fuck that. You've lost your damn mind. I'm not doing it."

"Yes, you will, or I'll tell."

"You go ahead and tell," Gary said, his finger in my face. "It's your word against mine, and who do you think my wife will believe? Her husband, or some damn psycho like you. Fuck you," and he turned to walk away.

"Um, Gary," I said, very coolly, pulling the videotape out of my inside jacket pocket. "I think there's something here that might convince you."

"Nothing will convince me to do what you're talking about," he said, stopping.

"Take a look anyway," I said, making sure there wasn't anyone in the aisle we were in, then sliding the videotape into the player. The screen went black.

"Keep watching, Gary. You're going to like this."

A second later, I heard him gasp when he saw the images of Faith on her knees giving him head, himself whining in ecstasy.

"Turn it off," Gary said, his face flushed. "Stop it."

"What do mean, stop it? You didn't want it to stop when you were actually getting it done to you."

"Turn it off!" he said, yelling.

I punched the Stop button, then the Eject. I took out the tape and slid it back into my jacket.

"Now, you'll do what I want?" I asked, confident that he would.

"I still can't," Gary said, looking defeated.

"And why not?"

"I fuck some freak in Faith's house, betray her like that, she's going to go right to my wife to get back at me, so I lose either way. I don't do what you want, you go to my wife. I do what you want, Faith goes to my wife. I'm fucked both ways. But I'd rather be fucked and still have Faith in my corner, than to have you."

"No, Gary. You can still do this."

"I told you I can't."

"I know you're sending your family down to D.C. in a few days, and I know you're going down there after them for a new job."

Gary looked at me astonished. "How did you—"

"That doesn't matter. You get busy with this woman in Faith's house after your family is gone, then you'll have nothing to worry about. You can't beat it, Gary. You'll get away with fucking Faith for two years, and still have your family thinking you're a faithful man. Hell, you would've even gotten a shot of some professional pussy. That should make you very happy, Gary. Because isn't that what you're all about anyway? Fucking around on your wife as much as you can."

Gary flinched at that remark, his hands tightening into fists at his side.

"Go ahead, Gary. Take a swing at me," I urged him. "So I can do to you what should've been done in that hotel room when I found you with Faith. Take a swing, please."

He backed off.

"There's something else I want to ask you before I take you back home. Faith still thinks you're getting a divorce, still thinks the two of you are getting married, doesn't she?"

Gary looked at me through evil, squinted eyes, not answering.

"Doesn't she?"

"Yeah, so what?"

"You didn't even tell her that you'd be leaving. You're just going to up and disappear on her. Do you know how much that's going to hurt her?"

Gary turned his face up to me, the angry scowl still there, and said, "Why should I care? She doesn't mean anything to me."

I wanted to put my fist through that man's head at that moment. I guess to defend Faith's honor. But then I realized, why would I do that when I don't mean anything to her.

34

Everyone and everything were gone, Asha thought as she sat behind the wheel of a rented Oldsmobile Alero heading east toward Indianapolis.

After receiving the news from Angie, Asha wandered about downtown, trying to stop herself from crying, but unable to. She didn't know if she was crying more because of Angie or Jayson, or if she was crying because she'd lost them both. She couldn't run to Gill either, to hide behind him again and try to reclaim her false identity.

Asha finally got a cab home and after failing at trying to relax in front of the TV and forget all about the past few days, she decided to get up and start packing. She wasn't able to make herself at home there anyway anymore, because it no longer felt like her home. Jayson wanted her gone, and now she had to find a new place.

Asha pulled armloads of clothes out of the closet still on the hangers, and dropped them across the bed. She dug out a dozen boxes of shoes, stacked them just outside the closet door, and all the while she was doing this, she kept telling herself not to think about Angie, not to think about Jayson.

Asha pulled purses, jackets, and sweaters out of the closet as well, placing them all on the bed. She stepped back, her hands on her hips and looked around her at the disarray her room—her life—was in. She couldn't believe it. If she had only maintained that she was straight. If she had only denied Angie the right to even speak to her after she'd made that initial pass at her, none of this would be happening. Jayson and Asha would still be friends. She wouldn't have been thrown out of her place, she would've voluntarily left, because she would've been moving into the house that Gill had bought her.

How she wanted to take it all back. But she couldn't. The tears started to fall again, Asha crumpling to the carpet, sitting there cross-legged, her face buried in her hands. She needed to talk to someone, be with someone desperately, and if she didn't think Jayson would slam the door in her face upon seeing the first glimpse of her, she would've run up there looking for him to comfort her. But there was no one. She raised her head, smeared the tears from her cheeks with the heels of her hands, and reached for a shirt off the bed. She shook it out, holding it out in front of her by the shoulders, then folded it neatly. She stood up, searched the bed for a pair of jeans, folded them, then two more pair, a few T-shirts, and a couple of nightgowns, and folded them all, tucking them into a duffel bag she grabbed from out of the closet.

Asha had been on the road for three hours now, and she was only three turns from her mother's house. She didn't know why it took losing everyone for her to think about telling her own mother her problems, but she hadn't seen her in months, and she knew her mother would understand. That is, she'd understand the part about Asha being upset by losing her best friend, and her fiancé. Asha would never tell her about the fact that she was a lesbian. Her mother was older, and Asian, born and raised in Japan, and still took issue with the philosophy Americans had regarding relationships—the freedom, and the willingness they had to act disrespectfully to each other.

Her mother had been totally submissive to Asha's father, a tall Native American. She never questioned any of his decisions, never talked back to him, and never disrespected him, publicly or otherwise. Her place was to help her husband be the best man he could be. To love him and care for him in whatever fashion he needed caring for. That was the place of all women in her mind, to be forever at their man's side.

Asha could see the expression on her mother's face if she were to tell her the only person she wanted to love and care for was a woman. Asha smiled to herself, pulling into her mother's driveway.

The house looked the same as it always had, and everything was still neat and tidy. The only difference was, instead of Asha's father doing the lawn and landscaping work around the house, Asha's mother now did it.

After Asha's father had died ten years ago, her mother went into a tailspin of depression. She normally woke up early, but after his death, she wouldn't crawl out of her dark room until some time in the early evening. She barely said anything more than good morning and good night to Asha. Asha remembered walking up to her mother's bedroom door, about to knock, but thinking twice. She placed her ear to it. She heard her mother in there sobbing, trying to muffle the loud sounds in a pillow. Asha had tried to open the door, but it was locked. She stood there another moment, thinking of knocking again, but knew if her mother locked the door, she didn't want to be bothered.

A week later, exactly seven days after her father was buried, Asha's mother called Asha down to the kitchen. The kitchen clock read 7 A.M. when Asha finally staggered into the room. A full breakfast had been cooked and was waiting for her. Her mother, looking healthy and bright-eyed, stood at the counter stirring up a pitcher of orange juice. After that breakfast, Asha had to ask her mother, "What happened? Why are you better now?"

Her mother reached across the table and took her daughter's hand.

"Asha, I loved your father. Loved him first day he speak to me. We had so much fun, every day like a fairy tale, until one day he gone. I had to grieve, Asha. Get all pain and hurt out now. To carry it with me for rest of my life, like casting huge shadow on his memory. So I took week, and let hurt do what it would to me. Now it's time is over. It's time to be happy self again. Your father would want it this way," she said, smiling at Asha.

Now standing outside her mother's house, Asha rang the doorbell, and realized this may have been the reason she'd packed up her things and come out here. She had two weeks to move, but figured it would only take her one. Like her mother had done when her father died, Asha would take a week to grieve over all the bad things that had just happened to her. She would get all the pain and all the hurt out now, accept who she was, the life she would live, and then get back to being herself again.

When Asha's mother opened the door, Asha was smiling, or at least the closest she had come to smiling in quite a while.

"Asha!" her mother said excitedly, stepping outside the door, throwing her arms around her daughter. "Why didn't you call? Tell me you coming?"

Asha didn't answer, pulling back from the embrace to get a look at her mother. She looked the same, physically fit, beautiful tan complexion, half the wrinkles of the average fifty-seven-year-old, and just enough gray in her straight black hair for her to be considered wise, but not old. Asha couldn't remember a time when she was more happy to see her mother.

"I didn't call because I wanted to surprise you, Ma."

"Well, yes. It's big surprise. Big, big surprise," her mother said, opening the door, bidding Asha in.

"You still got my bedroom upstairs, right, Ma?" Asha said, carrying her bag into the house.

"No. Turn into exercise room. But can put pillow and blanket on treadmill. Make very comfortable for you."

"Maaaa," Asha whined.

"Just joking."

35

Gary didn't know just how the hell he had gotten into the situation he was in. Faith was just a beautiful woman he saw at the perfume counter at Bloomingdale's one day trying on testers. She caught his eye immediately, and even though he was only there to buy a couple of pairs of boxers, which he had already purchased, he couldn't just walk by without saying a word.

Gary walked up to the counter, looking down at the women's perfume, at the same time feeling the woman next to him take notice of him being there. She turned away as if she thought nothing of him, but Gary knew that's how all women would've responded. It said nothing about how she felt about him.

"Which one are you trying?" Gary asked, still looking through the glass.

The woman looked around, as if she had to make sure the question was directed to her, then said, "Oh, um, Chanel Allure."

"That's a good one, hunh?" Gary said. "I need to know, because I want to buy something nice for this very special woman." Gary noticed that the woman in front of him now seemed to relax and smile a little.

"Oh yeah, it's my favorite. She'll like it a lot."

"Good."

The saleswoman in the white coat came back to the counter. "Have you been helped, sir?" she asked Gary.

"No, but I'll take the large bottle of Chanel Allure."

"Good. Let me get that for you," the woman said, taking a box from the beneath the counter. "Have you decided yet, miss?"

"Oh no, not yet," Faith said, smiling. "You can take care of the gentleman first."

The saleswoman took Gary's credit card and asked if he would like the perfume gift wrapped.

"Yes, please," he responded. He knew this would give him more time to speak to the beautiful woman with the gorgeous smile, and what he believed to be an equally gorgeous body pressing against the large sweater and loose pants she was wearing.

"Faith," she said, after Gary had asked her what her name was. He extended his hand, and she placed such a soft, smooth hand into his, that he knew one day he wanted to feel that hand on his bare body.

"Such a beautiful name, for such a beautiful woman," and yeah, he knew it was also such a corny line, but it always worked, just like it was working that very moment. Faith blushed, lowering her head to try and hide her wide smile.

"So here you are, sir," the saleswoman said, ready to slide the brightly wrapped box of perfume with the huge bow on top into a shopping bag.

"I won't need the bag, but thank you," Gary said, taking the box.

"Well, whoever the lucky woman is, she'll like that," Faith said.

"I'm glad to hear that," Gary said, presenting the box to Faith. "Because the lucky woman is you."

And that was the first step that led him on the path to here. Yeah, he had a wife whom he truly loved, even though things were rocky sometimes, and two sons whom he would kill for, but this, he thought, would just be a little tryst on the side, something to keep the spice in his marriage.

He never knew Faith would want to get married, and the only reason that Gary kept telling her that he would was because that ass had gotten so good to him that he didn't want to give it up. He knew it would all end if he told her that he would never leave his family, which he knew he never would. He and Lottie would get into it, and he would

leave temporarily just to hurt her some, make her feel bad, make her feel
he could live without her if he had to, when he knew he never could.
Faith provided a place for him to stay for a little while, but to live with
her for the rest of his life—he didn't think that was possible.

Faith had never really meant much more to Gary than just some
really good sex, so doing what this psycho Jayson had asked him to
wasn't that big a deal to him. Gary could almost understand why this
Jayson guy wanted it to go down this way, considering the look on his
face when he walked into that hotel room.

Gary hadn't even known Jayson was there. He just kept thumping
away at Faith, and he had to admit that that had to be the best nut he
had ever busted. When he finally did see Jayson, the boy looked
crazed, and Gary thought he was a dead man. But surprisingly, Jayson
did nothing, said a few words, and walked sadly out the room. But his
anger had to come out some way. All men have to get some sort of
revenge if they find their woman with another man, and Gary knew
this was Jayson's.

"It'll be five hundred dollars," Jayson said over the phone to Gary.

"Five hundred dollars!" Gary gasped, speaking as low as he could in
his home study, so his wife or kids wouldn't hear him.

"Judging by Faith, I knew you were into fucking beautiful women,
and I wanted someone so fine that when Faith saw her naked,
stretched out all over her sofa, getting boned by you, even she would
be jealous. Call them back, give them your credit card number. All
right?"

Gary didn't speak, but what he should've said that very moment
was fuck it, he thought.

"All right?" Jayson asked again.

"Yeah. Yeah. All right."

If he could've gotten his family out of the city by tomorrow, the
next day at the very latest, he wouldn't have gone through with this.
But something led Gary to believe, that since this Jayson guy knew
about him leaving in the first place, knew what city he was going to,
even knew where he'd be working, he would know how to get that
damn videotape to his wife, and that he could not allow. His children
meant everything to him, and he wouldn't lose them over a little sex
he had gotten.

It would go down in three days, Jayson told him.

"And when she walks in, when you get caught, you'll say nothing to her about my involvement. I had nothing to do with this. I told the woman everything, and how everything is supposed to go down, so you don't have to worry about her opening her mouth. Got that?"

"Yeah," Gary grunted.

"Now you call Faith and tell her that you'll have a surprise for her when she comes home on Wednesday," Jayson said, during that last phone call. "She's crazy enough to think it'll be that divorce from your wife you never had any intention of ever getting or an engagement ring. She'll come home happy, anticipating some life-altering surprise, and that's just what she'll get."

Gary heard the excitement in Jayson's voice as he spoke about the plan. "You're sick, you know that?" Gary said.

"I'm sick? I'm sick?" Jayson said. "I'm not the one who's cheating on his wife, has been for two years, lying to some woman, telling her that one day you'd marry her. I'm not the one knowing that there was another man with intentions of making that same woman his wife, but continuing to fuck her. You ruined my life with Faith, my plans to make her my wife, when you knew you'd be leaving town anyway. And you're calling me sick."

"Yeah. I don't love Faith, never have. But you're doing this twisted shit to her, and you still love her, don't you?" There was silence. Truthfully, Gary didn't care if Jayson did or didn't. He was just trying to find a way to make this weirdo call the whole thing off.

"Go ahead, you sick motherfucker. You still love her, and still you want to hurt her like this."

There was another long moment of silence. "Just be at Faith's at five sharp on Wednesday ready to fuck," Jayson said, and then hung up the phone.

36

I didn't know anymore. Was I doing the right thing? That son of a bitch, Gary, called me sick. But who in the hell said I still loved Faith? Wouldn't I have been some kind of fool to still have feelings for her after she did what she did to me? The mere thought of her, the mention of her name, should have driven me into a killing frenzy, but it didn't. When I thought of her, for some reason, I still thought of all the good things in our relationship.

Now it was Tuesday afternoon, and as I pulled my car in front of my apartment, I kept asking myself, why am I going through with this tomorrow? Because she needed to suffer as I had was the answer. Even if I did still love her, she needed to experience what it felt like to walk in and see the person she loved, whom she thought she was going to spend the rest of her life with, getting his brains screwed out and loving it.

I shut the car door and walked up the stairs to the building. I was steadily convincing myself that I was indeed making the right decision here, but I still wanted confirmation.

I opened the outer door of the building and walked inside. I stopped in the hallway outside Asha's door, telling myself that I was going to check my mail, even though I knew the mail had not come yet. I was just standing there, thinking about my old friend, wishing that I could talk to her now, and regretting how I had spoken to her last. It'd been four days now, and this had been the longest time we'd gone without saying two words to each other.

I was questioning myself again, but this time about whether or not I was right to kick her out of my building. Dammit, I don't know, I thought, walking very close to her door, trying to listen to hear if she was in there. She had lied to me, lied to me for all those years about who she was, and obviously about what I meant to her. I had loved her, and now I wondered did she ever feel the same about me, could she have? Did her sexual orientation stop her from loving a man the way she claimed to have loved me then? I didn't know.

What I did know was that I missed her. I missed her like crazy, and all the times I walked down the stairs thinking that I would see her, I hadn't. All the times I looked out my window, thinking I would spot her walking across the lawn, either toward the house or away from it, and then race downstairs, and pretend to bump into her, it never happened. Hell, we lived in the same building, and all the times in the past after a disagreement when she was the last person I wanted to see, she was popping up all over the place.

I raised my fist, prepared to knock on the door, telling myself that I had to be the big one here, since she obviously wasn't going to come upstairs to try to fix things. But then, just before my knuckles hit the door, I stopped myself. Hold it. She was the one who lied to me, so why was I down here trying to call a truce. Sure, she found me rummaging through her things, and yes, I was pretty harsh with her, but if she really wanted to stay, she would've come up and spoken to me. That's what has to happen, I thought, stepping away from the door. If she wants us to continue as friends, as neighbors, then she'll just have to come to me. I didn't think I was asking too much in light of the fact that her offense was far worse than mine.

Four hours later, after sitting on my sofa, allowing the television to watch me, I pulled a small business card out of my shirt pocket and set it on the coffee table in front of me.

The tiny red print on the card said, Discreet Escorts. I took the phone off the end table, leaned forward, and punched the number on the card into the phone. It rang only two times, then, "Hello, Discreet. This is Ginger, how may I help you?"

"I made an appointment tomorrow with Carmen . . ." I said, pausing, thinking of two things I could've said next. My conscience was telling me to say, "And I want to cancel it." It was telling me to say, "I want to cancel it, because for some insane reason, I still love this woman I'm about to set up. I still love her, and as much as I want to know that she has suffered like I have, I can't bear the thought of her feeling the slightest bit of pain." My mind was saying all that to me, when I was interrupted by Ginger.

"I'm sorry, sir. You said you made an appointment with Carmen, and . . ."

And what, Jayson? What? I asked myself, forcing myself to make a decision.

"And I just wanted to confirm. Just making sure we're still on for tomorrow," I said, feeling the slightest bit of sadness and remorse.

"Yes, sir. Carmen, tomorrow at five at . . ." and she rattled off Faith's address, and some other info that I really wasn't even listening to. I hung up the phone before she was even finished with her pleasant farewell and appreciation for calling Discreet.

It was the right thing, I kept trying to tell myself, sinking into the sofa. If for no other reason, this would let Faith know that Gary definitely wasn't the man for her. I kinda felt good about that. I just hoped tomorrow evening, after this was all over, there would be something else I could feel good about. Because right now, I mostly felt like shit.

37

Faith looked up at the clock in her office. It read 4:45 P.M. She was so anxious to get out of there that she didn't know what to do with herself. Last night, Gary had called her from his cell phone.

"So what time am I seeing you tonight?" Faith asked.

"Um, won't be able to make it tonight, baby."

It was probably some nonsense with his family, Faith thought, so she didn't even bother to ask why, because if he told her that one more time, she was gonna just bust.

"When will you be able to make it? For good, Gary."

"What are you talking about?"

"You know exactly what I'm talking about. You know how long I've been waiting for you, and it's always next month, or next week, even though you said, this time we'd—"

"Faith, Faith, hold it, baby," Gary said, trying to calm her down. "I can't see you tonight, but tomorrow I'll be there at your place, waiting for you to get home with a big surprise for you. How does that sound?"

"Oh, baby!" Faith said, sure she knew what that surprise was. She got up from her couch, wanting to jump up and down across the living room floor, but she'd save that for when she got off the phone, so her future husband wouldn't think she was totally nuts. "I can't wait to see you tomorrow!"

"Same here, baby," Gary returned coolly.

"I love you so much, Gary."

It took Gary a moment to reply, but then he said, "Yeah, me too." Faith found it odd, because when he said those three words, he sounded kind of down, and not too sincere. She didn't know exactly what it was, but something seemed to be bothering him at that moment. That thought only held Faith's attention for another second as she hung up the phone. Maybe there were really problems at home, but she wouldn't let that get to her, because her man had finally bought her a ring, and was going to spring it on her tomorrow.

Faith jumped around the room as she told herself she would, screaming, "Yes! Yes! Finally!" After thirty seconds of this, she stopped, her chest heaving, her legs a little weak. She flopped back onto the sofa, smiling widely, and extended her left arm in front of her, spreading out the fingers on that hand, and eyeing the ring finger, the ring Jayson had given her.

"Don't worry, little one," she said, speaking to that finger. "You'll be wearing the right ring from the right man come tomorrow." She took a closer look at the rest of the fingers, and told herself, even though she had gotten a manicure only a few days ago, she needed to get another, so the ring would look just right.

She threw her head back into the cushions of the couch, grabbed the one next to her, put it over her face as she writhed about, screaming joyfully into the pillow. After a while of that, she let the pillow fall from her face, the smile no longer there, but a deep, reflective look.

This is really gonna happen, she thought. I'm really going to be Mrs. Faith Robinson. She thought about all the time she had had to wait, all she had had to endure, the nights when after she and Gary had made love, she knew he was going back to be with his wife and his children. All the times she was making love to him, when she was pleasuring him, and he was moaning her name, Faith had to ask herself, might he be thinking about his wife at that moment?

She realized now that after Jayson had found out about Gary, he probably asked himself the same question about Faith. When he made love to her, was she really thinking about Gary? The answer to that was no. Jayson definitely did enough for her sexually that she didn't have to think about anything else. She thought about that, and couldn't stop herself again from thinking about how badly she had really treated Jayson. Nope, I'm not gonna do that, she told herself, kicking the thought out of her mind.

"Not gonna let that ruin this moment."

For the rest of the night she didn't think about Jayson anymore, although it was an effort. But the next evening, sitting there in her office, still ten minutes left on her clock till five, she couldn't keep her behavior toward him out of her mind.

She thought about him, and this time didn't try to rid herself of the thought, but allowed it to enter her mind. They had shared some good times together, she had to admit. She leaned back in her executive chair some, allowing one of the memories to come to mind. Then all of a sudden, she leaned forward, and started going quickly through her desk drawers. After digging into the final bottom drawer, she pulled out a small, wooden frame with a snapshot inside. It was of Faith and Jayson, on the lakefront, near Oak Street Beach.

It had been a beautiful warm night, and they were walking hand in hand, the tall buildings of downtown to their left, the calm, dark water of Lake Michigan to their right. It was well past 11 P.M. and they had been walking like that for at least an hour. They hadn't said a word the entire time, just enjoyed the silence of each other's company and the sounds of the city at night.

An old man with baggy, tattered clothes, and a long, dirty beard walked toward them carrying an old Polaroid camera.

"Take a picture of the sweethearts?" he asked, stepping in Faith's and Jayson's path.

Faith had looked up at Jayson and smiled. "Want to?"

"Sure," Jayson said, digging into his pocket. "How much?"

"Ten dollars," the old man said, preparing his camera for an exposure.

"Let's make it five this time. Okay?" Jayson said, handing him the five-dollar bill.

The man gladly took it, stuffed it into his pocket, then raised the camera up to his face.

Faith and Jayson stood there in front of it, still holding hands.

"Closer, c'mon," the man said from behind the camera. "You do love each other, don't you? Hug, kiss. Do something."

They both laughed, embarrassed, then moved closer to each other, face-to-face, placing their smiling lips upon each other in a kiss. Faith saw the quick, bright flash of light out the corner of her eye, heard the old man say to them, "Okay, that's gonna be a good one," but Jayson didn't stop kissing her, and she didn't want him to stop. She wrapped her arms around his waist, pulling him in closer, kissing him harder, and it was perfect. They had spent the entire day doing nothing in particular, just being around each other, but it was wonderful. And it all ended with this. This hug, this kiss, and at that moment, that very moment, Faith did know she loved Jayson. For whatever that was worth, she loved him. And there was a feeling of happiness inside her as they continued to kiss, but there were also underlying feelings of sadness. She knew one day Gary would do what he was supposed to. She knew one day she'd have to break Jayson's heart, and this would all be over, but as he gently pulled away from her, smiling in her face, she just smiled back, and told herself just to think about that one moment she was living in, and nothing else.

So she did really love him. Really, really love him, Faith said to herself, still sitting in her chair, staring at the snapshot. But she had always known that she just had to keep her feelings under control. It was hard though, seeing the man every day, spending at least three nights a week with him, and pretending that he was the only man in her life. And although her intentions were to always be with Gary, she saw Jayson more. Of the two relationships, it was more of a real one, so after a while, it was only natural for her to develop those feelings. There were even times during the relationship that Faith told herself, that if there was no Gary in the picture, she would've stayed with Jayson. No question about it.

But there was a Gary, and there is a Gary, Faith thought, still sitting in her chair, still looking at the snapshot of her and Jayson.

She had to do something. Faith set the framed picture on her desk and picked up her phone. He won't want to listen to me, won't want to hear this, but I have to tell him the truth, or at least some of it, she thought, dialing Jayson's phone number.

"Hello." Faith heard Jayson's voice, and it took her a minute to speak.

"Jayson, it's Faith."

"Faith. What . . . what are you doing calling me? What do you want?"

Faith noticed that he sounded very surprised to hear from her, but why shouldn't he?

"Jayson, I have some things to tell you. I haven't been totally honest with you. I've treated you really bad, and I want to let you know why, and try to apologize to you again, but this time the right way."

"Faith, why are you doing this?" Jayson said.

"What do you mean why am I doing this? Because I feel bad about how things ended between us. I thought about the times we had, and—"

"No, Faith. It's too late for apologies. You did what you did, and there's no just saying I'm sorry, and—"

"But, Jayson, I am. I know it doesn't sound sincere, considering how you found me, but—"

"No, it doesn't sound sincere," Jayson said, interrupting, refusing to listen to a word she had to say. "Why all of a sudden now? Why today of all days, this moment, do you want to call and try to set things straight?"

"I don't know, Jayson," Faith said, pausing, remembering as much as she could of their good times together. "I just realized that for all we had between us, I shouldn't have done you the way I did. So will you just let me tell you what I have to say?"

"No, Faith. You can't tell me anything. I don't want to hear a word from you."

"But, Jayson, just—"

"It's too late for that. Good-bye, Faith," he said, hanging up in her face.

Faith heard the click, then the dial tone. She pulled the phone from her ear, stared at it as though it could've been malfunctioning, then slowly hung it up. That was kind of strange, she thought, knowing that normally he would've at least heard her out before he hung up on her. Something seemed to be wrong with him, she thought, or maybe he was just tired of her continuing to pester him, trying to redeem herself for something there was no redemption for. Whatever it was, Faith had to understand that however sorry she was about everything, if he didn't want to hear it, it wouldn't get heard.

Faith took the snapshot of the two of them off the desk. It was something that she always kept in the drawer of her desk, only really taking it out and displaying it when she knew Jayson was coming to visit her. It was a prop, part of the play she was putting on. But on occasion, she'd take it out just to stare at it, and fondly remember that night like she was doing that very moment. But that all had ended now, even the memories, Faith thought, reaching behind her, and dropping the picture into the wastebasket.

She looked at the clock, and it was a few minutes after five. She shifted her attention back to thinking of Gary, to thinking about the surprise ring he had gotten her, was going to give her as soon as she got home.

Faith took her purse, got up from her desk, put on her jacket, shut off the lights, and walked out of the office, locking the door behind her. A moment later, she was unlocking the door, opening it, and turning on the light again. She walked over to the wastepaper basket, pulled the picture of her and Jayson out of the trash, as if she just made a simple mistake by tossing it there in the first place. She opened the drawer she had taken it from, put it back in, at the bottom, under papers and folders, then shut the lights off again, walked out of the office, and locked the door.

38

No, I can't hear that, I thought while Faith was trying to come clean to me on the phone a moment ago. Why was she telling me this now? Why was she trying to be honest the day that I was planning on getting revenge against her?

"What the fuck was that!" I said, aloud, pacing back and forth across my living room floor.

How was I supposed to react? What was I supposed to do? Was I expected to accept her apology, allow her to continue on with her life, guilt-free? Is that what she thought? Fuck no!

But how much of the truth was she going to tell me, I thought, halting my pacing, digging the fingers of both my hands into my scalp. Was she going to tell me everything, or was she going to just say enough to make her cheating on me seem justified? Probably the latter, but she did go as far as to call. For a second time. She was rid of me, and she had known that, but she called me anyway, even after still thinking that that clown Gary was going to marry her.

"Fuck!" I yelled as loud as I could, knowing that I couldn't go through with what I had planned. I had to abort this crap somehow, because although I still felt she deserved it, I could no longer do it to her. She showed remorse, and it sounded genuine, and there was no way I could knowingly hurt her after hearing that. Hell, I still loved her, right?

I raced over to the phone, punched redial, and waited for her to answer. After the third ring, her voice mail picked up. "Hi, this is Faith . . ."

I hung up the phone, looking at the clock. She had gone for the day. I picked up the phone and dialed her cell phone.

"C'mon, c'mon, Faith. Pick up the freakin' phone," I said. I wasn't going to tell her what was going on, what I had planned for her. I would've just come up with a diversion, an excuse for her not to go home just yet. All right. Meet me for coffee, and we can talk about it some more, I would've said. I would've kept her there as long as possible. Gary would've been fucking his little heart out over at her place, and when he and the escort were both finished, and tired of sitting around staring awkwardly at each other, they would've left, and everything would've been cool.

The cell phone continued to ring, but who was I kidding? I told Gary to give her the impression that he had her engagement ring. Why would she ever postpone receiving that from the man she loved and wanted to marry, to have coffee with the man she dumped?

"I'm sorry I can't take your call right now . . ."

"Shit!" I said, hanging up on Faith's cell phone. "Fine time to have your cell off, Faith," I said, grabbing for my keys and going for the door. I had to get to her place before she did. She could've only been gone a few minutes, and even though I was farther away from her house than she was, if I really pushed it, I could beat her. I had to.

I drove the car like a madman, speeding down residential side streets to avoid heavy traffic on the main avenues. I blew through two stop signs, almost ran over a soccer ball that some kids kicked in the path of my car, came close to hitting a dog, and would've gotten a ticket for running another stop sign if I hadn't seen the police car parked down the street. After all that, I headed for the main street that I knew would be fairly clear and take me to Faith's house. I kept my eye on the clock as I forced the gas pedal as far down as I thought I could get away with, and dialed Faith's cell phone at the same time. Still her voice mail, but the clock said, only 5:21 P.M. I was making spectacular time. There was no way that Faith could've beaten me to her place, unless she was driving just as wildly as I was.

I whipped around the last corner, putting me on her block, relieved I had beaten her, and that none of what I put in motion would actually happen. I continued down the block, slowing some. All of a sudden, just one door down from Faith's house, I slammed on the brakes, not believing I was seeing her backside slipping through the front door of her house and closing it behind her. My eyes quickly landed on the garage, and I saw the rolling door lower itself the final inch, closing completely. She had gotten there just moments before me.

"Dammit!" I yelled, throwing both fists down on the steering wheel.

39

Faith turned the key, but the lock wouldn't respond. Damn old key, Faith cursed, jiggling the key in the lock. Of all days the lock had to be jammed, it had to be today, she thought, wanting to explode with excitement. She felt that way all the way home, taking every shortcut she knew, speeding faster than she ever had before.

She just kept seeing Gary's face, kept seeing him as he reached into his pocket, lowered himself to one knee, pulled out that tiny blue, velvet box. And then she heard his voice, saying the sweetest words a woman could ever hear.

"Will you marry me?" Those words echoed in her head all the way home, and she answered him a zillion times. "Yes. Yes. Yes!" And they kissed, and they made love like they never had before, and now she was stuck outside her own house, jiggling this damn key, ready to just say screw it, and kick the door down if it didn't work on the next try. But then it finally turned, and as she pushed that door open, she knew that she was opening the door to her new life.

A new life where there would be sounds of a man and woman moaning in what sounded like exquisite pain. A new life where in her living room, on her sofa, the back of a woman's body was positioned toward Faith, her huge, round ass rising and dropping, up and down the length of some man's pole. She didn't know who that man was, couldn't see him from behind that very busy woman, but he was grabbing both sides of that woman's butt cheeks, and pulling them apart, trying to send himself as far up in her as possible.

Faith stumbled some, still holding on to the door, thinking that maybe, just maybe this was the wrong house. That's why the key didn't work at first, and it was possible that she jiggled it so much that the neighbor's door just opened, and as soon as they turned around, Faith was going to be so embarrassed, but Ted, her neighbor was *really* going to be embarrassed, because he was married, and Faith could see just by the size of the woman's butt that was shooting up and down his thang, that that wasn't Lauren, his wife.

But something pulled Faith out of that dream world she was in, and it was the sound of Ted's voice.

"Oh, baby," he said, and for some damn, strange reason, it sounded a little like Gary's voice. And then he said it again, and again, and with each time he said it, he grabbed that woman's behind harder. This wasn't Ted's voice, Faith realized, the corners of her mouth already starting to quiver with the fear that she knew exactly who it was on that couch.

She'd heard Gary say that a million times to her, the same throaty tone, the same lustful enthusiasm. But it couldn't be, Faith thought, swallowing hard, trying to suppress what was tunneling up from her stomach, threatening to erupt out of her mouth. It just couldn't be. And then she called out with what she thought would be a yell, but came out only as a shallow whisper.

"Gary?"

The screwing ended. No more up and down. Nothing. Both their bodies just stopped immediately, like they were playing musical chairs or something, and at the sound of Faith's voice, they just both sat and froze. Then the man's hands rose from the woman's behind, to her narrow waist, and moved her to the side.

Faith's heart raged within her chest, knowing that in only a second, she'd know for sure if it was truly Gary behind that woman. The second passed, and she was staring at him, dead in Gary's eyes—well, one of them, because one of those woman's huge breasts was blocking the other.

It was crazy that the first thing that came to her mind, the first question she wanted to ask him, was, did this mean there's no ring? Of course there's no ring, Faith answered for herself. There would be no ring, no wedding, no marriage, no having the child she had killed for this man. There would be nothing at all, and considering all she had done for this motherfucker, all she had endured, she wanted to kill him.

She wanted to make this known to him, but something had a grip on her vocal chords. Anger had a hold on her entire body, was controlling and pushing her over toward that woman, making her grab her by all that weave she had on top of her head, and yank her off Gary's dick.

The woman was caught off guard, lost her balance, and fell hard to the floor. Her thick weave probably acted as a cushion, and saved her from crushing her skull.

Gary sat there, his penis still erect, the condom glistening a pale tan color, looking like he was auditioning for the part of the new Trojan Man. He appeared unbelievably calm, not surprised or shocked at all, like he fucking knew this was going to happen.

This made Faith even angrier. It was bad enough to be screwing around on her, to bring the woman into her own house to do it, but to act as though it was no biggie when he finally got caught.

She was beyond anger, beyond rage, and she headed for him with intentions of gouging his eyes out, and making that bitch who was now climbing off the floor, eat them with a knife and fork.

But Gary didn't move, didn't jump, didn't throw his arms up like he was afraid he was in harm's way, but just raised a single hand, and softly said, "Don't, Faith."

She didn't know why, but she halted, almost afraid to take another step, and it had to be because of the tone he used, devoid of all fear, confident, like he had every right to be with that woman, and Faith was wrong for interrupting.

"Don't try to hurt me, and I won't hurt you," Gary said, getting up, and walking casually over toward her dining room table where his clothes were neatly folded and draped over one of the chairs.

Faith couldn't believe it, but she said nothing, just watched him walk over there and start to get dressed. The woman did the same, not saying a word, not yelling and cursing at Gary for putting her in this position, or not telling her that there was another woman.

Faith wanted to speak, wanted to ask so many questions like, why would he do this at her house when he knew she was on her way home? And worse, why did he tell her to expect a surprise? Was this the fucking surprise? Did he *want* to get caught? He had to. But why? Why the hell why! The questions screamed in her head, as she stood there stone-like, seeing that the two of them were now fully clothed and making their way toward the door.

The woman opened the door, and walked out, but when Gary passed Faith, she asked, softly, a tear from each eye rolling down her face, "Why?"

Gary looked up as if he hadn't even noticed she was standing there, and said, "Did you actually think I was going to leave my wife, and my two sons for you?" He said it in such a way that Faith believed that she was indeed a fool to ever have thought that.

"Just what kind of man would that make me?" He gave her a look that said he was offended that she even wanted him to consider such a ridiculous thing, a look that said it was her fault that they were both standing there that very moment. Faith looked away in shame—not for thinking that they could've been together, but because she had been used the way she had been.

Gary stood there another couple of seconds or so. It appeared to Faith that his glare had softened some, as if he felt the slightest bit of sympathy for her, that he didn't want this to be happening, but was in some way forced, then as quickly as it had shown itself, it disappeared.

"And if you have any desire to tell Lottie about this, she and the boys left the city for good, as I'll be doing in a couple of days. So call if you want, but you won't reach them. Good-bye, Faith," he said, then he simply walked out.

40

Damn, I thought, sitting parked down the street from Faith's house. There they were, walking out, not running, not hunched over, dodging objects that were furiously hurled at them. They were just walking out.

It made me worry what had happened in there, made me wonder that it could've been nothing. That when Faith walked in the house, Gary and Carmen were sitting there on the sofa, fully clothed, having a discussion, sipping tea, waiting for Faith's arrival to tell her just what I had intended for her to see. There could've been no other reason why those two didn't leave with a trail of blood behind them, or their clothes torn to ribbons, or squad cars skidding to a halt in front of Faith's place. She had a hell of a temper, and I knew that firsthand.

Carmen jumped in her Honda Civic and sped away without so much as saying a word to Gary. Gary approached his car, and I thought of going over there, asking him just what had happened, but I didn't want Faith to see me talking to him, so I let him go.

I got out of my car, stood outside it for a moment, wondering if I should just get back in and leave. Then I closed the door, telling myself I should go in and see what happened. What excuse I would use, I didn't know, but I'd come all the way over here, I might as well see her.

As I took cautious steps toward her house, I kept telling myself that if it didn't happen the way it was supposed to, if by now, Faith knew everything I had planned, it was for the best. Yeah, she'd hate me for life for even setting this awful thing up, but at least she wouldn't have suffered the pain of catching Gary in such a position. But if it did all go down as planned, then right now she would be devastated. Why did I even do it? Yes, she cheated on me, she used me to entice Gary to marry her, but I could've gotten over it. Did I have to go and do something this horrible? I stopped there in front of the steps, trying to decide if I should start up them, or just turn around and drive away, never speak to her again. If it really happened the way that I had planned, then I wouldn't even know if I could look her in the face, pretend that I had nothing to do with this, while I tried to convince her that everything would be all right.

I turned around and took a step back toward the car, telling myself, it was for the best that I just leave. But then I heard a faint sound of crying. It had happened. It happened just the way it was supposed to, I was sure, and I thought I couldn't have felt any worse than I did at that moment. But when I walked in, saw Faith on her knees, rocking back and forth, her hands covering her face, tears spilling out from between her fingers, I knew I had been wrong. I could feel worse.

41

It had been more than a week, actually ten days, that Asha had been at her mother's house. They were sitting down at the kitchen table, after breakfast, drinking tea. Asha's bag was packed and sitting by the front door.

She and her mother sat there in silence, their teacups held up to their lips, looking over the rims at each other, knowing that something had to be said. There was something wrong with Asha; something had happened that brought her here. Asha figured her mother knew this much, even though Asha hadn't spoken specifically about anything bothering her. Asha's mother never asked, and Asha appreciated that. While they went shopping, while they cooked dinner, or walked the streets of downtown Indianapolis, Asha's mother never stopped walking, took her hand, looked deeply into her eyes, and asked, "What's really wrong? Why are you here?"

Yeah, she was glad those questions weren't asked, because even if they were, Asha would've had to have lied to her mother, which she didn't like to do.

On a couple of occasions, she'd looked at the phone, thought about dialing Angie, asking her if she still felt the same way, if she still wanted nothing to do with her, but Asha had stopped herself. What good would that have done? There was nothing unclear about what Angie said that day in her car. She wanted a normal life, or at least

270

what appeared to be a normal life for her son, and Asha wouldn't disturb that.

One night she did call Jayson. Yeah, she'd found him snooping through her stuff. He'd said some awful things to her, and he was kicking her out of his building. Still, she knew they would always be friends, whether he acknowledged that or not. She called him with the intention of telling him that she'd move out of his place, no problem. She could've always used a little more closet space, the kitchen could've been bigger, and his floors were too thin, but after she was gone, they were still going to be friends. Like it or not, she wasn't giving up on their friendship.

But the phone rang, and rang, and then the voice mail finally answered, and Asha was in no mood to leave a message. He hadn't answered the phone, and in a way, Jayson not being there this one time, when he always seemed to be, made her realize just how alone she was. She had no more friends. Sure, she had acquaintances, people at the spa, but no more real friends, people who she could call and discuss her deepest, most personal problems.

For the next three days, she spent most of her time up in her room. When she did go downstairs for something to eat, or to walk outside, she would say very little to her mother, just smile at her, letting her know that there was nothing really to worry about. For those next three nights Asha cried, even when she felt she didn't need to, didn't want to. She forced herself, needing to get all that pain, that anger, and resentment out, so she could start new. She realized, when she returned to Chicago, she would be getting a new place, experiencing new relationships with women, and starting a new life.

On the tenth night, her final night in Indiana, Asha didn't cry. She didn't have to. Her grieving was done, and although she was still saddened by everything that happened, she knew she could put it all behind her.

Asha set her teacup down, and continued staring at her mother. Her mother set her cup down as well.

"What?" her mother said to Asha.

"You've been very good, Mommy."

"What you mean, very good?"

"You know what I mean," Asha said, smiling. "You never once

asked me what was wrong, even when you knew something was."

"No, no," her mother said, shaking her head, waving her hands in the air. "I know nothing. I think my baby come to see me, 'cause she love and want to see her mother, not 'cause something wrong."

Asha got up from her chair, walked over behind her mother, and wrapped her arms around her neck, giving her a kiss on the cheek.

"Aw, Mommy, you know I love and wanted to see you. Of course that's the main reason I came, but some things have happened that upset me, and I just needed to be somewhere safe, somewhere I felt loved, until I got over it. You understand, Mommy?"

"I understand," she said, rubbing her daughter's arms, then kissing one of her hands.

Asha sat back down across from her mother. "Mommy, the reason I was upset was because I broke up with Gill," Asha said, lowering her eyes, feeling somewhat ashamed because she knew how much her mother liked him.

"Good," her mother said. "I never like him, anyway."

Asha looked up at her mother, smiling. "What do you mean, you never liked him? You loved Gill. That time when we came down, you were all over him, like 'This my new son-in-law,'" Asha said, mocking her mother, complete with her Asian accent and dialect. "'He good man, and will take very good care of my Asha, and will give me lots of grandchildren.'"

"I don't talk like that," Asha's mother said. "You make me sound like man from *Karate Kid*."

"You mean, Mr. Miagi," Asha laughed. "You do sound like him. But that's beside the point. I broke up with Gill, Mommy," her smile quickly leaving her face.

"Don't worry. You two get back together," Asha's mother said, reaching across the table and patting Asha's hand.

"No we won't. I gave him back his ring and everything. We aren't going to get married. It's over for good. I don't know if I'll ever get married," Asha said, lowering her face again, feeling like a failure in her mother's eyes, considering how successful and loving her marriage with her father was.

"You will find other man. You beautiful, smart, funny girl. You my daughter. Man be crazy not to want to marry you."

"Naw, Mommy," Asha said, still looking down. She picked up her cup of tea, brought it her lips, and took a slow sip. It was cold and bland, but she drank it anyway while she thought about whether she should tell her mother the real reason why she knew she'd never get married. It would kill her, Asha thought. But then again, would it? She had never had a conversation about gays and lesbians with her mother. She had never heard her mother speak positively about them, but then again, she'd never been sitting near the television with her mother when a story about gays or lesbians aired, and watched her sling her bowl of noodles at the thing, cursing those freaks who were taking over the country. After hearing the news, she would react how she would react, Asha realized, as she lowered her cup to its saucer. Either way, this was her mother, and she should know the truth about her daughter.

"You will find man as soon as you get back to Chicago," her mother said.

"Mommy, that won't happen," Asha said, looking up at her now.

"It will. Why not?"

"Because I don't like men, anymore, Mommy."

Asha's mother gave her a knowing smile, nodding her head slightly. "I know what you mean. I feel same way, when me and your father break up for first time, but we get back together and—"

"No. I think I explained that wrong. It's not really because I don't like men, but because . . . because I like women," Asha said, and she made a point of not taking her eyes off of her mother's face, because she wanted to see the reaction she had as she was having it. But her mother's expression didn't change one bit, her eyes didn't widen, her eyebrows didn't fly up onto her forehead, and Asha knew although that wasn't happening on the outside, all that was going on just under the surface. Her mother had a way of hiding her emotions when she wanted to. A second later, a shaky smile spread across her mother's face. "What you say?"

"I said, I like women."

Her mother still wore her calm face, but looked at Asha as though she was trying to find out something more from her than what she was saying.

"How you know."

"Because I've been with one. I've had a relationship with one, and I loved her. I love her," Asha said, her voice shaking with emotion when she spoke the last few words.

"She don't love you back?" Asha's mother said, in the gentlest, motherly voice.

"No. I don't know," Asha said, batting her eyes quickly to stop the tears she felt ready to come. "There are a lot of things going on in her life, and I don't know if I fit or not."

Asha's mother got up from her chair, and walked over toward her daughter. She pulled her up from the chair and took her in her arms.

"This real reason you come to see me. Not because of Gill, but girl you in love with."

Asha didn't answer, but nodded her head, then lowered it onto her mother's shoulder, wrapping her arms tight around her waist.

"Mommy, I'm sorry to tell you this about me. I know how you must feel. I didn't mean to disappoint you, but I—"

"Asha!" her mother said, taking her daughter by the shoulders, and almost pushing her away from herself, so she could look her directly in the face. "Don't you say that. You my daughter. I love you. I could never be disappointed by you. Never. You hear me?"

Asha nodded, tear streaks lining her face.

"Do you hear me?" Asha's mother asked again.

"Yes, Mommy."

She pulled her daughter back into an embrace. "I love you, baby. You my best thing in the world. Who you love don't change you. You still my Asha. I just want to know you happy. Have you talked to her? She know how you feel?"

"She knows, Mommy," Asha said, still clinging to her mother, so relieved that her mother responded the way she did, but feeling just a little foolish for expecting her to have acted any other way. "She knows I love her, and I know she loves me too, but she's afraid of what other people will think."

"Then forget her. You will find other woman. You beautiful, smart, funny girl. You my daughter. Other women be crazy not to want to be with you." Asha's mother gave her the pep talk again.

Asha took her head off her mother's shoulder and looked into her eyes. "That's okay with you?"

"Of course, it's okay with me. But important thing is," Asha's mother said, touching one of her daughter's temples, "is it okay with you?"

And an hour later, while Asha was in her rented Oldsmobile, headed west, back to Chicago, she understood what her mother had asked her. Regardless of what anyone else thought, including her own mother, in her mind, in her heart, she had to know if she loved who she was. Was she willing to accept herself as that person? Asha thought about that for one more brief moment, not wanting to belabor it too much, not wanting her brain to answer it, but her heart, her soul. After that moment, a confident smile came across her face, because the answer had made itself known to her. That answer was yes.

42

It had been ten days since the day in the car when Angie told Asha they could no longer see each other. She hadn't called Asha, and definitely hadn't been back to the spa, because she knew if she saw the girl again, she might have wanted to go to her, hug her, apologize for what she had said to her, take her hand, pull her into the little massage room, and try to make love to her right there. But she couldn't do that. She had made a decision, and even though the decision was based on what her son needed, and not herself, she had to stick to it.

Since she had broken up with Asha, Angie had been quite grumpy, and things at home hadn't been right. Life in general felt like it was just lacking something lately. This had nothing to do with her son Kyle; they were fine as always. But Angie found herself examining Deric a little harder. When he came to bed the other night, wearing no shirt, just his boxer shorts, Angie noticed that he was looking a little soft around the middle. She didn't say anything, just lay there on her side of the bed, because she wasn't sure if he had recently loosened up some there, or if he had always been that way, and she was just now noticing.

He crawled into bed, moved very close to her, and leaned over, puckering to give her a kiss. Angie gave him a quick peck on the cheek, reached over, and turned her bedside lamp off, then lay back down. She remained that way for a moment, her eyes wide open, looking up into the dark space before her, feeling one of Deric's arms and one of his feet pushing against her. This is a queen-size bed, Angie thought, why did he have to be so damn close to me all the time? She scooted away from him some to the edge of the bed, and when both the bed and blanket ran out, because he was hogging them, as he normally did, she realized that she was just damn tired of it.

Angie sat up, leaned over, turning the lamp back on, and looked down at Deric.

"What?" he said, opening his eyes, the covers pulled up to just below his chest, a great deal of the blanket tucked firmly under his body.

"Look at all that space you have over there, and all the covers you got. What, are you expecting company? You saving that space for somebody?"

Deric looked at the space on the other side of him, and saw that almost a third of the mattress was there, empty beside him. He smiled sheepishly. "Sorry," he said, then scooted over some, relinquishing most of the blanket. He settled back in, rolling about a moment, making himself comfortable, then closed his eyes. But when the lamp didn't go off, he opened them again.

"What's up?"

Angie was still sitting up beside him, looking down at him, like he had borrowed something from her years ago, and had forgotten to return it. "Well," she said, "I don't mind you sleeping in here with me most of the time, but every now and then, I wouldn't mind sleeping by myself."

"What?" Deric said, sitting up.

"Yeah. I mean, I never really invited you to sleep with me. You just came in here one night, and you've been coming in here ever since. Like I said, I don't mind, but I'd like to feel my own bed, my whole bed, once in a while."

"Oh, so you don't mind me sleeping with you," Deric said, taking offense.

"No I don't, but—"

"I know, but sometimes you want to have the bed to yourself. Is this one of those times?"

Normally Angie would've said, hey, forget about it, not wanting to hurt his feelings. But lately she'd been feeling particularly edgy, so she said, "Yeah. This is one of those times."

Deric threw back the covers, stepped his marshmallow-middled self out of the bed, and stood there, his hands on his hips, as if he was about to make a speech. "Cool. There, you have your whole bed." And then he walked away. Short speech.

The next morning at breakfast, Deric had just as much to say to Kyle as he always did, but had not one word for Angie. The three of them were sitting there at the table, Deric asking, "So, Kyle, how did you sleep? Kyle, what are you going to learn in school today? And make sure you're a good boy today, Kyle." Deric wouldn't even look Angie's way.

When they were all finished with breakfast, Deric removed his plate, and Kyle's, but left Angie's there in front of her.

"Okay, Kyle. Daddy's got to leave for work, but I'll see you when I get home."

It was what he said to her son every morning, but when Angie heard that this time, she wanted to interrupt. She wanted to say, "Kyle, don't believe that shit. That man's not your father, never was, and never will be." But she just lifted her coffee mug and took a swallow to stop the words from coming out.

Deric kissed Kyle on the head, grabbed his briefcase, walked right past Angie without looking down at her, without saying a word. She didn't turn around to look at him. She just heard the door open, heard it close, and that was it.

Later that day, when she was on her way home, Kyle in the backseat, the phone rang. It was the same time it always rang, and she thought of not answering it, but why should she deprive her son of hearing from Deric, just because he was acting like an asshole, and she was pissed at him.

When she picked up the phone, it wasn't him, but her friend Chanda, calling to see if the shoes she had ordered last week had arrived. Angie told her they had, and quickly got off the phone, expecting Deric to call any minute, but he didn't. He didn't call at all. So now he wanted to play games, Angie thought. Cool. Fine with her. She'd have a long talk with Mr. Deric when he came in that evening. But then evening turned into night, night turned to late night, and late night into early morning.

It was 12:48 A.M when Angie heard Deric's SUV pull into the driveway. It didn't wake her up, because she had been sitting up, watching the last red number on her alarm clock continue to advance after each minute that passed.

Angie thought of quickly clicking off the lamp and rolling over, pulling the covers over her, as if she had been asleep. But hell no, she thought. She had been waiting up for him, and she wanted him to know that. She wanted him to know how angry she was for him just disappearing like that, for her having to come up with lies to satisfy Kyle every time he asked, "Where's Daddy? When's Daddy coming home?" Which happened to be about a thousand times.

So Angie sat there, the blankets just below her waist, staring angrily at the bedroom door, waiting for it to open, so she could let that man have a piece of her mind. She heard the downstairs door open, and after a few minutes, she heard Deric come up the stairs. Angie was getting herself ready, her speech prepared for him when he opened the door, but he never did. It was a five full minutes after he had come up the stairs, and he had not come into the bedroom. She knew he didn't go into the bathroom, because she would've heard that door close, water running, whatever.

Angie slowly crawled out of bed, and walked to the door. She opened it, walking into the hallway, and at the other end of the hallway, she saw the thin strip of light coming from beneath the door down there. It was the guest room that Deric used to stay in when he wasn't sleeping with Angie, and it was the room that Angie had relegated him to last night.

She marched down the hallway, knocked on the door.

"It's open," Deric said.

Angie pushed the door open, walked in, her hands on her hips.

"What the hell is going on?"

Deric was hanging up his suit in the closet. "What does it look like? I'm getting ready to go to bed. My bed. Remember, you kicked me out of yours," he said, not stepping out of the closet to speak to her.

"I'm not talking about what's going on just now. I'm talking about the whole damn day, since this morning. Ignoring me like I'm some stranger at breakfast, not calling after I got off work like you always do, and now walking in here at . . ." Angie turned to look at the clock that sat on the dresser, " . . . at twelve fifty-six in the morning."

"Well, Angie," Deric said, stepping out of the closet in a T-shirt, and boxers, "I'm surprised you noticed any of that. Over the last couple of weeks it seemed that I've been doing nothing but getting in your way. It felt like you didn't want me around. You half assed said two words to me, you were constantly nit-picking, and it all came to a head last night when you threw me out of your bed. Hell, I figured if I was gone three days, it wouldn't have made you a difference," he said, sarcastically.

"It wouldn't have. I was talking about Kyle," Angie said sharply, knowing she shouldn't have said it after the words had left her lips, because it wasn't what she really meant.

Deric gave her a cold, hard look. "I see," he said, and then made a quick line for the dresser, pulled out a pair of blue jeans, and looked like he was about to pull them on.

"Deric, no. I didn't mean that," Angie said, walking over to him.

"Then why did you say it?"

"Because I'm angry. I tell you I need a little space one night, so you get angry, and don't just take it out on me, but on Kyle too."

"I told you, for almost two weeks now, you've been getting your space. You've been zoned out, damn near every minute of the day. I'll ask you what's wrong with you, and you'll either lie and say nothing, or you'll bite my head off for always asking."

That was because Asha was always on her mind during those times, and when she looked at Deric, she would've so much preferred it to have been Asha standing, or sitting there, asking her what was wrong. But she was too much of a coward to do what it took to make that a reality, so she was disappointed in herself, and she directed the anger it caused toward Deric.

"But did you have to take it out on Kyle?" Angie said, stopping herself from further thinking of Asha. "Did you have to not call, come home so late, not even early enough to tell him good night?"

"Angie," Deric said, draping his jeans across the open dresser drawer. "Have you ever thought that maybe I needed a little space myself? Have you ever thought that maybe there were some things on my mind that I would've liked to think about. No. Hell no. I'm always calling while you're on the way home from picking up Kyle, because

I'm always offering to fix dinner, to do for him, to do for you. Maybe, I may have, for once, needed something. I'm always here, good ole' fucking Deric, and what the hell do I get for it? Thrown out of the damn bed."

"Deric, don't you think you're going a little overboard with this? I just asked to sleep in my bed alone one night because you were hogging the covers. What's the big damn deal?"

"What's the big deal? What's the big damn deal?" Deric said stepping right in front of Angie. "The big deal is that I have no say and no security. Today you don't want me in the bed because I hog the covers. What is it tomorrow, the bathroom, because I leave the seat up? Will it be the kitchen because I don't dry the dishes completely before I put them away? Or how about when you just get tired of walking in any one of the rooms in this house, seeing me there, will you throw me out of the entire house, Angie? Because it is yours. You can do that."

"Deric, no," Angie said, although that thought had been bouncing around in her mind over the last two weeks. "Of course not."

"And what about Kyle?"

"What about him?" Angie said, feeling defensive all of a sudden.

"I love him. You know that. I love him like a son."

"And he loves you like a father."

"That's the problem," Deric said. "The *like* part. He's not my son. I'm not his father. Technically, we're nothing to each other but good friends."

"That's not true. You two love each other. You're more than that," Angie said.

"Technically. Legally," Deric said, a very serious look on his face, "we're not."

"What point are you trying to make, Deric?"

"What if something happens to you? What if you get hit by a car or something? What happens to Kyle? He sure as hell doesn't come to me. *Like* a father doesn't stand up in court."

"You're catastrophizing, Deric. What if something happens to *you?* What if something happens to all of us?"

"Okay, how about a more likely event," Deric said. "I'm investing myself completely into Kyle, say one day you get tired of me, no longer want me in your life, what happens to me and Kyle then?"

Angie didn't say anything, couldn't say anything, because although she knew that was a possibility, and of late, a potential probability, she had never thought he would've considered that.

"What are you talking about? That's foolishness."

"Is it, Angie?"

There was a slight hesitation on her part, and then she said, "Yeah. I mean . . . just come out with it, Deric. What are you getting at?"

"Angie, we've been doing this for a little while now, and you know I love you. But for me to continue to do this, I'll need some sort of commitment from you, so I know that my life with you and Kyle is secure, and not just subject to how you feel from day to day."

Angie couldn't believe what she was hearing. This man was giving her an ultimatum. "What are you talking about, marriage?"

"That," Deric said, nodding his head. "And allowing me to adopt Kyle."

"Marriage," Angie said cautiously, as if the idea wasn't the most ridiculous thing she had ever heard. She knew she had to take it easy with how she proceeded, because she still wanted Deric around, he did serve a purpose for both her and Kyle, but she definitely wasn't going to marry him, or have him claim her child. "I'm not ready for marriage, and I think your relationship with Kyle is just fine the way it is. Why do you want to—"

But before Angie could finish with what she was saying, Deric was slipping on his jeans, tucking his T-shirt into them, and slipping on a pair of loafers.

"I knew you'd say that," Deric said. "But I know that you may not be thinking straight because this came to you as a surprise. So I'll give you a couple of days to think about it." He reached back into the closet and grabbed a jacket, threw it on.

"You know I want the answer to be yes, but if it's not, I'll understand, and I'll have my things packed and out of here in two days." He turned to go.

"Where are you going?" Angie said.

"I don't know," he said, his hand on the doorknob. "But I'll be back in time to have breakfast with you and Kyle in the morning. I don't want to disappoint him twice."

He walked out the door, closing it behind him, leaving Angie in the room by herself to think about what he had just asked her. But instead of thinking of Deric's proposal like she should've been, her mind was on how this turn of events might possibly affect her and Asha.

43

When I walked into Faith's house I found Faith on her knees, sobbing, rocking back and forth, mumbling something. I stood in front of her for a moment unnoticed, before she looked up and saw me. She covered her face with both her hands, turning away from me on her knees, toward a corner, trying to wipe her face, before looking back at me.

I got down on my knees, moved close to her, and put my arm around her. Faith jumped at first, as if she was afraid of my touch, but I didn't move my arm, and she just let it stay.

"Faith, what's wrong? What happened?" I asked, as if I had no idea.

She didn't speak, just continued wiping at her face, sniffling, and trying to pull herself together. When she finally did, she turned to me with puffy, bloodshot eyes and a pink nose, and asked, "What are you doing here?"

I was prepared for that question, had readied myself for it on the way up the steps. "After I got off the phone with you, I realized how rude it was not to accept your apology. I tried calling you back on your cell, but it was off, and there was no answer here, so I thought I'd come by and wait for you," I said, wiping a final tear off her cheek. "I wanted to tell you that I accept your apology."

Faith shook her head, pulling her face away from my hand. "No, Jayson. You shouldn't do that."

"Why not?"

Faith pulled herself up from the floor, and walked toward the screen door. She looked out of it, probably checking to see if Gary had really gone, if he had really left for good. Then she closed the big door and walked back past me, into the living room.

"Because I don't deserve for you to accept my apology. I shouldn't be forgiven," she said, turning to face me.

"You mind telling me why not?"

"Do you mind sitting down? It's gonna take a while."

I sat, and she sat across from me. She placed her palms together, as if in prayer, tapping her fingertips against her lips. She closed her eyes, exhaled deeply, probably recounting all that she was about to tell me. Seconds later, she dropped her hands, looked at me, and said, "This is what happened, Jayson."

She told me everything, and I reacted as if I hadn't heard all of this before from Karen, responded as if I hadn't known any of the players: Gary, his wife Lottie, or his two sons. I was surprised, but she was thoroughly honest with me. Everything she said jibed with what Karen told me, and what I'd found out from Gary. She finished by saying, "And the last thing he said was, don't bother going to his wife, because they were moving to another city." Faith looked at me sadly. "He never had any intention of marrying me." Then she said, as if to herself, "What a complete fool I've been."

And now she knew exactly how I felt, and although I was sorry for her in a way, I felt some satisfaction knowing that she could finally relate to what I had been through.

"Now I know how you must've felt, hunh?" Faith said, seeming to try to find some humor in it all.

"So you did all that for him?" I said, ignoring the comment she'd just made. "You spent all that time with me, pretended to want to marry me, pretended to love me, just to make him jealous?"

"Jayson," Faith said, getting up from her seat across from me and sitting beside me placing a hand on my knee. "It wasn't all pretend. We were together for a year. How could it have been?"

"That's what I'm trying to find out. Just what was real and what was pretend?"

"Okay, I wasn't planning on marrying you, because like I said, I was infatuated with Gary. But that doesn't mean I didn't love you."

"Right," I blew, turning my face away from her. "You wanted to marry him, but you loved me. That makes a lot of sense. Do you think I'm going to believe that?"

"Jayson, think about some of the times we had. That time on the lakefront when we had that old man take our picture. We walked for more than an hour, just holding hands, not saying a word. You didn't feel my love for you then?"

I remembered that time. It was a beautiful night, and she was right, we didn't say a word to each other, but it seemed fine. I was so close to her that night that communicating through words would've felt below us. It was as though we were on a higher plane, speaking telepathically. I did know she loved me that night, or at least thought she did.

"And how about those warm breezy nights when we'd make love outside on my patio, and we'd get so loud that all the dogs in the neighborhood started barking and howling. Remember those times?" Faith said, smiling.

I thought about those times, and how much fun they were. And yes, I remembered feeling as though she loved me then. I felt a smile spreading across my face.

"So you do remember that, don't you?" Faith said, seeing that smile on my face.

But the smile was gone when I recalled the image of her and Gary in that hotel room.

"Bullshit, Faith," I said, getting up from the couch. "You didn't love me, because if you did, you would've never used me like that."

Faith got up from the sofa, and stood in front of me, looking up into my eyes. "I told you, Jayson. I was a fool. I was so infatuated with Gary that I couldn't see what I had right in front of my face. I schemed, lied, played games with you, but that didn't mean I didn't love you, Jayson. Won't you believe that?"

I wanted to so much, but I couldn't. I just couldn't. I shook my head, too angry to say anything.

"What can I do to make you believe?" Faith said, reaching up, taking my face between her warm palms. I wanted to smack them away. I wanted to yell at her, telling her she had no right to touch me that way anymore, and never to do it again, but I couldn't. Her touch felt so familiar, reminded me of how things were before all of this happened.

"What can I do?" she asked again, moving slightly closer to me, her belly gently grazing mine.

"Nothing," I said, but my voice was faint, as though I had no power to speak.

"What can I do, Jayson?" she said again, and I felt her pulling my face toward hers, saw her bringing her lips closer to mine. Again, I wanted to stop her, wanted to stop myself, but there was something stronger in me wanting the kiss I knew she was trying to give me. It had been so long since I'd kissed her, and regardless of all the things she had done to me, I still couldn't say no to her.

Our mouths touched, and I felt my body start to react. I wouldn't let it go any farther, I told myself. This would be a simple kiss, nothing more than the surface of our lips touching. But then I felt her wet tongue pressing against my tight lips, trying to pry them open. I resisted, warning myself that if this kiss went farther, we could possibly wind up in bed, and from there, I could potentially be in the same position I was just freed from. In love with a woman who didn't love me, but was just using me to get something else she wanted.

But as I continued to try and fight, letting my lips part just the slightest bit, allowing her tongue into my mouth, feeling my knees go just a little weaker, I wondered why I was even trying to fool myself. I shouldn't have been wary of falling back in love with Faith, because I'd never stopped loving her. I loved her the entire time we were together, loved her when I saw her making love to Gary, loved her fifteen minutes ago, and loved her this very minute.

I didn't know exactly what was happening and exactly why it was. I didn't know if she still had feelings for Gary, and was looking at having sex with me as a way of getting revenge for his being with that woman. I didn't know if she saw losing Gary as something that she had to account for, realizing that if she couldn't marry him, marrying me would be better than not getting married at all. Or was she really telling the truth, that she really did love me then, and the reason why she was now steadily walking me back toward her bedroom as she continued to kiss me was because she still loved me now? I wanted to think that was the case.

So as we lay across the bed, and she kissed me gently on the ear and neck, undoing the buttons of my shirt, I didn't tell myself to fight her. I told myself to enjoy this, because whatever came of it, there was no place I would've rather been.

What came of it was our having sex three times that day, and never leaving the bed for the rest of the day, outside of going to bathroom, looking for the remote to the TV, and grabbing a pint of Ben and Jerry's from the freezer and two spoons.

The following day she called in sick to work, told them she wouldn't be in for the rest of the week. I stayed there. Not because she asked me to, but because she didn't ask me to leave. For four days, the majority of our time was spent in bed, making love or just talking. There were times when she'd just all of a sudden start crying. It had something to do with Gary, I knew, even though she denied it every time. She said it had more to do with the child she aborted than with him, and that that child was the reason she had been so infatuated with marrying him.

Again, I don't know if my vision was clouded because I was so in love with her, but what she was saying was starting to make sense to me.

"I saw him once or twice a week, Jayson," she said one night before we went to sleep. "All the other times I was with you. How could I have cared for him and not you? How could I have cared for him more than you?"

It surprised me how willing she was to talk about their relationship. But what really surprised me was how willing I was to listen. It could've been because I really believed it was over. It had been four days since he'd left here, I remembered counting, and in a few more, he would be gone. He would be gone, and Faith wouldn't know where he was, and I liked to think that she wouldn't even care if she could find out.

Neither one of us mentioned it, I guess for fear of jinxing what was now happening between us. It felt like a reunion, a homecoming of sorts. It was like one of us went away on a vacation for a while, then returned, and everything just fell back into place. All the old jokes we used to share were still there, the things we used to do to please each other in bed hadn't changed, and our bodies still contoured perfectly to the other's as we fell off to sleep.

On the fifth day, we decided to go to a movie. We both admitted that we had had enough of the house, and the bed, at least for a few hours. The movie was great. Something with Mel Gibson in it. Plenty of violence for me, a little bit of the sentimental stuff for her.

When it was over, we walked out the movie theater hand in hand.

"Oh, déjà vu," Faith said.

"What?"

"You know what." Faith smiled. "Look up. Where are we at?"

I looked up at the sign she pointed to. "Cineplex Odeon," I said, reading the sign. "Yeah, I saw that when we came in. I like it. It's a nice sign," I said, joking.

Faith looked sad, her bottom lip poking out. "You don't remember? This is—"

"I know, you big baby," I said, wrapping my arm around her neck. "This was where we met."

She immediately brightened up, then said, "Oh, oh. I have an idea." She walked away from me till she got to the door of her Camry, which was about twenty feet from where I was standing, stuck her hand in her purse, then without turning around, she said, "Okay, go."

"What?" I said, having to raise my voice a little so she could hear me. "Go what?"

"You know what," she practically yelled, still not looking directly at me, but at me through the reflection in the driver's side window of her car. "The day we met. Reenactment. For laughs."

"Oh no, no, no, no," I said, waving my hands, walking briskly toward her. "For laughs. That wasn't funny. I was a bumbling idiot that day. I'm not doing that again. It was hard enough the first time."

"C'mon, Jayson. It'll be fun. For old times sake."

"Heckie naw," I said, shaking my head.

"Okay, then. I'll do it. I'll be you, and . . ." Faith said, taking off her purse and throwing it on my shoulder, pushing me toward the car, " . . . you be me."

She ran back twenty feet away from me. "You ready?" she called.

"Yeah, I guess," I said.

"You gotta face the car."

I obediently turned around to face the car, clutching my—I mean, her—purse. I saw her approaching through the reflection in the car's window, and she was pimping, bobbing back and forth, swinging one arm around behind her back with each step she took.

"I don't walk like that," I said, looking at her.

"Shhhh. Turn back around and stay in character," she said, approaching.

Again, I did as I was told and waited.

"Uh, uh, excuse me, miss. Excuse me," Faith said.

"What do you want!" I snapped, in the highest-pitched voiced I could reach, pretending to be her.

"Uh, uh, uh. I was wondering did you like the movie? I was noticing how beautiful you are, and I was wondering what you liked about the movie and would you fill out a questionnaire, you beautiful woman you," Faith said, barely able to stop herself from bursting out laughing.

"Leave me alone, you . . . you wretched human filth," I said, clutching the purse even tighter. "You got rocks in your head? Do I have a sign taped to my back saying, All nice and handsome gentlemen please ask me about the movie? Now get away. Scoot, scat!" I said, shooing her off with my hand.

Faith raised her hands over her face, like she was Frankenstein being warded off by fire. "I'm sorry, beautiful woman. But when I saw you, I couldn't help but ask you about the movie, because I knew you'd have all the answers to my problems, and thought maybe I could get to know a beautiful woman like you, and then I would love you, and care for you, and we could have wonderful days together, and we could get married, and have lots of kids, and you would make my life complete."

"Okay, okay, okay," I said, breaking character. "I didn't say all that about the kids, and marriage, and wonderful days, and stuff."

"C'mon, Jayson. You were pouring your heart out to me, remember?" she said, straightening up, and losing the stupid look on her face, which was supposed to have been my look, I guess. "That may not have been exactly what you said, but that's what it sounded like then."

"Hmm," I said. "Well, maybe you're right. I guess maybe that's what I meant then."

Faith looked at me sadly, as if wishing we could've really gone back to that day and started over.

"I messed all that up, didn't I?"

I couldn't answer her. Exactly what did she mean by "messed all that up"? She'd done some serious damage to it. But if she meant destroyed what we had beyond repair, I just didn't know.

"You hurt me, Faith," was what I said. "And I don't know if I'll ever be able to forget that." I wanted to ask her, would she ever want me to? But that would be implying that I wanted us to get back together, and I wouldn't do that. She would have to approach me with that, and even then, I didn't know if I'd give it another shot.

Faith appeared even sadder, as if I had just punished her for ruining our relationship. I gave her a hug, and she hugged me back. We stood out there in the parking lot where we'd first met, almost a year ago, hugging for almost twenty minutes.

We didn't say a word to each other the entire ride home, didn't speak as we got ready for bed, and didn't utter a peep as we slipped under the blankets. There was total silence, but not the type we'd enjoyed on the lake that night. This was awkward, the type that had us questioning whether everything we had done up to this point, this new reunion, was a mistake or not.

"I'm going to be leaving tomorrow. I've been neglecting work. Gotta get back," I said, not looking at her but at the ceiling, as I pulled the blankets up to my chest. There was a feeling of finality to the words I had spoken, even though I hadn't meant them to sound that way.

We lay there, again in silence for a minute, then I turned to click off the light by the bed, when Faith said, "I don't want you to leave."

"Well, I gotta work, and I can always—"

"I don't mean my house, I mean me," Faith said, sitting up, turning to look at me. "I don't want you to leave my life."

I couldn't believe what I was hearing. After I got over my initial shock, I had to determine whether or not she meant it. Was she being sincere?

"What are you talking about?" I said, not really knowing.

"Jayson, I realize now, I made the biggest mistake a woman can ever make. You are such a wonderful man, and all you did was love me and want to make me your wife. I ruined that, but I know better now. What I had for Gary wasn't love, but regret for killing my child, and a hell of a determination to try to undo that. But what I have for you is love. It's truly love, Jayson."

"And how am I supposed to know that's true? You said that before, and I know you said you meant it then, but you still hurt me. How do I know that won't happen again?"

"You don't," she said, too damn quickly I thought. But she was right. "I can't guarantee anything, but I can say that I honestly do love you, and I think you still love me too. Don't you, Jayson?"

I didn't want to answer. I was actually afraid, feeling that keeping that fact from her somehow allowed me to maintain the ability to walk away if I needed to. But if I told her how I felt, I was scared that ability would leave me.

"Do you still love me, Jayson?" Faith asked again, and again, I said nothing, even looked away from her, as if her beautiful black eyes could pull the truth from me without my consent.

"I understand you not wanting to say," Faith said, snuggling closer to me, kissing me on the shoulder. I relaxed some, thinking that she was going to let the entire conversation go, when she said, "You know it's just six days away from it being exactly a year since we met."

I nodded slightly, almost unnoticeably, then said, "Yeah," not wanting her to think that I truly hadn't known.

"I'm gonna tell you something, Jayson. Then I'm going to ask you a question that I don't want you to respond to until tomorrow when you wake up. I don't want to talk about it anymore tonight. I just want you to think about how you feel and give me your answer in the morning. Okay?"

Immediately, I started to feel nervous, feeling a strange need to get up out of that bed and get out of there. I swallowed hard and said a shaky, "Okay."

"I love you, and all that nonsense that happened is behind us. Jayson, I promise that nothing like that will ever come between us again." Faith rolled more on her side, so she could stare directly into my eyes, and I hesitantly did the same. She gazed at me intently, then said, "You know that ring you gave me before?"

I tried to answer yes, but there was something in my throat. I guess it was fear. I cleared it, then tried again. "Yes."

"Then six days from now, on the one-year anniversary of our meeting, I want us to get married. What do you think?"

I lay there beside her, my entire body now covered in cold sweat. I didn't know how to react, had no idea what to say, and was so thankful that she didn't even want an answer at that moment, because I didn't think I was capable of speech beyond the "ga-gas," and "goo-goos" of a six-month-old.

"I want us to spend the rest of our lives together," she said, a slight smile appearing on her face. She leaned in close to me, kissed me quickly on the lips, then said, "Let me know tomorrow, if you want that too, okay?" She kissed me again and flipped over, leaving me there, my eyes looking like Grade A extra-large eggs, and my breath coming so fast that I thought I was going to lose consciousness right there in her bed. I slowly rolled over, clicked off the light, and turned back, pushing myself very close to her, holding her tight, fearful that if I didn't, I might lose a grip on all that was happening around me.

When I woke up the next morning, I had barely slept a wink, but I wasn't tired. I think I actually felt energized. From the moment I'd turned out the light, my mind had gone wild, thinking of all sorts of possibilities. Thinking, what if she cheated again? Thinking, what if she really didn't love me? Thinking, what if we were both just making a huge mistake? I raised my head and looked at her alarm clock and saw that I had been doing that thinking for six hours. All that time and I couldn't seem to come to any conclusion about what I would do regarding her and our possible life together. Then, because there seemed absolutely nothing else to do, I relaxed, and I realized it was actually all the *thinking* I was doing that was stopping me from understanding how I really *felt* about all this. So I settled down and asked myself what my heart thought. The answer came right away, and I fell right to sleep.

That was five days ago, and since then, all the arrangements have been made, and we've been excited as if this was our first go-round. I still can't believe I'm saying this, but I can't wait until tomorrow, when I make her my wife.

44

It was early evening when Asha finally made it back home. She took her time on the road, because she knew the ride was good for her. It gave her a chance to truly accept who she was, and not worry about what everyone else thought. She smiled as she pulled her overnight bag out of the backseat of the cab, there in front of her place.

She walked up the front steps, feeling glad to be home, or at least what was going to be her home for another week or so. She hadn't done too much looking, but she wasn't worried about that, because she knew she'd find something in that time, and if she didn't, then Jayson would just have to wait until she did. She was actually doing him a favor by complying with his wishes. She knew, and she was sure he knew as well, that legally, he couldn't just kick her out whenever he wanted to, especially without at least thirty days' notice.

Asha thought about their situation as she dug in her purse for her keys, before climbing the last step, and told herself she should say to hell with whatever reservations she had been having about speaking to him. She should just go up to his apartment, bang on the door, and tell him a thing or two. Exactly what those things would be, she wasn't sure. But why should she be tiptoeing around, just because he had a problem with who she was now; hell, who she had been all her life?

Yeah, that's what I'll do, Asha thought to herself, feeling confident. But when Asha pulled the outside door open, all of her confidence disappeared, because to her surprise, Jayson was standing just on the other side of the door.

Jayson seemed surprised too, for he jumped, almost dropping the paper bag he was carrying.

Asha wanted to say something, say anything. She was supposed to tell him how she was feeling. She was supposed to tell him that she was sorry for hiding who she really was from him for so long, and lying to him about it, but the fact that she had didn't mean they couldn't still be friends. She wanted to say that and so much more, but she just looked blankly into his face, unable to form a single word.

Jayson wasn't much better. Like her, it looked as though he wanted to speak but didn't. They stood there right in front of each other, staring into each other's eyes for a few seconds that felt like a few lifetimes. Then all of a sudden, they both seemed to snap out of whatever trances they were in.

"Excuse me," Jayson said, under his breath, lowering his eyes, as if he was trying to make his way past a stranger on a crowded subway train.

"Pardon me," Asha said, just as reserved, stepping out of his way toward her door, inserting the key, and getting in there as fast as she could. She closed the door, dropped her bag at her feet, then leaned her back against the door, shaking her head. What the hell was that? she asked herself. They'd acted like they didn't even know each other, like they hated each other. She once loved that man, still did, yet she couldn't even speak to him.

Asha turned around, opened the door, telling herself enough was enough. She opened the outer door and stepped outside, thinking that she would see Jayson there in the front yard, or driveway, but she didn't. When she looked down the block, she saw the back of his car, disappearing around the corner.

Asha dropped her head, disappointed, wishing that she could've resolved their differences then. She told herself, next time she saw him, she would end all of this nonsense that very moment.

Two hours later, Asha was standing in her bedroom mirror checking herself out. Her hair was done differently, corn-rowed, in shiny, thick, black braids, lining her scalp from front to back. She had on the huge, beautiful diamond stud earrings her mother had bought her for her twenty-fifth birthday. She wore a long-sleeve, button-down shirt, that hung just above her belly button, accenting her ample breasts, and her flat stomach. With that, she wore a pair of snug, denim capri pants, and a snazzy pair of Italian sandals. Asha's makeup was light, but brought out her cheekbones and eyes just the way she wanted it to.

She leaned into the mirror to get a closer look at herself, applying the last bit of makeup—her lipstick. It was a burnt orange that went with her copper complexion. She took a napkin, stuck it in between her lips, and pressed them together, blotting the excess off. She looked at herself and smiled.

"Girl, you look good," she said to herself, actually excited about going out.

Right after she'd returned home two hours ago, she'd thought about packing. But it was a Friday night, the weather was warm, and she told herself this would be the night she would start her new life. Asha tried to think of who she could call to do something with, but the friends she would've wanted to hang out with were no longer friends. That depressed her for a moment, but she told herself she wasn't going to let anything get her down.

She remembered a night spot that that girl Jackie used to talk about. Asha figured it was a lesbian club, considering that later Asha found out Jackie was a lesbian herself when she tried to give Asha a pelvic exam in her sleep.

Asha called information to get the phone number, then stood over the phone, the receiver to her ear, preparing to dial that number. As she stood there, she tried to imagine herself in one of those clubs, nothing but masculine-looking women and their very feminine-looking counterparts surrounding her. She imagined women dancing with women, women coming on to women at the bar, kissing in the corner, and doing whatever in the bathroom stalls.

Was that a place she could see herself in? After a moment, she thought, what the hell, and started dialing the number from the napkin she had jotted it down on. She wouldn't know if she could see herself in that type of place till she actually saw herself in that type of place.

Now she was ready to head out, and take the first step into her new world. She'd picked up her purse and a tiny, high-waist jacket, and was heading for the door, when the phone rang. Her hand was around the doorknob, and she looked back at the phone, trying to decide if she would answer it. At first she thought not to, telling herself that no one she cared about was trying to call her anyway. She had no more friends, no fiancé, so it was probably a wrong number, but Asha pulled herself away from the door and went to pick up the phone anyway.

"Hello," Asha said.

No answer right away.

"Hello," Asha said again, more forcefully.

Still no answer.

"Whatever," Asha said, about to hang up when she heard, "Asha, don't. It's Angie."

In a numb, dull kind of way, Asha was both excited and disappointed to hear Angie's voice again. Excited because she still loved this woman, but disappointed because Asha knew that she might abandon the big step she was about to take in her life just to sit on the phone for hours and talk to Angie.

"Asha, are you there?"

"Yeah. Yeah, I'm here," Asha said, clearing her voice, straightening her shirt, as if Angie could see that it wasn't clinging to Asha's body just right. "I'm just surprised to hear from you is all."

"I know. I mean, I knew you would be, but I had to call anyway. I miss you, Asha. I've been thinking a lot about you."

Asha smiled, feeling like a second-grade schoolgirl who'd just found out that the little boy who sat four rows over really did like her. "You have," Asha said.

"Yeah, and I wanted to say that I was crazy for breaking up with you like that. And I hope that maybe you might want to give me another chance?"

Boy, do I! Asha thought, smiling even wider, but only saying, very calmly, "Yeah, that might be nice."

"You sure about that, Asha? Because I thought you might've never wanted to hear from me again."

"Well, to tell you the truth, that's what I was thinking when I walked away from your car that day, but I've been thinking a lot about you too, and I told myself that if you were ever able to get past how your son felt about the two of us, be able to accept me in your life, I would take you back."

Angie didn't respond to that, didn't say a thing for a long moment.

"What?" Asha said, sensing something wrong.

"Asha," Angie said, very cautiously. "I think there may be a misunderstanding."

"What are you talking about?"

"I want us to take a second chance at what we had, exactly what we had. I guess I should've told you this first, but Deric, the man I'm with, wants me to commit to him, or he's leaving. I'm thinking about doing it because Kyle really needs him in his life."

Asha couldn't believe what she was hearing. "Then why are you calling me? Where do I fit into all this?"

"Because I love you, Asha. I don't love Deric like that."

"Okay, okay, okay, hold it," Asha said, shaking her head, waving a free hand. "Let me try to understand this. You're telling me you're going to marry this Deric only because your son needs a father, and no other reason. And you want to get back together with me so you can secretly visit me two days a week, so you can get your lesbian thang on? Is that what you're saying, Angie?" Asha was getting very angry.

"Asha, that's not exactly what I'm saying."

"Is it close? Is it anywhere in the ball park?"

"I guess," Angie said, shamefully.

"Fuck you," Asha said, coolly slamming the phone down into its cradle.

Not a second later, the phone was ringing again. Asha snapped it up.

"Asha, listen—"

"No, you listen. I'm good enough to have on the side, but not good enough to be with exclusively. Look, I love you, Angie. I've accepted that. And I've also accepted the fact that I'm a lesbian. I've accepted it so much that I'm all dressed up, about to go out to a lesbian club, get silly drunk, and see what happens," Asha said. "Angie, I'm better than just a warm body on the side, and until you can accept that, and get straight with your own issues about who you are, I don't ever want to speak to you again." Asha hung up the phone, and this time when it started ringing, Asha turned a deaf ear to it, and kept walking toward the door.

The club wasn't quite what Asha thought it was going to be. It was called the Liquid Cherry, not leaving much to the imagination, Asha thought, as she walked into the dimly lit spot. It was a huge, open room, with what Asha had to imagine were like thirty-foot ceilings. There were windows at the front and back wall of the place, extending up to ten or fifteen feet below the ceiling. There was a long, U-shaped bar to the left, and tables scattered around a clearing in the center of the room, where only a few couples were dancing to the blaring techno house music pounding out of the columns of tower speakers standing on the four corners of the dance floor.

All the tables were full with mostly women, chatting over pint glasses of beer, martini glasses, and short glasses of mixed drinks. There was smoke everywhere, coming from cigarettes, cigars, and Asha even detected the scent of marijuana. She could've used a quick hit of that, she thought, to make her relax some. As she made her way to the bar, she felt eyes on her. She didn't turn to acknowledge them, but strode confidently through the crowd of people, as if this wasn't her first time there.

She sat down at the bar next to an empty stool and waited for the bartender. When a lovely, thin woman with gorgeous eyes, the hair on her head no longer than the fuzz on a peach, asked, "What are you having?" Asha thought for a moment, then said, "Give me a Bombay Sapphire and cranberry, and two lemon drop shots." It was going to be an interesting night, she could feel it, and she wanted to start it off right.

45

Angie sat in her sitting room, a private place where she would go and think whenever something was bothering her, a place she could relax when she felt particularly stressed. This was one of those times.

Why did she even think Asha would've gone for what she had proposed? She should've known better than that. But she didn't think that Asha would blow up in her face either. Angie pulled the throw blanket up over her legs, smiling to herself, but only slightly. She told me to fuck myself, Angie thought. She told me to never call her again, until I get my thoughts about myself straight. I'll show her, Angie thought. I could actually never call her back again. I could stop thinking about her this very moment, and not let her image back into my mind, and that would be the end of that. She never really meant more than two cents to me.

But that wasn't true and Angie knew it. That had to be the reason this situation had her stressing, had her holed up in her little room, trying to think of the best way to handle this matter.

Every now and then, she'd holler up at the ceiling. "Cowboy, don't you tear the house down up there." Kyle was upstairs playing army men, or space heroes, or whatever he did to entertain himself when neither her nor Deric was around. Deric was acting an ass again. Angie guessed he was out somewhere making an effort to stay away. He was out somewhere, hoping Angie would think he was having the time of his life, trying to prove that he had a life outside of Angie, when he was probably really sitting in his car, staring out the window, checking his watch every five minutes, waiting till it was late enough so he could walk his ass back into the house.

Her son would understand was what Asha had told Angie a while ago. If Kyle loved her, he would understand the decision she made in letting go of Deric. But would he? Would he understand, and even if he did understand, would he ever forget that his mother booted out his father when he was six, to take in some woman?

Angie thought, okay, what if he did have no problem with it, and everything seemed fine. What if Kyle loved the hell out of Asha, and the three of them lived happily with one another for ten years? What would Angie think if Kyle walked in the house one day with an earring in his right ear, or wearing a pair of particularly tight, pink pants, or maybe had on his button-down shirt, not buttoned up all the way, but only halfway, and the lower half tied in a knot to expose his belly button. What if he came in the house one day hand in hand with Casey, the feminine-male looking Hispanic teenager from across the street? What would Angie do then? She'd blame it on herself, that's what. But who was to say that would happen? And who was to say that if she married Deric, it wouldn't?

Angie gave it some more thought, and understood that it really all came down to happiness. If she married Deric, that would make him and Kyle happy, but she would be miserable for the rest of her life. If she got rid of Deric, she'd be happy, but Kyle would probably resent her for some years. Regarding Deric? Well, she would hate to have to hurt Deric, but he would just have to understand.

Angie dropped her head back, letting it rest against the wall behind the couch. She wished her mother was still alive so she could speak to her about this, but she had died fifteen years ago. Angie had never told her mother about her being a lesbian, because she knew what her mother had sacrificed for her. Like so many parents, her mother had stayed in her awful marriage "for the sake of the child."

After Angie was old enough to realize what love between a married couple should look like, she could tell that her mother and father no longer cared for each other. They barely communicated with each other, and when they did it was through argument. Her mother had continued to deal with that marriage because she wanted Angie to have a whole family: mother, father, dog, and a stable future. If she only knew what Angie thought now.

She sacrificed all those years of her life for me, and after I finally finished college, left home for my own place, and allowed Mother to stop playing the role and divorce Daddy, what did she do? She up and died.

She never had the chance to be happy while she was with my father, Angie thought, and if she did, it had to have been during some quiet, stolen moment, when Angie wasn't around to see it, when her mother was locked away in some little room that she designated her private place. And then it hit Angie. She was doing the same thing, living the same life her mother had, and she hadn't even married Deric yet. That moment, she knew she couldn't go through with it. She would not sacrifice her happiness for her child, and she wouldn't deprive herself of love when it was right there in front of her, begging to be accepted.

Angie rose from the sofa, walked out of the room, and headed up the stairs. She came upon her son in his room, stretched out on his stomach in the middle of a sea of action figures, cars, and trucks.

"Kyle," Angie said, standing just outside the door of his room.

Kyle rolled over on his side, turning to look at her from over his shoulder. "Yeah, Mommy."

"Do you mind if I interrupt action figure time. I have something very important I need to talk to you about."

On the way back home from dropping Kyle off at Sherrie's house, her oldest friend from college, Angie thought about some of the questions she'd asked Kyle.

"Would you mind if Daddy no longer lived with you and Mommy? He would still see you almost every day, come to play with you and everything." Angie just assumed this would be the case, because she knew Deric would always love her son and never want to be completely out of his life. "But he just wouldn't live here."

Kyle dealt with the questions better than she thought he would, starting to cry after five minutes of their conversation instead of just a couple. She held him, rocking him, telling him, "It has to happen, baby. It just has to." His tears burned her like acid, his every sob cut through her like a knife, but just like Asha said, he would sense her misery in being with Deric eventually, and that would ultimately make him miserable, just like her mother's unhappiness made Angie.

When Angie walked into her house, Deric was sitting there in the living room, still wearing his work shirt and pants, the top button of his shirt undone, his tie loosened. He held a mixed drink in the palm of his hand, his legs crossed.

"Where you been?"

Angie closed the front door, ignoring him.

"I said, where you been?"

Angie hung her jacket and purse in the closet, then turned around, looking at Deric. "Same place you've been. Out."

"And where's Kyle?"

"He's not here, Deric."

"I can see that. That's why I'm asking where he is," Deric said, sitting up on the sofa, setting his drink down on the table.

"He's out too. I guess that place is pretty popular tonight," Angie said, turning and walking toward the kitchen.

"Well, don't you think I have a right to know? Out where?" Deric stood.

Angie turned to face him. "No, Deric, I don't think you have a *right* to know, and why would you think that anyway?"

"Because I treat him like a son. I—"

"But, Deric, Kyle is not your son," Angie said, walking toward Deric, raising a finger to make her point. "He's not yours, and he's never been your son."

"Well, you weren't saying that every time I took him to the park, played ball with him."

"Maybe I should've. Maybe I should've told you you couldn't stay here when you needed a place, because I knew my son would see you, and maybe get to know you, maybe become attached. And when he did do just that, maybe I should've told him the truth, that no, that's not your father, instead of going on with what you wanted and allowing him to call you Daddy, allowing him to believe that."

A concerned look appeared on Deric's face. "What are you saying, Angie?"

Angie lowered her head, trying to find enough courage to tell him what she knew would truly hurt him. "I'm trying to say that you can't adopt Kyle, and that we can't get married."

"But I'm practically his father. Kyle loves me," Deric said, an unbelieving look on his face.

"But I don't, Deric. I don't."

46

"Would you like anything else?" the bartender asked Asha. Asha looked down at the drink she had been sipping for the last twenty minutes, then took a slow count of how many she'd already had. Four lemon drop shots, and three Bombay Sapphires with cranberry, or was it four?

"Uh, no," Asha said, looking up a little blurry-eyed at the bartender. Her head was a little fuzzy, had been sometime after that third lemon drop, but Asha continued drinking considering she was doing nothing else but sitting there at the bar, those two empty seats forever vacant on either side of her.

This is some great club, she remembered thinking after she had been there for an hour and a half, and no one approached her. She went to the bathroom a couple of times, not only just for a change of scenery, but also because her bladder demanded it.

Once inside, she took care of her business, washed her hands, then did what women normally did—stood in front of the mirror, freshened up their makeup, and made small talk.

There was a short, athletic-looking sista in front of the mirror when Asha walked up to the sink. The woman was raking her fingers through her short haircut, when Asha said, "I like that hairstyle on you. That's cute. Where do you get it done?"

The woman didn't even turn around to give Asha the death stare, but delivered it through the mirror, gawking at Asha, like she had broken some sacred code of the Liquid Cherry club by speaking to her in the middle of straightening her hairdo.

"Excuse me?" the woman said, raising her eyebrows, and turning down one of the corners of her mouth. "Do I know you?"

"No," Asha said, wondering just what crime she had committed.

"I didn't think so," and the woman teased one more hair into place and left.

"Well, screw you too," Asha said, paying her no mind, leaning into the mirror, fixing her own hair.

But that wasn't half as embarrassing as when at the two-hour mark, Asha was getting fidgety just sitting on that bar stool, and decided something had to happen. She was having a lousy time just sipping on drinks all that night, but there was one thing positive about the club; the music was hittin'. They played a nice mix of hip-hop, jazz fusion, a little alternative rock, and R&B. But Asha couldn't continue to stay seated when they started on the Chicago house music. It was the funk, soul, disco hybrid of music that originated in Chicago in the early eighties, that Asha and so many other people fell in love with during their years in high school.

The floor started to get even more crowded than it was, when Asha's favorite house music song, "Inside Out" came on. She had to dance. She looked to her left, then to her right, and saw that no one was looking as though they were going to approach her. No one looked all that willing to be approached either, so Asha said to hell with it, and walked on to the dance floor herself. Hey, people in Europe did it all the time, she thought, as she closed her eyes, let herself relax, and started to let the music take over her body.

It was what always happened with house music. It enveloped her, got inside of her, went through her, and demanded that she move. Asha threw her hands up, spun in circles, letting her body be carried on the current of the music that reverberated all around her. She was no longer in that little club, but in her own little world, filled with the soulful melodies she loved, memories of her good times in the past, and good feelings about the future. She would open her eyes, see women jumping around, losing their minds as she was doing, smiling, laughing, enjoying the music, and then she would lower her lids again, let the music steal her away once more.

When she did that the last time, the song changed. The DJ played something that she hadn't heard since she was sixteen. It was a weird song that none of her friends liked back then, but that she loved. When Asha heard that song, she started to yelp on that dance floor, threw her head back, spun and jumped even faster. The entire night at the club up to this point had been a bust, but now it was all worth it, Asha thought, until she opened her eyes, and saw that the dance floor had totally emptied. Everyone had walked off, sat back down, or stood along the side, and they were all looking at her as she realized what was going on and slowed her spasmatic routine to a halt. She stood there in the center of the empty floor, felt a warm flash of embarrassment rush over her, and then quickly headed off into the crowd. As she walked, she saw people smirking at her from behind their glasses, heard them whispering from behind cupped hands. Were they smirking at *her*, talking about *her*? She didn't know, but it sure felt like they were.

Asha sat back down, throwing her elbows up on the bar, and sunk her head between them, trying to hide from the embarrassing incident. That's when the bartender asked her if she wanted another drink, and Asha said no. But a moment later, the bartender brought her one anyway, set the glass down on a paper napkin in front of her.

"Hey, but I said—"

"Girl over there," the bartender said, pointing down at the fine sister at the other end of the bar. She smiled at Asha, and even though Asha was now in a funky mood, damn if she couldn't help smiling back at her.

The girl stood up, and Asha realized she was going to come over. Asha quickly looked away from her, but not before taking a good look. She had the most beautiful body, curves Asha only wished she could've been born with. She wore jeans that clung to those shapely hips and thighs, a T-shirt that stuck like she just soaked it with a gallon of water, and her hair was done in that just-stepped-out-of-bed look, pinned up here and there with a million bobby pins, but it looked cute.

She walked up to Asha, and before she spoke, Asha saw how full and sweet her lips appeared. She had a beauty mark in the center of her right cheek, and she wore dark-framed glasses that were probably only cosmetic, but made her look cute in a studious kind of way.

"Is this seat taken?" she asked.

"Un uh," Asha said. "I mean no. It's yours."

The woman sat down, and Asha figured her to be somewhere between twenty-five and thirty.

"Thanks for the drink," Asha said, taking a sip and smiling, to show her appreciation. "But I really shouldn't be drinking anymore. I'm already making a fool of myself. I'm sure you saw that on the floor, right?"

The girl started smiling. "Fool? I don't know what you're talking about. If that was my song, which it obviously was yours, I would've stayed my ass right out there, forgot what everybody else thinks. They can't dance anyway, that's why they were looking. They were trying to pick up your moves." The woman took a sip from the drink she carried over to from where she was sitting, then extended a hand to Asha.

"My name is Beth."

"Oh, I'm sorry," Asha said, shaking Beth's hand. "Asha. It's good to meet you. I was starting to give up on this place."

"No, Asha. Don't give up on it yet, the night is still young."

Beth and Asha talked and laughed for another half an hour, and Asha didn't know if it was the alcohol, or just how beautiful this Beth was, but she couldn't keep her eyes off of her. She couldn't stop staring at those sensuous lips, that beauty mark on her smooth, flawless skin, and couldn't keep her eyes from dropping to the bustline of that tight T-shirt.

Beth had bought another couple of drinks, and was about to order another round, when Asha said, "No, no, no." She knew she was already way past her limit. "I want to stay, but I really have to go. I have clients in the morning."

"Really. What do you do?"

"I'm a massage therapist over at Phillipe Cozi."

"Oh, really?" Beth said, her eyes brightening.

"You know where that is?"

"Yeah, I'm familiar with it. But if I'd known you were working there, I've would've booked an appointment a long time ago."

Asha smiled, turning away, her cheeks growing warm. Asha stood up, lifted her jacket off the bar stool, and started to put it on. "So I guess I should be going."

"And what? That's it, no number, no nothing?" Beth said, smiling at Asha.

"Oh, yeah, of course," and as Asha grabbed a pen out of her purse, and jotted down her number on one of the napkins, she couldn't believe that this was happening. She came out to a bar with intentions of starting a new life, and it looked as though that was exactly what was happening. She felt proud, happy with herself that she wasn't afraid to come out alone like she had.

"Here you go," Asha said, giving Beth the number.

Beth took it, folded the napkin without looking at it, and slipped it in her jeans pocket.

"You know I really don't want this evening to end."

"Why, what did you have in mind?" Asha said.

Beth drank down the last of her drink, set the glass softly down on the bar. "We could leave, and I don't know, maybe go to my place. Finish our conversation. It was good, don't you think?

"It was wonderful conversation," Asha said, and as much as she felt she wanted to get to know this woman better, she knew she had to get up for work tomorrow. "I really think I better head on home. But give me a call, okay?"

"Sure," Beth said, looking disappointed.

Asha was about to turn to leave, when Beth asked, "Can I get a hug?"

Asha smiled and opened her arms. Beth moved into her, pressing herself very close to Asha. Asha felt Beth's warm, soft body pull her in, and at that moment, she felt herself reconsidering Beth's offer.

"How did you get here?" Beth whispered softly in her ear.

"I took a cab," Asha said, still hugging her, not making any effort to pull away.

"Well, let me take you home. I came by myself, and I was leaving anyway. What do you say?" Beth asked, holding Asha a little tighter.

"Okay. Who am I to turn down a ride home from a beautiful woman?"

o o o

Asha sat in the passenger seat of Beth's '87 Honda Civic, her eyes closed, her head spinning in dizzying, alcohol-induced circles, a wide smile on her face.

"How you doin' over there, girl?" Beth asked, turning down the volume on her radio some.

"Outside of feeling like my head's about to detach from my body and float up in the air like a balloon, I'm fine."

"Don't worry. I'll have you home soon," Beth said, taking Asha's hand, giving it a comforting squeeze.

"There's no rush. As long as you get me back by sunrise," Asha joked, opening her eyes and turning to look at Beth. Beth smiled back at Asha, and Asha turned away, looking out her window. It must've been the alcohol affecting her vision, she told herself, because nothing outside looked familiar to her. She lifted her head a little more, strained her eyes, focusing harder, and she was right, nothing was familiar. The street that they were quickly moving down was practically deserted, no houses, no buildings, just old, rusting warehouses on one side, an auto junk yard on the other.

"Hey, where are we going?" Asha said, sitting up, still looking at what was outside the windshield. "This isn't the way to my house."

"Yeah, I know. I'm taking a shortcut," Beth said, that same smile on her face, that Asha now was starting to question. "It'll just be—" Beth was about to say, but then the car started to sputter, to jerk, hesitate like it was going to cut off.

"What's wrong!" Asha said, really starting to get worried now.

"I don't know," Beth said, staring down at the gauges on the dash. "I don't know what the hell is going on." The car slowed a great deal, then came to a halt at the side of the deserted street.

"What's going on? What's happening?" Asha said, whipping her head about, her pulse racing, wishing that she had never gotten in the car with this woman, because something told her now that she might be in serious danger.

"I don't know, Asha. But don't worry," Beth said, grabbing the key out of the ignition. "Everything is going to go just as planned."

"What? What do you mean by that?" Asha said, now becoming even more scared.

Beth looked up into the rearview mirror, and Asha saw a bright light reflect off that mirror onto Beth's face. Beth turned to Asha, the smile no longer on her face, but a menacing expression that made her appear like no one Asha had ever seen before.

"You pretty little, stuck-up bitches think you can fuck over anyone you want, don't you," Beth said. And Asha couldn't believe what this woman had just said to her. Asha pushed herself back against her door, looking at Beth as though she had just been possessed, and was about to start spitting up split pea soup.

"But you fucked with the wrong dyke this time, bitch," Beth said.

"Beth," Asha gasped, more frightened now than she could ever remember feeling. "What the fuck are you talking about?"

"Shut up! My fucking name ain't Beth." She looked back up into the rearview, and that light became more intense, not only brightening Beth's face, but illuminating the entire car.

Asha quickly turned her head around, glanced out the back window to see a car pull up behind them, the doors open, and shadowy figures jump out. Asha went for her door, terrified, not completely understanding what was happening, what was about to happen, but something telling her that if she didn't get out of that car, she might die that night.

She grappled for the handle, felt it give, but the door didn't open. She looked toward the lock, seeing that it was pushed down. She raced to unlock it, but before she could grab it, she felt bolts of pain strike her from every root of her hair.

Beth had grabbed a fist full of Asha's hair, was yanking her away from the door. Asha blindly threw punches behind her, trying to hit whatever she could, trying to break out of that car before it was too late.

"Naw, bitch. You ain't going nowhere," Asha heard Beth grunt, as she sunk her other hand into Asha's hair, pulling her back with both hands now.

Asha continued to swing wildly, continued to kick at the door, at the window above it, until she felt her fist connect to something soft, but hard underneath. She heard Beth cry out. Asha felt Beth's grip loosen after being punched in the nose. This was her one opportunity, she knew, and she lunged for the lock, undid it, pushed the door open, and was about to race out of it, when there standing in the way of her escape was Big Les, and three other huge, evil-looking women.

"So you like getting motherfuckers fired, hunh?" Les said, holding something long and thick, slapping it into the palm of her other hand. "Well, we just gonna have to teach you what happens when you do shit like that."

47

Asha's phone rang over and over again with no answer. I told myself I shouldn't have been thinking about her while here at Faith's, but I couldn't help it. It was the evening before my marriage, and all I'd been able to do was think about my friend. It was because I was feeling guilty.

It was bad enough that I felt like an ass for telling Asha she had to get out in the first place, but then, when I finally bumped into her, I'd stood there staring at her like a mindless zombie, searching for words to say that I couldn't find, and even if I could've, I probably couldn't have spoken them. But I sensed that she wanted to speak to me just as much as I wanted to talk to her. I sensed that she wanted the mess that we'd been in to be over. As a matter of fact, I know that was what she was feeling. I'd known Asha long enough to be able to read it in her eyes.

I continued to let the phone ring, hoping that she'd pick up before her voice mail did. I had only been at Faith's house twenty minutes before I realized that I just had to call her and apologize for everything, tell her to forget about moving her stuff. She could stay there forever if she wanted to. I walked into the kitchen, leaving Faith in the living room, and dialed the number. That was five rings ago. The machine picked up, and I was about to leave a message when Faith walked into the room. I looked at Faith sadly and lowered the phone into its cradle.

Faith looked at me, shaking her head. "She wasn't home?"

"Naw," I said, and she could tell I was disappointed when I said it.

She walked over to me, rubbing my back. "Don't worry. You two will clear this up."

It was Faith's idea that I even call her. From the moment I stepped into her house, she'd noticed that there was something wrong with me. She'd kept on asking me to tell her, but I wasn't crazy. I thought if I even mentioned Asha's name, she probably would've had a fit, said something about the two of us still being together again, so I kept avoiding the question. Then Faith asked me what was wrong for what seemed the hundredth time, and I just told her. I couldn't believe her reaction.

"Then you should call her, Jayson. I know how much you care about her, and if it's bothering you this much, then call her up and resolve the issue right now."

What changed? I wanted to ask her, but didn't. I didn't care at that point. I was just happy there was a change.

Faith and I walked back into the living room arm and arm, and lay down on the floor in front of her TV. The room was dark, the only light coming off the tube, and from the low flames in the fireplace. Faith was on her back, me lying over her, looking down in her face. I smiled. It was a goofy, kinda daffy smile, and I not only knew that from the way it felt, but also by the way Faith was looking at me.

"Why the crazy grin?" she asked, looking up at me.

"It's not crazy, it's happy. I've been worried about everything between me and Asha for I don't know how long. Partially because she's my best friend, but also because I didn't know what our friendship, that is, if we ever got back to that point, would do to my marriage with you. But just your saying that I should call her, and your telling me everything would be all right, made me realize that things really would be all right—not only between me and Asha, but me and you too. And then all of a sudden I just felt every worry, every little disturbance or distraction just kind of lift out of me, leaving nothing but happiness about what's going to take place tomorrow. That's why the crazy grin."

Faith looked up at me for a long moment, her face displaying all sorts of emotions. First she looked like she was about to start bawling, then she grinned like she was about to laugh out loud, then it looked

as though she was fighting just to maintain one expression, finally settling on a very content-looking smile.

"Jayson, I love you. You know that don't you?" she said, placing a
hand on the back of my neck.

"Yes, I do," I said.

"No, Jayson. I really love you. Really," she said, pulling me down
some, raising up some herself to kiss me on the cheek, then on the lips.

"Yes, baby. I really do," I said, accepting her kisses, kissing her back.
"I really, really do."

"Good."

Nothing was said after that, she just started pulling at my clothes,
seeming to want to take them off.

"Isn't it bad luck or something to make love the night before the
wedding," I said, starting on her jeans, but having a hell of a time
unfastening them.

"No, baby," Faith said, helping me with the button, then sliding the
jeans all the way off. "I think it's the other way around. It's bad luck
not to make love the night before the wedding."

"Ohhhh," I said. "Well, in that case . . ."

We made love, fantastic love, and as we were doing that, I was
thinking about how much I loved her, and that it just kept getting better and better. Then a thought slipped into my head that I wished
never would've found its way there. And the thought said to me,
maybe she's gotten so good because of the practice she had with Gary.
I quickly shut my eyes, trying to quiet that noise in my head, and the
painful resentment that came along with it. I refocused on the love I
felt for Faith, the wonderful future we would have together.

Afterward, we showered. I put my clothes back on and she dressed
for bed. She climbed under the covers, and I tucked her in, kissing her
on the forehead.

"So tomorrow you'll be Mrs. Faith Abrahms, and it'll be the last
time you go to sleep by yourself. Is that okay by you?"

Faith smiled at me. "Yeah," she said, in a casual tone. "I guess that'll
be okay." Then she reached up, wrapped her arms around my neck,
and playfully pulled me down into the bed with her.

"Are you joking, Mr. Jayson Abrahms? I can't wait till tomorrow! And you better not be late."

"Be here to pick you up at eleven, and bells will be ringing by noon," I said. I pushed myself up from the bed. "Where we gonna live? Here or my place?" She smiled. "Let's just worry about tomorrow, mister. One day at a time, hunh?"

When I finally got in my car, I looked at the clock. It was fifteen minutes till midnight, and I told myself, I didn't care what time it was when I got home, I was going to have a talk with Asha and tell her just how much her friendship meant to me.

48

That long, thick object that Big Les was slapping across her hand was a dildo. As Les and the three other women were dragging Asha out of that car, she fought like hell, screaming, "What are you doing! What do you want!" They forced her into the car that Big Les had come out of, one of those huge Ford Excursions. The backseats were folded down, and they threw her in through the tailgate, two of the other big women getting in behind her, holding her down, punching Asha in the stomach and breasts, which hurt like hell, whenever she tried to fight her way out.

The truck went only a short distance, and when the tailgate door opened again, Asha was able to see through the little bit of space between the heads of the women that crowded around. She saw that she was behind one of those huge dilapidated warehouses and she didn't see anyone around at all who could help her.

Les climbed into the truck, hunched over her, staring down into Asha's face.

"It's like a dream, ain't it, baby? I planned on getting back at your ass, but never thought I'd walk in my spot and see your ass just waiting there for me," Les said, grabbing Asha's face and pinching it. "You must've wanted this just as much as I did."

That memory of Les seemed like an eternity ago, and it was so surreal, that if it wasn't for the pain, and the blood, crawling from the

R M Johnson

wounds on Asha's face, out the nostrils of her nose, the wide split on her lip, and from somewhere deep in between her legs and anus, she would've thought it was just a rumor about something that happened to someone else.

After the event, which was how Asha would term it forever in her head, she was rolled out of the back of the truck and fell hard onto the dirt. She lay there for a while, the star-filled sky spinning thousands of miles above her.

Her face burned as if she had been bobbing for apples in a tub of acid. Her arms, breasts, and middle were all so sore that with each breath, she felt that the bones there were breaking. And everything below her waist, she could not even feel, and didn't want to, because for the past however long it had been, she had been experiencing feelings down there far too much. Feelings of excruciating, mind-numbing pain, which she'd blacked out under a number of times.

After ascertaining that nothing had been broken, and she could move, she stirred about in the dirt awhile, doing nothing more than getting dirt in wounds on her hands, arms, and face. She pulled her pants and panties up, and seeing that she still had her purse with her, she slowly raised herself off the ground, and stumbled to a main street, where she was able to thumb a ride home.

Angels were looking out for her now, Asha thought, as she sat slumped, and shaking, hugging herself in the older black woman's car that picked her up.

"Are you sure you don't want me to take you to the emergency room?" the woman said, racing down the street.

"Thank you," Asha said, speaking into her folded arms over her chest, the words barely audible, "but I just want to go home."

The woman shook her head, her thick eyeglasses glued to the road. A second later, she looked back at Asha, determination on her face. "No, I'm taking you to the hospital," she demanded.

"Just take me home!" Asha said, raising her voice, turning to look at the woman, the blood starting to dry and harden with the dirt on her face. "Please."

∘   ∘   ∘

318

When Asha pushed her way through the door, it was 11:30 P.M. She didn't bother closing the door, just headed straight to the bathroom, wanting to see if she looked half as bad as she felt.

She paused a moment, just to the side of the mirror, bracing herself for what she was about to see, and then upon seeing it, she immediately started crying. Instead of being thrown out of that parked truck, it looked as though she had been tossed from one doing eighty miles an hour down the Dan Ryan, and had to use her face to cushion the impact of every bump she hit.

Both her eyes were black and puffy, splotches of purple floating faintly under her swollen cheeks, blood and dirt caked in her nostrils, in her ears, and in the corners of her mouth. Blood was smeared all over her, as if she had gone crazy, and intentionally painted her own face with her blood-covered fingers.

She undid only one button on her shirt, because that was the only one that had not been ripped off. She could only open it, because it was too painful to take it all the way off. Where the bra had gone, she didn't know, but as she looked down at her bruised breasts, she tried not to remember the awful pain she felt when two of those crazed women were biting down on them, as if they were mad dogs, tearing at raw flesh.

Asha smoothed a finger over the countless bite marks all over her breasts, most just superficial, a couple that had broken the skin.

She stood in front of the mirror, looking sadly at herself, her legs barley able to hold her up. But Asha did everything in her power to keep herself erect, because she had to take a good look at herself, figure out why all of this had happened to her. It was difficult, because her mind wouldn't let her think, wouldn't let her focus on anything but the event itself. And when Asha closed her eyes, and tried to force those pictures out of her head, the sounds would come. The sounds of her screaming. The sounds of those girls, cackling, hollering, cheering Big Les on. "Go on, girl! Show that little bitch that she can't fuck with you."

At first, Asha could make out each individual voice, the general direction each comment came from, but as Big Les continued to widen Asha's legs with her large hips, as Les continued pushing the thing strapped to her waist into Asha, the pain became so intense that everything started to become distorted, started to blur, the hateful sounds all rolling into one big ball of noise.

They're never going to stop. They're going to continue this until I die, Asha remembered thinking as she squirmed on her back, both her arms being held by two girls, pulled so hard that they had gone numb long ago. She could no longer feel much of anything down below.

It was the worst agony Asha had ever lived through, and she tried to move her mind away from it. She even tried to imagine she was experiencing a positive pain, like delivering a child. This was what it would feel like if she ever gave birth. This was what it felt like when my mother gave birth to me, Asha thought, as she felt Big Les's hot breath on the side of her face, heard her grunts as she went about causing Asha as much pain as she could.

But like Asha thought, there were angels looking in on her occasionally, and they would steal her away, allow her to black out. At times, Asha would wake up, feel nothing, no weight over her, nothing tunneling up through her, feeling as though it would erupt out of her chest. She would open her eyes, and think it was over, think that the torture would stop, and then she'd see a new face, a weird sick smile on it, mounting her, and the hollers, the chanting would start again, and her insides would be set afire once more till she blacked out.

When it was all over, when Asha was lying twisted on the ground, Les jumped out of the truck, and stood over her.

"You didn't have to get me fired. I was just bluffing with you about going to Margee. But no. You fucked with my money, fucked with me being able to take care of my son, so you had to get fucked with. You deserved this. Nothing personal though," Les said, smirking. Asha could hear the other girls from the truck, laughing, clapping their hands, thrilled with what they had just done.

"Oh yeah, and one more thing. I wouldn't think about reporting this, 'cause there's always more where this came from. But even if you do, it'll be my word against yours, because ain't no running no DNA on no rubber dick, bitch," Les said, then spit a heavy clump of saliva down on Asha's face.

Asha stood in the mirror now, slowly bringing her hand up to that place where she'd felt the spit hit her, wanting to wipe it away, but it had long ago dried in with the rest of the blood and dirt.

You deserved this, Les had said, and as Asha continued to look sadly at herself, she had to ask herself if Les was right. She didn't have to get Les fired, she could've just told her no, and that could've been the end of it, because, like she said, she wouldn't have gone to Margee. I probably did deserve this, Asha thought.

And then Asha thought about Gill. The man loved her and wanted nothing more than to marry her, make her happy for the rest of her life. But what did she do to him? Use him as a way to cover what she was most ashamed of about herself, instead of telling him the truth so he could walk away from her without investing so much of himself, so much of his heart, in a relationship that did nothing but break that heart. I deserved what they had done to me, Asha thought again.

Then there was her dear friend Jayson, whom she lied to as well. All those years they were together, she lied to him. The years after that, she lied to him. He knew her like no one else and still she couldn't tell him her secret. She'd allowed her lies, her infatuation with herself to go so far that now, he no longer wanted to be friends with her, and no longer wanted her in his building. "I deserve this," Asha continued to tell herself, but this time said it out loud as well.

And finally, there was Angie. Asha didn't believe she'd done anything wrong to her, but considering how many bad things she had done to everyone else, she was sure there was something. She loved Angie, but the woman didn't love her back, and maybe it was because Asha wasn't worth loving. Maybe because she had done so many people wrong, forsaken all the love that had come her way in the past, that now there was just no more.

Asha looked in the mirror, and realized that all of this, everything happened for a reason. This was her punishment for everything bad she had ever done. From the way she couldn't even speak to Jayson when she saw him earlier, to the night her sister died. That was the way Asha phrased it now. It was the way the therapist told her to. But Asha knew the truth, had never let it be forgotten. Her sister didn't die that night. Asha had killed her. She thought about that night, thought about her deep feelings of guilt and anger, and what she'd tried to do to make everything right for what she had done, and wished she had been successful.

Asha stared deeply into the mirror now, not looking at it, but through it, knowing what was there on the shelves behind it. She knew that what was there would make everything right, and if she'd just done it right the last time, none of what just happened would've ever taken place.

She raised a hand up to the mirror, opened the cabinet, and there before her in a cloudy orange prescription bottle, with a white cap, sat some sleeping pills for the nights when she couldn't fall asleep. She grabbed the bottle off the shelf, opened it, and dumped all the pills, which had to be twenty or so, into her hand. She turned on the water with the butt of the hand holding the bottle, filled it up till it over-flowed, then turned it off.

She raised both hands, the one holding the pills, and the other, the one holding the bottle filled with water, so that they were reflected in the mirror. She looked intently into her own eyes, and said, "I deserve this." Then in two quick motions, she popped all the pills in her mouth, then threw her head back, chasing them all down with the water in one huge swallow.

49

Deric put some things in a bag and left after Angie told him she didn't love him anymore. She didn't mean to hurt him, but she had to start being real with herself, and what was real, was that she believed she loved Asha. Angie called Asha's house several times, wanting to tell her that Deric was gone, that she had gotten herself together, and she was ready to pursue something with her. Something serious this time, but Asha never picked up her phone

It was 11:45 P.M. when Angie made her last call, and she stood in her living room waiting for the voice mail to click on again like it had every time. But this time when it did, Angie didn't leave a message, because she knew that Asha was probably there, checking the Caller ID. Angie knew Asha said that she was going out, but Asha wasn't that much of an "out" person, especially someone who stayed out this late.

So Angie decided she would go over there. If the girl didn't want to talk to her over the phone, then she'd have to do it face-to-face.

When Angie pulled up to Asha's apartment, she couldn't believe how excited she was, how burden-free and revived she felt, after letting Deric go. She felt like she was about to start her life all over again, but this time do it the right way.

She jumped out of the car, and actually skipped toward the building, she was so happy. As she climbed the steps, she was picturing Asha's face, how it would light up when she heard Angie's news. They would hug and laugh, and do whatever else they wanted to do, not fearing who saw, or who cared, or anything else.

Angie stepped up to the big door and pushed her way through, but halted when she entered the hallway, seeing Asha's door open. She looked oddly at the door, moving toward it cautiously, sensing that something was wrong.

"Asha," she called. When there was no answer, she stuck her head into the room, and said, again, "Asha. It's me, Angie." Still there was nothing. Angie took two more steps into the apartment, looking around the room, down at the floor, when she saw blood smeared across the hardwood floor.

"Asha!" Angie cried, knowing now that something was indeed wrong. She raced through the living room, checking the dining room, the bedroom, but saw no sign of Asha. Then Angie stepped in to the bathroom entrance. She shrieked at the sight of Asha's bloodied, bruised and beaten body, lying out across the cold tile floor. Angie didn't want to take another step closer at first, because she couldn't see Asha's head. It was hidden between the sink vanity and the toilet. She was afraid she'd be dead, that her eyes would be closed, and she would be dead, not breathing. But Angie stepped in anyway, and she cried out again. When she did see her face, it looked even worse than the rest of her body.

"Asha!" Angie cried, dropping to her knees, wanting to touch her, wanting to comfort her, but not knowing if that would cause her any more pain. That was, if she was still alive. Tears came to Angie's eyes as she looked around the small room for anything that she could use to help Asha, but she realized that even if there was something, she wouldn't know what it was. She threw her head down against Asha's chest, pressing her ear to her heart, listening as closely as she could.

She didn't hear anything at first, and the tears came to her eyes even harder then, but she persisted in her listening, until finally she heard a faint heartbeat. She was alive. Angie raised Asha's head off the floor gently, and was about to speak to her, when she heard someone entering Asha's apartment.

What was she going to do now? Whatever man did this to Asha was coming back for some reason, and now he would do the same to Angie. There was only one thing to do. Angie continued to hold Asha's head, but she slid closer toward the door, attempting to kick it closed and lock it before the man could enter. Angie moved herself as close as she could without dropping Asha's head back to the tile, and stretched her leg out, kicking the door. It swung almost completely closed, but was stopped all of a sudden. When the man walked in, Angie had Asha's head in her lap, cradling her, and defending her at the same time.

"Please don't hurt us. Just leave and we won't tell anyone," Angie pleaded.

But Jayson didn't know what she was talking about, didn't even know what was going on until he took the time to actually see what was before him.

"Asha!" Jayson yelled, throwing himself down toward Angie and Asha.

"Please!" Angie said, throwing her arms up.

"I'm not going to hurt you," Jayson said, gently pulling her arms away. "I'm Jayson, her friend. I live upstairs. What the hell happened? Is she alive?" he said, frantically.

"Yeah. But I think she got raped," Angie sobbed.

"Raped!" Jayson said, shocked. She was badly beaten, and he could see blood staining the space between the legs of her jeans. It certainly looked as though she had been raped, but there was no sign of a struggle, Jayson thought, looking around the bathroom. And if she had been raped, why did she still have her clothes on?

Jayson looked over the room again, and caught sight of the empty prescription bottle. He reached for it, read the white label, and knew there had been sleeping pills inside it. He immediately stood and hurried toward the kitchen.

"What is it? What's wrong?" Angie cried.

"Try to wake her up right now. I'm calling 911. She overdosed on sleeping pills."

50

"She tried this before," I told Angie, while sitting in the emergency waiting room. I had been thinking about telling her for the hour and a half we had been there, and kept telling myself not to, but it seemed like she really loved Asha, cared as much as I did about her, so I felt she should know.

"It was years ago, when her sister died in a car accident."

"Why would she try again?" Angie asked me.

"I don't know," I lied, getting up and walking away from her, knowing that it probably had something to do with me.

I walked to the nurses' station. "Can we see Asha Mills, yet?" I asked, and although I knew the haggard-looking female nurse was tired of me, I really needed to see Asha.

"I'm sorry, sir. As soon as the doctor is ready for you to see her, he'll let you know."

I looked at her for a long moment, letting her know that I was displeased with her answer, and then walked away from there. I didn't go back to Angie, but walked down the hall and stood in front of a snack-filled vending machine, looking at my sad, sorry-ass faint reflection in its plastic front.

If I hadn't allowed this shit between Asha and me to go on so goddamn long, this would've never have happened. If I'd just said something to her when I wanted to, instead of being so damn frantic to race over to Faith's house and be with her.

Damn Faith, I thought for a moment, but then corrected myself, telling myself that it wasn't her fault that I hadn't been there for Asha. It was mine.

I thought about the moment I'd walked in and seen her on the floor like that. I'd thought she was dead. I'd thought in that one moment that I had lost my best friend for life, and everything I did and said wrong to her came back screaming in my head. I thought I would never have a chance to take any of it back, to tell her how much she meant to me, how much I needed her to be there and never leave my life. I was so grateful that she was still alive, and I would tell her all this whenever that damn doctor finally let me see her.

I walked back down the hallway, toward the emergency waiting room, and when I entered, I saw the doctor talking to Angie. I walked quickly, almost ran over to them.

"What's going on? Is she going to be all right?"

"She's going to be fine. But you were right. She was raped. Unfortunately, she doesn't want to talk about it. She doesn't want us to call the police. She doesn't want us to do anything more than treat her."

"Can we see her, Doctor?" Angie said, worry on her face.

"Yes. Right this way."

He escorted us back to a curtained area. When we pulled it back and walked behind it, Asha was there dressed in a hospital gown, bandages on her face, arms, and hands, lying in a bed. Her face was still bruised pretty bad, but from what little I was able to see of it that moment, some of the swelling looked to have gone down some.

Her head was turned away from us, her arms crossed over her belly, looking as if she were still making a weak attempt to protect herself.

"Asha," I said. She didn't turn around to look at me. "What happened, and why won't you tell the doctor?"

Still she said nothing.

"Asha, baby," Angie said, stepping a little closer to the bed, enough to lay a hand on the blanket above her leg. "Tell us what happened. Tell the police so they can catch this man."

"I'm not saying anything," Asha said, her head still turned away from us. "And I never will."

"Asha, why not? Something has to be done, or this man's just going to go out there and do it—"

"It won't happen again," Asha said, turning to us, her face barely recognizable because of all the damage and repair that had been done to it. "And I'll never mention it again, so don't ask." She turned her face back away from us.

"Asha, baby—" Angie started.

"Why didn't you just leave me there?" Asha said, interrupting her.

"What are you talking about?" Angie said, walking around to the other side of the bed, so Asha would have no choice but look at at least one of us.

"Why didn't you just leave me there on the floor to die. That's what I wanted. Didn't you see the bottle of pills. Nobody shoved them down my throat. I took them myself because I wanted to die. So why didn't you just let me?"

Angie looked particularly hurt by the question, as she sat down on the edge of the bed, raising a hand to touch Asha's hair.

"Because I love you. You know that."

Asha turned away from Angie's hand. "You don't love me. If you loved me, you would've stayed with me. If you loved me, you wouldn't have called me tonight talking about—"

"That's over," Angie said, starting to smile.

"What's over?"

"Deric's over. I listened to what you said, girl. What you've been saying all along. I've been acting like it was no big deal for you to come out and accept yourself, but like there was no way in the world I could've done the same thing, like I had so much more than you to lose. It wasn't that. It was just that I was scared to death. I wasn't as strong as you, didn't trust myself to be able to deal with whatever negativity came from this. I also realized that I can't go on ignoring my feelings, my need to be loved, and love someone back. And I mean really, truly love them. Like I love you."

Asha looked up at Angie, her lips starting to quiver, her eyes starting to tear. She shook her head, back and forth.

"What's wrong, baby?" Angie said smiling, gently caressing the side of Asha's injured face.

"It's just that this has been so hard," Asha said, the tears rolling down her cheeks. "All my life I dealt with this, trying to be someone I wasn't, trying to be truly loved by someone, when there was no way, because I wasn't even being true to myself. But now you're saying that you love me?"

"Yes, baby. I'm saying that," Angie said sweetly, looking down into Asha's eyes.

"It just can't be happening. I just can't believe it," she said.

"It's happening, Asha," Angie said, leaning down to kiss the tears that rolled down Asha's cheeks. "Believe it, sweetheart." She kissed Asha on the lips, and Asha kissed her back. I thought seeing something like that, especially with it being done by someone so close to me, would've shocked me, but it didn't. Maybe because I could see that it was real, that it was true. The love that they felt for one another at that moment was so apparent that it transcended all that male/female, sexual orientation stuff. Hell, half the heterosexual couples in the world would be happy and proud to share a love like that, I thought.

"Well, I'm going to go to the ladies' room and allow you two a little time to talk. Okay?" Angie said.

"All right."

Angie got up and walked out of the room, leaving me standing five feet from the bed, looking stupid, both my hands sunk into my pants pockets.

"You can come closer, or are you afraid you'll catch the lesbian bug. I assure you, it's not contagious, not even through sexual contact," Asha said, and she was even smiling a little. I was never more happy to see that smile.

"No, no," I said, taking a huge, quick step forward. "I was just over here trying to think of how many ways I could apologize to you."

"You don't have anything to apologize for, Jayson."

"I went through your things," I said.

"I didn't tell you about who I really am," she said.

"Well," I said.

"Well," she said, nodding her head a little. "That kinda beats yours, hunh?"

"I don't think so. I think they're about even. Let's call it that."

"Okay."

I missed her so much, and just looking down at her, being next to her, speaking to her, and her speaking back to me, made me feel whole again. I don't know how I ever thought that I could go on without her in my life in the first place.

"You know I love you, don't you?" I said to her.

She smiled even wider. "Yeah. I know it, and I knew it all the time we were mad at each other. I even knew it when you kicked me out, and when we both stood in the doorway, looking stupidly at each other. I knew, Jayson. And I love you too."

She raised her arms, and I eagerly placed myself within them.

"And please, please, please, don't you dare think about moving out, all right," I said.

"Don't worry. I haven't found a place, and I haven't packed a thing," she said, chuckling.

I gave her a concerned look. "Asha, I gotta know what happened."

She gave me the look right back, looking like she was about to tell me not to even think about asking again, but said, "All right, Jayson. I've kept enough from you, so I'll tell you. But just allow me to do it in my own time. Is that fair enough?"

"Fair enough," I said, leaning in to give her a hug.

51

When Asha was finally released from the hospital, it was 9 A.M. the next day. The hospital had to call the police, and the boys in blue had to come anyway, even though Asha still wasn't talking and wasn't planning on filing any charges against whoever did this to her. There was also a counselor who had to come and speak to Asha, who surprisingly enough, Asha did talk to. She even made an appointment to start sessions regarding the rape and the suicide attempts.

I left her and Angie in Asha's apartment, telling them that I had to rush off.

"You seem excited. Where are you headed so early this morning?" Angie asked.

"Well," I said, knowing I was going to get it from Asha, "I guess I forgot to mention this, but I'm getting married this afternoon."

Asha looked at me, her eyes bulging, her mouth wide open. "Jayson. Who? Faith!"

"Asha," I said, throwing up my hands. "I know what you're going to say, but—"

"No, you don't," Asha said, shaking her head. "I was just going to say congratulations."

I said, "Are you sure you're okay with it?"

"Jayson," said Asha, "I know you're not a damn fool. I know you love that girl, and whatever happened over the last couple of weeks, it had to have been something huge, and something that made you know this is the right thing to do. So as long as she doesn't hurt you again, who am I to stand in your way?"

I hurried, putting on my tuxedo, watching the clock, and smiled into the mirror. The teeth were sparkling, I looked dazzling, so there was nothing else to do but call the bride, tell her I was on my way, and head out.

I hung up the phone feeling wonderful, wondering why I even entertained the foolish questions I had a few moments ago. Everything was fine. No, better than fine. Great! All I had to do was find my keys, and I would be on my way.

I looked over toward the TV, and there they were. I walked over there, grabbed them, but didn't lift them off the television. I let my hand rest there, because what my hand was next to was a tape that just happened to have recorded images of the woman I was about to rush off and marry.

No, don't do it, I told myself. What good would it do to start all that up over again? What fucking good would it do? None, I answered. But then I halted, my back to the videotape. It was like the thing was alive, like it was beckoning to me, tearing down my resistance, forcing me to want to view it again, to want to relive that horror that had changed my life.

I shut my eyes tight, summoned up every little bit of will power I had, and took steps away from that tape, to the front door, and out of my apartment.

"I now pronounce you man and wife," I heard the justice of the peace saying. He was smiling, as I looked up at him, Faith and I both anticipating his next sentence.

"You may now kiss the bride." I leaned in toward her, gently taking her veil, raising it over her head to see her beautiful face. I leaned in closer, and she did the same till our lips touched, and it was the most wonderful feeling I had ever experienced . . .

That's exactly how I imagined it would've happened if I hadn't broken down, opened the front door, gone back to that videotape, popped it in the VCR, and sat there on my wedding day, watching my soon-to-be wife sleep with someone else. I watched the tape all the way through.

I pressed the Stop button, unable to bear the sight of it anymore. I grabbed the tape out of the machine, walked out on my front porch, and just sat there with it in my hand. It was a beautiful, bright sunny day, too. A perfect day for a wedding, but I just couldn't bring myself to take another step after seeing what was on that tape again.

I sat like that for a long time, every now and then looking down at my watch, determining the points in time when I felt Faith would start getting suspicious, when she would start calling, and when she would jump in her car, and start heading over here.

By 11:20 A.M., I knew that any minute she'd be driving up in her beige Camry, all decked out in her wedding gown, like a woman going to a Halloween party in June. I looked down the street, in the direction I knew she would be coming from, and amazingly enough, there she came.

Her car screeched to a halt, she got out, whisked around the front of the car, but stopped in her tracks the minute she got close enough to see my face.

"Oh no, Jayson. Please, not wedding day jitters," she said, her shoulders slumping.

She walked closer to me, holding up her dress with both hands, trying not to get grass and dirt in it.

"You look beautiful," I said sadly when she stepped right in front of me. And she did, but she was probably barely able to hear me, because I was speaking into the hand that I had buried my chin and cheek in.

"Jayson, please don't tell me you started thinking about all that other stuff and now you're having second thoughts. Please don't tell me that," Faith said.

"I won't tell you that. But how about I say, I was *looking* at all that other stuff, and now I'm having second thoughts."

Faith looked at me oddly. "What are you talking about?"

I held out the videotape I had been holding. She took it.

"What's this?"

"Our wedding gift from your friend Karen."

"Come on, Jayson," she said, flipping it over in her hand, looking for a label to let her know what was on it. "Stop playing games, and tell me what's going on. I still wanna get married today, you know."

"It's a tape of you and Gary, that night in the hotel room. The night I walked in on you."

Faith's face went white, and the tape dropped from her hand, cracking in half, the ribbon unraveling some out onto the sidewalk. She looked down at it, jumped a step back from it like it was a snake that had bitten her and was trying to strike again.

"What?"

"She wanted me to see that you were cheating so that I'd want to be with her," I said, as though none of it mattered anymore.

"That bitch!" Faith said, shaking her head. "Why would she do all that to me? She was supposed to be my friend."

"It doesn't matter now."

"If it didn't matter, you'd have picked me up like you said you were going to," Faith said.

"I had planned to. When I called you, I was all ready to pick you up, but something made me watch that tape again."

"Jayson, how many times have you watched it before?" Faith asked, softly, moving closer to me.

"I don't know. I lost count."

"Aw, Jayson," she said, sympathetically, placing a hand on the hand I was holding my face up with. "I'm so sorry, baby. But you know that happened in the past. You knew about all that, and I thought we've gotten past it. Haven't we?"

"Yeah, I thought that too, but . . ."

"But what, Jayson?"

"What if this happens again?"

"It won't."

"How do you know that?"

"I'm not sure, but I just do."

"But what you did . . . you hurt me. Don't you know that!" I said, exploding at her all of sudden, not knowing where the outburst came from.

"Yes, Jayson, I know that. But what do you want me to do now? You know I'm sorry, and I'll be sorry forever. You'll know that firsthand, because you'll be there with me for the rest of my life if you just let this go. I'll tell you every day how sorry I am if you want me to, but what more can I do?"

What more could she do? She said it like she had made all sorts of efforts to make me trust her again, like after I found her out, she'd gone to Gary and told him to get the fuck out of her life because she had made a monumental mistake, and she had to find some way to repair it, as opposed to me setting his ass up. What more could she do, she said. And it was in a tone that suggested I stop crying like a baby, get over it, and either shit or get off the toilet. She was standing there looking at me, impatient, a hand on one hip, and I could imagine just under that dress, one of her toes was probably tapping impatiently as well.

"What more can you do?" I repeated the question to her. "What have you done so far outside of run around on me the entire duration of our so-called relationship, telling me one thing, but knowing good and well you had no intention of doing any of it."

"Jayson, c,mon. We already got past that. We both agreed," Faith said, her voice soothing, but worried at the same time.

"When did you see him, Faith?" I said, getting up from the steps.

"Jayson, what are you talking about?"

"When did you see Gary? What did you talk about? Did the two of you lie in bed afterward, smoking a cigarette, laughing at what a fool Jayson was to believe the bullshit you were filling my head with. Oh, but I forgot. He didn't know that it was just a game, just a setup. He thought you really did love me. But he was wrong, just like me."

"Jayson, I did love you. I told you that," Faith said, pushing her way into me, grabbing my tuxedo by the lapels.

"Right. Sure you did."

She rolled her eyes, and blew out a heavy sigh. "Why do you think I gave you all that hell about Asha? It was because I was jealous. I didn't want her to take you from me, because I loved you. I just didn't know how much then."

"You just didn't know how much then." I repeated the words, not believing one of them. "So what clued you into how much, Faith? Was it one day when we were together? One time when I told you that I loved you, and you thought, what the hell, I might as well tell him back? I mean, sure, Jayson's no Gary, you were probably thinking. But how hard could it be for him to flip me over on my stomach and fuck me like some two-dollar ho in a cheap motel room like Gary did for two years," I said, malice in my voice.

Faith looked at me like she didn't know who the hell I was, then sent a hand across my face with a slap that almost spun me completely around. She was huffing, chest heaving, on the verge of tears, and a little part of me wished I hadn't made that last comment, but it was obviously how I felt.

"Two-dollar ho," Faith said, quickly brushing a tear out of the corner of her eye. "That's what you think of me?"

"Faith, answer this honestly for me. What *else* am I supposed to think of you?"

Faith didn't answer the question, actually looked shocked that I had asked it. She looked down at her hands, as she picked at the polish on one of her fingernails. She raised her head, looking off down the street to the right and left of her, as if trying to find something out there that would make everything okay between us. But when she couldn't, she turned to me and said, "Well, I guess that's all there is to say, hunh? Who would want to marry a two-dollar ho, right?"

I nodded my head a little, then said, "That's right." Something told me that she was about to walk away at that moment, and I didn't care. It took her a second. I guess she had to let me see a few more tears fall, give me a moment to second guess what I had said, possibly come to my senses. But when she looked up at me, and saw that that hadn't happened, she slowly turned around and took a step toward her car. But that was the only step she took. She turned around and faced me again.

"You know, I really thought you had gotten over that," Faith said. Here we go, I thought, that final attempt to try and repair her fucked-up mistake. "Yes, it was wrong what I did to you. You were the man I should've been with all along, because Gary didn't love me, never did. I know that now."

"You only realized that when you walked in on him screwing in your house."

"No, Jayson. I didn't really know that he never loved me until a couple of days after that, when he called me."

"When he called you? Hold it, what are you talking about?" I asked her, feeling uncomfortable, knowing exactly what she was going to say, but praying she didn't.

"He called and told me everything, Jayson. That you were blackmailing him with some tape you had, that you had arranged for a call girl, and that if he didn't do it, you were going to go to his wife."

"That's what he told you?" I said, anger raging through my body, as I looked down at that broken tape, wondering if there was a way that I could fix it, and still get it out to that bastard's wife in D.C.

"Yeah, that's what he told me, and don't try to deny it, because I know he was telling the truth." She looked dead in my eyes. I looked away.

"He said that he would be flying into Chicago a lot on business, and he wanted to make up to me what had happened. He said he still loved me, Jayson, and he wanted us to get back together."

I whipped my face back in her direction, feeling a jealous anger starting to build in my body at what he'd said to her, and a very strong fear at what her answer was.

"And what did you say?" I asked, not even sure if I wanted to hear her response.

"That's when I found out Gary really didn't love me, and I told him so. If he really loved me, it would've never gotten that far. When you came to him with your plan, he would've told you to go to hell. He would've said that if his wife had to know, so be it, but he'd never hurt Faith like that. For that reason, and another, I told him he had to be crazy, and to never call me back again."

"What was the other reason?"

"I told him, because I love Jayson, and we're going to get married," Faith said.

"We hadn't talked about marriage, yet," I said. "How did you know then we would've been getting married today?"

Faith walked all the way up to me, placed her hands on my chest, and smiled sweetly. "I didn't tell him anything about *when* we were going to get married, because I didn't know, and it didn't matter. I just knew, whatever it took, however long it took, that we were going to be together, because that's what was supposed to happen." Faith leaned in and kissed me softly on the cheek. "At least that's what I thought, that is, before I became a two-dollar ho." She took a step back from me, looked at me as though it would be the last time, then said, "Good-bye, Jayson." She turned and walked across the grass to her car, not raising her dress like she did when she crossed the first time, obviously not caring now, because she knew it would never be used.

I watched her as she took those steps away from me, thinking about how she'd known all along what I had done. She had known it from the second day I was there and never said a thing. Maybe she was telling the truth about the child she had aborted, about being infatuated with that loss, and not in love with Gary.

I watched her as she continued toward her car, knowing that if she got in and drove off, there would be a chance that we'd never see each other again. I looked down at the tape, there on the ground. I bent down and picked it up. It was ruined, the images no longer accessible to me, no longer able to torment me. It was in the past now, as Faith had said earlier, and she was right.

She was walking around her car at that moment, opening the door, sliding in. I couldn't believe she had known all along about that evil thing that I'd done to her, and she hadn't said a word about it. Maybe she thought that it wasn't worth mentioning, considering how well things were going for us then. I didn't know, but I appreciated her for that. I loved her for that. I loved her for all that we'd been through, for all the horrible things that we'd said and done to each other, and strangely, for all the frustration that this love had caused us. After everything, she was still there sitting in her car, in her wedding dress, wanting us to get married.

She turned the ignition on the car, and it didn't start right away, but coughed and then stuttered, the familar sound trying to put thoughts in my head, but I fought them off. I called out my fiancée's name. She stopped for me, just as she was pulling away from the curb, and I ran out to her, watching her get out of the car, tears on her face again, running to hug me. And, on that day, I knew we would be husband and wife.

ABOUT THE AUTHOR

RM JOHNSON is the author of *The Harris Men, Father Found,* and the #1 *Essence* bestseller *The Harris Family.* He lives in Georgia.